T0356377

A BURNING IN THE BONES

ALSO BY SCOTT REINTGEN

A Door in the Dark
A Whisper in the Walls

A
BURNING
IN THE
BONES

SCOTT REINTGEN

Margaret K. McElderry Books

New York London Toronto Sydney New Delhi

MARGARET K. McELDERRY BOOKS
An imprint of Simon & Schuster Children's Publishing Division
1230 Avenue of the Americas, New York, New York 10020
This book is a work of fiction. Any references to historical events, real people, or real places are used fictitiously. Other names, characters, places, and events are products of the author's imagination, and any resemblance to actual events or places or persons, living or dead, is entirely coincidental.
Text © 2025 by Scott Reintgen
Jacket illustration © 2025 by Justin Metz
Map illustration © 2025 by Chris Brackley
Jacket design by Greg Stadnyk
MARGARET K. McELDERRY BOOKS is a trademark of Simon & Schuster, LLC.
For information about special discounts for bulk purchases, please contact Simon & Schuster Special Sales at 1-866-506-1949 or business@simonandschuster.com.
The Simon & Schuster Speakers Bureau can bring authors to your live event. For more information or to book an event, contact the Simon & Schuster Speakers Bureau at 1-866-248-3049 or visit our website at www.simonspeakers.com.
Interior design by Irene Metaxatos
The text for this book was set in ITC Veljovic Std.
Manufactured in the United States of America
First Edition
10 9 8 7 6 5 4 3 2 1
CIP data for this book is available from the Library of Congress.
ISBN 9781665930499
ISBN 9781665930512 (ebook)

This one is for Kate Prosswimmer.
There wouldn't be a Ren Monroe
without you. Thank you for the
early, unwavering faith you placed
in this series.

A BURNING IN THE BONES

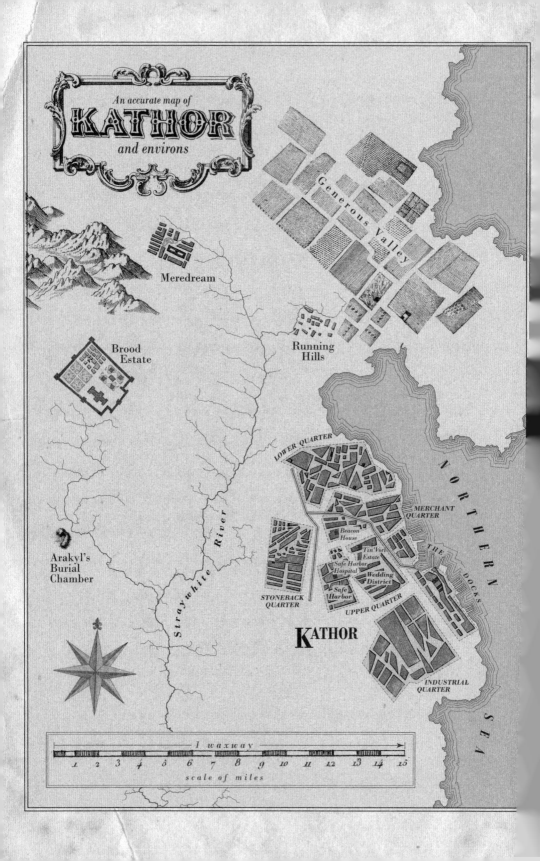

CONTENTS

PART ONE

PART TWO

PART THREE

PART FOUR

PART ONE

Bruising

1

MERCY WHITAKER

Mercy Whitaker was alone in the washroom.

She quietly scrubbed and soaped and scrubbed and soaped. Her eyes lingered briefly on the two fingers on her right hand. Both were shorter than the others. Stunted. The fingers had died just after her tenth birthday. Over the years, they'd faded to a grim black color. She flexed that hand experimentally, but the two fingers never responded. She had learned to live without them.

After drying her hands off, Mercy reached for a pair of double-thick leather gloves. Most students favored wands or orbs or jewelry of some kind for their vessels. She'd started wearing the gloves after her incident and only realized a year later that she could use them to store magic. They were just as fine a conduit as anything else. Rich with magic, the gloves had grown with her as she aged. Always a perfect fit. It didn't hurt that they also hid her biggest insecurity.

Ready, Mercy turned and entered the operatory. Dr. Horn was waiting within. She took her position on his left, set her feet in the proper stance, and nodded. The lights of the operating room flickered out a few seconds later.

Mercy stood in that sudden dark. All the nothing. She held her breath. There were rumors of outside contaminants ruining severance procedures in the past. Apparently, Colin Nearchase had sneezed during his own practical. One failed exam had landed him down in the basement of Safe Harbor with all the other castaway doctors. Assigned the worst patients. Given the least resources. Mercy had not risen through the class ranks to fail now. And so even though she was wearing a mask with three layers of sealing enchantments, she continued to hold her breath.

Her eyes slowly adjusted. Their patient took shape. A dark mound on a flattened, steel table. Her mentor—Dr. Horn—hovered on her right. Between them, a square table with dozens of tools. Mercy was starting to grow light-headed when her mentor cleared his throat.

"Begin."

Mercy exhaled. The first tool in her arsenal was the pair of gloves she was already wearing. She hadn't chosen them with this career in mind, but once she'd decided to become a doctor, she'd found the gloves perfectly suited to anatomical magic. They gave her meticulous control over smaller spells. A certain finesse. With quiet concentration, she began the required spellwork. It was no secret that Dr. Horn had invented this particular procedure. She could not afford any missteps in front of him. Silver light crept from her fingertips like fog. An eerie circle that expanded in every direction until Mercy used a second spell to ward herself and Dr. Horn from the magic. It cocooned the cloudlike substance into a sphere that now hovered directly over their patient.

"Very good," she heard her mentor whisper. "Maintain that radius . . ."

Mercy had a steady hand. She was not the smartest resident. She certainly didn't have the strongest family connections or the top grades in class—but she was steady. Always in complete control of her technique. An important skill when the slightest slip could slit an artery. She sealed the first layer of the spell before beginning the second, which led to the third, and then the fourth. The sphere around her patient grew thick. If she reached out to run a finger across its surface, she'd scrape away a substance that felt like translucent mud.

"Balance," Dr. Horn commanded. "Do not forget balance."

She had not forgotten it. She just wasn't as skilled at this part as Horn. Even so, she began the process of equilibrium. There had to be the perfect amount of each magic for the layering to actually occur. Otherwise, they would not merge properly and she'd be forced to start over. That wouldn't ruin the surgery, but wasted magic was wasted time was wasted energy. All the statistics showed that tired surgeons made more mistakes.

After a moment, her spells found their balance. All of the magic merged into a seamless unit. Mercy glanced once at Dr. Horn for confirmation. When her mentor nodded, she placed both hands—attempting to splay all her fingers—on the edges of the sphere. And then she *pushed*.

The movement was as mental as it was physical. There was a single flash of bright light. Mercy was forced to shield her eyes, and then the darkness stole the room back from them.

She waited in anticipatory silence. Long enough to start wondering if she'd failed. There was a flicker. Then another. A subtle glow began to illuminate the operatory. Mercy absolutely adored this part.

Threads appeared.

Every imaginable color. Some were colors she'd never seen in nature. The threads extended outward from the patient in complex patterns. Some were bone-thick, others no more substantial than silk. It was like looking at an entire person's life—a bright web of every connection they'd ever made in the world. Each thread represented a link their patient had with someone else in the world. Magical representations of naturally formed bonds. Smaller versions of true bond magic, which she'd never had the pleasure of witnessing in the operatory room. The hospital had only performed three procedures to sever such connections in the last two decades, and none since her fellowship began.

Mercy saw seven rust-red threads forking upward from the patient's abdomen. Those were kin threads. Blood relatives. She could even tell which ones were immediate family—or at least people their patient had spent every day with growing up versus more distant relatives. Near the patient's head, which was hooded for anonymity, Mercy spotted dozens of silver threads. A fickle color. These were connections to teachers, mentors, confidantes. Anyone who'd shaped the patient's thoughts. Mercy knew if she reached out and plucked them, they'd feel just like the strings of a violin—taut and resolute.

As she circled, she counted 131. The protocol for this procedure required her to document all of them. She circled back to the table and began taking notes. Her mentor did the same.

Both of them followed established patterns and categories. She finished a few minutes before him, and then they traded notebooks. Double- and triple-checking their work. This routine had been established after a doctor—who no longer worked at their hospital—accidentally severed a young boy's relationship with his twin sister. It had caused quite a stir in Kathor. But medicine could not advance without failure. The two were bedfellows.

Mercy's numbers matched Dr. Horn's.

"Confirmed. Here's your assignment."

Dr. Horn handed Mercy a small card. The doctor's handwriting was meticulous and cramped. Her task today was a fairly straightforward kin severance. When she'd first read about such procedures, she'd found the idea unfathomable. Why would anyone want to permanently sever their bond to a brother or a father? Even Mercy, who had a strained relationship with her mother, could not imagine severing herself completely from family. Horn had patiently explained that for some, those relationships were too painful to bear. Especially for those grieving the loss of someone they couldn't move on from.

After reading the note a fourth time, Mercy selected her favorite chisel scalpel. She maneuvered forward, carefully skirting around threads that were unrelated to her task. She determined her best point of entry, angled her body to match, and then located the third largest of the kin threads.

Mercy wrapped her free hand around the floating thread. That first contact offered a predictable mental flash. She saw a tall man with gray-faded hair. He was handsome, but in a cold way. There were rotating emotions at the sight of him. Love, then fear, then pain. Mercy's attention blinked back to the operatory. These "visions" were common. After all, she was touching the magical representation of their relationship. Mercy steadied herself and began.

The sharp blade of her scalpel bit into that fleshy thread. She found a groove for the tool and began working it back and forth, back and forth. Deeper with each motion. Every few seconds, she saw another image of the man. Dressed in black, standing at a funeral. Holding out a glass of wine on a balcony, the stars behind him like a cloak. A raised voice. A pinched expression. A threatening gesture. A brief kiss. Dozens of small moments shared between the patient and the man.

All of them on the verge of being swept away.

It was as if the patient realized this reality at the same time Mercy thought of it. There was more resistance now. She'd reached the very center of the thread. Back to the very beginning of their connection. She saw a younger version of the man. A boy at university, bent over his books, blond hair swept away from his forehead. The same boy jogging across the quad, wildflowers in hand. This was always the most difficult part. The part of their connection that wanted to survive and hold on and live forever.

But Mercy kept cutting. The man on the other end of this thread was nothing to her. She'd never seen him before and was unlikely to ever see him in the future. The scalpel slid back and forth until she was through the core. Gliding through the final section. The last images rotated back to the older version of the man. Beckoning the patient from the depths of a cozy library, his eyes slightly unfocused. Seated at a family dinner, though Mercy could not make out all of the other faces around the table. An entire lifetime. Until her scalpel found open air again.

She held tight to the thread with her free hand. She'd read about one operation where the operating doctor had accidentally let go of the severed thread. It had fallen and wrapped itself around another. The patient had woken up with an obsessive devotion to their neighborhood tailor that nearly resulted in legal trouble for the hospital. That would not happen in her operatory. Mercy held the thread tight until it disintegrated, then she carefully made her way back to the table.

Dr. Horn nodded his approval. "Perfect work. You continue to prove Balmerick wrong, Dr. Whitaker. Go ahead and begin the dispelling process."

Mercy couldn't help flinching a bit at the backward compliment. Horn saw her as someone who'd overcome adversity. He knew that she had a disability that had required extra testing by Safe Harbor. They'd forced her into a special "tryout" before even allowing her in the medical school. She had to prove her fingers would not be an impediment in surgical procedures. Once she'd gotten past that test, though, the overseeing doctors had been biased against her. Never quite believing she could be as talented a doctor as her peers.

After completing her finals, Mercy had not been chosen for the program. Not at first. Her score had somehow fallen *just* short. Literally. She had missed the qualifying cut by a single percentage point. Fifty other students had beaten her. She was number fifty-one. The first one to be left out of the program. Also, the first alternate.

That had been the single worst week of her life. Practicing medicine, caring for patients. That was the only thing she'd ever felt called to do. And Balmerick was not a school that believed in backup options. You performed well and made a name for yourself—or the school would quietly forget you'd ever graced its halls. Mercy had spent winter break chewing her nails down to stubs, unable to even break the news to her parents.

And then Cora Marrin had died.

That awful story about the six students who'd gotten lost in the wilderness. Four of them had died, and one of them just happened to be the best surgeon in their class. When Balmerick removed the girl's name from the list, Mercy slid up to number fifty. An invitation arrived a few days later. She was to be a doctor, because some poor girl had been killed. Horn had an unfortunate habit of reminding her of the fact that she hadn't been chosen.

She dispelled the magic she'd cast over their patient. One layer at a time. Then she followed the protocol for cleaning tools, carefully resetting the room for the next surgeon who would use it. The entire time, she thought about the man in those glimpses. How bright and bold he looked in the patient's memories—and now the patient would never think about him again. Such permanence.

Horn had finished in the washroom by the time Mercy stepped inside. She washed her hands again and then activated the cleansing spell in the room. She stood in that eerie white light and felt the magic washing over her body. As soon as the door gasped open, she marched out, determined to go home and sleep for as long as the world would let her.

"Whitaker." Horn was down at the other end of the hallway. "Need to see you in my office."

Mercy steeled herself as they walked. Had she made an error during the surgery? Maybe there had been someone observing the operation and she would now be weighed and measured for each small detail. The real answer was waiting in Horn's office, and not at all what she expected.

A young man stood in the corner. He was absurdly handsome. Carved from stone. Broad shoulders. As fine a human being as she'd ever set eyes on. The only problem was that she'd set eyes on him before. Far too many times for her liking.

"Brightsword Legion? What's the saying? Leave them better than you found them?"

Her ex's cheeks flushed in response. Dr. Horn plunked into the seat behind his desk, clearly unaware of the pointed nature of her comment. After all, that was the legion's standard motto.

"Dr. Whitaker, this is Devlin Albright. A paladin that Brightsword sent over to us."

Devlin extended his hand. *Actually* extended his hand. As if the two of them had never met. As if they had not dated for three wasted years. As if she had not let him in on secrets that no one else knew about her. Mercy's eyes drilled into his.

"We've met."

Devlin blushed again. His hand fell back to his side. He lifted his chin—gods, that chin—before settling back into a perfect soldier's stance. It was only then that she noticed the emblem on his shirt. Not just the markings of Brightsword Legion. According to the crest, he'd already achieved lightbringer status. Rising through their ranks fast. No surprise. Devlin's main concern had always been his own achievements and reputation. Dr. Horn finally seemed to pick up on the tension between them. He was not the most socially adept person on staff, but this was hard to miss.

"Right," Dr. Horn said. "As you know, Doctor, we do not

typically use paladins within the walls of this hospital. But when the outlying provinces reach out for help—it is protocol for us to hire protection for our doctors. None of you are specifically trained in combat. Paladins are. This way, you can go about your duties without worrying about safety. Understood?"

Devlin was to serve as her protector. Gods knew he'd love that idea. It was enough to make Mercy grind her teeth. She tried to focus on the other half of what Dr. Horn was telling her. The more important detail. "The outlying provinces?"

Horn nodded. "We've had word from a town to the north: Running Hills. It's a farming community. A report just arrived of a disease that their local medic didn't recognize. Our services are required. It's my understanding you need one more practical to advance to fellow."

Mercy nodded. "Yes, sir. That's correct."

"Consider this your first chance," Horn said. "I want you to travel north with Mr. Devlin here. Treat the illness. Assess the population. Perform your assigned duties to the high standard that we expect at Safe Harbor—and I'll sign off on your papers. You'll officially be named a practicing fellow at this hospital. One of the first in your year, I think?"

Another nod was all she could manage. She'd been waiting for this moment. It did not come as a surprise. Not to her. She'd tracked all of the other graduates in her year, noting their progress, and she knew she'd put in more hours than anyone. She was ready for this moment, but she also desperately wished that Devlin would not be there to witness her efforts. Briefly, she considered asking for Horn to send for another paladin. It was an obvious conflict. A request for someone else wouldn't be unreasonable, but Mercy also knew it would be a coin flip.

If the timing was urgent, Horn could just as easily assign the case to another understudy, rather than having to coordinate a brand-new paladin with an entirely separate organization. She wanted to move forward. This was her chance. All of the pride she felt was tangling with annoyance, however.

On cue, Devlin cleared his throat. "I'm completing my own practical. It would seem our ships are tied together."

Mercy threw up a little in her mouth. She could not unleash any of the snide comebacks she wanted to say. Not in front of Dr. Horn. It wasn't worth risking this opportunity. Better to take the high road. "Thank you for the opportunity, Dr. Horn. When do I need to be ready?"

Horn pushed a small file of notes across the desk. His smile was apologetic.

"You leave tonight."

2

REN MONROE

Landwin Brood was dead.

And yet, he still managed to annoy Ren with great regularity. After they'd shown his corpse to the other houses—confirming Theo's ascension as head of house—there'd been a flurry of activity. Documents to sign. Ceremonies to attend. An expensive funeral to arrange. Ren and Theo had initially been focused on the moral task ahead of them. What would it look like to steer an ancient house, built on brutality, toward a brighter future. It was all they had really discussed after the funeral. Their reign—how it would be different. Ren had never imagined it would all be so . . .

"Tedious," she spat. "That's the only word that fits. This is *tedious*."

Theo nodded and paced, nodded and paced.

"I mean, what is the point of scheduling a specific time? If that's *not* when the meeting is?"

Her bond-mate didn't respond. Ren could sense him trying to push soothing thoughts across their link—and she swatted them away with a mental backhand. She was in no mood to be placated. They had been waiting outside the viceroy's residence—Beacon House—for forty-three minutes. They stood on a sprawling verandah that connected the more famous government building with the viceroy's actual private residence. Guards roamed in and out of sight. All Brightsword paladins. If she walked to the very corner of the porch, she could see most of Kathor—stretched out before her like a dream. It would have been more inspiring if the man in charge of running the city understood the concept of time.

"Seriously, if it was your father standing here—"

The great doors swung open. She expected another guard, but it was the viceroy himself. He wore a simple charcoal suit that drew out the silver in his hair and beard. The only slash of color was a crimson scarf, artfully knotted at his throat. He offered Ren a perfunctory nod before his eyes landed on Theo. Everyone always looked to Theo. Never mind the fact that she'd been the one to bring the former version of House Brood to its knees.

"Am I terribly late?"

Theo said, "Of course not," just loud enough that Ren's less charitable answer went unheard. The two of them exchanged a glance. Her bond-mate offered her a quick smirk. That almost-smile calmed her more than anything else could. The viceroy gestured and they entered and Ren supposed a proper apology was simply expecting too much.

Martin Gray was one of the most well-loved viceroys in recent memory. He possessed the unique quality of belonging to the great houses *and* to the people. Those in power were always quick to hold him up to the rest of the population. See? This is what comes of hard work and brilliant magic. Be like him, and you can accomplish anything. The great houses left out the part where he was the second son of an incredibly wealthy merchant. They also didn't emphasize the fact that the viceroy possessed little actual power.

He was the official leader of the Brightsword Legion—though there were generals throughout those ranks who, if push came to shove, would swing loyally back to their original houses. He could also veto laws, arrange tribunals, and exercise emergency powers that allowed him access to the resources of any house. But all the research on the subject proved viceroys rarely did any of those things without the direct involvement of the houses themselves. Essentially, he was the stick they occasionally used to rap each other on the knuckles.

Gray led them into a room with high ceilings. There were cushioned chairs circling a war table—though the only war the viceroy appeared to be waging was against a stack of unsigned documents. A fire crackled in the background. Most of the room's light came from a run of copper-plated windows at the far end of the room. Once they were seated, he looked at them like old friends who'd spent far too long apart.

"Theo Brood. From exile to this. You've accomplished something that hasn't been done in over a century. The other houses were all so flustered about it, but I must say, I admire you. It was quite the move on your part. Bravo."

Ren wished she could roll her eyes. Theo had been incredibly bold, of course, but it never ceased to stun her how quickly they mitigated her role in the story. She could also hear the words just beneath all of the bullshit praise: *We could not find a way to deny you, and so with great annoyance, welcome to the club.* Theo appeared unbothered by this opening.

"That's very kind," he said. "We appreciate you taking this meeting."

"Of course." Gray leaned back in his chair. "Consider me at your disposal."

Theo nodded. "We have several matters to discuss. I know your time is precious. I'll let Ren take the lead and I'll chime in as needed."

Gray's attention flicked to her. His smile appeared more forced now.

"Of course. Ms. Monroe. Where would you like to begin?"

Ren set a folder down on the table between them. "First, there's the matter of the Betraskan farms," she began. "We'd like the original tenants restored to their positions. It seems that, in the past week, the Shiverians replaced them with some of their own house members. You and I both know that's an overstepping of the original accord that governs the southern provinces. I've highlighted the language in that contract here . . . and here."

Tedious. That was the right word for all of this. Ren and Theo had spent the last few months drowning in bureaucracy. They had not visited any local shelters to hand out food. There were no grand moments of justice or restoration. None of the past had been put right. Instead, they had discovered that Landwin Brood—for all his faults—was a damned busy man.

His responsibilities were so expansive that Ren was starting to think that he had existed outside the boundaries of time itself. Thugar had been running the Brood estate, but it appeared that Landwin had secretly been steering the ship for his wayward son. Landwin's wife—Marquette Brood—had no interest in day-to-day operations. She'd spent most of her time reading about obscure pieces of history or attending luncheons. At one point, Tessa Brood had been appointed to manage some of the Brood's minor houses—but she'd ceded those duties back to her father after securing a role at the opera house. Ren couldn't fathom how Landwin had managed everything. Ren thought about that often. What secrets had died with the family's patriarch? What small pieces of history had she killed when she'd cast that final spell?

Theo and Ren had divided his father's responsibilities right down the middle—and yet both of them felt stretched beyond capacity. She was sleeping less than ever. The two of them would sometimes work in the same room, but had enjoyed little time together beyond that. This meeting was a perfect representation of why everything took so long. A combination of archaic contracts that could be misconstrued, and a painfully slow process for lawful clarification.

It took nearly twenty minutes to resolve the tenancy issue of the farm that was co-owned by the Shiverians and the Broods. Another fifteen minutes discussing a tax on canal goods that had stopped benefitting their house, and instead penalized them for not "operating using their own privately owned crafts." Ren ended her part in the proceedings by successfully reminding the viceroy that ten trained legionnaires from Brightsword should have been enlisted to their house on the first day of the month. He agreed to send those soldiers without delay. When Ren closed her folder, the viceroy clapped his hands together.

"How efficient," he said. "If that's all, I'll see you out."

"Not quite." Theo reached into the folds of his jacket. He

slid a new folder onto the table between them. Ren's stomach turned slightly. She buried the feeling quickly. Better to not let her fears flow across their bond at all. The folder he'd just set on the table looked identical to the one Landwin Brood had shown Ren before his death. The same color. The same style. But when Theo opened this one, it did not contain the only secret she'd kept from him. None of the private research that had been conducted into what happened that fateful day in the portal room.

Theo's folder held just one document. "This is the city's official defense contract. We need to renew it. This should have been signed weeks ago."

Gray leaned forward, drumming his fingers on the tabletop, as he read through the contract. It felt like a delay tactic to Ren. This document had to be known to him. He'd signed it nearly a decade ago, though he'd been sitting across from Landwin Brood then.

"The contract, as I understand it, is a formality," Theo added. "The original agreement was made in perpetuity. We sign it every ten years for show, but I've learned that some of our contracted workers have reportedly been locked out of the buildings covered in this contract. There's really no reason it would need to be enforced that way."

Gray nodded, eyes still scanning the page. "What are you asking exactly?"

"Why is it being enforced that way?"

"Locked doors and all that?"

Theo nodded.

"Well, the contract is in perpetuity on our end," Gray explained. He tapped one of the first paragraphs. "As you can see, there's a loophole here that allows *your* family out of the binding agreement. If you so desire. When you didn't arrive to sign the contract, I simply assumed you might not be interested in continuing in that role for the city."

"That's quite an assumption," Ren interjected.

Gray shrugged. "I would have had to make an assumption either way."

"Oh, come on," Ren said. Theo cut her off with a calming gesture. She knew she was reacting heatedly, but the viceroy was clearly playing the fool. Theo's reply was more gracious.

"There would be no benefit in letting those contracts lapse," he said. "We would lose access to any number of benefits to our house if we allowed those positions to return to the Kathorian government. Not to mention those are citywide defenses. You're endangering people by leaving those buildings unoccupied."

Gray snorted in response. "You and I both know there aren't *actual* threats to Kathor these days. Not like the ones that existed when those documents were first created. This contract once existed to secure the city. Now it exists to pad the coffers of House Brood. There's no need for you to pretend otherwise. It's just us here. No one's going to put you on trial for your family's history." He shook his head. "Trust me, Theo, there was a great deal of discussion about this particular matter. The rumor was that you—and Ms. Monroe here—intended to run your house in your own way. You claimed you didn't want to be the Broods of old."

Theo offered a begrudging nod. "That remains true."

"Well, that's why I didn't push the contract on you," Gray explained. "I thought it was possible that you might not want to continue with it. Every single role in this document is technically an *inherited* title. Do you know what would happen if you decided to hand them back to Kathor?"

Theo frowned. "The other houses would eventually claim them."

"Wrong," Gray replied. "They would become government entities. Sure, the other houses might nudge me for appointments. Ask me for favors. But you'd be returning a number of wealth-creating industries to the benefit of the people. Not to one of the great houses."

Theo leaned back in his chair. His eyes swung to Ren. She'd combed through the document, as well as a few adjacent resources. Everything in that contract was functionally acting as passive income for House Brood. It represented money that she'd always imagined was better in their capable hands than in the pockets of the other houses. More funding for their future efforts—though she hated to admit that if their present results were any indication, most of what they would do in the future would only benefit House Brood. There had been precious little time for active altruism so far.

"I could sign this," Gray said. "Here and now. Or . . . you could go home and think about what you'd like to do. All of your workers are contractually covered for two more weeks. They'll receive their wages as if they're all performing their normal duties. If you decide all of this should stay in the hands of House Brood, I'll sign the contract. But if you'd prefer these entities revert to the people?"

He shrugged his shoulders as if he didn't care at all. As if he was not playing a song that he knew both Theo and Ren liked. While the viceroy had treated her like an afterthought at the start of the conversation, curiously he now fixed his attention on her. Almost like he knew that she was the one who could push something truly revolutionary into motion between the two of them.

"I want to see it in writing," Ren said. "Stipulations on how each property would actually function, who would benefit, all of that."

The viceroy nodded. "I'll have my people create a draft. I obviously can't make guarantees, but there's not a lot of mystery about what would happen. It's as I said."

Theo looked unsettled. Instead of voicing any further concern, however, he tucked the folder back into his coat and nodded. "Put a meeting on the schedule. Exactly one week from now. And it'd be nice if you were punctual next time."

That earned a surprised look from the viceroy, but Theo was already standing. Ren followed suit. She was learning a lot from watching him in these spaces. The difference between common defiance and polished authority. How power looked if you just changed the angle slightly, setting it just so in the light. Theo's political ability had always felt natural to her. Something he'd been born with. But it was a skill, and skills could be taught. There was a lesson dangling over this moment. It was this: no matter what the viceroy pretended to be the case, Ren and Theo were the ones in this room who possessed true *power*.

House Brood was still very wealthy. Reduced by their attack last year, but still a massive influence that demanded attention. Out on the verandah, Ren started to speak. Theo silenced her with a quick hand motion. *Of course,* she thought. *Eyes and ears.* This was another lesson he'd been teaching her. On anyone else's property, there was always a chance of being overheard. People who were hired specifically because they had a magical talent for eavesdropping. Overhead, she spied movement. A livestone monkey was scrambling across the nearest roofline. Definitely within earshot. A glance back showed the viceroy was still watching them through the window as well, in between glances down at the papers on his desk. Better to wait.

When they'd cleared the grounds, Theo nodded to her.

"What do you think?"

"I feel like he's overpromising."

"It's possible. I can't remember historical examples of the major houses losing control of an asset—and then that asset being handed back to the commoners."

"Gods," Ren said. "I'm pretty sure that term has fallen out of fashion, Theo."

He winced. "Sorry. That was my father's word. My grandfather used to call them peasants."

Such a grim ancestry. She'd been learning this, too. Theo's past had a natural way of bubbling into the present. Not his own sins, but the men who'd walked this world before him. Their cruelties had not died with them. Every time they reached into the past to undo the knots, they found themselves untying some vital part of the present House Brood. This issue was no exception.

"Is it bad that I want to say no?" Ren said. "The idea of losing all of those resources . . ."

"It would weaken us," Theo agreed. "Substantially. And that would obviously limit what we can do against the other houses. They're already standing against us. Even if it's been subtle. All of these random issues are creeping forward. I feel like it's intentional. They're testing the boundaries. Poking at this contract or holding up this treaty to the light. It's taking up so much of our time. You know, that was actually one of my father's favorite strategies. Force your enemy to *react*. He'd always say, 'Keep a man backpedaling, and he'll never be able to hit you with all of his strength.'"

"What a charming thing to teach a child."

Theo snorted. "Now that you mention it, I was about six. Anyways. I'm not sure what the right answer is. The point of all that we're doing is to return power to the proper hands. We want to reduce the influence of the great houses. Create more equal footing for all. What does it say about us, though, if when we finally have the chance to do that . . . we keep the power for ourselves?"

He shook his head. Clearly, this central question was bothering him. Ren realized it was bothering him more than her. She'd leaned so quickly into *keeping* the wealth in their hands. It made her insides squirm to think about how little she'd questioned her own thought.

"Are we just pretending to be different?" Theo asked, voicing Ren's exact concerns. "Pretending that we're benevolent, when really we're the same as them? Or is keeping that much power a necessity for long-term success? I'm worried that if we let too much slip through our fingers, we might be too weak to make a difference."

Ren said nothing. It didn't make her feel good, but she knew what her decision would be. *Keep the power.* She didn't trust the viceroy to keep his word. What person, with that much power and position, had ever made the right choice? All that influence would really return to the people of Kathor? She had her doubts. Still, the decision weighed heavily on her shoulders. This felt like an unmarked crossroads for the two of them.

"We don't have to decide yet," Ren pointed out. "You have a few days."

"True," Theo replied. "Come on. We have one more appointment."

His words proved how exhausted she was; she couldn't even remember what the final appointment was. Dutifully, she followed Theo through the Safe Harbor district. Past the library with the beautiful stained glass windows. Around the polite little market. Theo led her down a flight of stairs and into what looked like a back alley. Ren was surprised when Theo led her to an unmarked doorway.

"Here we are," he announced.

The interior was delightfully nondescript. There was another door leading deeper within the building—but no other features at all. "Is this where you brought all your girlfriends over the years?"

He snorted. "I didn't have any girlfriends. And there's not actually an appointment. I've arranged this just for you." He turned with a smile, looking painfully sincere. "I know we've been busy. None of this is how we imagined it would be. You've taken so much on your shoulders and without a single complaint. I just . . . I wanted you to know that I've noticed. I couldn't do any of this without you."

Ren smiled in return. She did not point out that Theo's father would still be alive—and thus he wouldn't *have* to do any of this—if it were not for her. Instead, she watched as Theo shoved the interior door open. There was a rush of cool air. A narrow passage led deeper underground.

"I've booked you an archive room."

That passage into the dark waited for her. Ren knew if she walked forward the tendrils of magic would appear in the air. A practice session. Theo had arranged a practice session for her.

"Only if you want to, of co—"

She cut his nervous backpedaling off with a hug. As a rule, Ren was not a hugger. This felt like a worthy exception. Theo had been so steady. All this time. And now he was throwing in a moment of pure thoughtfulness?

"Careful, Theo Brood. I might just fall in love with you."

The most violent blush she'd ever seen flooded his cheeks. So intense that Ren felt embarrassed herself. The only way to silence the sudden hammering of her heart was to plunge into that waiting darkness. She felt the magic stir in the air around her. The way the tendrils whispered to life. Theo did not call after her. He made no embarrassing declarations of love. Instead, he closed the door and left her in peace.

A man who knows to leave me alone with my magic? Yes, please.

3

MERCY WHITAKER

Her travel bag consisted of a few outfits and a select arsenal of the medical tools that she'd been quietly adding enchantments to over the years. She also hastily packed a copy of Strolle's *The Common Plagues* for quick reference. Mercy was hoping to beat Devlin to the hospital's waxway room, but unfortunately, she found him already seated in the glinting light of candles that had been lit hours before. He looked like the smuggest statue in the world. His eyes were closed in concentration, but she saw his lips quirk slightly at the sound of her approaching footsteps. She wanted to reach out and smack him square in the forehead. Tell him to vanish from the room the same way he'd vanished five years ago.

Instead, Mercy took the seat across from him. She stared at the nearest candle, watching as the flame danced from side to side. Next, she studied the provided painting. It was a barn. The fixtures were all rusted. A broken fence flanked its left side. Her designated landing zone was an overgrown field with small, half-faded flowers. Mercy memorized the details before allowing her eyes to drift back to the flame once more.

Now for meditation. The candle needed to burn down a little more to cover their intended teleportation distance. Mercy tried to think about anything besides the person seated across from her: Devlin Albright. The two of them had dated for three years. Long enough that she'd met his family and he'd met hers. Long enough to make mistakes and say words they couldn't take back. Devlin had told her that he wanted to marry her. He'd spoken those words, whispered them in quiet moments. Countless times. All before breaking up with her during their first year at Balmerick.

The image of her destination had slipped away. Sighing, she opened her eyes and began studying the painting again. The wheat-thin blades of grass. The picket fence . . .

"I'm sorry it worked out this way. I didn't know I was being assigned to you."

Devlin's eyes were open. She looked past the candles at him—and a part of her wished she could undergo her own severance procedure. Perhaps Dr. Horn could cut through whatever cord was still connecting her to this creature.

"Mercy, it's not—"

Anger burned hot in her chest. "Dr. Whitaker. You will call me Dr. Whitaker. I am your unwilling associate on this excursion. As far as you're concerned, there's no one named Mercy here."

"Fine. Dr. Whitaker. I'm just here to do my job. That's all."

Of course. Devlin Albright. Duty above all else.

Mercy realized she was too annoyed to keep speaking with

him. She centered that image again in her mind, and then reached out and snuffed the flame between two fingers. Her travel spell activated. She vaulted through space and time. Away, briefly, from Devlin Albright. Her chest thrummed unpleasantly. As always, she felt a particular sharpness in her two dead fingers. Like some invisible hand had clamped down on them and was *squeezing*. She also felt an aching in her lower stomach. Where she'd had surgery during her time at Balmerick. Ghost pains that were at their worst, for some reason, when traveling through the waxways.

And then she stumbled back into the real world.

Her feet set down in the same field she'd been picturing. It took a moment to get her bearings. The farm had a single road leading away from it. There was a small town glowing in the distance. It had to be Running Hills.

Mercy began to walk. She heard the vague sounds of someone else porting behind her. There was a sharp gasp, muttered curses, and then Devlin was jogging to catch up with her.

"Dr. Whitaker," he called. And then more intensely, "Dr. Whitaker, seriously? You can't break protocol. You know I'm supposed to port first. What if there had been a trap? What if there was something wrong with our destination? The guarding paladin always ports first."

Mercy made a show of patting herself down. "All my parts are still attached. The portal destination seems to be operating just fine. If you're experiencing any negative effects, do feel free to head back to Kathor. I'd be fine if Brightsword wanted to send a replacement."

He made an annoyed noise that pleased Mercy to no end. She also took joy in pushing the pace—forcing him to match her strides for once. Gods knew that never happened in their actual relationship. In the distance, Running Hills appeared to be a departure from Kathor in every way. Back in the city, everything was built tight and tall. The goal was to fit as many people as possible into limited space. Here, the buildings spread out. It was as if someone had taken them all in the palm of their hand and rolled them over the hills like dice, watching as they scattered randomly. What she'd assumed was the town center turned out to be a circle of just five stoic buildings. There was a man sitting on the front steps of one. Everything else was quiet. Not another soul in sight.

Mercy hesitated before glancing at Devlin.

"Do you remember the description of our contact?"

"Midforties," Devlin answered. "Light brown skin. Shaved head. That has to be him."

Their approach drew his attention. The man stumbled down the steps to meet them. Notably, he wore a mask covering his mouth and nose. It was a quiet reminder of why they'd been summoned in the first place. There was disease running through this town.

"You came!" the man said. "I didn't think anyone would actually come! Well, this is so exciting. I mean—the situation is obviously quite bleak—but to have a pair of Kathorian-trained doctors! Here in Running Hills. It's all just so unexpected! I'm Nance Forester."

He extended his hand. Devlin started to reached out, but Mercy pulled him back.

"Apologies," she said. "But infections spread in a variety of ways. Your mask is an excellent precaution. Limited physical contact is another. I'm Dr. Mercy Whitaker. This is my assigned paladin—Devlin Albright. Could you give us any more information on what's happening? All we were told is that your medic encountered a disease they didn't recognize."

Nance hastily withdrew his hand. "Right. Of course. My apologies. Let's talk and walk. Two wyverns with one stone as they say."

He turned to lead them through the heart of the town. The path diverged there, running in four different directions. Nance led them due east. Mercy kept a healthy distance between them for the sake of protocol. Devlin trailed them both like an unwelcome spirit. It was quiet. She could not remember the last time she'd left Kathor, but she'd drastically underestimated the noise of a proper city. Out here there was just the breeze and their footsteps crunching along the packed dirt.

"The first one to get sick was a boy," Nance said. "His name is Wells. One of the farmhands over at Mariner's place. Good kid. He went to bed looking as healthy as a fresh-picked apple. The next morning, he wakes up and —you'll see what I'm talking about—it looked like the other boys at the place had beat him in his sleep. All of them swore up and down that they didn't touch the kid. When he starts complaining about his 'insides burning,' they finally decided to call the local medic.

"So naturally she heads that way. Not a proper doctor, mind you, but she knew her business. She did some triage during the War of Neighbors. Not to mention she's delivered every baby born in Running Hills over the last two decades. Anyways, she assesses the kid. Treats him. The next day? He's worse, and *she* gets sick. Goes down with the exact same ailments. Everyone was hoping it would pass, but then all the other farmhands at Mariner's contracted the illness. We officially reported the disease to Safe Harbor when it spread to one of the other farms."

Mercy frowned. "Was there direct contact between the two locations?"

"That's a good question to ask the fieldhands," Nance said. "I didn't have time to conduct more interviews. I'm the chair of the farming union across this whole district. Which means I haven't slept a wink, between monitoring the disease and trying to organize getting extra workers out this way. We're smack in the middle of harvest season. None of our farms can afford to be short-staffed right now."

"You're bringing more people here?" Mercy asked. "From other towns?"

That wasn't exactly the best protocol when an unknown disease was spreading.

Nance shrugged. "What other choice do we have? The work happening this month amounts to about eighty percent of the town's yearly profit."

Mercy knew, if necessary, she had the authority to issue a lockdown. Safe Harbor's doctors could serve as temporary governmental authorities. She wasn't exactly sure what she could do to enforce such a command—other than having Devlin act intimidating—but her field guide made it clear she could do what was necessary to preserve the health and wellness of the wider civilization.

"So, two farms are involved. Your medic is sick. How many total patients?"

"It's actually four farms now," Nance corrected. "Last count was twenty-three, but I haven't been able to check in since earlier this afternoon. It could be higher."

Mercy was so shocked that she glanced back at Devlin. He looked surprised too. She hated that he was her only confidante here, but the reality was that those *were* shocking numbers. That was quite a wide spread compared to most diseases she'd spent time studying.

"Any social events recently? Dances or festivals?"

Nance shook his head. "Not really. I mean, it's a small town. There are only so many folks to socialize with. The tavern stays busy, I suppose. People coming in and out. But no event that the whole town would have attended at the same time."

Mercy was deep in thought when the farm finally appeared. The main building was surprisingly large. Sprawled out in the heart of a small valley, surrounded by endless rows of a crop she could not quite make out in the dark. Nance didn't lead them toward the main house in the distance. Instead, he directed them to a series of smaller cabins. Residences for the farm's hired hands, she guessed. Mercy signaled to their host before he knocked on any doors.

"Would you give me a moment? I want to discuss the proper spellwork with my associate. Just to make sure we're on the same page about how to proceed."

Nance nodded. "Yes, of course."

He stood there for a moment before realizing Mercy desired a private conversation. There was movement on the opposite end of the cabins. A man appeared, hauling two massive buckets of water. He was barrel-chested and towering. His eyes fixed uncomfortably on Mercy until Nance trotted off in that direction. They exchanged a few words she couldn't hear, and Nance helped him with the buckets. When they were out of earshot, Devlin nodded to her.

"You want to discuss spellwork?"

"Of course not," she answered. "I'm almost a fellow at Safe Harbor. I know what spells to use. I just wanted to get your take of the situation."

Primarily because she had no one else she could ask, but still, Devlin looked pleased to be included in the discussion. "Twenty-three seems like a high number in such a short time."

"It is," she agreed. "But I'm more concerned by the fact that it's spread to so many other locations. It's one thing for a dozen men sharing bunks to all get sick. That's common enough. The leaps from farm to farm suggest a rapid-spreading contagion. Which is bad . . . but only if it's *bad*."

Devlin frowned. "You lost me."

"The nature of the disease," she said, thinking out loud. "If the disease results in an intense head cold, no big deal. That happens every winter. But if a truly deadly disease can spread this rapidly, you're looking at something far more dangerous. Let's put on masks. Triple-layered sealing enchantments over everything. We'll refresh the spells every fifteen minutes."

She looked over expectantly, and realized she was waiting for Devlin to add his two cents. It was muscle memory from their time together. She'd always been so uncertain of herself back then. Lacking in proper confidence. She'd looked to Devlin for the final word on every topic they discussed. His opinions had quietly stolen in and replaced her own. But now, they were standing squarely in the heart of *her* expertise. She didn't need any notes from him. Really, she'd just needed to talk through it out loud to someone—a method for sorting her thoughts out.

"Let's begin."

She offered Devlin one of her own surgical masks before setting to work on casting every protective enchantment she thought would be useful. Nance and the other man were still delivering buckets of water, and Mercy couldn't help noticing how the other man's eyes slid back to her again and again. His attention crawled uncomfortably over her skin.

"He keeps staring," Mercy whispered.

Devlin replied quietly, "I suspect you're one of the only women to visit the farm in a while. I also suspect you're one of the prettier ones to ever step foot in Running Hills."

"Doesn't make it any less creepy."

Ready to get on with the work, she signaled for Nance. Their host set down a final bucket and hustled back to their side. "All sorted out?" he asked.

"What's with the buckets?"

"All of them are thirsty. An almost unquenchable thirst. Holt's been delivering water to them all afternoon. He's a hand-for-hire in town," Nance explained. "Works odd jobs for me every now and again. Mostly maintenance, but right now, there's no one else left to help with this. All the farmhands are sick."

Another disconcerting symptom. Almost as disconcerting as the way Holt kept glancing at her between deliveries. When the silence stretched, Devlin cleared his throat.

"I'll make sure it's safe to go inside."

Before Mercy could nod her approval, there was a bright flash—like a miniature sun. Out of that brightness, a hound emerged. She could not tell if he was fully corporeal or made of light, but the creature briefly cocked its head back toward Devlin. An unspoken command traveled between them. The hound trotted forward—and blurred straight through the still-closed door. Nance actually clapped in delight at the summoning. Mercy glanced at Devlin.

"That's new."

"My divinity shield," he replied, clearly proud. "Just one of the forms it can take."

She restrained herself from calling the hound cute. Inside, they heard a brief yelp that was entirely human. She supposed that a dog made of golden light would be a shocking thing to wake up to. Hopefully, the young man didn't think he was hallucinating. A few more seconds passed, and then the hound returned. Mercy thought it was rather convenient to have a creature who could walk through walls at your disposal.

"All clear," Devlin announced. "It's just the boy inside."

A single touch from him had the hound vanishing like a puff of golden mist. The substance soaked back into his skin. Absorbing like sunlight. A shiver ran down Devlin's body. Mercy saw his neck muscles straining. His chest rising and falling.

No, no, no, she thought. *Don't look at that. Don't notice that. Not today. Not ever again.*

"Let's get started," Mercy said, flustered by the distraction.

Nance rapped on the door. "We're coming in, Wells. Make sure you're decent."

Their host shouldered inside. It was a decent-sized space. Far nicer than what her expectations had been. Three bunks with six total beds. A candle burned at the center of the room and she suspected it was enhanced by a small cantrip, because its glow curled through every nook and cranny. More than bright enough to read a book or journal by. Mercy's eyes found the only occupied bunk. A boy sat there, shirtless but otherwise covered. That first glimpse drew a shocked gasp from her. His entire body—from head to hip—was covered in bruises. The colors were fading, but that did not make the painful constellations any less terrible. She'd never seen so many contusions on one body—and she'd once treated a wyvern flier who'd slipped from his mount and plummeted hundreds of feet, his body rag-dolling through the branches of the forest below. This was worse. As if the patient had been subjected to thousands of miniature stun spells. Mercy carefully schooled her expression as Nance made introductions.

"Wells. A doctor has come from Kathor. She'd like to talk with you."

Devlin took up his post in the corner of the room. Mercy knew that the mask likely made her appear more frightening. She did her best to smile with her eyes.

"Hello, Wells. I'm Dr. Whitaker."

He smiled at her and the sight was nearly enough to break her heart. It was a lovely, boyish smile. A reminder that he couldn't be a day older than fifteen. The bruises had made him seem more mature somehow. As if pain like that could only knock on the door of someone old enough to face it. She removed a journal and a pen from her pocket.

"I'm just going to take some notes while we talk. Would you mind telling me about your symptoms? How you're feeling?"

The smile retreated some. "Better. A little better. It hurt like hell at the start. The first thing was the bruises. I'm still sore, but when it started, it felt worse. Like I was burning inside."

"No pain on the exterior of your body?"

The boy shook his head.

"So, no one hit you? There were no physical altercations?"

"No. Nothing like that. I get along fine with everyone here."

"Not even with magic? No one struck you with a spell?"

Again, he shook his head. "Nothing I can remember. Besides, none of the boys here know much magic. A few spells to make our work easier. Weight reversal charms or sunshade spells maybe. You learn the spells that'll help you survive harvest week, you know? Are there really spells that can do this?" He gestured to the bruises covering his body. "Are there?"

He looked afraid. Mercy was quick to shake her head.

"No, you're right. I haven't ever seen a spell do this. What else? Besides the bruises?"

She hated to ask that question. Weren't the bruises enough? It looked unbelievably painful to hold that much damage inside a single body. The boy scratched at his collarbone before answering.

"I'm thirsty. My tongue just feels so dry. And I'm exhausted. More than just tired. It's like I'm just . . . empty inside."

"That's common when you're sick," Mercy offered. "To not feel like yourself."

He nodded. "And sometimes . . . I wake up and I'm not sure where I am. You know, kind of like a fog. It's like . . . I think I'm back at my mom's place. Even though I've been here for a couple of years. Longer than a lot of the other boys. I forgot some of their names too. Even this morning, I was trying to do a little spell just to heat my tea back up—and I couldn't remember any of the steps. I don't know. It's like my brain is all turned over."

Mercy scribbled down everything he was saying. It was a strange set of symptoms. Not what you'd typically see with a communicable disease. "Any fever?"

"Maybe on the first day?" Wells shrugged. "But like I said, it was more like . . . I was burning *inside*. Not just heat. It was pain. I've had fevers before. Been every kind of sick. Working on farms like these, you catch a little of everything. But this didn't feel like that."

She nodded. "Any tightness in your chest at all?"

"Not that I've noticed."

"All right. I'd like to listen to your heart and your lungs. Do you mind?"

She held up her stethoscope, the same way she might to a small child, so that he could see it fully in the light and know it wasn't anything that would hurt him. Wells nodded in return. When she gestured for him to come a bit closer, he obeyed, swinging his legs over the side of the bunk. He wore leggings that ran down to his midcalf. She noted small bruises on the skin there as well. He sat up nice and straight, shivering only slightly when she set the tool against his wiry, birdlike chest.

Mercy followed the standard protocol. Listening to the boy's heart, his lungs, his intestines. Trying to hear any murmurs or oddities. His heartbeat was almost normal. So very close to the normal thump, thump, thump of a healthy patient. If she had not been so thoroughly trained, she wouldn't have heard the difference. But it was there. Right there.

An echo.

The sound was unlike anything she'd ever heard. Back during her training, students were given a series of enchanted stethoscopes. According to their overseeing doctors, every known abnormality could be studied by listening to the sounds in that room. She'd trained through all of them, learning each rhythm, understanding what was an abnormality and what was not.

This was something else.

An absence. Like something is missing.

"Everything sound all right?" Wells asked. His voice was so earnest.

"Yes," she answered automatically. "Yes, you sound normal."

No point in breathing out the unknown at this point. It would only make him more afraid. Mercy smiled reassuringly, earning one more of those boyish smiles in return, and then she stood. Her eyes swung over to Nance, who had been watching the exchange closely.

"I'll need to see the others. And I'll need to visit the other farms. Tonight."

4

NEVELYN TIN'VORI

Nevelyn Tin'Vori felt most at home in a library.

When she was little, she used to sneak into her father's study. His collection had been extensive. She would hoist herself onto the ledge above the lower cabinets and walk from end to end, her fingertips tracing the spines. They'd had their childhood home publicly returned to them—but all the books had been stolen. Every cabinet was emptied. The scavengers had come and gone over the years, picking the entire house clean. Down to the bone.

Lacking an alternative, Nevelyn walked to the nearest library every morning. It was in the opposite direction of the playhouse. Away from any trace of Garth. She visited the Safe Harbor district instead. Access to the library there was restricted, but Theo Brood had happily petitioned on her behalf. A kind gesture, even if it bordered on negligence.

After all, Nevelyn spent every hour in that library researching the Broods. She read through archaic business contracts.

Squinted at the minutes of historical legislatures, hoping to see how they'd voted on various issues. Land purchases, leasing agreements, execution notices. It wasn't dissimilar to the work they'd done in Ravinia. Their apartment closet had been papered from top to bottom. Even a whisper of the Brood name would have found its way onto that wall. They'd been so hungry for news that any scrap tasted good.

Now she had the opposite problem. An abundance. The meal that was on the table now felt so large that if she started eating it from the wrong direction, she'd never get to the best parts. That was her current task. Figuring out which books or essays possessed information of true value. Her task was made difficult by how public the Broods' lives were. Society knew so many of the family's sins. Not just whispers in back alleys. Documented atrocities. Most of them overlooked because for generations the Brood name had been synonymous with the city's survival.

Nevelyn was not pursuing skeletons. No, she needed flaws in the machine that the Broods had built. Surely, they must exist. No family could grow that powerful—span that wide an empire—without unintentionally creating weaknesses. Nevelyn wanted to nestle into those cracks. Dig around. Maybe help them grow a bit wider. Week after week, she returned to the same library. Researching until she could barely keep her eyes open.

It took a month to find the first worthy curiosity.

She was at her favorite table. Documents sprawled the length of it. The title of the book that had her attention was *In Defense of a City*. The introduction was written like a story. It followed a specific point of view that Nevelyn eventually realized was Theo Brood's grandfather. The account had been quite gripping, but now she saw it was a foreword. An introduction. One that invited her into the reading of yet another tiresome city contract.

She was on the verge of tossing the book aside when she saw the final pages. Every ten years, two separate parties signed this document. One was always a member of House Brood. She saw Theo's grandfather, then his father. On and on through the decades. The other signee was a rotating list of Kathor's viceroys. What truly caught Nevelyn's eye, however, was the last entry. It was unfinished. The word "EXPIRED" had been etched across that entire section in someone else's handwriting.

"What the hell . . ."

According to the record, the ten-year mark should have been two weeks ago. The contract had lapsed. Even though the Broods had signed it a dozen times over the course of more than a century—always on the exact same day—this time it had lapsed? That realization begged an absolutely crucial question. "What is this even *for?*"

Nevelyn scanned back through the contents of the contract. Words like "civilian" and "domain" and "sovereign" threatened to drag her thoughts down into the mud. Nevelyn read the entire thing three times. It took that long to understand what she was reading. This was the city's primary defense contract. The document that committed Kathor in good faith to their ongoing relationship with the Brood family. More specifically, it was the contract that gave the Broods permission to occupy, control, and profit from a number of publicly owned facilities.

Nevelyn had already found evidence of this strategy during

her research. For the other great houses—the Shiverians, the Proctors, the Winters, and the Graylantians—private wealth was the heart of their endeavors. The Broods were not like them. They had been too busy protecting the city to accumulate piles of wealth. They were warriors and guardians, rather than builders or doctors. But they had wisely extracted promises from the wealthier houses they protected. A share of profits here. Free access to this canal or that theater. All in perpetuity.

Which meant this document was unique.

"Why didn't you re-sign the contract?"

Her question was for an imagined version of Theo Brood. Or maybe even for Ren Monroe—who Nevelyn knew far better. She was not the sort of person to miss a detail. Especially not one as pivotal as this. From what Nevelyn could see, the unsigned contract would leave loyal Brood workers without access to some of the most functionally important facilities in the city. That alone made it feel like something that would bubble quickly to the surface of Brood's attention. If his guards were being kept out of their normal workspaces, wouldn't they report back to him?

There was one potential flaw in her discovery. The text she was reading was a *bound* manuscript. A copy that was magically linked to the original text, which was located elsewhere. Nevelyn knew the translating spells took time. And the older the documents got, the larger the gap between the original and the copy. She had no idea if the missing signature was still accurate.

This concern led her to the librarian.

During her visits, she'd never seen the man away from his desk. He looked as if he'd been nailed down in that chair a decade ago, and someone simply came to change out his wardrobe every few days. Today he wore one of his less frumpish cardigans. When Nevelyn cleared her throat and held out the book in question, he looked at her like she was offering him a plague.

"Yes?"

"This book. It's bound to the original. I wanted to make sure it's current."

He stared at her. "Current?"

She nodded before setting the book on the desk in front of him. "Current, yes. There are contracts within the text that appear to be incomplete. I wanted to know if there might be a delay in the magic. Between the original and this one."

"A delay?"

"Yes, a delay. Are you going to start using your own words, or are you planning on repeating mine for the remainder of the conversation?"

The man leaned back in his chair, incredulous. She was about to apologize when his face split into a grin. "You don't have to make such a big fuss about it. Look, I maintain the magic here. If there's a delay, it would be a reflection on *my* spells. It would mean I'm not taking time each week to update the charms that currently link my collection to the others around the city. Do I strike you as a man who does not maintain order?"

She squinted at him. "You have three *different* stains on that shirt."

He glanced slowly down, and then belted out a laugh.

"Damn it. This is my favorite shirt, too." He rubbed at the most glaring stain before looking up at her. "I visited the food stand for lunch. Just one of my many sins. Anyways. Everything in the library is current. I can show you how to check for yourself. That way next time, you don't have to come here and be a brat about it."

Nevelyn couldn't help grinning. Were they becoming friends? With practiced care, the librarian flipped to the front of the book. There was a section with very small writing. She saw it had details about the book's publication—and she also saw that there were details about the book's physical location, first printing date, and more. His finger traced down to the very bottom line in that thicket of text.

"The magic was refreshed two hours ago. It's current, dear."

She accepted the book back from him. "Thank you. And I'm not your *dear*."

The two of them exchanged smirks before Nevelyn retreated back to her section of the library. A small thrill filled her steps. This was something. It might be something. At least until Theo Brood realized his error and amended it. Now she just needed to know which buildings around the city were currently unoccupied. The next hour saw her feverishly turning the pages of various reference books. She managed to identify seven books that would have the information she needed. Rather than spend the evening hunting them down, she took the list back to her new friend.

"You never mentioned your name," Nevelyn noted.

"A good librarian never would. We are neutral arbiters of information. Faceless servants of the masses. It is not our duty to be known. . . ."

Nevelyn rolled her eyes.

"Oh fine. My name is Robert."

"Suits you."

He smiled before adjusting his reading glasses and eyeing

her list. She watched as he flipped through a massive reference book. It served as a catalogue of all the texts in the library's possession—as well as a detailed account of patron activity.

"The first one isn't here," Robert said, already turning the pages. He hummed a small tune to himself. "And the second one . . ."

Already claimed. So was the third, and the fourth. Nevelyn found herself nodding along as Robert quietly confirmed that every single book on her list was in someone else's possession.

"All by the same person, too," Robert said. "You must be studying the same subject."

Nevelyn craned her neck. "Who has them?"

Robert smiled as if her question was a joke. When Nevelyn did not laugh, he shook his head like a man who'd just stepped through cobwebs. "I can't share that information. There are privacy laws that protect the patrons here. I could lose my position."

"Perhaps you could take a bathroom break," Nevelyn suggested. "For just a moment."

That was all it took to ruin their friendship. Robert's playful expression shut down.

"It isn't permitted. Do not ask it of me again."

He turned away from her, looking forlorn. Like the opportunity to make a new friend had slipped through his fingers. She watched him close the reference book before resuming his own work. Nevelyn retreated back to her corner of the library. It would not do. She had to know the name of the person who'd borrowed the *exact* set of books she wanted.

After the briefest of hesitations, Nevelyn reached for the heart-shaped charm dangling against her collarbone. She turned it so the dark side was facing out—then went right back to the librarian's desk. Before Robert could look up, she *pushed* her magic in his direction. *Do not see me. Look elsewhere. Behold me not.* The older man's head jerked unnaturally to the left. His eyes fixed on the window that overlooked a courtyard outside. She knew he would sit there transfixed for another thirty seconds. More than enough time. Nevelyn flipped back to one of the pages she'd seen him inspect. Her finger traced down the page until it landed on a familiar title. On that same line, the patron who'd checked out the book.

Ren Monroe.

That had to be wrong. Was she imagining the name? Even though she could feel the tension of her maintained spell starting to grow fraught—Nevelyn turned to another page. Searching. She had to confirm the truth. Sure enough, the next entry matched the first.

Ren Monroe.

A moment's hesitation—and then Nevelyn ripped the page out. The sound nearly dragged Robert's attention back to her. She could see the way his body wanted to resist the magic. It was time for her to leave. Before this all went awry. Nevelyn shoved the page into her pocket, closed the reference book, and glided toward the exit. Only when she was safely in the outer alcove did she release the spell—gasping as the tension in her shoulders began to unknot. Both of her hands shook, but she didn't have time to recover. There was one more detail she needed to check.

Nevelyn skipped her favorite market stalls on the way home. She did not dally by her favorite storefronts. Instead, she bustled through the front door of their home and started immediately up the steps. Ava called from the kitchen. Nevelyn ignored her. There was a lonely-looking dresser in the corner of her bedroom. She opened the top drawer and fished through the various trinkets until she found what she was looking for.

It was the note Ren Monroe had written her last year. She unfolded the ripped entry from the reference book and held them both up to the light. The handwriting didn't match.

Someone else had the books.

". . . lose your hearing?!"

Nevelyn whipped around. "What?"

"I've been shouting for you," Ava said. "There's a visitor."

There was a brief slash of a second where Nevelyn thought it might be Garth. But of course it wasn't Garth. He was dead. Buried just outside her window. If she looked, she could see the small mound of his grave—but she never looked. Her eyes cut back to Ava instead.

"Why would there be a visitor? You're not supposed to let anyone in."

"I didn't let him in," Ava said. "I found him lurking in the gardens."

Nevelyn frowned. "Spying?"

"Maybe," Ava replied. "It's hard to say. He's kind of . . . small for a spy."

"Small how?"

"What do you mean *small how?* Physically small. He's a child, Nevelyn."

It was hard to process that response. One part of her had been hoping for Garth. The other part had been dreading the thought that Ren Monroe might show up. Their former partner had a knack for appearing whenever her name was mentioned.

Like a spirit who'd been summoned. For some reason, the idea of a child waiting for her was the only more disturbing possibility.

"I don't like children," she muttered as she passed Ava.

The two of them took the stairs together. Her sister's hair was slowly growing back. She'd kept it trimmed short during her time in Nostra. It was not quite shoulder length yet—which meant it still wasn't quite long enough for her to walk the streets of Kathor without being recognized. Nevelyn knew her sister was growing restless, but the decision to remain hidden had been Ava's idea. It would only be a few more weeks before she could roam more freely.

"You know, I wouldn't just let someone in," Ava said, clearly annoyed. "I did manage to survive for two whole years without you pecking me up and down like some sort of mother hen."

Nevelyn nodded. "You're right. I'm sorry. Old habits."

It was so good to have Ava back, but they couldn't let anyone else know she'd returned safely. After the dust had settled with the Broods, Dahvid had made an official inquiry. What had happened to Theo's castellan? Dahvid had revealed that the girl was in fact their sister. They'd offered Brood a carefully rehearsed story. Why had they chosen to hide her existence? Well, if the two of them died during the attack, they'd wanted one Tin'Vori to survive. Theo had put on quite a show in return. His claim was that Dahl Winters—as he had known her—vanished right after the army passed through Nostra. He claimed that he had not seen the girl since.

It would have been a perfectly reasonable lie if Ava wasn't alive to counter it. She had ported directly to the Tin'Vori estate and told them the entire story. How close she'd been to killing Brood. How Ren Monroe had appeared out of nowhere to save him. They'd walked back through the details a hundred times, all of them confused by Ren's ability to be in two places at once, but in the end, all that mattered was that they'd agreed to keep Ava hidden. If Theo and Ren believed their sister was dead, it was like having a piece on the game board that no one knew about. Now it was simply a matter of making the right moves.

The two of them reached the landing. Nevelyn glanced around the room.

"Is the child also invisible?"

Ava rolled her eyes. "He's still out back."

Frowning, Nevelyn followed her sister. The sun was bleeding toward the horizon. She could see the clay-red light pressing through the great run of windows along the back of their house. And she could also see the boy in question. He was *very* small. Nevelyn had been expecting, or perhaps hoping, for someone over the age of twelve. Someone that age could at least be spoken to and dealt with in a reasonable manner. But as they stepped outside, she saw that he was no older than eight or nine.

"Why didn't you just tell him to leave?" Nevelyn whispered.

The sound of her voice must have carried. Just enough to be heard. The boy turned—and Nevelyn saw why Ava had not asked him to leave. The shape of his face. The thick limbs and the wide shoulders. He even had Garth's deep-set eyes. But when he turned, his face didn't frame itself in that lovely smile she remembered. Instead, his eyebrows knitted together in suspicion.

"You're Nan," he said.

Nevelyn could barely breathe. She felt Ava hovering beside her.

"Nevelyn. My real name is Nevelyn."

The boy studied her. His dark hair tossed slightly in the wind. He reached a small hand up to swipe it away from his eyes. "My brother liked you."

Those words struck her square in the chest. An unintentional reminder that Garth was gone. He had *liked* her. Once. Before. Never again. But the word that eventually drifted to the surface of her mind was "brother." She hadn't been certain at first glance. Garth had always felt like he was the same age as her, but she'd never bothered to ask. It had been possible that this was his son. Now she had an answer. The two were siblings.

"Where are your parents?"

The boy's eyes fell to his feet. "Mum's no good. Dad was worse. Garth took me in as soon as he found a place of his own."

"He lived in an apartment. Near the theater. Is that where you live?"

The boy's chin dipped even farther. "They told me I couldn't stay."

"They who?"

"Paladins," the boy said. "Garth wasn't paying the rent. Our landlord reported me. The paladins came and said I have to leave. I told them it wasn't fair, because Garth was dead. That's when they took me away. To one of those places with all the other kids."

Nevelyn exchanged a glance with Ava.

"An orphanage?"

He nodded, but still wouldn't make eye contact. She did not need to ask him how he liked it there. She could guess. The three of them had passed through plenty of orphanages after leaving Kathor. Nearly every time problems would find them. An abusive nurse. A gang of boys who wanted to put Dahvid's strength to the test. One place had been infested with tiny, flesh-eating bugs. Their skin had itched for weeks afterward. Nevelyn knew those places were rarely full of light. At least not enough light for a quiet boy like this.

"What's your name?"

"Josey."

Nevelyn nodded. "How'd you find me, Josey?"

The boy fished through the pockets of his coat. There was a thick-cut paper, folded many times over, with small rips and a number of stains. He unfolded it with such tender care. As if it were a map that might lead to treasure. But when he showed her its contents, she saw it was not of a place—but a person.

"Whoa," Ava said. "Is that you?!"

Nevelyn saw herself in the delicate brushstrokes too, but it was like seeing herself as Garth had seen her. Her hair was not the unruly nest she'd always imagined, but a waterfall of dark curls. He'd captured her shape, too. He had not imagined her any differently than she was. The fullness of her was there on the page, something cherished and lovely. In the image, she was bending slightly. Reaching for something. Nevelyn's heart caught in her chest. It was the mail wall from the opera house. A stolen glimpse from their past. A past that had no possibility of a future.

"Gods," she muttered. "I didn't even know he could draw."

Josey cleared his throat. "I looked for you. In the markets. Every day. One day, you walked past the theater. I wasn't sure it was you, but I . . . I followed you. Here."

She stared at him, unable to say anything at all.

"I thought if you liked him, maybe you'd like me, too."

There was enough sincerity in his voice to shatter Nevelyn's heart all over again. She imagined him searching for her each day. Imagined him folding up that portrait, sneaking through their backyard, and knocking on their back door—hoping someone in this world might care for him. She was not one for physical touch, but she held out her hand. He took it without hesitation.

"Are you hungry?" she whispered.

Her touch seemed to unlock him. Almost like he'd been guarding himself until he was certain what her answer would be. He started rattling off his favorite and least favorite foods. His hand was so small and warm. She couldn't help thinking of the way Garth's hand had swallowed hers. How safe it made her feel. Now it was her turn to be that for someone.

"Take a seat over there. We'll get you fed."

She gave his hand a quick squeeze before releasing him. Nevelyn started pulling out ingredients. Ava rustled through the other drawers helpfully. Outside, the sun was setting over the harbor. The boy threw his elbows on the table and then lowered his chin into the crook of his crossed arms. Like he was too tired to sit up straight for even a second longer. Nevelyn's and Ava's eyes met. They spoke without speaking. Ava set down the knife she'd been chopping carrots with.

"I'll go get his room ready."

Nevelyn nodded once. Darkness was creeping over the yard

outside. Shadowing the three graves there. Before she could even finish cutting the rest of the vegetables, the boy was snoring softly. Which was a kindness. It meant no one was there to watch as she began to weep.

5

MERCY WHITAKER

After a grueling night of visits and examinations, Mercy and Devlin were led back to the center of town by Nance—who looked as tired as she felt. They were guided to the back of one of the larger buildings. There was a basement entry that led to an unused apartment. Nance claimed to have hosted "foreign dignitaries" there over the decades, though Mercy could not imagine a proper politician staying in this place for long. The apartment would be theirs as long as they stayed in Running Hills. It was nice to have a proper base of operations, she supposed.

Mercy took two steps inside and stopped dead in her tracks.

"There's . . . only one bed?"

Nance craned his neck. "Wonderful. I knew I shouldn't have trusted Holt with this. Gods, that man has a brain the size of a stunted pea sprout. We have extra mattresses, I promise, but the supply closet is locked at this hour. Can you make do for tonight? I'll be back here bright and—" He was cut off by his own, stifled yawn. "Early. I'm very sorry. It's completely unprofessional."

Mercy was too tired to voice her complaint. Of course they couldn't just make do with one bed. That was absurd. But their host interpreted her silence as compromise. He departed with a wave over one shoulder. Devlin glanced at Mercy, who had decided that looking anywhere else in the room was preferable. Both of them set to work immediately. Cleansing enchantments, security checks, but with all of the enthusiasm of two people who had been awake for far too long.

Thankfully, there wasn't a whole lot to check. A small bathroom. An even smaller closet. Aside from the bed, two mismatched tables made up the only other furniture in the space. When their tasks were complete, Mercy realized they were in the same awkward position as they'd been in upon arrival. Devlin broke first.

"You take the bed."

"Oh. Right. And you'll take what? The corner?"

He snorted. "I slept on far worse during my training. Take the bed."

Devlin was the son of a posh merchant in Kathor. She highly doubted they'd been too rough on him during his training. Still, it annoyed her just how classically Devlin this moment was. He always took the high road at the start. A rampant sort of kindness. He would build himself up through good deeds and heartfelt gestures—but she'd also learned that the point of Devlin's kindness was not how it made others feel. The point was how it positioned him in the relationship. When they'd dated, he would build up a resume that he could later wield against her in crucial moments. During every argument, he'd fall back on his good deeds, leaving her constantly on the lower moral ground. Which meant even when she was right, she somehow felt wrong.

The difference now was that they weren't dating. When their tasks in Running Hills concluded, they'd go their separate ways. He would report to Brightsword. She would report to Dr. Horn. There was nothing he could possibly gain from his garish sacrifices. Why not let him make them?

"Fine," she said. "I'll take the bed."

She saw a flicker of surprise, but then he turned and began preparing his own makeshift sleeping arrangements. Mercy grabbed her travel bag and went to the bathroom. She stripped down to nothing, cleaned her face, and put on the most comfortable clothes she'd brought. Briefly, she debated whether or not to put back on her gloves. It felt so nice to have them off while she slept. Besides, Devlin had seen her fingers when they'd dated. He was one of the few people who knew about the incident that had caused them. But that didn't completely take away her insecurity. After all, he'd broken up with her. She always wondered if her abnormality had played a part in that.

In the end, she decided to keep the gloves off. Let him be uncomfortable if he actually was that shallow. When she emerged, however, Devlin was already asleep. He'd claimed one of the pillows from the bed and curled up in a pitiful corner. With a sigh, Mercy sunk into her own bed.

For a while, she could not sleep. Her mind kept dredging up the images of each of the farmhands. All covered in bruises. There had been thirty-one patients in total. Consistent symptoms in each case, though one of the older field hands had grown far sicker than the younger patients. That was relatively normal. Stronger bodies tended to fight diseases better. She'd also noted that the newer the case the fresher the bruises looked. One of the girls at the fourth farm had been covered in welts the color of midnight. The newer patients also reported ongoing pain. That "burning on the inside" feeling had been a constant refrain. But there were no other signs of internal damage. No one was coughing up blood. No one had passed out or had a seizure. Not a single report of dyspnea. It seemed, too, that the earliest victims were well on their way to recovery.

The only detail that haunted her was the sound. As she'd listened to each of their hearts, the same echo surfaced, again and again. At first, she thought she was just imagining the noise. But when she'd listened to Devlin's heart and her own for comparison—they'd been normal. No echo. What could cause something like that? And more worrying: What were the long-term risks for each patient? The disease hadn't killed anyone—but would there be other lasting symptoms?

She turned restlessly. Sleep proved elusive.

Her eyes eventually flicked over to Devlin. He was no more than a dark mound in the corner. Barely there at all. An image of Holt surfaced in her thoughts. The watchful eyes. The way he looked at her in every spare moment. One fear led to others. What if she contracted this disease? What if she failed to treat the people in this village? Those thoughts were answered by a flash of unexpected light.

She bolted upright in bed, reaching for her gloves on the bedside table, when the hound appeared. Devlin's divinity spell. In its glow, she could see that her ex was still fast asleep.

His conjuring crossed the room all on its own, pacing back and forth like an actual hound might.

Mercy snorted before patting the bed. The creature had been waiting for that. It leapt up and curled into a perfect circle against her side. It was a warm thing. Calm radiated from the creature's touch. An overwhelming sense of safety. Mercy's eyes fluttered shut. Sleep tugged at her limbs. Once, twice, and she was swept away.

The hound protected her that night—but it could not protect Running Hills.

Morning brought new cases. Another farm had fallen ill. But the worst news came just as Mercy and Devlin were sitting down to a meager breakfast: the town medic had been found dead. She had seen bodies before. Worked with hundreds of cadavers. This felt different. No matter how many wards were summoned between her and the dead—the air felt thick with potential disease. A disease that she now knew *could* kill. Mercy performed a routine examination, but her hands moved hastily through the procedure. She didn't want to be in that room a second longer than was strictly necessary.

Her findings: the woman's internal damage was far worse. Even more bruises than the other patients. A distinctly concentrated pattern around her upper chest. She was potentially older than any of the other patients, which meant it was possible she was more vulnerable than the rest of them. She also might have had preexisting conditions. It was not a conclusive data point, but Mercy quietly noted her own theories before ordering the body to be moved to the nearest morgue. Holt was the one who arrived to perform the task. His eerie presence was as good a reason as any for her to head back to the town center.

Issuing a quarantine was the next move. The command went out through Nance Forester. She was requesting that the people of Running Hills spend the next two days in their respective homes. Especially the elderly. Anything to reduce the spread of disease.

Nance was an exception to the rule. Their host was permitted to come and go, relaying messages from every corner of the county. Mercy asked him for a map so that they could see everything on a large scale. He was quick to deliver that and more. The map, two buckets full of water, and the most threadbare mattress she had ever seen. In any other circumstance, she would have taken quiet glee in Devlin's situation, but death had forced her to bury the old grudge. The two of them had quietly transformed into partner detectives instead. A development that Mercy could not bring herself to completely hate.

"Where do you want the map?" Devlin asked.

"On the table, please."

He set out the partially faded document as Mercy uncapped a pen.

"All right," she said. "Let's mark all of the infected farms. . . ."

One by one, she circled the locations. Four of the five farms were clumped in the eastern hills. Apparently, this was a consequence of history. Running Hills had been home to one of the northern farming tribes that opposed Kathor in the past. The Broods had actively raided them—and thus the farms were built close enough that they could come to each other's defense whenever the city bells rang out sounding an attack.

The last farm—owned by the Locklin family—had been

built nearly a century later, well after the Graylantians had made their famous pact with Kathor, and so they had chosen the most fertile ground, rather than concerning themselves with defensibility.

"Here's our big mystery," Mercy said, tapping that location on the map. "All of the other farms trade workers. There are friendships and romances and families. A lot of traveling back and forth. It makes sense that the disease spread between those four locations. It's harder to understand how it spread to the Locklins at the exact same pace."

Devlin leaned in closer to examine the map. She felt his shoulder briefly brush against hers. He was close enough that she could even feel the vibrations of his voice.

"But one of their workers went into town that night."

She nodded. "Patient Twenty-Eight. According to his testimony, he didn't visit the tavern. He just went into town to pick up the post for the Locklin family. Didn't talk to anyone from the other farms. Minimal physical contact. He's not exactly an ideal host candidate to spread a disease."

Devlin reached out and tapped the same spot she had. "What about visitors *to* the farm?"

"Three new workers arrived this week," Mercy confirmed. "But all of them were from out of town. From Peck. West of here. Seems unlikely that they'd stop by the other farms."

She traced a finger inland to the neighboring town of Peck. According to Nance, that was the source of most of their extra workers. If not from there, then seasonal workers from Kathor would travel up to take on harvest work when their occupations in the city slowed.

Devlin made a thoughtful noise. "But all it would take is one moment. If the disease moves as fast as it seems to. Maybe Patient Twenty-Eight downplayed his visit. It's possible he thought he'd get in trouble for spreading the disease to Locklin."

Mercy chewed on her lip. "Maybe."

Maybe was the most scientific answer they could summon at the moment. The disease did appear to move at a rapid rate. Almost too easily, if that was possible. She reached for her notes and started flipping back through everything she'd written down during the interviews.

"I'm confused by the time line," she said. "Our first patient developed the disease six nights ago. He felt feverish when he went to bed—and then he woke up covered in bruises. That's also when we have our first report of the 'burning insides' symptom."

Devlin nodded as he followed her thoughts.

"That same night, most of the field hands at Mariner's develop similar symptoms. Quick fevers. Burning insides. The next morning, every single one of them is covered in bruises. And the progress of the disease is completely uniform across the entire group. Even though some of them have significantly less contact with the others."

"The baker in the fourth cabin," Devlin noted. "He had his own room and worked different hours than the others, but he still contracted the disease at the same time."

That was the exact patient she'd been thinking about. The baker was the most curious case at Mariner's. His symptoms should have developed after the others. Or at least at a slower rate. Why hadn't they?

"I'm even more interested in Patient Twelve," Mercy mused.

"The old man?"

She was impressed Devlin had kept up with all her notes. As

they'd made their way from location to location, he had stood watch over the proceedings. A statue in the background. She wouldn't have blamed him for drifting off—especially given how repetitive the interviews got after a while. It was clear, however, that he'd paid close attention.

"Patient Twelve's bruising has the most consistency with our first patient. His marks were already fading when we treated him. Which leaves just two possibilities: either he contracted the disease close to the same time or older bodies process the disease at different rates. Based on his interview, his bruises appeared less than five hours after Wells's did."

She shook her head in frustration. Every doctor knew it was a mistake to start thinking they were on a first-name basis with their patients. Only misery waited down that road.

"After Patient One," she corrected.

"Do you think someone from Mariner's visited the night before?" Devlin asked. "Maybe they didn't realize they were sick yet?"

"Anything is possible, but that seems unlikely. Most transferable diseases have a clear sequential element to them. Patient A gives the disease to Patient B who spreads it to Patient C and so on. We should have a very clear flow from where the disease began to where it moves next. But these are the two data points that just don't fit. It's almost like they're not sequential at all."

Devlin was pacing the room. Normally, that was Mercy's strategy, but she felt it would be weird if both of them were walking around the cramped space. Instead, she busied her hands, flipping back through the details of her journal. Looking for something she hadn't previously noticed. She saw Devlin cross over to the door and was briefly distracted by his broad shoulders, his muscled back. Who even had a muscular back? What was the point of having that?

He knelt down to lift the two buckets Nance had left them. Mercy watched as he ferried them to the bathroom, trying not to notice the way his triceps stretched beneath his shirt. She was still staring when the answer hit her right in the stomach.

"Water. Devlin. *It's in the water.*"

He paused midstride. "Because . . . all of the patients . . . were thirsty?"

"Not that." The theory came tumbling out of her. "I mean, maybe that's a part of it? But no. Think about it. Drinking water. That's the only common thread they all share. Everyone would have different diets. Different exposure levels. Different social groupings. Those factors *should* cause variation. We should be seeing clear sequence. Instead, we have uniformity. The only possible explanation is that every one of our patients is drinking from the same water supply."

Devlin looked skeptical. "I don't know, Mercy. These are big farms. They're all spread out too. Don't you think they have their own wells built? It doesn't seem like they'd be able to share the same water source."

"But what if they do?"

Devlin shrugged. "Let's ask Nance."

Lacking any other leads, the two of them thundered up the stairs in search of their host. He wasn't hard to find. The town was in quarantine. They found Nance seated on the front steps of the same building where they'd met him when they'd arrived in Running Hills.

"Nance," Mercy called. "A question for you."

"Fire away, Dr. Whitaker."

"Do all the farms share a water supply?"

He frowned thoughtfully. "Sure. I mean, there's just one treatment facility. It's up north. Right where the town limits brush up against the Straywhite River. There's a small tributary and the water gets pumped out to all the farms from there. It's one of those—passive magic facilities? Is that the word for it?"

She nodded. "Meaning no one physically works there."

"Exactly," Nance confirmed. "An engineer from Kathor set the place up about ten years ago. All we're supposed to do is perform an annual check—but this year's inspection isn't due for another month or so."

"Can you take us there?" Devlin asked.

"No. I'm sorry. I can't. I'd love to, but I just found out there's a whole crop of folks coming here from Peck. I need to be here to turn them away, what with the quarantine and all. But I could always bring a carriage around for you. Either of you know how to drive horses?"

Mercy glanced immediately at Devlin—who snorted in response.

"Guessing that's a no," Nance said. "Holt could take you. Well, as long as you're fine giving him permission to break quarantine."

Mercy fought off a shiver. She did not mind him breaking quarantine, but she minded everything else about him. Still, what choice did they have? Her guess had been correct. The entire town shared a water source. This was a proper lead in the investigation. If she could get out to that building and test the water levels—they might make a huge break in fighting this disease.

"Send for Holt. We need to test the water."

6

REN MONROE

Pure adrenaline.

Ren felt as if her entire body was vibrating as she exited the archive room. Gods, she'd forgotten this feeling. How breathless it was to shape magic in new ways. To alter her footwork slightly or adjust the final sweep of her wand hand as she released a spell. Ren's deep love for spellmaking had first blossomed at Balmerick. That was a secret she'd never admit to anyone. When she'd first set out to avenge her father, magic had been a stepping stone. Get good grades. Perform solid magic. Work hard enough and she'd land a scholarship. It was the first step in a plan.

Balmerick complicated everything. It was there that she'd fallen in love with magical theory. Developing new spells could shape the actual world around her. The only true limits were the wizard's imagination and ability. Magic felt like a path toward transforming life itself. During her time at school, she would occasionally forget about her father and his murder and the cruelty of the Broods. Normally that happened inside an archive room. She'd be so focused on working out the small, but necessary details of how to perform a spell that she'd lose sight of her true purpose at Balmerick. She'd always felt so guilty after. But not this time.

Ren stepped into the alleyway after roughly three hours of practice, completely reinvigorated. That familiar guilt never arrived. Of course not. Her father had been avenged. Landwin Brood was entombed in a vault not far from where she stood. The realization tingled down her spine. It was like coming up for air after holding her breath for a decade. The next steps of her journey could be anything. She could do *anything*. Chase after spells. Practice new magic. Study any subject she desired. There was no longer a secret creed guiding her steps. No dark cloud hovering above every action. She was bonded to Theo, of course. She was charged with helping run House Brood—but for the first time she realized she was free to do whatever she wanted with her life.

It felt like a beginning.

Theo came bustling around the corner. He was wearing a plaid jacket with a lovely charcoal tie and matching slacks. Everything tight and buttoned and sharp. He smiled at her as he came down the steps, deeper into the heart of the alley. No doubt he'd sensed her satisfaction across their bond. Even if he could not read her mind, Ren knew he could see it in her expression. Some door finally unlocked. A long-hidden room finally open. His smile stretched into a grin as he reached her.

"Was the room booked after me?" Ren asked.

Theo shook his head. "I don't think so. If you want more time I could . . ."

Her hand found his collar before he could find the end of his sentence. She pulled him down into a kiss. Theo hesitated for a second, and then his hands slid to her waist. Ren drove him backward through the still-open door. In that unlit space, Theo kissed her hungrily, as if he'd been waiting for this moment. Ren answered. One hand running down his jaw. The other tugging his tie loose. He found the clasp of her cloak. The fabric whispered from her shoulders as she pushed back his jacket. A loud clattering sounded in the alleyway. The two of them briefly froze, then they fell to laughter—gods, how good it felt to laugh like that. Ren led Theo down the hallway and into the actual archive room. They found each other again in that thicker darkness. He lifted her off the ground. Pressed her pleasantly against the chilled walls.

"Why . . ." She kissed him. ". . . are there so many . . ." Again. ". . . buttons."

He laughed before setting her down. There was a forming light in the room. No brighter than moonlight. This was one of the few places in the world where a person could see literal magic in the air. Those subtle tendrils were stirring all around them. Like lightning that briefly illuminated a distant shore. She saw Theo in that soft glow. His pale skin. The runner's frame, tight with corded muscle. Even the wound he'd suffered in their battle with the wyvern. Her hands reached for that spot first. Fingertips tracing the tapered scar. She saw him shiver and it was hard not to enjoy the small noise that escaped from his lips. Ren's hands trailed from the scar to his waist. Theo shivered again.

"Ren . . . are you sure . . ."

She answered his question with a kiss. Once, twice, a third. And then she guided his hands to where she wanted them. Theo needed little help, fingers digging lightly into her skin. Ren's shirt slid away from her shoulders. They pressed together and more magic pulsed in the air. Bright and brief. Reacting to both of them. Weaving itself between touches. Ren realized it was displaying their bond. The magic that existed between them—made visible for a moment. For so long that connection had been a pleasure on the verge of pain. It overwhelmed. Something too sweet or too bright or too sharp. Not this time. No, this was pleasure on the verge of pleasure.

"More," Ren whispered in Theo's ear.

And he gave her more.

There was no shame to their walk home. It did not feel like it had at times during undergrad. Slipping back through the hallways at odd hours, hoping not to run into any of your fellow classmates. Instead, Ren and Theo crossed town together, barely capable of maintaining a sense of decorum. This was the sort of joy that Ren wished she could bottle and stopper. Not to be sold, but to be handed out for free, for all. Everyone deserved to feel like this at least once in their life.

It was not until they arrived back in the Heights that their feet seemed to set back on solid ground. An unwelcome shadow waited on their front stoop. Ren saw the figure long before they reached the stairs, but it took that entire approach to recognize who it was.

"Aunt Sloan?"

It had been quite some time. Ren realized she'd last seen the woman in line. Down in the Lower Quarter, the two of them had chatted before refilling their vessels with the monthly allotments. It had not been a pleasant conversation. Ren recalled a few cutting remarks. Normally, her memory of such moments was quite good. But the conversation had happened *before*. Before the portal room. Before her friends died because of her. Before everything that came after with Theo.

Another world entirely.

"Ren. I've been looking for you."

Theo was a knot of anticipation at her side. Ren sensed the sudden tension in their bond—and she realized he didn't know if this was a threatening situation or not. She dispelled the notion that Aunt Sloan might hurt them by shoving reassurance across their bond.

"Why have you been looking for me?" Ren asked. "Did something happen to my mother?"

"Not like that. It's still urgent that we speak."

There was something dreadful buried in her words. *Not like that.* Ren turned that particular phrase over again and again before realizing she hadn't invited her old neighbor inside.

"Please. Follow me."

Ren unlocked the door. Theo trailed them, still radiating uncertainty. She walked Sloan straight through the living room and opened the door that led to the balcony. As the woman stepped outside, Ren had a brief moment alone with Theo.

"That's your aunt?"

"No," Ren replied. "It's a term of endearment. She's someone who lived in our building. An old friend of my mother's. I need to talk to her. Alone. She might shy away if you're with us."

"And you'll be safe?"

She nodded. "Of course. Aunt Sloan is harmless."

"Right. All right. I'll wait inside."

Ren stepped out, closing the door behind her. The entire property was warded—so they would not be overheard by neighbors or spies. Guilt was creeping into her thoughts. She took a moment to tamp it back down. She truly believed Sloan might talk more without Theo there. After all, he was a stranger to her. But the real motivation was that she didn't want Theo to hear anything about her mother before she heard it first. That way she could edit the story as needed.

Will I ever be free of secrets?

She led Aunt Sloan to a pair of cushioned chairs. The seats offered the best view of Kathor below and of the sea beyond. The last two years had not been kind to the woman. Ren felt as if she'd aged rapidly in that time. Her gray hair looked frayed and the corners of her lips pinched. Even her eyes were notably baggy. It softened Ren to see her this way. A reminder that life in the Lower Quarter was far from easy.

"What word do you have of my mother?" Ren asked.

The woman bristled. "No tea? Nothing to eat? Your generation's concept of hospitality . . ."

Well, so much for softness. Ren pivoted. "I did not invite you here, Aunt Sloan. You arrived at my door unannounced. I suspect this visit will bring unwelcome news. If, on the other hand, you have come to deliver good fortune, I will rush inside and put on the kettle."

Ren waited patiently. When Aunt Sloan remained silent, she nodded.

"That's what I thought. Go on then. Tell me what you know."

At heart, Aunt Sloan was a gossip. Ren knew she would not

come all this way to keep her mouth closed. Sure enough, the words began spilling out. Smooth as a stream of poured tea.

"My daughter-in-law vanished. Two weeks ago, she disappeared without a trace. My son spoke with Brightsword Legion. He talked to people she knew. Everyone dismissed it as a runaway case. I need your help, Ren. I know you have resources the rest of the Lower Quarter can't access. I wouldn't ask this of you if it weren't serious. My son's afraid that Lana might be dead."

Ren leaned back in her chair. "Why does he think that?"

"What do you know about the Makers?"

"They're a support group," Ren answered. "A place that people go when they've been through trauma. Like my mother. She's been attending those meetings ever since my father died."

"A support group," Aunt Sloan bit back. "That's the public image. Just a few sad souls gathering to help each other out. But they're more than that, Ren. The group has rituals. Rules that they demand their members follow. If you want to join, you have to forfeit your magic. . . ."

Ren nodded. "I know my mother doesn't use magic. That's a choice that she made a long time ago. I've no issue with it. Spellwork isn't for everyone. Why should it matter to you or me what they choose?"

"Because it is one thing to stop using magic—and quite another thing to believe no one should use it at all. Did you know that's what they preach at their meetings? That magic is the chain that binds the hands and feet of the lower class. These are not monks who've taken a vow of silence, Ren. They are zealots who would like to cut out everyone else's tongues as well."

She could hear the urgency in Sloan's words, but there was a gap between the woman's claims and her own experiences. "My mother's been attending those meetings for a decade. She doesn't use magic, but she's never asked me to set my spells aside. Not once. And she's had plenty of opportunities to say something. Trust me."

Aunt Sloan brushed that aside. "Well, of course not. You are uniquely gifted. You had a scholarship to Balmerick. What Lower Quarter mother would deny her child an opportunity like that? She wouldn't ask you to stop. But that's not how it goes for most of us, and you know it. We toil down here. A few spells for back pain. A little magic to pass the time. How many of our folk go as far down that road as you? Where magic is what we live and breathe?"

The question didn't require an answer. Ren knew there weren't many. Guilt crept deeper into her thoughts. She also knew that just a few years ago, several of the exceptions to that rule had died in the wilderness. Timmons Devine. Cora Marrin. Avy Williams. All three of them gone because of one mistake. Ren had to mentally shake those thoughts away and focus on what Aunt Sloan was suggesting. "You're making them sound like zealots," Ren said. "But my mother never changed. She's always been the way she is now. As far back as I can remember."

"She's older. More set in her ways. The Makers recruit the young and impressionable these days. Like our Lana. My son's wife . . . she's the sweetest girl I've ever met. A wonderful person. But she was fired from her job last year. She felt hopeless. She went to one of their meetings—and it was like she'd joined a cult. Swore off all magic. Talking about the city's injustices all the time. My poor son, he was worried to death. He said they made promises to her. Tall talk of a future where *she* would have all the power. My boy said people would knock on their door late at night. Lana was assigned to tasks, ordered not to tell him any of the details. Not unless he'd join them too. One of those late-night visitors . . . was your mother."

Ren's insides twisted. Until now, the connection had felt innocent. Sloan's missing daughter-in-law had attended the same meetings. So did hundreds of people. The odds of the two of them being connected had felt so slim. Now her mother was directly implicated.

"What exactly are you suggesting?"

"Nothing," Aunt Sloan answered quickly. "I know your mother isn't that kind of person. At least, not the Agnes that I always knew. I can't speak for the person they call 'Old Agnes.'"

It was the second time Ren had heard that name. Last year, she'd stolen away to Ravinia. Her mother had quietly arranged a "double" that would draw the attention of the Broods' spies. The girl had rendezvoused with Ren in an apothecary shop. She'd referred to her mother as Old Agnes and it had sounded like an established nickname. As if everyone down by the docks called her that. In truth, Ren had been a bit stung. She'd felt like a neglectful daughter for not knowing that side of her mother's life. But as she rifled back through the memories of that journey, she realized that moment was just one of many strange details.

For example, her mother had arranged a fairly complicated decoy. Why had Ren never questioned that? Agnes Monroe had spent her entire life working on the docks. She wasn't trained in espionage. How had she known what to do? And what about the boat they'd secured passage on? Or the fact that she'd found an entire apartment for Nevelyn Tin'Vori to live in? Free of charge?

Ren could not help the creeping sense of paranoia. Maybe she was just looking back with a view colored by Aunt Sloan's accusations. Or maybe there was something hiding in Ren's blind spots. A truth she'd never seen. She felt certain of one thing.

"My mother has her faults, but she is not in the habit of making young women disappear."

"Of course." Aunt Sloan averted her eyes. "Of course she's not. I didn't come here to accuse her. I came here to beg you for help. My son said your mother visited them. We don't know why. Please, ask her. If she knows *anything* that might offer my son peace of mind, I would be grateful. And if you don't want to ask her—there is something else you could do."

Aunt Sloan reached into her bag and set out a pair of threadbare shoes. The soles were nearly worn through and the sides had been scuffed.

"A pair of old shoes?"

"Enchanted with a mimicry spell."

Ren recoiled. Much like chain spells, mimicry magic was illegal. The government occasionally granted exceptions—often to the major houses—but that branch of spells was banned because it opened the door for all sorts of potential abuses. For example, a jealous husband might use a mimicry spell on his wife's shoes. Such magic would allow him to track her steps. He could follow her anywhere—no matter how far she went. The concerns with such magic felt obvious to her.

"You do understand how that looks? Magic like that doesn't reflect well on your son."

Sloan nodded. "I know. Trust me, I know. He was desperate. Imagine the person you fell in love with just . . . changing overnight. Into someone else entirely. He thought the Makers were doing something to influence Lana. And so he cast that spell."

Ren frowned. "Then why do you need me? Can't he just follow the shoes and find her?"

"Jon's a metalworker. He's one of the best at Peckering's workshop, but he has no skill with magic. He linked the shoes. We know the spell worked because the new shoes transformed. Looked just like hers." Aunt Sloan tapped the dirty laces. "But he can't get the second part of the spell to activate. We know how talented you are, Ren. One of the most skilled wizards to come from the Lower Quarter in a decade. And you're a part of House Brood. The government . . . they grant exceptions to people in your position. You wouldn't be arrested for this. Would you?"

It was a reasonable guess. Likely Sloan was right. Ren might receive a polite slap on the wrist, but truly, there wouldn't be any real consequence for her. "Why should I risk my reputation for you? You've come here and all but accused my mother of kidnapping."

"No, no, no," Aunt Sloan said quickly. "I promise this isn't about your mother. It's about Lana. It's about my son. I would do anything for him. I came to you because who else would I go to? We don't know the Broods. No one in House Shiverian is going to meet with someone like me. Even the Brightsword commander assigned to protect our district told us to stop bothering him. He dismissed Lana's case in less than two minutes. There's no one else, Ren. If you can't help us, who can?"

Ren didn't know what to say. She had little love for Aunt

Sloan, but she had quite a bit of love for what Aunt Sloan repre-sented: the Lower Quarter. Her people. It was where her father had made his reputation. The very people he'd died helping. It was where she'd grown up and where her mother lived. Fire burned to life in her chest. A forgotten loyalty stretching its limbs and stirring back to life. She had not risen to this posi-tion just to ignore the people she'd grown up with. She could not simply walk away from the ghosts of Timmons and Cora and Avy, either. She owed it to every single one of them to make sure that the power she'd gained when they died would not continue to pile up in the vaults of the great houses. That would be like leaving unpicked fruit to rot on overfull vines. She had vowed to change Kathor—and perhaps it started in moments like this.

Quietly she reached out and accepted the shoes. She slid them inside her own bag before locking eyes with Aunt Sloan. "I will investigate. I can't make promises beyond that."

Her old neighbor burst into tears. Ren could hardly bear the sight. She stood and led the woman back inside. Out the front door. Each whispered "thank you" shivered uncomfortably down her spine. Ren had never been good with emotions. Cer-tainly not the emotions of others. The second the door closed, her mind began racing through everything she'd just learned.

Theo was trotting down the stairs. She had no doubt that he'd have a million questions for her. Not that Ren had any answers. Looking back, it was staggering to think through all the help her mother had given her while she attempted to take her revenge on Landwin Brood. As soon as Ren had invited her into the plan, a fountain of resources had been made available.

As if she'd already been plotting something . . .

Ren had assumed each action was a representation of her mother's resourcefulness. Agnes Monroe had looked after herself for nearly a decade. She was self-sufficient, street-smart. A survivor—like Ren was. Not once had she considered a deeper explanation. This felt like a startling weakness in her own defenses. Was it really possible her mother was living some other life?

Theo reached the landing. "Everything all right?"

"We need to go back to the archive room."

That drew out a smile. "That's . . . well . . . I don't know if it's been long enough. . . ."

Ren snorted. She brushed his cheek with a kiss.

"For work this time. Not pleasure."

"Right," Theo said. "Of course. Wait. What work?"

Ren walked past him, holding up the shoes so he could see them.

"We're looking for the owner of these shoes."

And we're hoping that she's still alive.

7

MERCY WHITAKER

It didn't take long for the carriage to arrive.

Nance gave his hired man instructions, and within minutes they were bounding north. Holt made no attempts at small talk. He didn't glance back either—which made Mercy feel even more uncomfortable somehow. All that staring the night before, and now he wouldn't even look her way? For the first time, Devlin's presence was an undeniable comfort. If something happened, she could trust him to handle it. Her ex had plenty of shortcomings. Landing a blow was not one of them.

Mercy felt like they went up and down every single one of the town's famous hills. They heard the river long before they saw the actual treatment plant. A distant and pleasant sort of thunder. Nance had mentioned a tributary branching off from the Straywhite River—and now she spotted that stretch in the distance. It was a slash of white-foamed water that ran headlong into the treatment plant.

As they drew closer, Mercy saw the plant consisted of several buildings. Three total structures. First, a pair of identical, one-story buildings. They ran from east to west. Those two buildings were windowless and blended with the hillsides. The third building was more notable. There were flashes along the roof that indicated sun striking metal. There was also an active smokestack. Great puffs of white churned skyward, merging with the clouds above.

"The main building is locked," Holt announced, the first words he'd spoken the entire ride. "But there are pump basins around back. You should be able to take samples there." They crested a hill. Holt reined the horses in with ease before gesturing to their right. "The tanks are that way."

Devlin helped Mercy dismount. She felt a sudden thrill. The idea that the answer could be waiting for them here was exhilarating. A footpath led around the buildings to the back. Holt was making an inspection of the harnesses, and offered no sign he planned to go with them. Devlin summoned his hound. Mercy smiled at the creature. She hadn't mentioned the midnight visit she'd received. She still didn't know if Devlin had sent the creature knowingly or not.

That doesn't matter. Focus. You have a job to do here.

They rounded the corner of the building. She'd never seen a water treatment facility, and yet she felt she knew the purpose of everything she saw in front of her. The "tanks" looked more like large pools. Each one was rectangular, separated by walkways with protective railings. In the distance, there was a dam or a canal. It was responsible for redirecting the tributary's flow toward this building. Where they stood was the second step in the process: cleaning the water. She could see that each tank possessed mechanisms for release. Once the water had been purified—separated from waste and other contaminants—it could be released through the main building, then on to the farms for consumption.

She was considering what to do when Devlin's hound darted away from them. Like a golden arrow shot at the central of the three buildings. It reached the outer wall and vanished in a brief shiver of light. The two of them exchanged a glance.

"Must have caught a scent."

Mercy frowned. "What kind of scent?"

Another pulse of light announced the creature's return. It padded back to Devlin's side. He frowned at the creature, then frowned at her. "There's a body. Inside the building."

"A body," Mercy repeated, dumbfounded.

"Inside the building."

"What do you mean there's a body? There can't be a body."

"He says there's a body."

"Your magical dog *told* you there's a body?"

"Yes."

"He's a dog, Devlin. He doesn't talk."

Devlin scowled. "Mercy, I promise you: there's a body in that building."

She didn't bother correcting the use of her first name. It wasn't quite annoying enough to break through her confusion. What he was saying did *not* make sense.

"Nance said this is a passive magic facility. No one even works on-site. The last inspection would have been almost a year ago. You think a body has been in there this whole time?"

In response, Devlin reached for the glinting half hammer hanging from his belt. There appeared to be only one access point along the backs of the buildings. He stalked toward it, his hound falling in step with him. Mercy quickly made her own modifications. She adjusted the strap on her medical bag so that it was hanging behind her, out of the way. Mentally, she cycled through a few defensive spells—not that her arsenal was at all designed for combat.

When she was ready, she followed Devlin.

He heard. "What are you doing?"

"Coming with you."

"Can't you just stay out here?"

"Who's going to inspect the body, Devlin?"

He made a disbelieving noise, but it was hard to argue with a doctor when it came to corpses. They reached the entrance. He gave the handle a testing tug, clearly expecting it to be locked, and the door groaned open. Devlin shot her a look before pulling it the rest of the way. Inside was dark. Nothing but shadows. Until his hound slid past him. The creature acted like a lantern cantrip, casting its glow over the interior of the building. They stepped into what appeared to be a cleansing room. The next door led into the primary chamber. The sound of rushing water dominated the space, drowning out other noises. Mercy assumed that all the clean water from the outer tanks would eventually release through here. Sure enough, a single channel cut through the heart of the room. When it reached the southern wall, it divided into four separate pipes, all of which vanished underground. This was the lifeblood that pumped to each of the town's farms.

Mercy was the first one to see the body.

"What . . . is . . . that?"

Devlin stumbled to a halt. The corpse was in the water.

Floating perfectly on the surface. She saw a pair of stiff legs set tight together, arms neatly folded over the victim's chest. It would not have been strange to find a body like this in a motionless pool, but the channel was more like a river. The currents looked incredibly strong. All that water should have been battering the body against the walls. Even someone who was alive, actively swimming against the current, would have been dragged in the direction of the pipes. Instead, the corpse sat immobile. Untouched.

"A stasis charm," Devlin said. "It has to be."

He was right. It made no sense, but he was right. There shouldn't have been a body here at all. Much less a body that had been enchanted to remain perfectly in place. The two of them had stopped to observe the scene, but Devlin's hound had reached the platform below. As she watched, the glow from its skin finally illuminated the edge of the channel. All that light trembled against a darkness that was unnaturally thick.

"Look at that. Above the body."

As the hound paced, Mercy could make out the borders of some kind of fouled magic. It wasn't anything she'd encountered in her time at Safe Harbor. Corpses decayed, of course. Bodies eventually rotted and fell apart. This was something else. It reminded her of . . .

"Dragon corpses look like that," she blurted out. "We studied one in graduate school. We visited Ayana. The Winter Dragon. Her corpse is buried to the south of Kathor. It used to be a drug farm, but they ran off the harvesters and turned the whole chamber into a museum. I've never seen a human body decay the same way. There are fumes leaking from every wound."

"Is it safe?" Devlin asked. "To go closer?"

She shook her head. "No. We're fully warded, but no. I can't guarantee that we won't get sick from whatever the hell that is."

Devlin's face was half-shadowed. He'd been so confident this entire time. Now she saw the first trace of doubt. It was a very reasonable fear. Not cowardice. This was clearly unknown territory for both of them. He eventually cleared his throat.

"Do we turn back then? Wait for someone else?"

"Who else would know what to do?"

Her question echoed off the walls until it became an answer. This was the risk that every doctor was called to when they swore their vows. To serve and protect, even if it meant endangering themselves. Both of them started down the stairs, which curled around, leading back to the platform that banked the channel. If the body's arrangement had looked unnatural, the wounds were even more so. Matching slits ran down both biceps. Twin wounds cut across each exposed thigh. The woman's chest—and she felt certain now that it was a woman—had caved in before being split open. Another slit ran vertical from collarbone to chin. It was difficult to see, but when she squinted, she was certain that a strange substance was leaking from each wound. A smoke that pooled in the air above them.

"How do we actually get the body out?" Mercy asked.

The corpse had been magicked into place at the very center of the channel. Just far enough that they could not reach out for it without falling in. She didn't think it wise for either of them to leap in themselves, and was preparing to talk Devlin out of that thought when his hound jumped into the rapids instead.

"Wait, wait, wait," Mercy sputtered. "We can't risk damaging the corpse."

"Don't worry," Devlin replied. "He knows."

As she watched, the creature sank its teeth into the soggy hood of the deceased's cloak, then turned to swim back to them. The body held in place for a moment, but the stasis spell had been conjured with the river in mind. A resistance cast in a very specific direction—which was not the way the hound was pulling. It managed to tow the dark cargo back to them. Devlin reached down to drag the body onto the platform. She could see how uncomfortable this made him. Touching a body in this state, warded or not, was enough to send a shiver down her spine. Mercy was grateful for their efforts, however. She could perform a much better inspection at this range.

"Hold this."

She handed off her surgical bag and performed her favorite revelation charm. It was a spell that Dr. Horn had taught her. A very basic casting, but well loved for the fact that it could help a doctor without altering the magic that existed in the actual patient. Her eyes would be drawn to the most important details. Mercy finished the casting and bent to inspect the body again.

"Interesting," she said, letting the sensory magic guide her. "These wounds are clearly surgical. They're so clean. You don't typically see wounds like that if there's a struggle. Moving bodies don't allow for such clean cuts. Which means these were likely made on a corpse. Or someone who'd been unconscious. More likely she was dead already. Each one is intentional, too. There's a lot of precision here." She frowned. "I still don't understand what would cause this kind of decay. I mean, these wounds are literally leaking right now."

Devlin was pacing the platform, her bag clutched in one

hand and his hammer in the other. Mercy gently turned the body over. More wounds. A slit down the spine. Two others running the length of the victim's calves. There was something almost ceremonial about this. Or if not ritualistic, then medical in some way? Not that she could think of any reason a doctor would need to do this. Unless this fell into some kind of experimentation. A person with minimal experience attempting to learn more? That wasn't unheard of—but it would have been far more common a century ago. Schools of medicine had been established for exactly this reason.

Her mind returned to the thought of breath farmers. They approached their dragon corpses the same way. Like surgeons. Making precise cuts that would allow a very specific amount of the hallucinogen into the air. Was this similar to that somehow? What would the purpose be?

"I feel like you're focused on the wrong thing," Devlin said, surprising her.

Mercy frowned. "What do you mean?"

"Mercy, someone *put a body here.*" He said those words with urgency. "This was planned. Think about it. They killed this person. Or she was dead. Either way, they brought her body down here. Cut her up like that. And then they put her in the water supply. *On purpose.* The same water supply that they knew the rest of the town would be drinking. I know you want to figure out why she's decaying and what magic this is and all of that, but the reality is that someone intentionally poisoned the people of Running Hills. This is how the disease spread. And it seems it was spread on purpose. This isn't a medical case anymore. It's criminal."

Devlin was right. She wanted to dive into the parts she knew best. How the incisions had been made. What magic was causing this specific decay. How the disease could travel through water and whether or not the people who'd positioned this body knew what kind of illness would manifest when they first placed this woman in that exact location. There were a thousand medical questions to ask—but Devlin had already arrived at the most important conclusion.

This needed to be reported to Kathor as soon as possible.

"Hello?"

Mercy almost jumped out of her skin. Devlin's entire body tensed. They both watched as Holt made his way across the catwalk above them. The man squinted down, taking in the scene.

"I saw the door was . . ." He blinked. "What the hell is that?"

Devlin answered, "We found a body, Holt. We need to report back to Nance. Immediately."

The bigger man kept walking down the catwalk. "Who is it? A man or a woman?"

"A woman. Looks to be around thirty or so?"

"The Chathams," he said. "Their girl disappeared a while back. Everyone thought she'd run off to Kathor. Gods be good. Let me come down and see if it's her."

Mercy wasn't sure what to do. She wanted to warn him that if he came closer, he might risk getting the disease. But for the first time, it dawned on her that Holt had already been exposed quite a bit. The bigger man had been to every single one of the farms, making deliveries and providing water. It was surprising he hadn't caught the disease already. She watched him adjust to get down the curved part of the staircase, turning his bulkier frame sideways, before reaching the platform.

"Last time anyone saw her was a few months back," Holt said, crossing the room.

In the hound's glow, Mercy saw Holt fully for the first time. He'd always been a sideways glance for her. Someone whose gaze she was trying to avoid. His skin was pale for a farmer. The kind of skin that burned before it tanned. She saw discolorations on the backs of his right hand. Near the veins. Even more of them below his collarbone. Exposed by the deep V of his tunic. Squinting, she realized what they were—long-faded bruises. Nearly invisible.

"Holt, did you . . ."

He moved faster than she thought was possible for such a big man. Like the crack of a whip. He brought up his right leg and the flat of his boot found Devlin's unprotected chest. The blow sent her protector flailing backward—into the water with a splash. Mercy had never studied combat training. Her instincts were all about preservation. Keeping people alive. Her fingers flexed as wide as they could inside her leather gloves. She cast the first shield spell she could think of. Holt's next blow slammed into it. The shield was barely strong enough to turn him aside, but that spare second gave Devlin's hound a chance to enter the fray. The creature's jaws closed around one of Holt's ankles. She heard him cry out in pain before shaking the creature loose. It skidded to a stop at the edge of the platform and all of time froze with it.

Mercy saw everything at once.

Devlin struggling against the river's current. The hound with teeth bared. Holt settled into a wrestler's stance. Even the small gap between her attacker and the stairs. Every detail stretched out in front of her like a painting. Devlin's hound broke the spell first. It lunged. Holt made no effort to sidestep the creature. Instead, he caught the hound in the air, arms closing in a tight hug. The creature snapped at the air, teeth clacking, and then Holt heaved it across the room. It struck the far wall with a yelp before splashing down into the water. Mercy saw the light flicker below the surface, then gutter out completely. She couldn't tell if the creature was dead or if it had been sucked through the nearest pipes. Mercy was afforded a single, distracted moment. She darted for the stairs, but in that blossoming darkness, she missed her mark. Her shoulder struck the railing, causing her to gasp with pain. It was just loud enough for Holt to hear. Before she could move again, she felt a hand close around her arm. The man's voice rasped in her ear.

"Oh no you don't."

Mercy screamed as she was dragged back onto the platform. Her cry was answered. A golden light split the room in two. Devlin stood on the platform, drenched from head to toe. Unnatural light was gathered in his right hand. Golden threads ran through the crevices of his hammer before extending past the grip and wrapping around his forearm in a crisscrossed pattern. Holt was forced to drop Mercy as Devlin cut the empty air with his hammer. Magic pulsed out in a wave. Their attacker shielded himself with a forearm, just barely keeping his feet against the blast. Devlin repeated the motion, again and again, sending those crescent-shaped pulses of light in his direction. Holt kept inching forward, though, like a man walking straight into the jaws of a hurricane. How was he resisting that much magic? Mercy saw a knife in his right hand.

"Devlin!"

Her shout drew his eyes to the weapon just in time. Devlin sidestepped the first blow, spun around a second, and then the two were circling. The hammer's light kept pulsing. Like the beating of a heart. It left the room in a rotation of perfect darkness and blinding light. Mercy could only see half of their attacks. Devlin landing a blow to their attacker's hip. Holt slitting his forearm in response. Back and forth like that. It took Mercy about fifteen seconds to remember she still possessed magic. Her gloves. She was thinking through what spell might be helpful when it happened.

Devlin brought the hammer across in a terrible arc. The flattened metal found the side of Holt's skull. The bones there didn't break—they shattered. She saw the man's eyes bulge outward. Ripples raced beneath the skin of his forehead, away from the impact point, like a boulder dropped into the center of a lake. Then his head snapped sideways with a sickening crunch. She knew Holt was dead long before his body slumped to the ground. But their attacker had landed a final blow too. Holt's knife was buried in Devlin's stomach. He fell back, his hammer tumbling helplessly away. The light kept pulsing as Mercy collapsed at his side and said, "Shit, shit, shit. Devlin. Hold on!"

He was losing blood. A lot of blood. Mercy set one hand on the knife's grip and the other against the flat of his chest. Using a quick count in her head, she ripped the blade free. Devlin screamed before slamming his eyes shut against the pain. His mind was clearly trying to close down. The pain must have been unbearable. Mercy quickly cast spells to numb the air and to staunch the bleeding. Next, she needed to inspect the wound. Assess any interior damage before stitching up the skin. It was hard to see with her lone light source pulsing on and off, but as she squinted, she saw something that made her curse again. "The blade is poisoned. Damn it."

Devlin didn't respond. Either he'd passed out from the pain, or he didn't have the energy to speak. Mercy reached for the knife that she'd cast aside. There was definitely something coating the blade. She didn't know the exact poison, but it looked cheap. Something that would take time to course through his body—and she could work with that. She'd been trained for this. Turning, she scrambled on all fours. Searching the platform. Where had her surgeon's kit fallen? She made one quick loop before the answer hit her square in the gut.

I handed Devlin the bag.

Right before Holt's arrival. She had shoved the bag into his arms. Devlin had been holding the kit in his off-hand. He'd fallen back holding both the bag *and* his hammer. Instinct would have forced him to clutch tightest to the item that seemed the most vital to their survival. He would have held tight to the hammer, and he would have let go of the kit. Mercy dropped down to her knees at the channel's edge. Her eyes searched the churning rapids. There was something dark bobbing near the pipes. Her bag was there. The strap had caught between the second and third pipe. It was holding for now. Mercy eyed the churning waters, knowing if she did not retrieve that bag, Devlin would almost certainly die.

Taking a deep breath, she leapt.

8

NEVELYN TIN'VORI

Nevelyn did not dream that night.

In the morning, she tiptoed down the stairs. A part of her hoped the others would still be asleep. Maybe she could set to her morning tasks uninterrupted. Instead, she found their kitchen lamp already glowing. She crept through the shadows of the hallway. A peek around the corner showed Dahvid was seated at their kitchen table. So was Josey. The two were sizing each other up.

After a long pause, Josey whispered, "You're tall."

Dahvid nodded. "I am."

"And you have a *lot* of tattoos."

"I do."

"Did they hurt?"

"Pain is a road to power."

Nevelyn rolled her eyes at that, but Josey nodded as if that made perfect sense.

"What's that one?"

Dahvid held out his wrist for the boy to see. "It's a sword."

"How old were you? When you got it?"

Her brother leaned forward conspiratorially. "Five."

Josey's eyes went wide as a pair of winter moons. "But I just turned nine! I can get one!"

Nevelyn took that as her cue to enter the kitchen. "You're not getting a tattoo. Dahvid is unique. He's an image-bearer. Those tattoos are magical."

The denial earned her a world-class scowl from their young guest. "That's what adults always say. When they don't want you to have something. It's magic. It costs too much. Maybe next time."

In response, Dahvid reached out and swiped a finger against the skin of his wrist. A second later, the weapon materialized in midair, settling smoothly into his grasp. Josey's eyes shocked even wider. The boy reached out to try to touch the blade with the tip of one of his pale fingers.

"Hey," Nevelyn said. "Don't touch that. You just said you're nine years old. You're not two. Don't nine-year-olds know they can't touch sharp things?"

Josey shrugged. "I'm hungry. Your brother tried to make eggs."

Nevelyn glanced over to the stove. There was, indeed, a gathering of scorched remains in one of their skillets. Entirely unsalvageable. "Do you like honey bread, Josey?"

The boy nodded. Dahvid raised his hand like a child. "I'd like some as well."

"It's early, but Marta's stand should be opening soon. I'll be right back."

She could not help smiling to herself. This was the most she'd heard Dahvid speak since Cath's death. He'd thrown himself into training and practice duels. Anything physical to help him forget the pain of that loss. She supposed she'd been doing the same thing—except she was using books instead of swords. The appearance of a random child in their house would not have been her first bet for what might draw them back to their former selves—but she wasn't going to ignore the possibility that Josey's arrival could be very good for them.

As she walked back through the unlit front hall, she could hear Josey launching into a new round of questions. Nevelyn was about to open the door when he asked: "What about *that* one?"

This time the answer was silence. Nevelyn had no visual on them, but she knew exactly which tattoo the boy had pointed to. It would be the hand reaching toward the surface of the water. The tattoo that Dahvid had used in his duel with Thugar Tin'Vori. The one that had unintentionally drained Cath's life to heal him. She heard her brother mutter an answer. A quick dismissal of the subject. Being only nine, Josey moved on without question, barely noticing at all.

Nevelyn slipped out their front door.

After breakfast, Nevelyn asked Ava to watch Josey.

"What am I supposed to do with him?" her sister had asked.

"I don't know. Play games with him. Kids like games."

Ava looked thoughtful. "Hmm. I guess I could show him how to pick a lock."

"No criminal activity."

And with that warning, she headed out to participate in some criminal activity herself. She made her way north, past some of the busier markets. The route led her to Stepfast Street. It was not a road she'd have visited as a child. She thought about that sometimes. The fact that Ren Monroe—whatever her position now—had grown up here. A step above poverty. Nevelyn turned the heart charm dangling at her collarbone so that the black side faced outward. For the second time in two days, she activated her magic.

Two long strides brought her to a pearl-blue door. She trotted up the steps, skirting an elderly woman who did not even glance her way. The apartment she was looking for was already unlocked, though Nevelyn knew Agnes Monroe was not home. She'd checked the work schedule three times just to be sure. The older woman would not be on break for another hour. That gave Nevelyn plenty of time. The door swung inward with a small groan.

Nevelyn listened for sounds within. Nothing. She ducked inside, closed the door behind her, and released the magic that had been veiling her presence. Thankfully, the place was small. Agnes Monroe's possessions were meager. One of the bedrooms had been half-filled with food. Like an extra pantry. There were boxes of noodles and jars with pickled vegetables. Another set of crates was filled to the brim with way candles. Nevelyn found the stockpile curious, but it wasn't why she was here. In the main bedroom, she found the stack of borrowed books. Each one matched what she'd seen listed in the ledgers. It was as Nevelyn had guessed: Agnes Monroe had pretended to be her daughter. That facade had granted her access to the Safe Harbor library. The woman had signed out these books. There was a chain of events that Nevelyn could follow, if she could just get her fingers around the logic of the first link.

And the only logical conclusion was that Agnes was also researching the Broods. Unbeknownst to her daughter. That was very curious. Nevelyn didn't have time to formulate proper guesses about the woman's motivation. All she knew was that she needed to borrow from the borrower. She began turning through the pages, searching for the volumes that might prove most fruitful for her own plans. As she did, a small square of paper fluttered free.

Nevelyn watched it twirl in the air before settling on the ground. She turned the pages and another one fell. They were notes. Each one packed with Agnes Monroe's cramped handwriting. She saw lists, questions, commentary. Even a few drawings. This wasn't a brief survey of the Broods' defenses. It was proper research. Thorough research.

"What are you up to? . . ."

Back in the main room, a soft click sounded.

The main door opened with that same groan. Nevelyn's hand slid instinctively up to her locket. She gave her magic a practiced shove forward. All while backpedaling into the nearest corner, one of the library books still clutched to her chest. *Do not see me. I am not here. Do not see me.*

A second later, Agnes Monroe appeared in the doorway. No more than a few paces from where Nevelyn had just been standing. The woman's entire body went rigid.

Gods, it's the stray note. She's spotted in on the floor.

Nevelyn cursed her own carelessness. She stood in the corner, waiting for Agnes to search the closet or under the bed. Instead, the woman looked up. Right at her. Eyes seemingly piercing the great veil of Nevelyn's spell. Agnes smiled.

"You can release your spell, Nan. It won't work on me twice."

Nevelyn's eyes shocked wide. She shoved an even stronger wave of the magic forward. Briefly, she thought of poor Kersey, who'd never fully recovered from the strength of the spell Nevelyn had used against her. But the second casting didn't strike Agnes in the same way. She was not rocked back on her heels. There was no dazed expression on her face. Instead, the woman lowered one shoulder. Like she was determined to walk into a hurricane. The magic dispersed all around her. Agnes smiled through gritted teeth.

"I told you. Magic that worked once will not work again."

Nevelyn could only stare. "How are you doing that?"

"We can talk about the magic—or we could talk about that book you've got in your hands."

Nevelyn had forgotten she was clutching it. She accidentally fumbled it to the ground. The book landed with a dull thud. Agnes was slowly closing the distance between them. The same way a person might approach a feral cat that had snuck in through an open window.

"Or," Agnes said, "if you're ready, we can talk about the future."

Nevelyn frowned. There was a strange tone to her voice. It felt odd. As if Agnes Monroe had somehow arranged this meeting between them—rather than Nevelyn being the one who had infiltrated her home. It had the feeling of a conversation that was long overdue. But they were not friends. They'd spoken only a handful of times, and never with even a hint of partnership.

"The future?"

Agnes nodded. "The time is coming. People like you will have to make a choice. Do you want to walk down this road?"

She gestured to an imagined path with her right hand before lifting her left. "Or this one? You aren't like the other elite in this city. You might have a home in the Wedding Quarter—but you've lived with despair. You've gone to bed not knowing when your next meal would come. You are as much like us as you are like them. You know both worlds."

Agnes came to a stop in front of Nevelyn. They were standing in striking distance of each other. The older woman bent down. She collected the fallen book and set it on the edge of her own bed. Patiently, she turned the pages. Nevelyn saw flickers of blueprints, great blocks of texts, all in brief snapshots.

"I'm inviting you to make your decision now. Before everyone else."

"How charitable of you," Nevelyn remarked. "Do tell, what am I deciding?"

Agnes only smiled. She stopped on a very specific page. It unfolded neatly from the book. Nevelyn saw it was a map of the entire city. Kathor, rendered quarter by quarter, district by district. It was detailed enough that if she looked closely, she'd be able to find the exact corner on which the Tin'Vori home was etched. Agnes tapped the map with one finger.

"Everything," she whispered. "We are deciding . . . everything."

MERCY WHITAKER

When Mercy was little, she raced her sisters.

Out in the field behind their house. They'd choose a tree, settle into their stances, and sprint breathlessly forward to see who could get there first. Dresses billowing behind them, heartbeats elevated. She remembered how they always fought afterward, arguing about who'd actually won the race. Now, Mercy was in a race against time itself.

She'd pulled herself back onto the platform, soaking wet, but with her tools in hand. There were enchantment in some of the tools that helped. She made quick work of the internal damage, sealing this and healing that. If it had just been a knife wound, Devlin would already be right as rain. The problem was the poison. It was seeping through his body and none of her tools would work as an antidote. She could limit the spread—and she did—but she could not stop it until they returned to Safe Harbor for proper treatment.

Dr. Horn had always preached the idea of using one's environment when treating outside the walls of the hospital. She was pretty sure he'd meant using a turned-over stump as a surgeon table—rather than what she did now: searching the dead. Mercy picked over Holt's body. Their attacker offered nothing of great use. She found another blade, sheathed down by his ankle. There was some kind of birdseed in his jacket pocket, but nothing else.

Next, she padded through Devlin's pockets. His utility belt seemed equally useless. Until she found what he'd tucked against his back, left hip. A pair of way candles. *Of course.* His role as designated protector called for more than dueling. It also meant he needed to have an escape route ready, a backup plan. The wicks of both candles were damp from his plunge in the water, but not so bad that they wouldn't light. The problem was fire. Mercy searched the bodies again, hoping to find some matches. Anything that might get the candles burning.

Halfway through her search she remembered she had *magic*. She was literally wearing a pair of gloves that served as a vessel. Hastily, she cast the first warming spell that came to mind. She was so nervous that she almost scorched the sleeve of her shirt—but it worked. The wicks lit. Mercy carefully leaned both candles against the first step of the staircase. After a moment's thought, she plucked one of them back up. Crossing the space, she set the candle against the side of Devlin's hammer instead. If a wind blew through the space, hopefully just one of them would flicker out. When she assessed the scene—the second candle's swaying flame was barely visible in the flickering glow of the abandoned weapon.

Next, she checked Devlin's vitals again. It seemed his heartbeat was a perfect match for the continual pulses of light in the room. He wasn't losing blood anymore, but he was losing time. The poison would keep spreading through his body. If it infiltrated the vital organs before she could get him back to Safe Harbor, his chance of survival would drop significantly.

I will not let you die. I will not let you die.

Her stunted fingers began to itch wildly. She could feel, too, the phantom pain in her stomach. Where doctors had removed an organ during her sophomore year. A burst appendix. She ignored the feeling as she paced the platform once more. The first hour passed.

Devlin woke once. Long enough to sip water, murmur restlessly, and pass out again. Mercy noted a small dip in his heart rate. That worried her, but it was not a conclusive sign that the poison had reached any of his organs. The candles had both burned down to the three-fourths mark when she heard a sharp rattle. It was just loud enough for her to hear above the numbing churn of the water. Her eyes darted to Holt—thinking he'd somehow survived Devlin's deadly blow. His body was motionless, though. Another rattle. It took a moment for her to place the sound.

It was coming from above.

She called out. "Hello? Is someone there?"

"Dr. Whitaker?!"

The rattle transformed into footsteps. Nance appeared on the catwalk above, though Mercy's angle made it hard to see more than slivers of him. Their host rushed down the steps, nearly slipping as he descended. His eyes shocked wide when he saw the scene waiting on the platform.

"Holt! Good gods, look at his face!"

And then his eyes landed on the other body.

"Who the hell is that?"

Finally, he saw Devlin.

"Is he *dead?*"

Mercy shook her head. "Poisoned. He's still alive. For now. Holt attacked us."

"Attacked?" Their host looked shocked. "He fixes gutters. Repairs doors and windows. He's never—I've never seen any sign—"

"We found that other body down here," Mercy answered. "Holt must have been involved somehow. Maybe he's the one who killed her. She's been down here for some time."

But even as she spoke those words, she knew they fell short of the truth. There was something about the placement of the body, the intentional nature of what had been done here. Holt had obviously been involved, but this was no crime of passion. He hadn't murdered the girl and dumped her body to hide the crime. The corpse's placement was part of some larger design.

"I have to take Devlin back to Safe Harbor."

Nance's eyes slid from her to the way candle by the stairs.

"But what will the town do?" he asked. "What do I tell every-one about the quarantine?"

"I'm not abandoning you," Mercy promised. "You have my word. Devlin's been poisoned. I have no other choice. I have to get him back to Safe Harbor. Once I'm there, I'll make a full report. They'll send an entire team out to investigate. A squad of doctors. Soldiers, too. Enough people to figure out what really happened here."

Nance nodded. "Of course. Yes, of course. That's all very logical."

There was a whisper in the air. A word she could not quite make out. *Ar-kill-ar-kill-ar-kill*. She could not figure out where the noise was coming from. Was it something in the water? She watched as Nance made his way back across the platform. Her host paused by the foot of the stairs. Using his boot, he knocked the way candle sideways. Mercy's eyes widened as it rolled once along the metal platform—and then the heel of his boot came down. The flame snuffed out. Useless now. Nance looked back over one shoulder, his face half in shadow.

"I am afraid I cannot let you leave this place."

The words slithered down her spine. His voice sounded strange. All the light was gone from it. He turned around to face her, but made no move to attack. Instead, he placed himself between Mercy and the stairs. Cutting off her only escape—or so he thought.

It took all her effort not to look to the right. The other way candle was hiding in the glow and afterglow of the hammer's pulses. No more than two paces away from her. Instinct screamed that she should lunge for it *now, now, now*. She could escape easily. The hard part would be taking Devlin with her. She would have to dive in his direction, get a solid grip on him, and then physically reach back to extinguish the candle. All without Nance stopping her. And if she did succeed, it would be two people traveling on a shared candle. She would be stretching the magic to its outermost limits. Mercy's heart pounded as she considered her options.

"I can see your thoughts," Nance said. He tapped a finger against one temple. "Which spells to use. What magic might help you escape. Go on . . . try them."

He spread his hands out. Offering himself up as an easy target. Mercy hadn't been thinking of spells. Truly, she doubted that she possessed any magic that could actually overpower him. She'd been trained to heal people—not hurt them. Nance's smile stretched in the silence. Mercy needed to buy herself more time.

"Why would you do this?" she asked. "I don't understand."

It was obvious now that Nance was involved. He and Holt had killed the girl, and then they'd intentionally set her body here. For what purpose? Did they intend to poison their own townspeople? It was incomprehensible, but she desperately hoped Nance would explain it. Anything that might give her more time to think.

"We needed to know if it worked."

Another shiver ran down Mercy's spine.

"If what worked?"

Nance gestured to the girl's body. "The disease. You could call this a trial run."

As he spoke, Mercy edged closer to Devlin. Nance noticed the movement, but made the wrong read again about what she was thinking. "Wouldn't jump if I were you. Those water pipes run all the way to town. No access points between here and the farms. Are there any spells that would help you hold your breath for fifteen minutes?! And that's if you're not bludgeoned to death inside the pipes first."

Mercy had no intentions of testing her abilities as a swimmer. She'd only been hoping to reach Devlin. *Reach him, reach the candle, port away. Reach him, reach the candle, port away* . . .

"Tell me," Nance continued. "What did you learn? About the disease?"

The light of the hammer pulsed, spinning shadows in every

direction. Mercy reached mentally back for the notes she'd taken. Anything to buy more time. Let the candle keep burning.

"Low mortality rate. Just one death so far. At first, I thought it was one of the most rapid-spreading contagions I'd ever researched—but if it was moving to them through the water, it didn't really have to spread, did it? All of them were going to eventually get sick."

Nance nodded. "All of them. Yes."

"I thought you and Holt were evidence that the disease didn't spread to every potential subject. I was wrong, though. You've already had the disease. Haven't you?"

Nance tugged down the collar of his shirt. Even though his skin was darker than Holt's, she could still see a pattern of long-faded bruises below his collarbone. "Correct again."

"So, you intentionally spread a disease. . . ." She still couldn't fathom the bigger picture. "A disease you've already experienced. All these people. You put them in harm's way."

"As you just said, the mortality rate is low."

Nance's casual tone dug under her skin. Mercy couldn't accept that. One casualty was too many if the disease could have been avoided. Besides, there wasn't just one dead person.

"But this girl . . ."

"Volunteered," Nance said. "She's one of ours."

Mercy highly doubted that. People didn't just sacrifice their lives like that. Not when death was waiting for them. They must have forced her into this somehow. At the very least, she'd been manipulated. There was another pulse of light from the hammer. Mercy noted how the beats were continuing to slow. Devlin was running out of time. Her scarred fingers itched again. She could save Devlin—but only if she escaped

SCOTT REINTGEN

first. There was another whisper in the silence. That same strange sound cutting through the air, on the very edge of hearing. Nance briefly cocked his head as if he were listening, and then his eyes fixed back on her.

"Did you hear it?"

Mercy frowned. "Did I hear what?"

"The echo. I know you were trained at Safe Harbor. Educated at Balmerick. You've worked with some of the very best doctors in all of Delvea. I know you heard it."

"Yes. I heard an echo."

Nance smiled again. "In all of them?"

Before Mercy could answer, the light of the hammer went out again. She waited for that next pulse—but this time it did not come. As the afterglow faded, the candle's light was finally visible. Nance's eyes briefly widened. Mercy lunged for Devlin. Her body slid across the water-slick platform and she almost overshot her mark. One arm wrapped around his neck, though, as if she were trying to choke him. Certain her grip was tight, Mercy fell backward, reaching for the candle.

Nance was coming. He shouted something, but the words tangled as Mercy's fingers closed on that waiting flame. A quick sequence of pain followed. First, the burning. Fire pinched between both fingertips. The sound hissed in the air. Next, a sharpness in her side. Skin tearing. Muscles ripping. Something hot and sudden cutting a path toward her organs. Both of those smaller pains were followed by the full-body compression that always happened when entering the waxways. How the magic seemed to shape a person, folding briefly into some other form, so that it could ferry them through that dark world and set them down elsewhere. She heard a whisper in the shadows.

Ar-kill, ar-kill, ar-killllllllll.

Eventually, the sound faded. Her pain multiplied. When Mercy's feet set back down in Kathor, it felt as if someone had put their hands inside the wound in her side. Gripped the edges and pulled them wider and wider and wider. Until the entire world was pain. She blinked her eyes open to candles. She was back at Safe Harbor. Home. It would have been far more pleasant if someone wasn't screaming. Bloodcurdling. Echoing off the walls. She could hear people scrambling to get inside the room. Bodies suddenly filling that space. Shadows and movement.

Mercy ignored them. She was looking to where Devlin should have been. Clutched in her arms. Sprawled across the floor. But there was no one else with her. She shoved to her feet, eyes searching the room. Devlin was not there.

"Gods, look at all that blood."

"Give her space! Back the hell up and give her some space!"

The screams were getting louder. Mercy closed her eyes as the world began to spin. A small part of her mind accepted the fact that she was losing blood rapidly. That was why she was so light-headed. More importantly: Where the hell was Devlin? Why hadn't he come through the waxways?

She couldn't think with all the screaming. She wished the person would stop. She wanted them to shut up. *PLEASE! SHUT UP!*

And they did.

PART TWO

Breaking

10

REN MONROE

The mimicry spell grated against her senses.

A prickling up and down the spine. Small sensations running the length of her arms. Anytime she stepped in the wrong direction, her discomfort would spike. That was how this particular spell had been designed. The magic was encouraging her to follow Lana Dawson's footsteps. Theo trailed behind her like a dutiful ghost—and five soldiers trailed him. Three were assigned paladins from the Brightsword Legion. The other two were guards loyal to House Brood. The retinue was large enough to draw attention from other morning commuters, but Theo had insisted on proper protection.

The prior evening, Ren had taken several hours to find the correct spellwork. Another few hours to acquire and master that magic inside an archive room. Each attempt had pointed her thoughts back to Timmons. After all, the last time Ren had labored over magic like this had been the day before the portal incident. Her friend had offered her enhancement power to Ren so casually and made the magic feel so easy. It was hard not to imagine what it would be like to have her best friend with her now, walking through all of this together. Would it be easier? Would she have found some other way to where she stood now? Some better path?

Ren had been forced to push those thoughts aside. She couldn't allow herself to be lured into a world that would never exist. This world still needed her. After finalizing the spellwork, she'd been ready to rush out into the night and follow the scent until Theo politely pointed out that pursuing a missing person in the middle of the night to an unknown location was not a rational decision. Ren had acquiesced.

Morning was more reasonable. They'd been on the trail for an hour now. The spell description from the textbook had claimed that wearing the shoes would provide the best results, which meant Ren's feet were jammed inside the too-tight simulacrums. The shoes led her first to a small apartment in the Dock district. Aunt Sloan had mentioned this was where the girl had lived with her son. From there, the route had gotten more interesting. The trail led them to a magic house. Not the usual entrance for refilling vessels, though. An unmarked back door with no exterior handles. Ren had wanted to press on, but every next step she tried brought the itching sensation back to her skin. It took a moment to figure out what the mimicry spell was communicating.

"She waited here. For several minutes at least. Meeting someone perhaps?"

Theo nodded in response. "We can wait too."

Ren wasn't sure that was true. Was time on their side? Was Lana out there somewhere, waiting to be rescued? Or had she simply left behind a life that she no longer wanted? Ren paced until she felt a subtle urge onward. West down Humming Street until it dead-ended into Parsons Avenue. There was a gradual shift in the buildings around them. From residential to commercial. Houses transformed into shops. Then the smaller shops eventually ceded ground to the industrial sector of the city. Full-on factories dominated the area. Workers came and went from unmarked buildings. It was like walking down the city's metaphorical spine. All the industries to which their lives were attached. On her left, two women were scaling a rusted silo. On her right, a new construction was going up—the base pillars were exposed and a small crew was there, arguing about some logistical issue. The area was truly bustling.

"This is a strange place for her to visit," Ren murmured, but she kept walking.

The buildings did not grow any smaller. There was no shift back to a residential neighborhood. The factories ran all the way up to the eastern gates. Ren had never visited this section of the city. It felt like the sort of place that you visited on purpose—or not at all.

Finally, Ren felt hives bubbling along her upper back. She tested each possible turn until the shoes responded. The itching subsided. Ren found herself standing before a hunched building.

It was not tall but it was certainly long—stretching from where they stood and all the way to the eastern gate. There were no markings other than the address: 52 Prosswimmer Circle.

"She came here."

Theo frowned. "This building . . . it's one of ours. Well, we don't own the property—but we've run it for decades. It was one of the buildings included in that city defense contract. Our men have been locked out. I forget what kind of building it is. . . ."

Ren could see the file in her mind. "Water treatment."

Theo nodded. "That's right. The crew is small. Maybe five people? They're posted here for general oversight. It's a passive magic facility. So, the place is still running. The viceroy wouldn't have risked a facility like this stalling out. It's too important to Kathor's infrastructure. I'm pretty sure our people haven't been in there for over six days now. It should be empty."

Ren frowned. "But this is where Lana came. I can feel the shoes tugging me forward. She's either still inside there—or she visited this place and left."

"You're certain?"

Ren tested right and left. Both options sent unpleasant ripples down her skin. When she stepped toward the door, the effect subsided. "Yes. I'm certain she went inside."

Now Theo was pacing. "Right. A girl goes missing. We follow her trail—and it brings us here? To an unmarked building that most people don't even know exists. Not to mention it's a building that *should* be locked. How did she even get inside?"

Curious, Ren reached for the handle. The door groaned open. Darkness waited within.

"It's just open?" Theo asked, disbelieving. "Why did our people report that it was locked?"

"Maybe it was," Ren said. "But you said it's been six days. I doubt the workers walked through town every morning to check the locks. They were probably waiting for official word from you. Clearly someone's visited since then. Lana went in there. We need to go in there too."

Theo shook his head. "No. They can go first. That's why we brought them."

He signaled. All three of the paladins trotted forward. It was strange to watch Theo give them orders, considering all of them were at least a decade older. There were no complaints, though. They accepted his authority easily. Each of them activated divinity shields. The bright lights reminded her of Devlin. She wondered if he'd risen through their ranks and where he'd been stationed. A second later, the paladins ducked inside the building. Theo signaled for his own soldiers to come forward next.

"Head for the back of the building," he ordered. "Report back if you find anything. No one exits without our permission. Detain anyone who tries."

Both men thundered off obediently. Theo turned back to Ren.

"I don't like this. It doesn't make sense that she'd come here."

Ren could feel his unease across their bond. She suspected that she was producing her own doses of that emotion. Why had Aunt Sloan's daughter-in-law come to this particular building? Her initial guess had been that this was a bunch of smoke with no fire. She thought Lana had potentially fallen in love with someone at one of her meetings with the Makers. But this was not the sort of place you rendezvoused with a lover. No, this felt like the beginning of something darker.

Less than two minutes later, one of the paladins returned.

"You'll want to see this, sir."

Theo and Ren exchanged a glance before entering. The first room appeared to be a storage room. She saw a table with a scattering of random items, likely left behind the last time the guards had been on duty. The next door opened directly onto a raised catwalk. A network of catwalks, Ren saw, as she looked ahead. Rushing water dominated the space. Echoing off the low ceilings. The building's exterior made a lot more sense now. It ran all the way to the eastern gates, because that was one of the three locations in the city where the Straywhite's tributaries ducked under Kathor's outer walls. This was a water source for a large portion of the city. Lost in thought, Ren ran right into Theo.

"Whoa, sorry—"

"Gods."

Their raised platform had emerged into the heart of the facility. Below were a series of rectangular tanks—more like narrow pools. Basic logic told her this was where the city's water was treated for disease and that the cleansed water would funnel out through a network of pipes to the populace. But all the textbook details faded to the back of her mind.

Ren saw why Theo had stopped.

There were bodies.

Bile started rising in her chest. Theo vomited first. Over the nearest railing. The three paladins were gathered on the lower platform, having a quiet discussion. Ren fought off the nausea and set a hand on Theo's back, urging him forward. He wiped the corners of his mouth before taking a spiral staircase down to the main level.

"How are they just . . . sitting there like that?" was his first question.

She'd noticed the same detail. The tanks weren't stagnant. Water flowed in and out of those spaces at a rapid pace. The currents should have been tugging the bodies all around. Instead, they hovered perfectly at the center of their respective pools. The answer felt obvious.

"Stasis spells. I'd guess these currents are very consistent. Always the same amount of water churning through each tank. No outside factors to consider like wind or erosion. It would be fairly easy to create a countercharm if you knew the exact flow rates."

"And the bodies would just float like that?" he asked.

"Some kind of buoyancy magic. Probably lining their clothing. That's how I would do it."

Theo offered a grim look in response to that. One of the paladins backtracked to them.

"There are four bodies, my lord."

Ren had only noticed the first two. In the distance, there were two other tanks, separated only by a narrow walkway. One body per tank. That detail made all of this even stranger.

"Not just dead," Theo corrected. "They've been mutilated."

He was right. Ren had been careful to look at them out of the corner of her eye instead of straight on. Her best angle was on the tank to the left. The corpse was a young man with a shaved head. Maybe five years older than her? Whoever had done this had opened up his chest cavity. The skin was flayed at the edges. . . .

Ren saw a flashing sequence of images: Clyde's burns. Tim-mons falling. Cora with an arrow punched through her chest. Even Landwin Brood—his eyes dead and his throat marked by those dead-black veins. She spun around in time to throw up in the nearest corner. When her stomach settled, she called back to Theo.

"Describe what you're seeing. I don't . . . I don't think I can look."

"Right," Theo answered. "I don't know. It's odd. All the wounds on the bodies are a perfect match. Open chests. Gashes on the upper thighs, the upper arms. I can't see the other two corpses from here—but I'd imagine they're the same."

"Is one of them a girl?"

Theo was quiet for a moment. "Yes. In the front right tank."

"Short hair? Light brown?"

"Yes. About shoulder length."

Gods. Aunt Sloan was right. Lana Dawson was in trouble—and now she's dead.

Ren was about to ask another question when her mind frac-tured. A new fear pulsed to the forefront of her thoughts. Aunt Sloan had connected Lana to Agnes Monroe. Ren's mother had been one of those late-night visitors. This—whatever this was—had happened at night.

What if . . . what if . . .

She pushed back the nausea and checked the first two bod-ies. One was a young man. The other appeared to be Lana Daw-son. Ren started down the narrow walkway that ran between each of the tanks. The paladins tried to stop her, maybe to protect her from having to see the carnage, but Ren's voice cracked like a whip. "Get out of my way."

They parted like a golden curtain. She took the path, ignoring Theo's questions. She had to know. She needed to see. *Please. Don't let it be her. Gods, it can't be her.* The path between the tanks was slick. She almost slipped before reaching the spot where the first two tanks ended and the next two began. The bodies came into view. One was a man. She dismissed him immediately.

But the other one . . .

"Oh gods . . ."

Ren's eyes hunted through every detail. An older woman. Her skin deeply tanned. A scattering of freckles. She could feel her shoulders starting to slump under the weight of this impossible, impossible truth. Her stomach curling up. Her throat constricting. Like there was no more air left anywhere in the world. But then she saw the woman's hair. It streamed out where it met the water, flat and dark, but the woman's bangs were dry. And they were tightly curled.

A ragged breath escaped from Ren.

She fell to her knees. It wasn't her mother. It was someone else.

"Ren?"

Theo was behind her. He set a cautious hand on her shoulder.

"Ren, what is it?"

She shook her head. "I'm sorry, Theo. I had to know. My mother . . . she visited Lana . . . I just thought that it might . . ."

He pieced it together. "But that's not her."

"No. It's not her."

His hand squeezed her shoulder in relief. He was kind enough not to mention the other truth that was waiting for them. Like a bridge neither of them wanted to cross. The worst possible fate would have been to find her mother here, sacrificed like these other victims. But the other option was not much better. The reality that, somehow, Agnes Monroe was involved in this.

Not as a victim, but as a perpetrator.

"Let's get you home," Theo whispered. "We don't have to be here."

Ren shook her head. "No. This is important. We need to figure out what's going on."

"Mr. Brood. Ms. Monroe."

It was one of the paladins. He'd trailed them down the center walkway.

"Pardon the interruption. If I could have a moment."

"What is it?" Theo asked.

"I think we need to evacuate this building."

Ren frowned. "Why? Whoever did this is gone. . . ."

"It's not that. One of my colleagues just pointed out something about the bodies. It appears that they're . . . leaking."

After the terror of thinking her mother dead, the corpses didn't look nearly so grim as before. The bodies were just bodies. The wounds just wounds. She and Theo squinted at the nearest one. It took a slight adjustment of her angle to see what the paladin meant.

A faint, but unmistakable gas.

"Until we've identified the substance, we shouldn't be here," the paladin said.

Ren unconsciously tugged the collar of her shirt up over her nose. They didn't need any more convincing. Both of them were led back down the narrow walkway. This scene was unlike anything Ren had ever witnessed. Even Clyde's death didn't compare. That had been gruesome, certainly, but it was not designed with the *intention* of being gruesome. It had been an accident. Magic gone awry. These bodies with their matching wounds and strange posturing felt more like a form of cruel artwork. Ren found herself hoping that her mother had nothing to do with them.

Outside, Theo ordered the paladins to head straight to Safe Harbor. He wanted their best coroner sent to the facility—as soon as possible. His own men conferred quietly. Ren was still thinking about her mother. The role she'd played in this. As always, Theo had a knack for looking at the larger picture.

"Do you remember the details on this building?"

She nodded. "Most of them."

"How much of the city's water supply comes from here? I know there are four treatment facilities, but I can't remember which sections of the city they're each responsible for. . . ."

Ren closed her eyes. She could see the pages turning in her mind.

"This one supplies the northern sector," she recited. "Wedding district, the Stoneback Quarter. Maybe some of the Lower Quarter, too? I'd guess about a third of Kathor."

Theo was deep in thought.

"And we run two of the other three facilities. Buildings that are unoccupied. What if . . . what if they were targeting the water supply, Ren?"

A sharp whine cut through the air. All four of them paused, looking around, when a bolt of amplified magic struck the ground between them. Ren saw it happen in slow motion. The way the ground warped. A ripple running over the stones like an earthquake. It shook them off their feet—and while they were still airborne, the magic *exploded* outward.

Ren felt like she'd been punched with four armored fists. One struck her shoulder. The other her stomach. Two more struck the meat of her upper thighs. If she had not been wearing several of House Brood's protective signets, she would have died.

The shield activated in time to catch most of the blow, but she was still launched backward through the air. Right into the stone wall of the water treatment facility. Theo suffered the same, thumping into the wall beside her. His guards were not as well protected.

Ren saw the magic rip them into pieces. One lost a limb. The other slumped, his hands pressed to a gaping hole in his stomach. What the hell kind of magic was . . .

Hooded figures flooded into the streets. Two . . . four . . . ten. More than she could even count in such a small space. Ren saw that all of them had vessels raised. Spells were forming on the tips of their wands or staves. She cast the fastest spell that came to mind. It was the concentrated light cantrip she'd used against the wyvern.

The great blast of light blinded their enemies. Ren was moving in the aftermath of its glow. She seized Theo by the front of his cloak and shoved him back onto his feet. The two of them stumbled into a run as their attackers shouted, trying to get their bearings. Ren thought it might actually work. They were about to reach the nearest alleyway when another masked figure stepped out from those shadows. As if he'd been waiting for them there.

He brought his wand slashing downward in a harsh motion. She saw the air fracture strangely. A flickering glimpse of something. Her shield would have protected her from a direct blow, but his magic was aimed downward. The cobblestones threw her briefly into the air. Theo's hand slipped out of her grasp. Ren saw her momentum was about to bring her down right on top of the masked wizard. He brought a second wand up at the last possible moment. Her wards flashed bright, parrying his first spell, but the timing of his second casting was *flawless*. It slipped by her defenses entirely.

That isn't possible.

Bone-crushing pressure seized her. Like she was a plaything in the hands of an angry god. She locked eyes with the masked wizard and saw two slashes of an unnatural green—and then he flung her sideways. Straight into the wall. Ren felt pain running through her entire body.

And then the darkness took her.

11

NEVELYN TIN'VORI

E veryone was staring.

Nevelyn could not find it in herself to care. She kept the front of her shirt pulled up over her mouth and nose. Her heart had not stopped racing since she'd departed from Agnes Monroe's flat. The woman had unveiled so many intimate details. A secret organization. A plan that felt impossibly large in scale. A disease intended to infect the entire city. She had also invited Nevelyn to join their cause. To be one of the houses that supported the new society they wanted to build.

The woman had drastically misjudged Nevelyn's capacity for sympathy. It was true that House Tin'Vori had been dispossessed by the city's elite. It was also true that they had lived in poverty for nearly a decade. Monroe clearly believed there was a natural bridge between them and the plight of the common Kathorian. But the truth was that their house and holdings had just been restored. Their way of life was returning, piece by piece. After all this time, she had no intentions of turning around and giving it all up for some *cause.*

She hadn't said any of that to Agnes Monroe. She'd seen the glint in the woman's eyes. This was someone acting not just with purpose, but an uninhibited faith that what they were doing was the right course of action. Nevelyn had no desire to be in league with zealots.

"You have my full support," she had said. "Just tell me what you need me to do."

Wait. That had been Monroe's only demand. Sit and wait. A time would come when someone from their group would arrive with instructions. Be ready to act then. Nevelyn had lied through her teeth, promising every support. As soon as she'd departed, however, she'd marched straight to the nearest market.

She was still in the habit of carrying most of her money on her person. A victim's mentality. Their hovel of a home in Peska had been robbed twice. Once she reached the market, she began spending every coin in her possession. She bought food she knew would last. Again, her time on the run came in handy. They'd often chosen foods that they could stretch well past their expirations. Anything that could travel easily. She bought those same foods now.

Small pouches full of nuts. Dried beans in hollowed-out tubs. Bags full of rice or noodles. She piled these items up until the nearest vendor began eyeing her suspiciously, worried she might try to bolt with the goods before paying. She assured him by thumping the correct coinage on the countertop. Her purchases still drew attention. She didn't care. As long as Agnes Monroe didn't walk down the street and see her—it would not matter.

Only when she'd loaded three bags to the brim did she carefully sling the straps over her shoulders. She winced at their weight and how the fabric dug into her skin, but after a quick adjustment, she began the short but arduous walk home.

People stared. Small children pointed. A few shopkeepers even came to their front windows, curious at her passing. Nevelyn could not help staring back. Agnes Monroe had claimed a disease would be spreading through Kathor. Would it happen today? Tomorrow? In a week? Was it already coursing through their veins? The woman had claimed it would spread to everyone. Nevelyn had been skeptical. The older houses possessed so many protective wards. Magic that most common folk could only dream about. Monroe had smiled in response. "It's coming. For all of them."

She eyed the people she passed for signs. Symptoms. A hacking cough or a rash of some kind. By the time she'd reached their home, though, she felt uncertain of reality. Was she overreacting to a madwoman's claims? Every single person she'd seen appeared to be perfectly normal. Their lives rumbling on as if this were any other day. Ava answered the door.

"Finally, I'm tired of entertaining this little . . ." Her eyes widened. "What the hell is all of this? Nev, he's like half our size. He can't eat *that* much food."

Nevelyn ignored her. "Help me unload everything. I'll explain inside."

Ava scowled before reaching out and slipping one of the bags from Nevelyn's shoulder. The two of them hustled through the halls. Josey was at the kitchen table, looking as if the entire world had failed in its sacred duty of entertaining him. His eyes widened as items spilled onto the counter. He wasn't impressed for long, however. "Beans? I don't like *beaaaaans*."

Nevelyn rolled her eyes. "Let's start sorting everything. Where is Dahvid?"

"In the bath," Ava replied. "Are you going to explain why you bought ten *pounds* of noodles? You were on your stepstool preaching about modest spending just last week."

"Get Dahvid first. I don't want to repeat myself."

That earned a world-class eye roll, but her sister skulked off down the hallway. Nevelyn heard her calling for their brother. She turned back and nearly jumped out of her skin. Josey was mere inches away from her. His fingers were frozen on a box of dried cookies. He smiled innocently.

"Sorry. Didn't mean to scare you."

"Don't do that again, or I'll enchant your shoes so that they squeak when you walk."

His eyes widened. "You can do that?"

"I can do far more than you might imagine. Come on. Help me with these."

To her complete surprise, he obeyed, accepting every small task she assigned him. It was a quiet reminder that he'd spent several years living with Garth. Likely the two of them had split the household tasks, which meant he was more accustomed to this work than many children his age. That might be useful. Ava returned with Dahvid, though he arrived shirtless and annoyed. When he saw the piles of food, he offered a single raised eyebrow.

"Starting a restaurant, Nev?"

Ava snorted. Dahvid looked quite pleased that his joke had landed. It had been like this ever since her sister had returned. The two of them were thick as thieves again, which annoyed

Nevelyn to no end. "We are preparing," she answered. "I've just been to visit Agnes Monroe."

In the quiet of their kitchen, she relayed everything she knew. A plan ten years in the making. A door that they had unknowingly opened when they defeated House Brood. The city that they'd finally returned to—after all these years—was allegedly going to suffer through a blight. Monroe promised it would spread to every household. No spell could keep it out. There was no ward it would fail to break through. And according to Agnes Monroe, the disease would alter the very fabric of their society once it arrived. Bold promises. Perhaps too bold.

When Nevelyn finished the story, Dahvid shook his head.

"Most people overpromise and under-deliver."

"Ah," Nevelyn replied. "Didn't realize Father had returned from the grave."

Dahvid rolled his eyes, but Ava was eager to pick at the same thread. "Agnes is a dockworker, right? It's hard to imagine she has the resources to work on a scale of this size. Let me guess. She wanted your help. A few donations would go a long way?"

"That's actually what convinced me," Nevelyn answered. "She didn't want our money. She didn't even ask for my help. She said the disease was already on the way. Plans were already in motion. The way she talked . . . she made it sound inevitable. Nothing will stop it at this point. She wanted our support for what happens after. When the city gets back on its feet. She wanted us to support the Makers then."

"The Makers?" Josey chimed from the table. "I know them!"

All their attention swung his way. Nevelyn had forgotten he was sitting there. He beamed at the three of them. "Don't you?"

"No," Nevelyn admitted. "Who are they?"

The boy's smile widened as he realized he possessed knowledge they didn't. And like any child who knows a secret, he relished the moment. "Come on. Everyone knows the Makers."

"Quit milking it," Nevelyn snapped. "Tell us what you know or I'll have Dahvid use one of the tattoos he hasn't told you about. You might not like that kind of magic."

Josey actually looked more tempted by that. "Fine. They have meetings down in the Lower Quarter. Garth went once. He said that they were . . ." And here he adopted a deeper voice with almost effortless effect. "'A bunch of raving-mad lunatics who gibbered on about a future that won't ever exist.'"

Nevelyn swallowed. It was a decent impression. Decent enough to remind her of Garth's real voice, and the mint he often had on his breath. The warmth she'd felt whenever he stood close to her. She looked down and realized she was clutching a bag of rice so tightly that the seams were starting to tear.

"But now that future is coming," Nevelyn concluded. "According to Agnes Monroe."

"That last bit is the important part," Ava said. "How could we possibly trust her?"

"Why would she lie to me? What would she gain from that?"

Ava shrugged. "Father always said there were two kinds of lies. People who lie to someone else—and people who are lying to themselves. She *thinks* a change is coming. How many people have believed the same? Most revolutions die before they can even take their first breath."

Dahvid had sat in silence. Now his eyes fixed on her. "Last time, we trusted my gut. Look where it got us. This time we'll go with yours. What does your gut say, Nev?"

Nevelyn met his gaze. "My gut says that a storm is coming.

And I think if we're prepared, we might be one of the only houses in the city who doesn't get knocked off their feet by it."

Ava was shaking her head, ready to complain. Dahvid silenced her with a look.

"We follow Nev's lead on this one. What else do we need to do?"

"More food," Ava said. "This is a good start, but you'd be surprised how quickly this will vanish. We only had a few people living at the castle in Nostra but the food stores always ran out earlier than expected. If the city falls into proper chaos, there will be shortages. We should probably buy twice this amount. We also need to work on the house's defenses." She gestured to the run of windows overlooking the harbor. "Half of these don't lock. We'll want to repair everything. Magical wards, too. It's a lot of work but I know the spells we'll need to use."

"Good," Nevelyn said. "That's decided then. Josey. You're up next."

The boy blinked. "Me?"

"Yes. You. If a disease comes, we're going to lock the front doors and we're not going to open them again. It could be a long time. This is your last chance to go somewhere else. If you stay with us—you're staying for the long haul."

He looked around at all of them.

"Where else would I go?"

His question echoed. All of them knew the answer. There was nowhere else. She'd just wanted to make sure he was the one who made the choice. That way, if they really did have to isolate, she could remind him that he'd wanted to be here. Asked to be here.

"We wouldn't want you to go anywhere else," Nevelyn said,

standing. "Ava. Make a list for me. I'll go buy more food. Maybe I can go to a different market—just to avoid any unwanted attention."

Her sister reached inside her coat. She froze as she did. Confusion transformed to panic in less than a few seconds. "I put it in here this morning . . . what the hell . . ."

Josey's face went bright red. The same kind of blush Garth always wore when he was fumbling for what to say. The boy set a small sack of coins on the table. Nevelyn saw how he was already slowly backpedaling. "I was just seeing if I could! I promise I wasn't going to keep any of it!"

Ava darted forward, but Josey was surprisingly fast. He ducked her and shot off into the unlit hallway. Dahvid was already belly-laughing. Nevelyn couldn't help smiling. It wasn't often that she had the pleasure of witnessing someone outmaneuver Ava. Their chase took them upstairs. There were a number of carefully crafted curses. Shouted apologies wove in and out of those. From the sound of it, Josey had managed to lock himself in one of the closets.

When Nevelyn glanced back, she saw that Dahvid was watching her. The weight of that stare wiped the smile from her face. "What?"

"I'm sorry," he whispered. "I haven't been looking out for you or Ava. Not since . . ."

"You were mourning. That is not the same as neglect, Brother."

He swatted her words away with a lazy backhand. "We both lost people. I know how much you were hurting, Nev. But you kept your eyes open. You've been watching out for us. Thank you. I won't neglect my duty again. You have my word."

There was another thunder of footsteps above. Josey sounded as if he'd escaped the closet. Sure enough, he came sprinting down the stairs and past them. Out the back door. Ava was hot on his heels, half-laughing and half-furious. Nevelyn started forward, all too prepared to separate them. Dahvid set a hand on her arm as she passed, though.

"If a storm is coming, let them enjoy the sun."

Nevelyn turned away from the window and set to work.

12

MERCY WHITAKER

In her dreams, Dr. Horn sat in the corner of the room.

He asked her questions. Repeatedly. That patient, tight-lipped smile of his. After a few questions, though, his face would shift into the carved-stone features of Devlin Albright. Mercy found that dream version of him achingly handsome. But then his face would melt into Nance's softer features. And then the medic who died. A rotation of freckles and bruises and lips and chins that would blur until Mercy opened her eyes again. Her mother was there.

The two of them hadn't been on good terms in years. Ever since Mercy's grandmother passed away. They'd had a terrible argument right before the funeral. Her mother had pressed in on her, demanding and suffocating, and Mercy had refused to help her. No matter how many times she'd explained the situation, her mother—consumed by grief—hadn't been able to accept the answer. The bickering got so bad that her father had stepped in. When he took Mercy's side, her parents' relationship had begun to unravel. A few years later they separated. Mercy hadn't felt guilty about it. Her mother had behaved like a petulant child.

In the dream, Mercy's mother was speaking with Dr. Horn. That was how she knew she was dreaming. Her mother never visited the hospital. Not once had she come in for a glimpse of how her daughter's life had unfolded over the past five years. It had to be a dream—in spite of how realistic the colors all looked. How textured and vibrant. Her eyes would fixate on a specific item in the room, trying to assess its reality, and that was when everything faded.

Back to darkness.

"Mercy? You have to eat, my sweet."

Now the face belonged to her father. Another impossibility. He never came within pecking distance of her mother. The two had not spoken in years. His voice urged her again.

"Go on. Have a bite to eat."

Mercy felt something in her hand. She frowned down. Pudding. Her hand was *in* pudding. Cold, mushy, disgusting. A chill ran the length of her spine. She held the hand up for inspection. There were dark streaks. Not unlike blood . . .

"Get it off! Get it off of me!"

Her father rushed forward. Mercy saw the world fill in around him. She was at Safe Harbor. She could see the small bird emblem, with its protective wing outstretched. She was seated upright, with pillows on either side for stabilization. Her father held her tenderly by the wrist, wiping the streaks away from her upturned palm. When he finished, he set the tray back on her bedside table.

"I'm sorry," he whispered. "I was just trying to be helpful. Mercy? Is that you, sweetie?"

She nodded. Her throat felt raw. She signaled. There was a pitcher nearby. Her father hastily poured water into a cup. Mercy drank. One cup after another after another. Only after she'd drained half the pitcher did her mind connect this small detail back to what had happened.

Water. The disease is in the water! That's how it spreads. . . .

Horrified, she threw the cup. It narrowly missed her father's head, striking the wall at the far end of the room. The door opened. Her mother peeked inside. She was not a figment of Mercy's imagination after all. Her parents were actually in the same room for once.

"What happened?" her mother asked.

"I don't know," her father whispered back. "She just threw it."

"I'm sorry," Mercy said. "It's just . . . the disease. The disease is in the water. That's how they're planning to spread it. The water isn't safe."

Her parents exchanged glances. Mercy felt a surge of annoyance.

"What? The two of you don't speak for years and now you can read each other's minds?"

Her father snorted. Her mother, of course, did not smile.

"You've woken up several times," her father explained. "Every time, you seem to forget that you've talked to us before. It's like you're drifting in and out. Water has been a common theme."

Mercy nodded. A mistake. She felt a small spike at her temples. Her mind was very sluggishly attempting to link pieces of memory back together. Water. She remembered the water.

And Devlin.

She had reached for him at the last moment. Then reached for the candle. Shit. Wait. Was that how it had happened? It helped to go back. The two of them had been at a water treatment facility. They had discovered a body inside. A girl. Murdered. Holt had arrived and he'd attempted to kill them both. Devlin had been stabbed. Poisoned. Mercy . . . was going to save him. She had intended to bring him home, because she was the only one who could save him if he died. Her stunted fingers began to itch wildly. Her stomach twisted with pain.

". . . but when I ported, he wasn't with me. He . . . he didn't travel through the waxways. The only reason he wouldn't travel through the waxways . . . is if he was dead."

Mercy finally realized she had been speaking aloud. These weren't just thoughts. The words were tumbling out into the open air. Her parents exchanged another concerned glance.

"You've said all this before, dear. About Devlin. You keep figuring out that he's dead."

Mercy frowned. "Nance. He was one of them. He almost stopped me from porting."

Her parents exchanged a glance.

"You've brought this Nance character up a lot as well," her father whispered.

One link connected to another connected to another. Her thoughts ran ahead of her like a chain spell. She recalled the disease and all its symptoms. How fast it spread to the farms. The town that had been named Running Hills. Someone intentionally spreading a disease.

"I've said all of this already?"

Her parents nodded.

"To who?"

"You've said it to us," her mother said. "To the nurses. The doctors. The paladins who came to investigate. You've told pretty much anyone who's walked into the room. It's like your father said. You drift in and out."

"Devlin's dead," Mercy said stubbornly. "He was killed. Someone has to investigate."

A nod from her mother. "Oh, Mercy. The paladins took your claim very seriously. They look after their own. When they heard what you said, they sent a full company to Running Hills. Less than an hour after you ported. They found a lot of sick people up there, but when they visited the water treatment facility . . ."

Mercy nodded. No pain this time.

"They found them. The bodies."

"No, my sweet." Her father's voice sounded so infuriatingly patient. "They didn't find any bodies at all. Devlin wasn't there. They did . . . there were townspeople who claimed you'd sent him away. A few people claimed they heard you fighting. About what happened when you dated."

Fury pulsed to life inside her. "That's not true. That didn't happen."

"Mercy." Her mother looked exhausted by the conversation. As if this were all a grand inconvenience to her. "The paladins investigated everything. They couldn't find anyone named Nance. There was no sign of Devlin. Dr. Horn is worried about you. We're all so worried. This . . . this is like before. Remember the story with your cousins? You always said you rescued them. . . ."

Her anger multiplied. A deep and terrible rage.

"Mother, I *did* rescue them. You know that."

"I know what you told us, but those boys . . . they were never the same after. Then there was what happened to your friend at Balmerick. Come on, honey. You have to admit that this kind of drama follows you. It's not normal. I'm worried. We're all worried."

Mercy's fingers itched again. Her fury had grown with every word. Bright to the point of blinding. She had *not* imagined the events that had unfolded in Running Hills. She could remember the sight of Holt's face caved in. The wound in Devlin's side. The girl's body and those terrible mutilations. It was all real. She'd seen it with her own eyes.

"You didn't believe me," Mercy said. "But you came to me after grandmother's funeral. . . ."

Her mother's voice sharpened. "Do not go there."

The two of them stared each other down. As always, her father intervened.

"Look. Mercy. We believe you. We do. We just want you to feel better. That's all. Your mind is recovering from trauma. Dr. Horn agrees. We just need you to . . . rest. Recover from this."

Her mother's tone. Her father's placating. It was all too much. She knew there was nothing she could do from a hospital bed. She'd have to show them her journal. All her notations. If necessary, she'd go back to Running Hills and walk them through what happened. She didn't know how Nance had moved the bodies that fast but she'd figure it out.

Determined, she swung her legs over one side of the bed. Her parents both started to protest before she felt it. A sharp tug at both wrists. Magical binding appeared. Activated as she attempted to leave the proximity of her bed. They normally reserved these spells—these particular hospital rooms—for dangerous or unstable patients. Mercy stared down in horror.

"What the hell is this? Why am I bound?"

Her father looked away in shame. Too weak to speak the truth. Her mother had always been far better at delivering a blow. "Because you are a suspect, dear."

"A suspect of *what*? You just told me there aren't any bodies. I reported three people killed—and your response was that no one died. You're acting like I imagined everything. So tell me, what could I possibly be suspected of doing?!"

"Devlin is missing," her mother answered. "He never returned to Kathor. You arrived at the waxway station covered in his blood, Mercy. You also have been describing someone else murdering him to anyone who would listen. The paladins believed . . . you might be conflating the stories. Subconsciously hiding what happened through . . . through a fiction you've created. Mercy, it's just us here. No one else. You can tell us the truth. If something happened out there, you can tell us."

Mercy couldn't help testing the bindings. There was no give to them at all. The magic bit into her wrists like teeth. She felt a spike of claustrophobia before remembering the magic was built around a proximity charm. It would deactivate if she remained where she was supposed to be. She leaned back against the pillows, settling into the center of the hospital bed, and the bindings vanished from sight. It was a shame, really. Because right now she would have loved to strangle the condescending woman standing across the room from her.

Nance Forester had outmaneuvered her. Even her parents were half-convinced of her guilt. She was trying to figure out some way to exonerate herself. "My journal. It has all of the notes I took. About the town. About the disease. I took notes about Nance in there."

They shook their heads sadly.

"There was no journal with you," her mother said. "Not when you ported."

Damn it, Mercy thought. *I left my notes in our room. If Nance got rid of the bodies, he would have disposed of the journal, too.* Her mind was still tracing back through their final conversation. Picking over the details of what he'd said. There had been so much specificity to his questions. He'd asked her if she heard the echo, which meant he *expected* an echo. That detail linked to another. What had he called Running Hills?

"It was a trial run," Mercy said. "He didn't think I would escape. That's the only reason he told me anything. He thought I was as good as dead. He . . . he called Running Hills a trial run. That means they're planning to do it again. The target would be . . ."

Her parents traded glances again. She knew how she sounded. Like some kind of deranged conspiracy theorist. But the pieces were lining up now. There was only one logical target. All the towns to the north were identical to Running Hills. A scatter of farms. Small populations. If you were performing a trial, you'd first attempt it on a small scale—then you'd know what to expect on a larger one. There was only one city that fit the profile.

"Kathor. The target is Kathor. I need to speak with Brightsword. We have to send paladins to check every facility that feeds water to the city. There's still time. We can stop this. It's not too late."

Neither of them would meet her eye. She saw hope slipping away. Her father stood just in reach. Close enough that she could slide her hand into his without setting off the proximity spell. That small touch brought her father's eyes up to hers.

"Father. I'm telling you the truth. I've never had a good imagination. You know that."

He smiled through his heartbreak. "That's true. You're not the creative one in the family."

Her mother remained unmoved. "Briar. She's sick. Our baby girl is sick. It's been going on like this for a month now. We can't just . . ."

All Mercy's pulsing anger went cold. She blinked rapidly, as if that might be enough to reset her mind so that she could hear her mother correctly. That couldn't be right. It couldn't be.

"What did you just say?"

"I said that you are sick, Mercy. I won't pretend otherwise. You are unwell."

"Not that. How long? How long did you say I've been here?"

Her father squeezed her gently. "It's been . . . over twenty days. Longer maybe."

Mercy sank back into her pillows. Her hand slipped out of her father's grasp. The room was spinning. Maybe the entire world was spinning. *Over twenty days. I've been here for over twenty days.*

"Get the paladins."

When her parents didn't move, Mercy reached for the food tray. She flung it at her mother. It struck the poor woman's shoulder, knocking her back into the wall. Mercy followed that with a rage-filled scream. The outburst rattled them both. Forced them into a terrified retreat.

She did not care.

They were running out of time. If they didn't act now—it would be too late. The people she'd vowed to protect were vulnerable. Nance—and whoever he was working with—could already have infiltrated the city. She would not fail in her duty to the city.

A plague is coming.

13

REN MONROE

Ren licked her lips, trying to make out the shapes and shadows that stirred outside the dense fabric of her hood. There were three voices. A steady stream of conversation, but even though the words were audible, Ren couldn't understand them. She'd initially believed it to be another language. Some sort of Tusk variant? But eventually she realized the clipped syllables and strangely elongated vowels were the result of magic. An enchantment was at work. Hiding their exchange from unwanted ears.

Mentally, Ren began working out how she'd create such a spell. The exercise kept her terror at bay. This was the third time she'd been taken captive in the last two years. First, on Della's drug farm. Ren still carried the mental scars of her torture in the darkest corner of her mind. Next, she'd been captured by Zell Carrowynd. The city's warden had been a far more pleasant jailor. Their conversation had been a crucial step in the destruction of Landwin Brood. Ren found herself hoping—and doubting—that this capture would be more like the latter.

A small pop sounded.

Magic had been dispelled. Ren could feel the weight of it vanishing from the air. One of the voices spoke—and now she could understand the words. "Can you hear us?"

It was not a voice she recognized.

"Yes. I can hear you."

"Good. Do you have any idea where you are?"

Ren weighed how to respond, and decided that whoever had kidnapped them was *powerful* and powerful people wanted to know they were dealing with someone else who was powerful.

"My first guess was that you were connected to what we discovered inside that water treatment facility. . . ." She let that dangle in the air. It was ideal to keep them curious. Trading useful information could matter in a situation like this. "But that theory fell apart. Our captors were all using magic, which means you're not with the Makers. The next clue were the masks. The eyes I saw were an unnatural shade of green. The fabric is enchanted. Weaving magic that modifies eye color and voice pitch. That particular pattern belongs to the Graylantians."

One of her captors snorted. "Well done. You've narrowed your attackers down to a house that has roughly three thousand members."

"Oh, it wasn't them," Ren replied. "The masks were a distraction. You were trying to hide the identity of the wizard who led the attack, but he spoiled the secret. He was *very* good. Clever enough to get around some of the protective wards I was wearing. But the most interesting detail was the illusion he had over his wand. It's one thing to wear masks. Hiding your identity in an attack like that makes sense. But how many people in Kathor have a vessel that's famous enough that someone might recognize it on sight?"

Ren waited. No one snorted this time.

"I can think of . . . maybe five or six. Combine that knowledge with the other details—height, casting style, standing posture—and it's pretty clear that Able Ockley led the capture party."

Again, no one spoke. Ren knew they were still in the room. She could see those deeper shadows through her hood. "Which means House Shiverian organized the attack. If I had to guess, Seminar is in the room with us now. She hasn't spoken because I'd recognize her voice."

Ren knew she could stop now, but she figured she might as well finish the trick.

"But your question was where are we. The Shiverians have countless properties, but I'm a student of history—so I know that their house prefers to keep their hands clean. If you have to be involved in something criminal, you normally distance yourselves through your minor houses. You use them as shields. Which means I'm in a building that belongs to the Ockleys, the Arvinasks, the Marthins, or the Bearings. Able would never let you use his family's home. Not if he's already risking his reputation by participating in the actual kidnapping. The Arvinask family doesn't know how to keep a secret. That leaves just two options—and based on the very faint scent of candle wax, I'm going to go with House Bearing. Specifically, we're on the third floor of their workshop . . . on the corner of Conning Street."

A rough hand pulled the hood away. Ren blinked against the light, and then blinked up at the familiar face of Seminar Shiverian. Her onetime mentor and her current captor.

"Gods," the woman said. "I wish you'd chosen me. You could have learned everything I know. How bright that future would have been for you. Instead, you get this."

Seminar gestured. Across the room, she saw Theo. Bound and hooded. There was no sense of panic across their bond, which meant he was likely unconscious. Either that or the charm was blurring their words. Two other people were in the room. The first was a man of middling height. His dark hair was receding. His eyes were wide and pronounced beneath rimmed glasses. The stranger was circling Theo while holding an old lamp in the air. It produced no light, but he squinted as if he could see some invisible substance in the air around them.

The second person stood half in shadow. Her bird-thin arms were crossed in front of her. Predatory eyes glittered as they met Ren's. Prison had not dulled Tessa Brood's natural beauty. This was what they deserved for showing mercy. The Broods ran most of the prisons around Kathor. A natural consequence of acting as Kathor's bloody knuckles for the better part of a century. Theo believed that if he sent Tessa to one of their prisons, it might have been a death sentence. After all, her family was responsible for everyone's horrible existence in those places. Mercifully, Theo had chosen to send his sister to the only facility that was run by the Proctors.

And now that decision worked against them.

"This is your plan?" Ren asked in disbelief. "You can't just replace Theo. His ascension was public. The city views him as the rightful successor to House Brood—so do all of the minor houses that serve him. Removing him now would start a war. It's one thing for an inheriting member of the house to usurp his father. Quite another for one of the other houses to force a change in leadership. I'm pretty sure that's why the War of Neighbors started."

Tessa's smile stretched. "That's the problem with being so smart. You start acting like an ass, and you assume no one else knows what you know. You finished what . . . fifth in your class?"

Ren nodded.

"I finished first in mine. How about you, Seminar?"

Her old mentor smiled. "First. As if there were any other option."

"We know how the War of Neighbors started," Tessa continued. "We've memorized those textbooks too. We know all the treaties and the major casualties. Little Ren Monroe stepped out of poverty and rose above her station . . . and now she thinks she has no equals. That's not how it works. I'd dare to say that you actually have several superiors in this game we're playing."

Tessa crossed the room so that she was standing fully in the light. She spared the outside world a brief glance before looking back to Ren.

"Let's put that mind of yours to the test. Tell me, Ren Monroe, what was the primary mistake that led to the War of Neighbors?"

Ren could almost hear Professor Sasser's voice echoing in her mind.

"Secrecy. One house attempted to sway the internal mechanisms of another—but without the express involvement of the other three."

Tessa offered a mock clap. "Very nearly an exact quote. That's correct. Look at how we learn from our mistakes. What clever people we are. Seminar represents House Shiverian. Dr. Horn is here on behalf of House Winters. The Proctors were the ones who facilitated my release and the Graylantians, as you pointed out, offered the masks and tracked your movements alongside Able Ockley. Every single major house is involved this time. Which means no war."

The Brood heiress looked at Ren as if she were the smallest, most insignificant creature in the universe. "You said you're a student of history. Now you get to be an entry in a textbook. I'm sure we can find someone to write up a little paragraph about the genius Ren Monroe. You'll be an answer on a Balmerick midterm. I just hope they actually remember what your name was when they take the test."

Ren was shaking her head. "You can't just get rid of Theo. It won't work."

"Get rid of Theo? We wouldn't dare. No, dear, we're getting rid of *you*. Dr. Horn?"

The third person in the room finally disengaged from his work. He retreated to where they were standing and set his strange lantern on the table. "There's an opening," he said. "The slightest crevice. Some small matter of distrust between them. A disagreement or an old wound or a lie. I'm not sure, but it doesn't matter. It's there. Enough to get me inside. The surgery will be lengthy, but I feel confident it will work."

She had no context for what he was saying. Crevice? Wound? Surgery? She was about to ask what he meant when the answer clicked into place. Tessa Brood's eyes glittered with delight.

"Good girl. Knew you'd figure out the answer."

"We are bonded," Ren spat out. "Literal magic courses between us. You're really going to attempt a severance? That's been done . . . twice in all of Delvean history."

"Four times, actually," Dr. Horn answered. "The first two successful procedures were performed by my father—and the next two were perfected by me. I am very good at what I do, Ms. Monroe. After assessing your bond, I can assure you that it is quite possible."

His voice was so calm. As if he were explaining normal symptoms to a normal patient. Ren's own panic started to rise in response. A wild thrashing in her rib cage. There was no response from Theo. No pulse of emotion. No protective surge of power. It was a confirmation that he was unconscious still. She thought she felt *something*. Some distant entity opening its eyes in response to the raw emotion thundering through her veins, but that presence was flicker and gone.

Like any caged creature, Ren thrashed back at them.

"This could destroy Theo. You risk doing permanent damage to him. There are stories of failed cases." She shook her head. "Please. You can't do this to him."

"We can," Tessa replied. "We will. If it works, Theo will never know. He'll forget you ever existed. You could knock on the gates of our estate every morning—and he'll look out at a stranger. It's so delightfully tidy, no? We keep the capable heir of our house—and in the same breath, we get rid of you. The fucking mud on our favorite pair of boots."

Ren had no answer. It was a disturbingly intelligent plan. She'd always known that Tessa was the most dangerous Brood. She'd also wondered—though never dared say aloud—whether they should just kill the girl to avoid future trouble. And now that trouble was here. Ready to devour them both. Tessa swept in for one final word.

"After it's done, you don't get to die." She tapped Ren's nose. "I think I'll keep you."

She marched out of the room. Seminar and Dr. Horn were still there, conferring quietly. Ren's final hope rested outside the room. *Vega. She wasn't with us during the attack.* Her eyes darted to the windows. Her view was of the tops of distant buildings, a steadily dimming sky. She watched and watched, but there was no rewarding sweep of stone wings. Instead, Dr. Horn crossed the room with a needle in hand. He smiled, as if she were any other patient in his care.

"This will pinch slightly," he warned her. "But after, you won't feel anything."

"Wait."

The word thundered out. It was not meant for Horn. Her once mentor turned back before leaving the room. Ren knew her only hope was to delay. She had to give Vega and the rest of House Brood a chance to find them. There was only one way to do that.

"You never asked what we found in that facility."

Seminar humored her. "Go on then. What did you find?"

"Bodies. One in each water tank," Ren said. "They were set there on purpose. Their wounds had been created after death. Like surgical openings. There was a substance leaking from each corpse. It was unlike anything I've ever seen. Almost like the dragon corpses."

Seminar listened without any change in her facial expression. Surprisingly, it was Dr. Horn who reacted. He reeled back a step. His face gone pale.

"We were following a tip. It led us to those bodies. Theo was worried that what we found there might be in other facilities around Kathor. He didn't think it was an isolated incident. It's possible that someone is targeting Kathor's water supply. Poisoning people."

Ren knew she was stretching the truth. Inventing wildly. Anything to plant the seeds of a bigger conspiracy in their minds. She was surprised again by the intensity of Dr. Horn's reaction. He looked like he'd seen a ghost. As if she'd just predicted the exact date of his death.

Seminar was less convinced. "'If ever you are captured, distract and delay.' That quote comes from Homa's treatise on interrogation and warfare. A clever girl like you would know that text by heart."

Ren shook her head. She could sense the door closing.

"Ask the paladins who were with us! They would have reported it back to Brightsword."

"Unlikely," Seminar replied. "We intercepted them before they could report anything."

Another hope gone. Like a bird shot out of the sky with an arrow. No one else knew they were here. All they had now was Vega—and each other.

"You are charged with the protection of this city," Ren said. "Kathor could be in danger."

"One wyvern at a time," Seminar answered. "Put her under, Dr. Horn."

Ren felt the promised pinch. A flood of deceptive calm. Quiet reassurances whispered her panic into a corner. Subdued those feelings until they didn't exist at all. Her extremities went numb. She could just barely make out Dr. Horn's words to Seminar.

"I must . . . the hospital . . . Her story . . ."

". . . the procedure cannot . . . delayed."

Sound and color faded. Ren felt like she was falling through time itself. Drifting back to some ancient before. Back, back, back. Gone. Into lightless nothing.

14

NEVELYN TIN'VORI

One of her father's favorite stories to tell them as children was the tale of Gathraxes.

For the first century of Delvea's existence, their ancestors interacted with dragons. Not often. Even then, the dragons had begun their retreat into the Dires. Their already dwindling numbers continued to decline rapidly. But every now and again, a story would make its way back to the general population. Travelers would encounter them on the deeper forest trails. Expansion into new territory would occasionally be stymied by their presence.

One of those stories came from a man named Crawley Shiverian.

Eighth son of the legendary Hara Shiverian—he stood to inherit little. Backed by a generous sum from a family patron, he led an inland expedition. Not all the way into the Dires, but near enough to be considered a risk. He established a small outpost that grew into a small town. Crawley's mission looked successful until one night, he came face-to-face with Gathraxes.

The dragon unfolded from the shadows. Crawley knew better than to fight or run. He immediately bowed. Pleased by that subservience, Gathraxes offered mercy.

"In seventy-three days, your town will flood. Many will die. Prepare and you will survive."

Crawley took the news back to his people—and his wisest advisors all rejected him. His prophecy wasn't logical. Their town was elevated. Far away from any flood plains. It had hardly rained at all since they'd settled in the region. His encounter was dismissed as a fever dream. Pure imagination. Crawley prepared his house and the rest of the town smirked at him from their front doors. Once their leader, he was denounced. Stripped of command. Others stepped in to replace him. Crawley labored on in spite of their judgment.

The day finally arrived. Seventy-three days since his encounter. Crawley woke up to an empty sky. The advisors passing his home pointed at the stray light cutting through the forest trees. All that wasted effort, because of a dream, or else because of the mischief of a dragon. Crawley was the town's newest fool. Until they heard a distant rumble. The rumble became a roar.

In less than an hour, the town flooded. Historians would later confirm what none of the townspeople—not even Crawley— knew. Gathraxes had spent those seventy-three days toiling. Every day and every night. He'd been in the mountains using his claws to carve a new valley. That gap in the mountains diverted one of the major riverways, slowly but surely, until the entire waterway broke through like a shattered dam.

Hundreds died. Crawley was one of the lone survivors. The

story's lessons always depended on who was telling it. Patience is a virtue. Dragons are assholes. Wisdom can only be found in hindsight. A younger version of Nevelyn had considered everyone in the story to be utter fools. If she'd encountered a dragon—she would not have stayed and worked on her house like Crawley had. She would not have grinned in mockery like the advisors. No, she would have left the next morning and never returned to that place. But now she found herself walking in Crawley's metaphorical footsteps.

She was a mortal in possession of prophecy.

Their home was prepared. A dozen different wards had been cast. Magical protection layered over the entire property. Physical reinforcements had been installed as well. Nevelyn had replaced every lock. Doubled the thickness of the exterior doors. She'd even ordered special windows. As they made their modifications, the neighbors took note. She saw them watching from windows, or else pausing in the front of the street to assess their bulky new door. One woman had muttered to her partner that it all looked rather out of style. No one asked what they were doing, though. Maybe the answer seemed obvious. The Tin'Vori family—once raided and ruined by the greed of the great houses—was taking steps to see that the same fate would never befall them ever again.

A decent guess, even if it was inaccurate.

Now that preparations had been made, Nevelyn felt like Crawley must have felt on the dawning of that seventy-third day. Waking up to a bright sky. Not one cloud on the horizon. Looking out at a world that showed no signs of what had been promised.

Nevelyn had taken over the master bedroom when they'd

first moved in. No one else had wanted the room. One too many ghosts for their tastes. It was on the second floor with a big bay window that overlooked the entire neighborhood. Their estate stood on the corner of two streets. One ran down to the nearest market. The other was a residential street that was often full of small children and their sometimes-watchful parents. Looking out now, she saw the makings of a normal Kathorian day. Markets full. Commuters passing by on their way to work. Bright scenes that had her pacing her bedroom and wondering why she ever chose to trust anyone besides her siblings.

Agnes Monroe was Nevelyn's own personal Gathraxes.

Had the woman lied? Or was she, like the dragon, working in the background to fulfill her own dreadful prophecy? Downstairs, Nevelyn heard Josey rattling dice in a small cup. He poured them out onto the hardwood floors. Dahvid groaned at whatever the result was. She'd visited a specialty stall and bought dozens of different games for them to play. Childish things, but what else was there to do? True isolation meant there was only the house and the outer courtyard. Ava had secured a stack of novels from the library for reading. Dahvid spent most mornings training. Each of them had activities to occupy their time. All she knew how to do was brood and over-think.

It wasn't until the following morning that Nevelyn witnessed the first proverbial trickle of water into the village. She had dozed off in her rocking chair. She woke to the sound of boots. A team of paladins were hustling up the street in the morning light. Nevelyn watched them until they turned the corner and the rhythm of their footsteps on the stones faded. Sometime later, they returned with a gurney held between them. A woman writhed atop the stretcher—though it was hard to see more than her outline through the thick barrier of golden light that sealed her off from the rest of the world. It might have been a normal injury. A heart attack or an overdose of the breath. But Nevelyn saw, as they passed just beneath her window, the bruises. The woman's body was covered with them. Across her face. Running along her collarbone. Far too many to count.

And then the paladins turned onto the next street. Moving in the direction of the Safe Harbor hospital. Agnes Monroe had promised this would be the first sign.

"It's beginning," Nevelyn whispered to no one. "It's here."

15

MERCY WHITAKER

An older paladin hovered in the corner of Mercy's room. Mercy's restraints were gone, but only because this woman had been left to shadow her movements. She'd been allowed to shower. Her guard had watched from one corner. It was the most shameful experience of her life. An invasion of her privacy and her dignity. Mercy had already felt exposed without her gloves. The fact that this woman was allowed to see her this way, to see the scar running down the lower right side of her stomach. It was too much to bear.

Her only grim satisfaction was the knowledge that she'd done everything in her power to help the people of Kathor. After her outburst, the paladins had returned to the room. She'd demanded they investigate the local water treatment facility. Post guard rotations. Anything that might stop Nance from the next step in his plan—if that next step hadn't already happened.

The paladins had made their promises, but her assigned guard spoke volumes about how they currently viewed her: a madwoman, a murder suspect. Mercy was starting to feel that way. The biggest shock had been the discovery of how much time had passed since she'd ported back from Running Hills. Weeks and weeks had slipped by without her notice. Enough time that the city might truly be in danger—and yet they seemed content to treat her like the criminal in all of this.

Mercy had little appetite, but her wits had returned to her. It wasn't smart to refuse food. Sustenance was what fueled the body. How could she properly face whatever was coming if she deliberately weakened herself? Instead, she quietly chewed and swallowed, chewed and swallowed. All for the sake of gathering her strength. Bracing for a blow no one else believed was coming. She also demanded that her water be boiled first. She'd already been exposed—drinking water during her delirious state *and* tending to the actual contagion in Running Hills—but no symptoms had come. There was no point risking further exposure.

She was permitted to walk the hospital wing once every few hours. When she did, her entire body protested. Aches in her calves. A sore lower back from too much bedrest. She kept expecting bruises to appear on her skin. Maybe she was getting sick? But the dark marks never came.

A sense of desperation formed in her mind. A feral sort of fear. What if she was never released? What if the hospital sent her straight to one of Kathor's prisons? Falsely accused of Devlin Albright's death. Unable to prove the truth. Those thoughts began to haunt her waking moments.

Until Dr. Horn shouldered into her room. "Dr. Whitaker. You're needed."

Her guard scoffed at that. "No way. She's a murder suspect. She's not going anywhere."

"We've discovered proof of her claims," Dr. Horn said. "Your commanding officer has been informed. Dr. Whitaker was right. About everything. The water treatment facilities in the city have been compromised. Which means she's innocent. It also means we *need* her. Our hospital has twenty-two new patients who've all arrived in the last hour. All with signs of heavy bruising."

Mercy wanted to pump a fist in the air. She wished she could beat her chest and shout in their faces. She was right. They were wrong. As glorious as it felt to have her sanity proven, she knew she couldn't celebrate. The cost of her freedom was a plague knocking at the gates of the city.

It was here. And it was only the beginning.

"Have attendants start filling up buckets of water," she said. "As many as we can spare."

Horn frowned. "I thought water was the mechanism for how the disease is spreading."

More vindication. Clearly, he had been listening to her all along.

"It is," Mercy said. "But if they're arriving with symptoms, there's no risk of further exposure. All of them are going to be thirsty. It's a common symptom. I also think we need to go ahead and isolate one wing of the hospital. Clear out every bed in one of the units. I'm thinking . . ."

"The North Wing," Dr. Horn finished with a nod. "You're right. It's mostly empty anyways. We'll consolidate beds, move people around. I'll have our nurses start casting the standard wards. Mask enchantments. All of that."

Mercy started to rise, but the paladin shadowed forward from the corner and took up a protective stance in front of the doorway. "I have orders to keep you here. I cannot disobey those orders until I've heard directly from my commanding officer. We can wait until—"

Dr. Horn cut her sentence off with a shockingly powerful spell. The paladin attempted to raise her divinity shield, but she was a second too slow. The spell punched her square in the chest. Knocked her backward. Mercy gasped when the guard slumped unconscious to the ground.

"We'll deal with this later," Horn announced. "Come with me, Dr. Whitaker."

It felt good to be called by that name again. Mercy stumbled after Horn. Into the waiting hallway. Her mother was there, peeking nervously around the corner.

"Mercy? I thought I heard a noise. . . ."

"Go home, Mother." It was impossible to keep the heat out of her voice. "We have confirmation that it is no longer safe in the city. The disease that you didn't think was real is now spreading. Go home. Make sure father is safe. Boil any water you drink. I wish you all the best."

She made it sound like the dismissal it was. Her mother's mouth opened, but Mercy and Horn took the corner at speed. They marched straight to his office. He pulled open the top drawer of his desk. Mercy's gloves were there, along with her uniform. He set both items on his desk before excusing himself to give her privacy. She changed out of the patient gown she'd been wearing. Putting on her official Safe Harbor uniform felt like donning armor. A protective layer that stood between her and the lies she'd almost started believing during her imprisonment. When she slid her enchanted gloves on, pulling them tight over her fingers, it felt as if she were ready for battle.

Horn nodded once when she reappeared and then they were marching back down the main hallway. Nurses were ducking in and out of sight. Mercy heard conflicting orders. Horn's voice boomed above them all.

"Listen up! We are going to clear this wing. Now! All current patients go downstairs. New arrivals who show signs of bruising will be funneled to this wing until further notified. Let me walk you through what we're dealing with. Dr. Whitaker, correct me as needed. . . ."

He explained the situation, the symptoms, everything Mercy had detailed to him over the past few weeks. He also explained that the majority of them, if they'd had any water at all, were likely already exposed to the disease they would be treating. The staff were urged to boil their water until symptoms appeared. As he spoke, Mercy maneuvered in the background, preparing her own intake station. Quietly casting enchantments over her cloth mask and her uniform. As soon as Dr. Horn's speech stopped, the staff began to move. Fulfilling requests. Following orders. Horn turned to her.

"What else? We're following your lead here, Doctor."

Mercy nodded. Her confidence was being restored, moment by moment. "It might be smart to reach out to the city's governors. We're about to use a lot of magic in this hospital. We should have them divert emergency stipends of ockleys for our staff. Free vessel refills for anyone who comes bearing the Safe Harbor sigil."

Dr. Horn frowned. "We haven't activated that protocol since . . ."

"The War of Neighbors," Mercy said. "I know. Better safe than sorry."

"I'll make the necessary arrangements. Can you organize this wing in my absence?"

She nodded. "Are we using the Nelson method? Assess, contain, stack?"

"Precisely what I would do."

He began marching down the corridor before pausing. When he looked back, there was a mixture of despair and pride in his expression. "Mercy, I'm sorry. I should have never doubted you."

She'd craved those words an hour ago. All she'd wanted then was for one person to believe her story and to confirm she was sane. Now it hardly mattered. There was work to do.

"It's behind us. Let's focus now."

Her response steeled something in him. Dr. Horn nodded before disappearing down the hall. Mercy turned her attention to the nearest attendants. "How many patients are on their way?"

"We're starting with forty. But there's more in the line outside. Tons of request for transport. Too many for the triage teams to handle. Gods. It must be chaos out there."

Mercy was the only one who knew how bad this was about to get. Kathor had more resources than Running Hills. Bigger hospitals and hundreds of talented medics at their disposal. Those were marks in their favor, but everything else was stacked against them.

This was a proper city. Across all Delvea, there wasn't a

larger population that existed in a smaller geographical footprint. Even though the casualty rate had been low in Running Hills, that didn't mean the disease would cause no damage. It had been temporarily debilitating for its victims. Scale that kind of illness across Kathor and the city's industries would grind to a halt. She knew there were facilities that relied on passive magic. Those locations would remain operable, but much of the city had been designed with a working populace in mind. It required people to run.

Was that Nance's endgame? An attack on the city's infrastructure? Her mind was still chasing through those rabbit holes when the double doors of their wing burst open. Teams of paladins bustled inside. Each pair had a gurney held between them. Mercy took a deep breath and then called out in a commanding voice.

"All patients come to me first. I'll assess and assign. Everyone, follow my lead."

Her work began. Asking quick, concise questions. Checking vitals. Everyone in the room was watching her. Mercy's hands did not shake. Her voice did not tremble. She had spent years training for exactly this moment, for exactly this reason.

"First room on the left," she ordered. "Next patient!"

16

REN MONROE

R en's eyes opened.

She was on an operatory table. Her hands and feet were bound with leather straps. Like a goat being prepared for sacrifice. To what god, she wondered? Did the city of Kathor count as a deity? Were the great houses minor gods in that imagined pantheon? The air in the room was heavy with magic. Sterilization spells. Some kind of visual enhancement charm. A table with medical supplies and instruments was set against one wall. Her eyes were drawn to her right.

Theo.

He was bound on an identical table. As she stared, his eyes blinked open. It took a moment for them to swing in Ren's direction. An invisible force pushed against her senses. Racing across their bond. So powerful that Ren couldn't help recoiling. Theo looked confused, small, vulnerable. She had seen that exact same look before. On Avy's face just before Clyde dragged him under the surface of the water. Again, when the revenant seized Timmons by the hair, dragging her off the side of that mountain. It had been on Cora's face too, just before the crossbow bolt found its mark.

This was how an innocent creature looked before it died.

Protectiveness and anger roared across their bond. She felt him try to pull her. The same magic he had used to drag her from the Brood estate and all the way to Nostra last year. But this time, counterspells thundered to life. Bright and brief and more than strong enough to keep them on their separate tables. Ren saw Theo open his mouth to speak. He tried again. The sound would not reach her. Magic, she realized, was muting his side of the room from hers. It was an unexpected blow. Tears began to stream down Ren's face. Pinned as they were, she could not even reach up and wipe them away. Theo tried to send assurance across their bond, but that only brought more pain. He had no idea what was about to happen to them. Ren had no way of warning him.

Instead, she said the only words that mattered.

"I love you."

Over and over, she shaped those words until Theo understood. He nodded, repeating the phrase back to her. Finally, those words belonged to them. After all they'd been through, Ren could say them without hesitation. Words she'd only said to her mother and father and a few close friends. *I love you.* Those three words should have been theirs to claim for years to come. Spoken just before falling asleep. Whispered before walking into parties. Gasped after making love. Scribbled in notes left on coffee tables. All she could give him now was the shape of those words. Not even their sound, their fullness.

That realization brought more tears streaming down her face.

Dr. Horn arrived. Theo tensed as the man entered. He looked his question at Ren, but how could she possibly answer? How could she explain who this man was and what he'd come to do? The doctor circled. Judging some invisible quality in the air. Satisfied with what he saw there, Horn returned to the entryway.

"I'm ready. Make sure the assistants rotate every hour. Listen for three taps on the glass before entering. Never two people at the same time. Understood?"

Someone out of sight must have signaled their approval. Horn closed the door and strode to the heart of the room. The lights flickered out. Ren blinked against the sudden darkness. Terror gnawed at the edges of her mind. She found herself retreating deeper into their bond as silver light crept through the air. An eerie-looking substance coalesced in a perfect sphere around her.

In that light, she could just make out Dr. Horn. He wielded his wand like a baton, conducting the progress of the fog, shaping one sphere over Ren's table and another over Theo's. She could sense how detailed it was. A second layer, a third, a fourth. Until the air felt too thick to breathe. Horn performed a final sealing spell. Ren marveled at how each of his layers merged. Flawless precision. His promise from their last conversation echoed in her thoughts.

I am very good at what I do, Ms. Monroe.

Horn's next spell was a pulse of darkness. It left her briefly blind. She could not see Theo. She could not even see her own hand held out in front of her. As if the world had ceased existing.

And then the most beautiful magic she'd ever witnessed. A lavender thread emerged from her abdomen. Followed by apple reds, stray silvers, fickle golds. The most curious one was a cord of bronze that looked half-there and half-not. If she focused on it too much, the thread would vanish from her vision. The threads reminded her of walking into an archive room. Magic made fully visible to the naked eye. Each of the threads extended out from her, reaching for the walls or the ceiling. She stared in wonder until the final thread emerged.

A river of white fire.

Our bond. It's . . . beautiful.

She watched it course across the room, connecting her to Theo. It was hard to believe that was coming from her. She'd spent so many years with a fire burning in her chest that she'd assumed there was nothing left there but ashes. Seeing her bond, though, made her feelings for Theo undeniable. *I really do love him. Those aren't just words. They are the truth. Written in magic between us.*

Her eyes found Theo's again. There was enough light in the room to see him properly now. She was forced to watch as the joy on his face twisted into horror. Dr. Horn had set aside his wand. He lifted a small, silver tool. A scalpel. The room, their bond, the glinting silver. Those three clues pointed to a specific answer. Theo finally saw why they'd been brought to this place. All she could do was say the other words that he deserved to hear.

"I'm sorry."

She was not sorry that she'd met him or that they'd bonded, but she hated that their tangled lives had somehow led them to this place. She hated that Cora and Avy and Timmons and Clyde had all been casualties of her efforts. Deep down, she'd imagined having decades to figure out a way to put their spirits to rest. She knew there was nothing she could do to make it right, but for all of this to end here and now? They deserved more. Theo deserved more.

Dr. Horn began his dark work.

Most of the other threads appeared to be bone-thick. Their bond was over four times that size. Wider, but also less contained. The edges spilled light outward, like a river on the verge of overflowing its banks. She realized it was still in the process of growing. Horn tested the edges of that thread, scraping here or there with his tool, searching as much with his hands as with his eyes.

Finally, he seemed to find what he was looking for. He hunched over a specific spot. Beneath the bright pulses, she saw a hairline fracture. Barely discernible at all. Horn set his scalpel to the spot and started to cut back and forth, back and forth. Their bond roared in response. Hungry and pulsing and defensive, but the counterspells quelled the magic quickly. Their vessels had been taken from them, which meant they were powerless to stop him.

Horn ignored the bright flashes and continued to *cut*.

Her view of the operatory vanished. Ren found herself seated before Landwin Brood. He was leaning back in a familiar armchair. On the table between them, a folder. Ren knew what was inside. The details of the waxways accident. The revelation that it had been Ren's magic—her binding spell—that eventually stranded all of them in the Dires. It was the one secret she'd kept from Theo. The operatory flickered back.

Horn was still patiently sawing at that small break in their bond. She recalled what he'd said to Seminar Shiverian. When he'd assessed their bond, he'd claimed to have found an entry point. A weakness. Ren wept now, because she knew the one flaw he'd found was her secret. Her eyes swung to Theo. She expected shock or anger, but there was only an unspeakable sadness.

A boy on the verge of something worse than death.

The operatory vanished. She stood in ruins. Great piles of shattered stones. She saw books and broken furniture and an active fire burning some thirty paces ahead. Ren watched breathlessly as Theo picked his way through the debris. It was his memory this time. In the same location, but Landwin Brood was gone. The library had been demolished. The one consistent detail between the two memories was the folder sitting on the table.

Theo reached down and picked it up. Quietly, he began to read. Eyes drinking in every detail. Ren waited for that ancient Brood anger to surface. It would be fair. She'd lied to him. Instead, Theo closed the folder. He continued through the wreckage, knelt down, and set the evidence against her in the flames. They both watched as smoke curled into the air.

Theo looked back at her. She knew this was not a part of the memory. It was him, right now, telling her what had happened. He had already found her most damning secret. Her very worst fear—and he'd destroyed the evidence. Once again, he'd fought for the best version of her. It was the most devastating realization of all. The final secret—the only barrier left between them—was gone. There was someone in this world who loved her exactly as she was with no equivocations—and she'd discovered that life-altering truth just in time to watch that person be ripped away from her.

The operatory returned.

Horn was there, cutting deeper. As he did, new memories appeared. All the little moments that defined their relationship. Ren found herself with Theo in that dark alleyway. She grabbed his coat as he grabbed her waist as they pushed back into the archive room. Her blood was racing, his lips were soft, and the shadows cradled them both just so. Flicker.

Ren was dressed in black for Landwin Brood's funeral. Theo stood solemn at her side. They were in the same church where they'd mourned Clyde Winters the year before. Her eyes traced the stained glass windows on her left until she found a scene depicting the founding of Kathor. There were small details intended to depict each of the major houses. The one for the Broods was a dagger that dripped with freshly drawn blood. She stared at that dagger until the ceremony ended.

Back to the operatory.

The dagger transformed into a scalpel. The hairline fracture had tripled in size. The place where Horn was focused on appeared lightless. Almost as if that was what Horn was severing. The light that existed between the two of them. More memories followed.

A party with Theo. Their duel with his father. A glimpse of Nostra, where they'd curled under a blanket together and watched the sun rise. She saw the argument they'd had in the cobwebbed library. The moment his father exiled him. Moment upon moment upon moment.

Ren was dragged like a prisoner through the halls of their relationship. And in between each glimpse of their tangled lives, she saw Dr. Horn—like the steady hand of a god—cutting it all away. Theo was being drowned by the same memories as her. Forced to relive all that bound them, good or bad. Horn had reached the halfway point when his scalpel broke. It was a small stab of hope. Ren watched as he retreated to the door. He was sweating profusely. Absolutely exhausted by the effort required so far. How long had they been down here? Minutes? Days?

Horn knocked three times. An attendant opened the door. They offered him a replacement tool—a toothed saw this time—and vanished as he set to work again. Ren found herself on the bridge where they'd fought a revenant. She walked through the dragon burial chamber with him. Huddled for warmth in a mountain pass. Between each gasp of memory, Ren whispered prayers. She begged gods that she'd never believed in: *Please. Come. Save us.*

The worst memories were the ones where she was in Theo's perspective. Seeing his version of events. Often, they were the same memories, just shaded with new colors. In those, she was always the focus. And what could be more painful than to finally see herself through his eyes?

Beloved. Desired. Delighted in.

It should have been the greatest joy of her life to witness it, but Dr. Horn was there, severing every single glimpse—cut by precious cut. Ren saw that he'd reached the final clinging strands of the bond. A chasm of darkness had been left in his wake. Ren watched him stumble back in the direction of the door. He paused, bending over like a man who'd just run a lap around the city's outer gates. Even with a foothold, their bond was no easy thing to kill. His entire shirt was soaked through with sweat. He'd replaced his gloves twice—and his tools as well. Ren saw a slight tremor in his hand as he lifted a glass of water to his lips. He drank the entire thing. Pausing, he went to the door. Three knocks.

"More please. Bring me more water."

They returned—and he chugged the second glass. Horn shoved the glass into those waiting hands. He closed the door and crossed over to examine the final strands of their bond. Ren's eyes found Theo again. She didn't know what to say, what to do. And then she heard it.

The gentlest of thuds.

Dr. Horn was on the ground.

17

REN MONROE

What do we do? What do we do? What do we do?

That was the panicked thought that echoed between Ren and Theo. No one came to the door to help. Ren realized the sound of Horn's fall had been barely loud enough for her to hear. This would be their only opportunity. Both of them began testing their bindings. Tugging, pulling, twisting. Groaning with effort. No matter what they did, however, the leather straps held tight. Horn had dropped his saw, but it was well out of reach. Ren was still searching the floor for some other option when she realized Theo was signaling her. He mouthed a single word, over and over. She couldn't make it out until he paired it with hand movements. He held his hand flat and shoved his palm outward as far as his binding would allow. This time when he mouthed the word, she understood. *Push.*

She nodded. It was their only chance. They'd tested it at the very beginning, and the counterspells had swatted away their effort. Hours had passed, though. The magic would have waned. And the first attempt had been one-sided. Theo desperately pulling at her. If they *both* worked together, could that overcome the wards? Her bond-mate closed his eyes in concentration.

Ren felt that familiar tug. The same beckoning voice that had drawn her from Ravinia to Nostra that first time. She shoved headfirst into that sensation. Counterspells flared, bright and brief, but she was already moving. It wasn't pleasant. She'd traveled along their bond easily before. It had always felt similar to traveling the waxways, but this time she was passing through a reduced version of their magic. The final threads connecting them. All of her compressed into that too-small space. And then she was there. Beside him. Half-there and half-not. One final pull of magic from Theo solidified her form. She was free—and falling.

"Shit!"

She had been lying down. The magic kept her in that position before dropping her. Her back collided painfully with the stone floor. She rolled over on one side, groaning against that pain, and then she was pushing back to her feet. She spared a glance for Horn, to make sure he hadn't woken back up, and then she set to work on Theo's bindings. Loosening each strap in spite of her trembling. When his hands were freed, she moved to the bindings down by his ankles.

"You knew," she whispered. "About the portal room, and you didn't say anything."

Theo nodded. "Yes. I knew."

"You must hate me."

She knew those words weren't true—or fair. Guilt made her

say them. It hurt that that flaw Dr. Horn had found in their love came from her heart and not his. Theo had no such flaws in his affection. It had been her decision not to fully trust Theo that nearly doomed them. And might still.

"I could never hate you," Theo whispered. "I read my father's report, and then I assumed the best of you."

Ren frowned. "Theo. The portal room *was* my fault, though. It was."

"It's behind us," he said. For the first time his brash confidence felt like a salve on old wounds. "Look, you're not the only one who's smart, Ren. I knew you'd never put Timmons at risk like that. Which means the binding spell you performed—it was meant for me and Clyde. My father's notes made your position clear. An unfair lack of offers from the great houses, in spite of your performance at Balmerick. The desire you showed for a new position. What better audience than two heirs? I still don't think it was a wise decision, but you're assuming everything that happened after that was your fault. Think, Ren. What happened to Clyde? That would have happened no matter what you did. He was casting a spell. Magic was coursing through his veins when the waxways activated. Your binding spell was irrelevant. He would have died no matter what. Either in that forest or in the streets of Safe Harbor. It wouldn't have mattered. His death isn't on you."

"But the others . . ."

"Weren't supposed to be there! Your binding spell drew them in completely by accident. What do you want me to do, Ren?! Hate you for the things you never meant to do? Despise you for being so desperate that you felt like you had no other choice but to do something drastic? I'm sorry, but I'll never hate you for that. I'm not sure I could if I tried. I mean, just look at that. . . ."

He pointed. Their bond was still visible in the air. Even marred by Horn's work, the spell remained breathtaking. Ren noticed that in the few seconds they'd been speaking, the magic had already started restoring itself. As if Theo's words were healing the damage Horn had done, word by precious word. "Look, I'm in love with you," he said. "Now, let's get the hell out of here."

Ren felt like a fool. How much time had she wasted worrying about that secret? When love had already propelled Theo past it? She watched as he collected Horn's tool from the ground before handing her the spare wand from his pocket. There was little chance she could use it. Accessing someone else's vessel without permission was enormously difficult. It took years of training, but Ren accepted the wand anyways. It was possible a guard might not know it belonged to someone else. She could at least create the pretense of being armed.

"Are you worried he'll wake up?" Ren whispered.

Theo shook his head. "I don't think so. Besides, now he has no wand. Come on."

They crept over to the door. Staying low the entire time. Theo's voice was so quiet that it barely reached her. "I wish I knew who was involved. We have no idea what's waiting out there. If we're in a basement or a loft. Outside the city or somewhere downtown."

Of course. He didn't know. He'd been sedated for the entire conversation with Tessa.

"It was your sister's idea. We spoke. While you were unconscious."

Theo's eyes shocked wide. "The Proctors released her?"

Ren nodded. "All of the great houses were involved. This was a state-approved coup."

"To remove me?"

"No. They wanted to keep you. The goal of this was to remove me."

"A severance procedure. Gods. I would have forgotten who you are."

His eyes were bright in the surrounding darkness. Ren felt burning anger begin to fill the space between them. The kind of fury that led to the destruction of entire cities. It was the most attractive thing she'd ever witnessed, and she'd once seen him perform a ceremonial dance shirtless. It had her smiling in the dark.

"Save that anger for later," she suggested. "Right now, we need to stay focused."

He nodded. "We knock three times. They come to the door—and then what? Do you know how many guards are out there?"

"I've only seen attendants. Rotating. Maybe two or three of them."

Theo regripped the saw. "We'll have to move quick. Before they can get off any spells. Are you ready?"

When she nodded, he knocked on the door. The same rhythm Horn had used. They stayed out of sight as the answering footsteps approached. The door swung open and they thundered out of the shadows like a pair of revenants. There was a clipped scream before Theo seized the person by their collar and put the saw to their throat. Ren darted past, her stolen wand raised high, but there was no one else in the room.

"Where are they?" she asked. "The other attendants?"

The young woman burst into tears. She'd dropped her own vessel to the floor. Ren collected it, keeping her eyes on the adjacent hallway the entire time. Theo's borrowed weapon had grazed the girl's neck. There were small rivulets of blood staining her collar.

"Tell us where they are," Ren repeated.

The girl stammered. "No one else . . . I was . . . Arlo just went home sick. He wasn't feeling well. Someone was supposed to come an hour ago. My shift . . . over. My shift should be over. I was supposed to be home. It's just been me. No . . . no one else came."

"Where are our vessels?"

The girl pointed at the nearest wall. Ren frowned, but moved in that direction. It appeared to be empty. She ran one finger across the cracked paint, though, and found a spot that sent vibrations back across her skin. Goose bumps ran down the length of her arm. There was magic here. She tapped the wall three times and a cloaking spell fell away like shed skin. A hidden door.

"Got them," Ren announced.

All their vessels. Their coats, too. Ren traded Theo his wand for the saw. It fell to the ground with a clatter. She slid the dragon-forged bracelet over her wrist, then adjusted her grip on the horseshoe wand she'd used since she was little. *Gods, it feels good to have my magic again.*

All that was missing from their arsenal was Vega.

"You will lead us out of the building," Theo explained. "You will tell us everything you know about where we are in the city. If you want to live, you will be quiet and helpful.

Hesitate for even a moment and we will leave you here for your colleagues to clean up in the morning."

That had the girl shaking violently. Theo forced her to start walking. Ren trailed them both. They found themselves strolling through a private medical wing. The entire place appeared to be empty. Ren assumed that was intentional. Fewer witnesses for their illegal procedure. Now that decision worked in Ren and Theo's favor. No one sat at the intake desk. No one was watching over the lobby. They slid like wraiths toward a set of double doors with stained glass panels on either side. Ren thought she saw a figure waiting outside.

"How many guards are there?" she whispered.

"T-two. Usually two."

Ren and Theo edged quietly forward. She silently counted to three—and then they burst through the doors. There were two chairs set on a dimly lit porch area. The left one was empty. The right one occupied. Ren was preparing to unleash a concussive blast when she realized the guard was asleep. She gestured to Theo, who understood, slapping one hand over their attendant's mouth.

The girl struggled before remembering that her life was very much in danger still. Slowly, they edged away from the guard. Ren saw that he was sweating. His face had turned pale. Not just tired, but sick? The grounds were extensive. All draped in shadow. They reached the darkest corner of the courtyard, but Ren still felt terribly exposed by the terrain. It ran flat in every direction with very few trees. They would have nowhere to hide if someone stumbled upon them, but at least it was night. Visuals would be low. They were shadows walking inside shadows.

"Is this the Whisper Garden?" Theo asked.

Their captive nodded frantically.

"You've been here before?" Ren asked.

He nodded. "Once. For a luncheon. It's a reward for the Shiverians' vassal houses. There are underground baths. That place they had us . . . it's a rejuvenation center."

"How lovely," Ren whispered back. "Where the hell is the exit?"

A third voice cut into their conversation.

"Stop where you are. I am a member of House Shiverian. Do not move!"

The missing guard. Shit. He'd made his approach using the same shadows as them. Several spells rotated through Ren's mind. It would not be easy, she knew, to spin around and cast magic. The guard had the drop on both of them. Their one advantage was that they had the numbers. Two of them to just one armed guard. Unless he was uniquely skilled, he'd have a hard time hitting both targets. All they had to do was move in opposite directions. Ren glanced at Theo, who glanced at her. Understanding passed between them. The guard noticed.

"Hey! None of that . . ."

Ren saw that he'd lifted his wand into the air. It was the clever solution. He didn't need to stun them both or attempt to duel them at all. One firebright spell and he'd have the rest of the guards on this estate joining the hunt. She flinched in expectation of the bang. Magic launching into the sky, bright and bold and beckoning.

Instead, she watched the man's entire wrist *detach.*

Blood poured out. The pain was delayed, but when it arrived, it arrived in full. The man fell to his knees and Ren had the split-second awareness to cast a silencing spell. The gossamer wave of magic struck him just in time. There was the briefest slash of a scream, and then nothing. Just a man with a stump for an arm, screaming without making a sound. Theo was more merciful than her.

A stun spell thundered out from the tip of his wand. Too wounded to resist, the man took the full force of Theo's casting in the chest. He slumped unconscious to the ground.

"What just happened?" Ren asked. "Did his spell backfire?"

Theo shook his head. "Look."

A small cry echoed above. Ren spotted Vega swooping in tight circles, the gruesome appendage still clutched in her talons. Focused on her flight, they'd forgotten about their captive. She was sprinting back in the direction they'd come from. They watched her vanish and knew the countdown was on. Ren followed Theo into the night.

Vega winged overhead like a talisman of hope. They encountered no other guards. Eventually, the gardens began to narrow. From sprawling sections to a sort of stone labyrinth. Ren did not like that feeling—of being trapped as she'd just been trapped on that table—but Theo moved like someone who knew where he was going. There was a lone gate between hedges. He led them through that archway and out into the public streets.

He knew this area better than she did. They walked parallel to the property, still too close for Ren's comfort, until the road began to slope down into a market space. Theo pulled up short when they reached that waiting square. "There's no one here?"

"It's the middle of the night, Theo."

"I know. They call this the Midnight Market. It's popular with Safe Harbor residents. It doesn't usually empty out until sunrise. There should be hundreds of people here. . . ."

Ren frowned. "Holiday?"

"National Day is still a few weeks away. This is something else. Let's keep moving."

As they continued, her paranoia flared. Kathor was a massive city with a large enough population that it never truly slept. Being raised in the Lower Quarter had taught her that much. As a child, loud conversations and passing footsteps had served as bedtime songs. The perfect amount of noise to lull her to sleep each night. But Theo was right. These streets were more than quiet. They were dead.

"People are watching," Theo muttered.

Ren saw what he meant. The windows. Eyes peeking through slats. A hastily pulled curtain. As if the entire city knew something they didn't. It was unnerving.

"What are those markings?"

Dark *X*s were chalked across a door on their right. As they walked, Ren noticed more and more of them. One *X* here, two *X*s there. Right now, all it meant was an unhindered walk to the nearest portal access. The station was empty. Normally there was at least one attendant. City protocol dictated that there be someone here to oversee waxway transportation. More troubling, the candles had all been stolen. It took some rummaging in a back closet to find a few spares. The two of them lit the wicks and counted down the minutes, half expecting someone from House Shiverian to stumble into the room with their wands raised. But that didn't happen.

Empty streets greeted them in the Heights. More chalked doors. Ren felt as if they'd been kidnapped in one world and set down in another. Like the old fairy tales where people would travel through mirrors and stumble upon entirely separate universes.

Their first priority was safety. The two of them trotted up the front steps. Theo made quick work of the lock. Once they were inside, barriered to the outside world, they both sagged to the floor, their shoulders pressed together. Death had come for them again, and it had come away empty-handed yet again. Neither of them spoke. What was there to say?

All that mattered was that they were safe.

The nightmare was over.

18

NEVELYN TIN'VORI

It was like watching the end of the world.

Over the course of the day, Nevelyn and her siblings and Josey had sat together by the bay window in her room. Witnesses to the fulfillment of Agnes Monroe's dreadful prophecy. First there were the medics and paladins. Brightsword Legion activated every reserve unit. She'd never seen so many uniforms on the streets. It took less than an hour for the conditions of the city to outpace their efforts. Recovery units stopped visiting homes. Patients were forced to make their own way to Safe Harbor's hospital.

Next came the market rush. People abandoned their work posts, or else slipped out of their residences, to buy everything they could. Long queues formed. The queues led to crowds. And the crowds quietly stumbled into something more like a mob. As they watched, a fight broke out near the back of one of the lines. The food stalls were running out. When the first punch was thrown—spinning a man unconscious to the ground—Nevelyn decided it was time for Josey to go to bed.

He groaned and mumbled but his own protests were interrupted by several ill-timed yawns. She tucked him in with a quiet good night. Nevelyn wasn't one to pray—but as she closed the door, she paused on the threshold and muttered a proverb her mother had always spoken to them.

May darkness not knock at your door.

She wasn't sure why she said it. She didn't believe in prayers or fate. Nor did she fully understand the protectiveness she felt for Josey. It wasn't until she walked downstairs, passing the secret door near the library, that Nevelyn realized he was the same age she'd been when a group of masked men crashed through the front doors of their estate all those years ago. It was hard to imagine sweet Josey hunched in that same darkness, hoping his hunters would not find him.

Nevelyn made a mental note to show Josey the passage. Tomorrow. Just in case.

When she returned to her room, Ava had dozed off in one of the armchairs. Dahvid had covered her with a blanket. The two older siblings sat and watched the events below, stoic and silent. The fighting in the crowd had intensified. Proper brawls were breaking out. Nevelyn spied a patrol of paladins approaching from the south. The trio had a brief discussion—then started walking in the opposite direction.

Now it really begins, she thought. *The darkest hours come next.*

If society's normal shields would not step forward, the rule of the street would become law. All that mattered then was who was the biggest or who had the best magic. A glance in the other direction showed the neighborhoods of the Wedding Quarter. She saw families herding children back inside. Partners conversing. Many of them seemed unaware of the violence unfolding just around the corner. Each couple would send one person out. Perhaps in search of some final item the family needed. Bread or cheese or apples. She watched them walk past the Tin'Vori estate before turning the corner and coming face-to-face with the market scene. Some were wise enough to retreat. A few went forward, thinking they could help, and not realizing just how much danger they were in. . . .

"Do you feel bad?" Dahvid asked quietly.

Ava was snoring.

"For what?"

"We have an excess of food," he said. "They don't have any."

Nevelyn had already traveled down that particular rabbit hole. "You're right. Let's go open the front door. We can hand out care packages. How much of the crowd do you think we can feed before we run out? And do you think everyone will wait in a neat line to take their rations? Or do you suppose that it will end up looking like *that*?"

Her words were punctuated by the outbreak of a magical duel. One man slashed the air with his vessel. There was a spray of blood. She thought she saw a severed finger, but she couldn't be sure from this distance. Maybe it was a hand. A bright flash answered, sending him crashing into the nearest crate. It didn't take long for the fight to echo. A stone dropped into a pool. Duels, both physical and magical, rippled across the whole market square. Chaos in a matter of seconds.

"Do you know how many people live in Kathor, Brother?"

Dahvid shrugged. "It's been a long time since primary school."

"Nearly three hundred thousand, according to the last census. What we're watching is a small fraction of what is to come. There are still people at work that don't even know a disease has reached the city. The next wave will be much worse. And the wave after that?" She shook her head. "We cannot shield an entire city. We can only try to survive. Do not make me apologize for saving the people I love the most in the world."

She could see Dahvid wasn't fully satisfied by that answer, but he made no reply. It was as much of an agreement as they could hope to reach on the subject. Below, the streets were emptying. The market had been picked clean. Most of the stalls had been damaged. Streams of people moved toward the Lower Quarter—perhaps hoping some of the other, larger markets were not yet overrun. There were warning bells ringing out over the city. They didn't use them often, but she knew it was signaling for people to return to their homes. A curfew was in effect. The city's leadership was asking for people to begin a quarantine.

Nevelyn could feel her eyelids getting heavy. It did not help that a light rain was beginning to patter on the rooftops. The city grew quiet and gray until her vision of it faded entirely.

Later, she awoke in discomfort. She'd fallen asleep in the chair. A massive knot had formed in her upper back. Her throat had run dry. Ava had slipped off to her own room. Dahvid too. She could not have said what time it was. The night lamps were all on. Nothing moved in the world beyond her window. The city a still painting stretching in every direction. All the doors looked like eyes that had been shut. The buildings like soldiers with slumped shoulders. Guards meant to be watching the city, derelict of their duties.

Nevelyn pushed to her feet, dreaming of curling up in bed, when movement caught her eye. Out along the rooftops. Nearly invisible. She squinted and saw that it was a gargoyle. One of the livestone creatures charged with protecting the city. She followed the direction it was heading and saw smoke quietly rising over the tops of buildings. A flickering red in the distant windows. There was a fire beginning to rage in the dark. She shook her head.

Better there than here.

Nevelyn stumbled wearily to bed. There was a half-filled pitcher of water on the table. She poured one cup, drank the entire thing, and then poured a second. She glanced one more time through the distant window. All the world was framed there with all its troubles.

"Stay out there," she warned. "Leave us alone."

And then she sank into the comfort of the pillows. Sleep took her. When morning came, she walked downstairs to find that the world had not listened: Ava was sick.

19

MERCY WHITAKER

The hospital was a nightmare.

Overrun would have been a generous description. However, Mercy thrived in the chaos. She hadn't stopped moving, assessing, treating. Eventually they'd activated emergency protocols. Patients who were not there because of the disease had to be sent home, unless they'd been previously labeled as critical. Dr. Horn should have been the one to sign off on the decision, but he'd gone home for a family issue and still hadn't returned. She feared the worst. Only a true crisis would have taken Horn from the hospital at a time like this.

Three of four wings were converted into isolation centers. All focus went to victims of the disease. The first floor transformed into one big intake station, as well as a holding area for the cases with the mildest symptoms. Several factors were involved in the opening assessment. First, the spread of the patient's initial bruising patterns. Mercy was surprised how accurate this was as a measurement of degree. More bruising led to more severe symptoms, and less bruising usually meant a mild case. She'd seen no exceptions to that rule.

Next, they factored in the relative health and age of the subject. They moved patients based on their degree of risk. The second floor was for anyone with debilitating symptoms. The third floor was reserved for potential mortalities. The most at-risk patients. There had already been three casualties the last time she'd checked with the morgue. She made a mental note to check again, but for now the living demanded her attention. She entered a room occupied by a family.

The mother was tending to her husband and two children with all the focus of a trained nurse. Mercy introduced herself. The children—twins—smiled shyly as she put her stethoscope against their bruised chests. The echo was there. It was always there. Mercy winked at the little boy before moving to his father and beginning the process again.

All of them had the echo, didn't they?

Nance's words haunted her. She could not escape him or the near-death experience in Running Hills. Those memories were like a spot of blood she could not rub out, no matter how often she held her thoughts under the water and scrubbed. Hindsight made it clear that Nance had been there to monitor the results of an experiment. Designed by him? By some other entity? It seemed likely a larger group was involved. Creating and spreading a disease would be difficult. Nor would it have been a small task to remove all the evidence she'd left behind in that water treatment facility. She couldn't help wondering how they'd created the disease in the first place. And more importantly, to what end would they spread this plague? Her mind always lingered longest on that question. *To what end?*

There was evil in their world, but it rarely existed without purpose. She'd witnessed all sorts of tragedies during her time at the hospital. Spells that blinded or tortured or maimed. Nearly every one of those patients had a story for *why*. A thief stealing a purse. A spurned lover, seeking revenge. It was a rule of human nature to act in one's own best interests. This Nance—whoever he was—would not spread the disease simply to watch the world hold its breath. There had to be a *why*.

Mercy finished with the family. None of them were severe enough to be advanced to another floor. Very young children seemed especially resilient against the disease. Often showing just a few bruises. She was grateful for that small silver lining. She suggested the family head home, if they felt they could reach home safely. From there, she returned to intake. Her point person—a nurse named Bathly—was filling out a series of charts. Mercy had given the command to skip most of the usual paperwork the hospital required, but basic information was still a requirement for basic organized treatment.

"Where do you need me next, Bathly?"

The woman shrugged. "Intake is down to a trickle. Now's as good a time as any to visit the morgue. I know you wanted to get a look at some of the casualties. No sign of Horn yet by the way."

Mercy eyed the first-floor waiting room. There were fewer than a dozen people there. It was always possible another flood of new patients would hit them in the middle of the night. Bathly was right, though. She would not have a better opportunity to set triage aside and focus on the other elements of the disease. "Who's on rotation down there?"

"New guy," the nurse answered. "Williams."

Mercy eyed a few of the charts before thanking Bathly and heading downstairs. The basement floor was the quietest wing of the hospital at the moment. She knew there were patients in these rooms, but the normal flock of nurses and doctors had been pulled into the chaos upstairs. The only mild discomfort came from the lighting. Cantrips had been installed overhead. She suspected the original castings had covered the entire walk, but no one had refreshed the magic recently. The unhappy consequence was that the radius of each light fell just short of the next and she found herself walking through brief slivers of perfect darkness. Each time she expected something to leap at her from the shadows.

Gods, I'm losing my mind.

Another set of stairs led down to the morgue. The sub-basement offered a natural chill. The perfect environment for reducing the rate of decomposition. Mercy shouldered through the door to find the new guy sound asleep. He had long hair that had started graying at the temples. He wore a crimson-colored mask and was nestled inside a winter coat to ward off the cold. Mercy crossed the room as he continued to snore. The first form had been signed by Arthur Bow. Their longtime coroner. The other two finished forms? Also signed by Arthur. Which meant their newest hire had done nothing since his arrival.

"Hey," Mercy called. "What the hell is this?"

The new guy bolted awake. "Huh? Oh. *Oh.* Hello. Sorry. I am so sorry. I was just . . ." A yawn rolled through the middle of his sentence. "Just trying to catch up. I'm new. Dr. Williams."

"Catch up?" Mercy repeated. "You haven't actually done

anything. You haven't processed any of these patients."

He eyed the row and looked surprised by the number of bodies waiting there.

"Shit. More corpses came."

"You *are* in a morgue. And there *is* a plague going around."

"They could have woken me up," he grumbled.

"You could have also chosen not to be asleep. Look, the rest of us are working triple shifts up there. You're not the only one who needs rest. Pull it together."

He nodded. "Of course. I guess I just kind of assumed they weren't going anywhere."

She stared at him. "The bodies?"

"Well, yeah . . ." When she said nothing, he finished the thought. "Because they're dead."

Mercy didn't laugh. The awkward silence forced him to his feet.

"Right. Sorry again. I'm on it."

"Good. I need to see all of them. Rapid check."

He blinked. "Really? All of them?"

"Yes. There's an unknown disease ravaging the city. We now have multiple corpses and multiple corpses—"

". . . creates a pattern, and patterns provide strategic response. Understood. I read Pulliver's manual too. You're right, you're right. Let's open them up and take a look then."

At least he was trained. Borderline derelict of his duty, but properly trained. He walked the row, unzipping one patient at a time. As always, her scarred fingers itched slightly when she stood near the dead. There was also a brief sharpness in her lower stomach area. She knew it was where, five years before, her appendix had burst and needed to be removed. Mercy ignored those phantom pains and focused on what was in front of her. She picked up her replacement journal and began taking notes on each of the victims.

The first patient was seventy-four. An older man with bruises scattered across delicate, olive skin. A fit for her profile. The next two patients, however, were in their twenties. It was surprising enough that Mercy paused to read their case files. One was an elemental engineer. Mercy didn't know much about that branch of magic, other than that they worked with weather patterns and shaping raw materials in landscapes. The other was a classically trained weaver. Mercy frowned at what she read in that file, then moved on to the next corpse. Of the nine dead, five were under the age of thirty.

"The original profile isn't holding up."

"Really?" Dr. Williams asked. She'd almost forgotten he was there. "I thought this was a new disease. How could there be an original profile?"

"I investigated the same blight in Running Hills. About a month ago. There was evidence that it was more dangerous to the elderly—which fits with most communicable diseases. The only casualty there was an old nurse who served as the town medic."

He frowned. "You assumed a pattern from one casualty?"

"Of course not. There was also a pattern amongst the living patients. At the time, it appeared that older victims suffered the worst symptoms. Fastest onset as well. But this new data runs in the opposite direction."

Before Williams could respond, the double doors at the back of the room slammed open. Mercy jumped, but it was just a team of Brightsword paladins. They filed in with another body.

Safe Harbor's tenth official victim. Mercy knew it was still a relatively small mortality rate—but the sight of another body reminded her of how Nance had responded to her accusations. That careless shrug. As if the death of innocents simply did not matter to him.

To what end?

"Bring the body over here," she ordered. "We'll go ahead and take a look."

Williams signed off on the transfer. Mercy didn't wait for him to perform the unzipping. A small pull from her and the metal teeth parted. The fabric opened. She let out a shocked scream that had the paladins pausing at the doorway, their hands drifting down to their weapons. Dr. Williams was there in a heartbeat, placing himself between her and the body, but it was not that kind of threat. This was no revenant. No foul magic was at play. She'd screamed because she recognized the casualty. The tenth victim was none other than Dr. Horn.

20

REN MONROE

Morning dawned, bright and beautiful.

They watched Vega wing in the direction of the sunrise. The livestone bird clutched a message in its talons for House Brood. There were protocols Theo could activate that would summon hundreds of their sworn guards into the city. A proper escort back to the estate. But the two of them agreed that discretion was the better move. They needed to get their bearings after the attack, and the bird's-eye view from up in the Heights provided that.

Besides, this location was as well warded as any Brood property. Even after being kidnapped, Theo functioned as a proper gentleman. He'd procured pastries from gods knew where and the tea he poured for Ren smelled like wild oranges. She settled into a cushioned chair and felt as if she'd been given a second chance at . . . everything. A life with Theo. A chance to honor the dead. Rather than being shaken by how close she'd come to death, Ren felt more determined than ever to step into her role in changing the city. But that couldn't start until they figured out the right first step to take after their narrow escape.

"So, my sister was behind all of this?" Theo asked. "I guess I shouldn't be surprised. Of the three of us, she was always the one who had the most in common with my father."

"It says a lot that their big move was to *solidify* your position. That tells me that the other houses like you. They didn't want you out of the equation. Just me."

Theo surprised her with a wicked sort of smile. "Which tells me that you've left an impression. How many people have earned the collective fear of all the houses, Ren?"

She snorted. "I hadn't thought of it that way."

"You've earned their attention. And now they have earned mine."

Theo spoke those words in a tone that was darker than she'd ever heard from him. This was no petty annoyance. The feeling that radiated across their bond was a cold sort of fury. There was a deadly promise in his eyes. Ren had never seen him look so much like a Brood. He must have sensed her trepidation, because he shook himself. "Too dramatic? Too dramatic. I only mean that the great houses are all tied to us in one way or another. They depend on House Brood. If we want to apply some downward pressure, we could."

Ren was nodding. "A bridge to cross later. Right now, there are more pressing concerns. Both involve family. There is the matter of where your sister is hiding—and then there's the matter of what we found in that water treatment facility."

Theo frowned. "I assumed that was a trap. A dark one, but I

thought they used those bodies to lure us to that location. Once we were inside, they surrounded the building. . . ."

Once more, she'd forgotten he'd been unconscious during that reveal.

"Seminar didn't know about those bodies. I spoke with her. I was trying to use the information we'd learned to delay them. It didn't work, but I could tell from her reaction that she had no idea what we were there to investigate."

Theo set his tea down, dumbfounded. "It was just a coincidence?"

Ren nodded. "I think so. Remember, it was Sloan's tip that led us there. She linked Lana to the Makers. A group known for *not* using magic. It's hard to imagine House Shiverian would partner with them. No, I think what we found in that facility was something else entirely."

Before Theo could respond, there was a crackle of static. Noise on the verge of meaning. Their eyes were drawn to the back patio. He'd left the door open. Just a sliver. The two of them set down their teas and crossed the room. As soon as they stepped outside, the noise resolved itself into a voice. It was as if someone was standing right beside them and giving a speech—and that someone was Viceroy Gray.

". . . are officially extending the previous edict. I repeat, we are officially extending the quarantine issued two nights ago. This order impacts every Kathorian citizen."

It was the government's amplification system. A spell that Ren knew had been painstakingly woven into every street, every building, every corner of the city. It was one of the viceroy's only true powers. He—and he alone—could activate the spell during a crisis, communicating with the entire populace.

"Breaking this quarantine is a punishable offense. The only exemptions are for hospital personnel, Brightsword soldiers, government officials . . ."

As they listened, Viceroy Gray offered several missing pieces to the puzzle of their last few days. Dr. Horn's sudden collapse. The missing guard. All the empty streets and vacant markets. A plague had reached their city. The markings on the doors were providing information to government officials. Who was sick and in what neighborhoods and to what degree?

The viceroy encouraged people to continue to keep open lines of communication so that their teams could appropriately react and offer help. Kathor's leader relayed a detailed list of symptoms. Then he shared the current status of the local hospitals and what capacity they had for taking on patients—and which patients *needed* to go there.

Ren knew this was not the first disease to ever knock on Kathor's gates. The earliest settlers had nearly been wiped out by swine fever before they finished building the outer walls. The most devastating pandemic—in terms of mortality rate—had been the Quiet Pestilence. It killed eight thousand at the turn of the century. The disease's origins were famous. A story of warning told to children—and every newly hired sailor. A merchant ship had spotted an abandoned vessel floating along the shoreline north of the city. Everyone on board was Tusk. And every single one of them was dead. Signs of disease clearly marked each corpse. Still, the merchants could not resist a free supply of goods. Down in the hold, they found crates of rare Tuskan cloth. Instead of burning the ship, they ordered their deckhands to begin unloading. That cargo would eventually kill a tenth of the city's population. Naturally, the city had advanced since then. There were safeguards that should have limited the spread of any plague. Most of the great houses had properties that were so heavily warded, in fact, that diseases usually skipped past them entirely. Viceroy Gray's next words answered that very question.

"Initial reports indicate the disease traveled through the water supply. We have secured all such facilities across the city. If you have consumed city-provided water anytime in the last week, you've been exposed to the disease. We suggest that everyone boil their water in the coming days, as a precaution, but the water supply should present the city no further danger. Please remember, we are Kathor. Brightest city on the hill. Our light will not be dimmed. Not now. Not ever."

His booming voice guttered out. Ren's eyes were drawn back to the tea they'd been drinking. Thankfully, they'd boiled it. Heat normally destroyed bacteria, but did it work for a plague like this one? Neither of them were exhibiting symptoms. Had they been exposed *before* finding the bodies? She supposed only time would tell. Theo was the first one to break the silence.

"The bodies," he said. "We found them in the water supply."

"Which means what's happening is connected to what we found."

Shit, shit, shit. My mother is potentially connected to the plague.

"I need a way candle," Ren said.

Theo frowned. "Why? You heard him. There's a quarantine."

"We need answers. And I think I know where to get them."

21

NEVELYN TIN'VORI

Nevelyn did not get sick, regardless of how much she hyper-focused on every soreness or ache. Josey also avoided the plague, though he seemed to be suffering from the incurable disease of boredom. Dahvid had initially seemed sick, but it turned out that he'd eaten some expired cheese. When Ava found out she was the only one, she'd instantly transformed into the world's biggest brat. Nevelyn was genuinely worried for her—after all, it was an unknown disease—but the demand that they transport every book in the house to her room felt rather dramatic.

She didn't have any sympathy until things got much worse. For lunch, she was delivering a tray of food and happened to spy Ava through a crack in the door. Her sister was leaning back against the cushions, teeth gritted, sweat running down her forehead. They'd all agreed to not enter the room, but Nevelyn could not do that. Not to Ava.

"I'm filling a bath," she said, gliding into the room. She had her mask on with all its wards. That would have to be enough. "Come on. The warm water will feel good."

Ava didn't protest. She allowed her older sister to guide her. It was clear that without Nevelyn's help, she would not have had the strength to pull herself over the rim of the great claw-foot tub. Ava groaned with instant relief as she was lowered into the frothing water.

"You can go," her sister said, teeth still gritted. "I'll be fine."

Nevelyn ignored her. She went to the bedroom and found the book that Ava had been reading. She turned to the ear-marked page, set out a stool, and began to read. Her sister didn't ask her to leave after that. She sank deep into the water with her eyes shut against the pain. For the first time in weeks, Ava didn't whine or complain. A temporary peace was found.

Afterward, she wrapped the poor girl in a towel, helped her into her pajamas, and ordered her to bed. She could hear the snoring before she'd even reached the door. As she turned the corner, she saw Josey at the top of the steps. He adjusted his body slightly as she approached, and she thought it could not be clearer that he was hiding something.

"What is that?"

He shrugged. "What is what?"

"In your hand. What have you got?"

He shrugged again, but this time he slowly turned to reveal a knife. Their father had kept it on one of the shelves in his study. A gift from a merchant who'd worked with him? In truth, she'd forgotten most of those stories. His words were always there. His face and his smile and his anger. But so many of the other details had already fallen through the cracks of her mind.

"Who let you have a knife?"

"Dahvid."

A voice called from below. "That's not true!"

That earned a third shrug from their ward.

"If you keep shrugging like that, your head's going to roll right off your shoulders. Why do you need a knife?"

"There's a mouse."

She lifted one eyebrow. "And you're going to catch it with that?"

A fourth shrug. *Gods, he must be going for a record.*

"Will this keep you entertained?"

His eyes widened hopefully. "Yes."

"Don't damage the house. Don't damage the knife. Don't run down the stairs. Don't accidentally stab yourself. . . ." She thought that covered most of it, but then she remembered that he was only nine and creatures that age lacked basic logic. "Don't lick it either."

He made a face at the last one before nodding. "The mouse or the knife?"

"Both."

He nodded. "Deal."

She watched him stalk down the hallway and knew it would only be unpleasant if he actually caught the poor creature. Sighing, Nevelyn headed back to her room. Their own drama felt small in comparison to what was unfolding outside. As the day spun on, the city seemed to briefly recover. Vendors ventured out to inspect the market. Some attempted to restore their stalls before a roaming group spotted them. There was a brief conversation, an even briefer snatch of violence. The two shopkeepers were forced to empty their pockets. The group shoved them away before continuing on to some other section of the city.

No paladins appeared. Kathor was still subject to a different set of rules. How long, she wondered, would this sort of anarchy last? The only real surprise was the total absence of the great houses. None of them had stepped in to establish any kind of order. She wondered if they were counting on these smaller forces that had formed in the city to batter against one another. Tire each other out, then they could return to put their boot down on the city's neck just as the dust began to settle. It was also possible that Agnes Monroe's boldest prediction had come true. Maybe the great houses had been hit by the plague with consequences just as devastating as everyone else.

The next phase was as predictable as the first. In the early afternoon, people were forced back into the streets. She knew only one thing could motivate such a risk: sustenance. She watched them knock at the back doors of local restaurants. Tapping windows of the local grocers. In some cases, they'd break the glass if no one answered. All of them searching and searching and searching. And it was all in vain. Every scrap had been claimed. For the first time, she felt guilty for how prepared they were—how little these people had. But the same problem existed now that had existed before. If they opened their doors and helped even one of these desperate wanderers—how quickly would the rumors lead back to their house? How long before they faced an angry mob of their own? All that mattered to her was their survival. Weather this storm. Make it to the other side.

As evening approached, she spied movement again.

A large carriage had pulled into the market. She watched the horses circle until they found a spot big enough to settle. Several people hopped down and began unloading. Their arrival was like carrion for vultures. In minutes, scavengers began to circle the location. Others crept out of their buildings in pure desperation. The packs returned too. Smaller groups who'd been working other sections of the city and now appeared to have found a proper prize. There was a collectively held breath, where everyone appeared to be waiting to see who would strike first. The people unloading took note. She saw pointing back and forth.

It would come to violence.

She waited for the first punch. The first slash of magic to cut through the air. Neither occurred. Nevelyn watched as the tops of the crates were popped open. Everyone was handed a few items. And then, to her surprise, they went on their way. Word spread quickly. More crates were unpacked. More boxes and cans passed out. For the first time, Nevelyn noticed that the original crew all wore the same red scarves. If not around their neck, then tied around a thigh or tight around one bicep. Maybe they'd been sent by the viceroy? Everyone who came was given food without argument. She watched until the crates had all been emptied.

Now, she thought. *Now is when the violence resumes.*

But she was wrong again. There was an initial reaction from the crowd. People pushing forward. That same desperation she'd witnessed in the market. A woman raised both hands, though. She called for quiet and they actually listened. Nevelyn was too far away to hear anything, but the woman spoke with emphatic hand gestures. When she finished, the crowd did not rebel. They didn't try to steal the carriage or kill their unlikely benefactors. Instead, they dispersed.

Quiet as a dream.

Nevelyn bolted to her feet. She went to the window and started working at the latches. A pair of women who'd been in the crowd were passing on the street below.

"Wait! Excuse me!"

Both women looked up.

"What was that?" Nevelyn asked. "Who were those people?"

An exchange of glances. They were deciding whether or not to share what they'd learned. "Free food," one of the women finally said. "They had free food for anyone who really needs it. Extra rations to see people through the next few days. But only if you're hard up."

"What did they say?" Nevelyn asked. "At the end?"

"Told everyone they'd be back tomorrow with more."

"Who were they? Brightsword Legion?"

Nevelyn's guess jolted a laugh from the woman. "Of course not. Those assholes retreated into their barracks and never came back out. The people handing out food were the Makers. All Lower Quarter folks. Through and through. Gods, I hope you weren't holding your breath waiting for Brightsword to come and rescue you."

And with that the two women continued down the street. Nevelyn's eyes swung to the market. The group had finished loading the empty crates back into their carriage. Again, she noted their bright red scarves and ribbons. It was a clever touch. A memorable feature that others could see and recognize immediately. There was still a small crowd around them. The Makers waved, spoke briefly, and then allowed the horses to draw them away.

So, this was Agnes Monroe's group. Nevelyn had been waiting for this next phase in their plan. A plague had spread. As promised. As *intended*. And she'd just witnessed step two. Nevelyn thought it was one of the cleverest kinds of violence she'd ever seen. A plague would be viewed as a natural disaster. No different from famine or drought. Few would know or believe that a specific group could play a role in the spread of such a disease. If the cause was seen as naturally occurring, then what mattered was the *reaction* to the plague. The Makers had perpetrated violence with their unseen right hand, and now shielded the population with their visible left hand. After all, who better to rescue from drowning than the one who'd been holding your head under water all along?

"How diabolical," Nevelyn murmured.

Her eyes traced the tops of the buildings. At this hour, they were beginning to merge into a shapeless gray mass. A plan was clearly in motion now. First, the plague. Now, recovery and charity. What was the natural next step? Agnes Monroe had told her that everyone would have a choice. They would need to decide which road they wanted to walk down. As if this were some great turning point in all of human history. Which made the answer to Nevelyn's question obvious.

Create a disaster.

Rescue the city.

And then? Ask for a reward.

The final step of the plan would be *power*.

22

MERCY WHITAKER

The hospital transformed into a battleground.

Her senior advisors vanished one by one. Two went home with the disease. The other two checked themselves into rooms in the basement—useless except for answering the occasional operational question. It didn't help that their staff reached a critical shortage at the same time. Even working double shifts, there simply weren't enough nurses. Normal protocol had to be abandoned. Everyone did the best they could to treat patients while maintaining a relatively sterile environment.

Down in the morgue, bodies were beginning to pile up. The city's massive population was finally becoming more apparent. In Running Hills, there had only been one casualty. A deceptive result. Now the percentages applied themselves to a city with more than two hundred thousand people. More corpses arrived each day. The hospital was forced to hire runners to send out to the families. The deceased needed to be claimed to make more space. Of course, most were too sick to even receive a summons, which left them in a terrible circle of grim tidings.

Dr. Williams had not left the morgue. To her knowledge, he'd been sleeping down there. Safe Harbor's normal coroner had never returned. The rumor was that he'd died in his flat. Grim word like that spread more and more. And it was made even more grim by the fact that none of them had time to mourn anyone. Mercy's own mentor had died and she'd barely spared a thought for him. There was not time to fret or to sneak away for a good cry. Every person left standing had to keep their feet moving, or else the hospital would fail.

Their first ray of hope came when patients actually started recovering. Mercy began processing dismissals on the first floor. Bruises were fading. Not fully gone, but no longer causing pain. Other symptoms vanished. She prescribed rest, medicine, and continued hydration to every patient they discharged. More helpful news came from Brightsword. A paladin arrived to let them know that all water treatment facilities had been cleared. The city's water was officially drinkable again. Mercy might not have been able to keep going if not for those two small positive turns.

She had dismissed nearly two hundred patients before a pattern began to emerge. Something curious that had not been visible to her at first. Two patients in a row made the same complaint. Just a coincidence, she thought, until the third patient echoed their words.

"I can't do magic."

The man was in his late forties. Sharply dressed. According to his chart, he was a structural engineer who worked for House Proctor. Mercy had given him the normal speech for discharge, but he'd stopped her before she could leave the room.

"None?" she asked.

"None. I've tried everything. Spells I use at work. Spells I use at home. I've tried magic that I've known since I was a boy. None of it works."

Mercy nodded. "Sickness often dampens magical ability."

"I don't feel sick," he said. "That's why you're discharging me. I'm better now."

"That's true, but how you perceive your health isn't always a perfect indicator of what's actually happening inside your body. There are likely remnants of the disease in there. You've won the battle, but that doesn't mean your cells have finished killing everything. I'd expect your functionality to return after a few days. Give it a week. Try those spells again then."

Mercy discharged him and moved on. The repeated details continued to prickle at the edges of her thoughts as the day wore on. Unfortunately, she could not do what she'd always done when a mysterious ailment presented itself. If Dr. Horn discovered something in the middle of a surgery, there had always been time afterward to visit the hospital's library. She'd research there as long as she liked, knowing the next shift was days away. The idea of spare time for a bit of reading was laughable at this point. She was forced to pivot her inquiry to the patients themselves. Before each discharge, she began asking a series of questions.

Did they have their vessel with them?

If they did, could they attempt a small cantrip? Any spell at all?

Not one patient who'd suffered from the blight could perform magic. The current intensity of their symptoms didn't matter. Time since infection was irrelevant. Not one patient could still access their arsenal of magic. Some complained they were too tired. Their minds too foggy. Others grew intensely concerned. Why couldn't they remember the proper steps? It was as if the information had been cut away from their minds. Once she'd gathered a convincing amount of data, Mercy handed her duties over to one of the younger residents and headed for the basement.

Dr. Williams was there. Awake, this time, but surrounded by even more bodies than she'd realized were at the hospital. At a glance it looked to be at least seventy casualties. A number that she knew would only keep growing.

"Question for you."

He opened his arms in welcome, briefly looking like the king of the dead.

"Fire away."

"Do you know the occupations of the deceased?"

"Some of them," he replied. "It's on the intake form that the next of kin fill out. There are a few that haven't been identified, but yes, I have that information for roughly half of them."

"How many would you consider high-volume users of magic? People that go through a large number of ockleys each month?"

Mercy knew that most of the government allowances had to do with economic levels, but exceptions were always granted for specific jobs. If you simply *needed* more magic to do your duty to the city, you were often able to secure it through a quick petition. Dr. Williams considered her question. "You'd have to track down their allotment information to know for sure. But generally, I'd say . . . a lot of them? The first victim was a weaver. They use magic over long periods of time. There were a bunch of engineering types. People who are essentially walking around the city mending things all day. Most of them have high usage rates and get assigned extra ockleys to cover all the spellwork, but these days, who doesn't use a lot of magic?"

"Gods," she said, ignoring his question. "That's the echo."

Williams was watching her with concern. "Have you slept at all?"

"Not really, but this isn't me losing my mind. I've finally landed on an answer. All of our patients upstairs, even the recovering ones, can't access their magic."

"Sickness dampens magic," Williams supplied. "That's well documented."

"Which is exactly what I said—but all of them are that way. Every single patient. Without exception. And it's not just a dampening. They can't do *any* magic. We also know that many of the deceased are high-volume magic users. Think about that. In school, they teach that magic is . . . it's this invisible substance, right? We can use magic because it's in the air. It's in everything. Including inside *us*."

Williams was nodding. "We are conduits. Very powerful conduits."

"Exactly. People have magic in their veins. It's present. At all times. Even if you're not actively using the magic, correct?"

"Theoretically, yes."

"If magic is present inside us, then that means it takes up space, right? Even if that space is infinitesimal, there would have to be some physical space that it occupies inside each of us."

"I suppose so?" Williams frowned. "This is all very theoretical."

"Okay. Theoretically, what would happen if the magic inside you was *destroyed*? Let's say it's burned out, for example. What would that mean for the space it previously occupied inside you?"

"That it's . . . empty."

Mercy banged one fist on the nearest table. "And that would create a *damn* echo!"

It felt wrong to revel in this moment, down here surrounded by the dead, but it was such a massive breakthrough to such a tormenting question. Magic was at the heart of all of this.

Why was there an echo? Because the absence of magic created *space* inside the body and that space produced a new sound in each victim's heartbeat. Why the burning? That was likely what it felt like to have magic physically destroyed inside a person's body. It was painful, but not so damaging that it caused a high mortality rate. Why the bruises? Well, magic existed throughout the entire body. It would naturally cause pain—and the evidence of that pain—to appear everywhere. And why did most of the casualties happen to be high-volume magic casters? They had more magic flowing through them. More to burn. More pain. More bruising. Put simply, they were more at risk. That also explained why the nurse in Running Hills had succumbed. She was likely the only one in the town who actively used magic every day.

It felt so good to finally have answers. But those naturally led to even more questions. How long would the magic be absent? Was the condition permanent? Or more like a rup-tured muscle? Could it be retrained slowly in each patient?

She also could not help wondering how she'd avoided getting sick. The initial exposure alone, back in Running Hills, should have been enough for her to catch the disease. Not to mention she'd been chugging contaminated water for weeks after arriving back at Safe Harbor. Was it that she'd followed protocols? Or was luck involved? Some sort of immunity?

All those curiosities eventually gave way to dread. It was impossible to forget that this was no normal plague. Rats had not boarded a ship and brought it to their shores. This disease had not festered beneath the skin because of some invasive, microbial bug. This had been *deliberate*. Engineered. It had creators— and its creators had a purpose.

Disrupt magic.

23

REN MONROE

As Theo focused on making contact with House Brood, Ren lit a wick in the privacy of the guest bedroom. Even seated and focused, she could not stop mentally pacing. It was like her problems were all competing for which one could be most devastating.

Was it the looming threat of the plague? Or the fact that the most powerful houses in the world had collectively tried to dispose of her? Oh, or perhaps it was her mother's potential involvement in a dark conspiracy? *Gods, it's just so hard to pick a winner. . . .*

The candle was nearly finished. Ren's mind fixed on the image of her bedroom. The chalk-colored rug. Her bed with its pale yellow covers. The empty walls. She'd never been one for much decoration. Reaching out, she pinched that waiting flame between her fingers. Darkness claimed her. There was the briefest moment of discomfort. A slightly longer hesitation than normal where she thought she felt something in that dark space. A shadow nestled inside the larger shadows—and then she blinked to life and found herself in a room she hardly recognized.

It was not at all how she'd left it. From floor to ceiling, the room was filled to the brim. Bags of rice piled up. Boxes full of uncooked noodles. There was enough food to feed a small army. The only space left was where she stood. A small circle and an even smaller path that fed to the door. The hoarded goods felt like an ill omen. How had her mother gathered all of this during a plague?

"Ren? Is that you?"

Agnes Monroe's voice echoed through the walls. Ren took a second to steel herself, then opened the bedroom door. There was even more food stacked up here. Boxes and crates filled the entire space. Her mother stood in the kitchen. She wore her normal, sparing outfit. Black clothes with relaxed fits. Only what she needed to cover herself and still move about her work on the docks with ease. The only notable addition was a piece of bright red cloth. The scarf was tied fashionably around her neck, knotted perfectly at her throat.

Ren didn't see anyone else in the apartment, but there were obvious signs of previous company. Cups littered the counter. Like the aftermath of a party, or perhaps evidence that a group of revolutionaries were using their home as a safe house. When Ren finally spoke, she could not keep the accusation out of her voice. "What have you done, Mother?"

"Come. Sit with me."

Ren did not move. "I had a visit from Aunt Sloan."

Her mother waved the name away. As if their old neighbor

was no more than a petty gossip. Idle chatter was easy to deny. Ren decided it would be easier to cut straight to the heart of things.

"I also found Lana."

Her mother's face went blank. No feigned surprise. No attempts to dismiss the truth. Instead, she smoothed out her features. Erasing any emotion.

"Mother . . ."

"It is not what you think."

"We found four corpses," Ren replied heatedly. "What else could that be?"

"A willing sacrifice. For the greater good. Every person you found volunteered to be there, because all of them believe in what we're doing. They believe in what comes next."

"Mother, you are frightening me."

"Oh, grow up, child. Are you really going to stand there and act as if your hands are clean? I watched you murder a man not long ago. Did you forget I was there to witness that?"

"That was the man that killed my father. *Your* husband."

"He did—and you called his murder justice. Isn't that right?"

"It *was* justice."

"Then tell me, what punishment would deliver justice to the houses that have oppressed an entire population? For generations? None of them have ever had to stand before the world and answer for their sins. So tell me, if Landwin Brood deserved to die—what of them?"

Agnes Monroe had always been a beautiful woman. Now that beauty sharpened into something else entirely. Her eyes had gotten darker and darker as she spoke. The normal honey-brown color verging on black. There was anger woven into her voice.

Aunt Sloan had referred to her mother as Old Agnes. How long had this version of the woman existed? The truth was that Ren didn't know. She had stopped paying attention years ago.

"You got your revenge," her mother said. "A position with House Brood. A precious new life. Is that where justice stops? Once *you* are satisfied, no one else deserves to reach for the same?"

Her mother shocked her by spitting on the floor between them.

"Roland Monroe did not die for that. Your father was killed because he stood up for everyone. He was not seeking a personal reward or a better job. He was fighting for the people who lived in the Lower Quarter. Ren, we have waited a generation for this moment. The chance will not come again. Not for a hundred years."

Ren's stomach churned uncomfortably. Her hands trembled. It was hard to recognize the person who stood before her. "I felt guilty coming here," she whispered. "Like I was betraying you for even asking. I thought surely, my mother would never involve herself in something like this. Lies, conspiracy, the death of innocents. Those are the tactics House Brood used against us. Mother, I saw the bodies. People are *dead*. The city's hospitals are overrun. Are you really going to stand there and tell me that this was all a part of *your* plan?"

"Our plan," Agnes corrected. "Our precious work."

Those words echoed through the room. That darkness had returned to her mother's eyes. The air in the room felt weighted. She knew her mother didn't use magic, but there was something almost palpable looming between them. If not a spell, then a threat. It was the first time in Ren's entire life that she wasn't sure if her mother was on her side.

"The Makers are not the city's castaways. We are the people. We are the blood that beats in this city's heart. We are Kathor." Her mother thumped one fist to her chest for emphasis. "Our numbers are in the thousands. And I promise you this: thousands more will join. The people of this city have always dreamed of change. They just didn't know they could reach out and take it for themselves. Your target was the Broods. You hit the mark. I was proud of what you did. But we are aiming at every single house left standing. Tell me, if we succeed, what is the difference between us and you? What made your pursuit so noble? And ours so worthy of disdain?"

Ren opened her mouth to speak, then snapped it shut again. She was about to point out the growing number of casualties, but then she remembered: her own plan had plenty of those. Death had trailed her footsteps from the beginning. How many guards and soldiers had died during their raid of the Brood estate? How many had they buried afterward? There were other casualties too. Cora and Avy and Timmons. All completely innocent. Each one of them had been dragged into the wilderness because of *her* mistake. The truth was that she had no moral ground to stand on. For the first time, she saw that with perfect clarity. The only difference was that her plan had been successful. She'd possessed the requisite skills to actually succeed. Her mother and this group of magicless rebels? The truth was that Ren simply could not fathom a world where they would win. The great houses were too strong.

"All right. The plague has arrived. Tell me, how does that impact the major houses? I studied pandemics in our Cities and Empires course. Mortality rates run evenly across every population in the city. Most of the time, they're slightly worse for the poor. Since there are more of us than there are nobles, you can almost guarantee that there will be more casualties amongst the lower class. That's just basic math. You've succeeded in bringing the city to its knees, but true Kathorians will suffer the most."

"It would seem that way. From the outside looking in."

"Then let me in."

Ren was growing tired of the back and forth. Either there was something of substance here—or she was about to be invited into the beginnings of a monumental fuckup.

Her mother repeated her first invitation. "Come and sit."

This time, Ren obeyed. They settled into their favorite seats. How often had they sat like this over the years? Discussing homework or politics or crushes. Now their eyes met and they began to discuss the fate of an entire city.

"Death is not the goal," her mother said. "It is an unfortunate byproduct of any disease. Trust me, we did everything in our power to minimize the number of casualties."

"Then what? What was the point of all of this?"

"What is the one power the great houses have over us?"

Ren knew the answer. Her professor had asked the same question during a first-year seminar—although he'd done his best to frame the situation in a more positive light for the wealthy. After all, a fourth of the students in their class were direct descendants of the great five houses.

"Magic," Ren said.

Her mother pounded the table between them with a fist.

"Magic. The great inequality of our age. The ancient houses own *all* of it. They're the only ones with access to the supply.

They control the entire market. It is what separates us from them."

Ren couldn't hide her disappointment. "So, you're targeting the magic warehouses? Controlling the distribution centers is a decent strategy, but I think you're underestimating how many of the great houses have private caches of magic. House Brood has storehouses on their estate that could refill every vessel in the city dozens of times. I can only imagine how much House Shiverian has hoarded over the years. Even if you secure every facility in the city, the wealthiest houses *will* survive. And then after the disease fades, they'd have the firepower to take them all back from you. This won't work."

Agnes Monroe only smiled in return.

"Gods, you're smart. It took me four years to figure that out. Our master . . ."

Her mother's words trailed briefly away. Ren saw her head tilt slightly, as if she were listening to some distant voice that Ren could not hear. It seemed clear that she wasn't entirely sure how to navigate the moment. Ren was her daughter. Someone she'd always trusted, but there were still some details she probably didn't care to divulge at this point. Ren watched until her mother's eyes fixed back on her.

"Let's just say we knew we had to dream bigger. It wasn't enough to change the curtains or paint the walls. Not with a problem like Kathor. If you want to change a city this big—you knock the entire house down. You don't leave a single brick standing. And when you're sure the job's finished, you build a new one."

Ren felt trapped by her own knowledge. Her mother's passion was plain. It was all too clear that she believed this would work.

But how could they understand the history of events that they'd never bothered to study? The ancient houses could not be swept away by a simple plague. If anything, previous large-scale diseases had solidified their grip on the city. It was the smaller houses who were left compromised, unable to withstand the storm. Ren was trying to figure out a way to explain all of that when her mother spoke again.

"The great houses will see soon enough. The plague isn't designed to kill people."

Her mother leaned forward. The same way she had when Ren was a child. When she was hiding a piece of candy behind her back. As if she possessed a secret that was just for her.

"It kills the magic inside of them."

24

REN MONROE

Gods, she's lost her mind. They all have.

"That's not possible" were the kindest words she could summon. "Mother, there is no way to *destroy* magic. It's in the air. It's in the ground. It's soaked into the stones and the buildings. We've been using magic for so long that it's in our bodies. Woven into our bloodstreams."

"Not after this," her mother replied. "Not after the disease finishes its work."

Agnes Monroe tugged down the collar of her blouse. There were discolorations at the base of her throat that had nearly faded, but not quite. Ghosts of some previous pain.

"I am proof of what happens next."

Ren recoiled. "You were a test subject."

"Hundreds of us volunteered, yes," she confirmed. "You know that I swore off magic years ago, but when I tested the disease, I sacrificed my ability permanently. Ren, I promise you, the disease works. I have tried every old spell I've ever learned. Spells I used when your father was still alive. None of them work. No magic runs in these veins. It has been burned out."

It was the first time that Ren felt a genuine pulse of fear. She could sense Theo across their bond, gently probing her with his concern. Her mother's words—however improbable—struck at the heart of all that Ren was. Her stomach tightened uncomfortably. Sweat began to run down her neck. Ren shoved to her feet. She backpedaled slowly away from her mother. Everything felt like a threat now. She'd spent far too long developing her magical arsenal to lose it to whatever this was.

"I know you're scared," her mother said softly. "I know that for someone like you, it sounds like a death sentence. Magic is how you advanced. It's how you beat the odds. But consider this, Ren: the removal of magic is how everyone else moves forward. You achieved so much. Just think about what might happen if we make the door you walked through wide enough for the rest of us."

Ren shook her head. "Mother, this won't work."

"It already has."

"I have to go. Please don't ask for my help. I will take no part in this."

"You've already helped."

Ren looked up sharply. It felt like something was lodged in her throat. The words she wanted to speak simply would not come out. Everything was choking and clawing at her.

"In a way, you were the one who started all of this," her mother said cryptically. There was that weight between them again. Something dark and unspoken. Then her mother went on, "You sacked House Brood. Your work with the Tin'Voris advanced our cause by decades. I wasn't sure I'd ever get to see my own revolution. Not until you. The Broods' protection of the city was nearly flawless. Landwin Brood, for all his sins, was a damned good shield for Kathor. When Theo took over their house, there was chaos. However brief. The contracts for several key city defenses lapsed. You and Theo . . . you left the door wide open. All the Makers had to do was walk through it."

Gods, the water treatment facility.

Her mind traced back to the meeting they'd had with Viceroy Gray. They had discussed the buildings then. Loyal members of House Brood had been locked out for almost a week. Such a small window of time, but now the city was suffering because of it. Ren did not like the implication. Her mother's words were almost threatening. Accuse us of this, and we can accuse you. The entire situation had Ren feeling backed into a corner. It drew out her claws.

"Father would be ashamed of you. Using me to advance your cause. Sacrificing the innocent to a plague. All for what? To destroy magic? He loved magic. He taught me my first spells. He was always asking what I was learning at school. He wouldn't do this. . . ."

He wouldn't do this to me.

She couldn't bring herself to say the selfish part aloud. Ren understood there were grander implications, but in the heat of this moment, she could only think about the fact that her mother had started something that would destroy Ren's most treasured possession: her magic. And what was the point of all of this if she did not have that? She expected mercy or sympathy. Instead, her mother aimed right back at her.

"You didn't know the real Roland Monroe. How could you? You were so young when he died. Sure, he liked the occasional spell. He delighted in clever magic. But that was not what he spent his evenings debating. That was not what he read about in the morning paper. Your father was a quiet man—but when he raised his voice, it was always against injustice. He voted, time and again, to limit the magical expansion of the great houses. He did not fight for *magic*, Ren. He fought for *people*. And now it's your turn to choose. Will you defend magic? Or will you defend freedom?"

"Freedom," Ren threw back. "Right. Look, if you remove magic something else will rise up to replace it. That's just human nature. Have you asked that question yet? Who will rule next? Because there's never been a world where everyone was equal. Someone *always* ends up with a little more power than everyone else. Who will it be this time? People with physical strength? Or military prowess? The families who have the most farmland or the best weapons? What you're imagining is a utopia. Set aside magic and the people of Kathor will hold hands by the fire and sing. Nothing like that has happened in the course of our people's history. The Makers are offering you false gold."

Her mother sank back into her chair. "What an answer. The great houses keep us underfoot for centuries—and your answer is to do nothing? Attempt no change? Ren, our city has a rotten limb. If we do not amputate, the rest of the body will die. The rest of the body *has* been dying."

"That's a surprisingly perfect analogy," Ren replied. "A century ago, amputation was the only treatment for certain diseases. If there was rot in a limb or an infection in someone's foot—doctors would cut it off without a second thought. But then amputations decreased by seventy-three percent. There had been an advancement in the world of medicine. Any guess what it was?"

Her mother said nothing. But Ren, of course, knew the answer.

"Magic. They invented new treatments using magic. Spells that could keep people *whole*. That's what magic does. It provides new paths. Better solutions." Ren's voice was shaking now. She could feel tears rolling down her cheeks, but she didn't care. "Let's say your plan works. Magic vanishes. Do you know how much of this city depends on it? Our ability to travel, gone. Our ability to purify water, gone. Our ability to irrigate large tracts of land, gone. Our ability to stabilize old buildings, gone. Our ability to treat the sick, gone. Our ability to protect ourselves, gone. The plan you're suggesting would throw civilization into one of the darkest ages it's experienced since we set sail for this continent in the first place."

Her mother only shrugged. "There are alternative methods for every single issue you've mentioned. We can survive without magic. I have for a decade. But tell me this, Ren. If we succeed—if all of this works—what would happen to the great houses?"

It was Ren's turn to bite her tongue. She could not bring herself to answer the question.

"Gone," her mother said into the silence. "Our tyrants would finally be *gone*."

She had no counter to that. Her mother was right. If they could truly destroy magic, it would decimate the entire social structure. All the great houses would be reduced with devastating swiftness. It would give the general populace a chance to overrun them. As Ren imagined that possibility, she felt like a fraud. All these years, she'd claimed to want the destruction of the great houses. It wasn't long ago that she'd looked up at the Heights and compared the great houses to the dragons. She'd silently promised to guide them to the same extinction. Why did she flinch now? Was it simply because she doubted her mother's ability to beat them? Or was it because the solution—neat and elegant as it sounded—would take the one thing that she had ever truly loved?

The weight of all those questions finally broke her.

Ren's normal talent for compartmentalization failed. Tidal waves of consequence swept through her mind, ripping past her defenses, drowning every thought. It was too much. It all weighed too much. Her mother caught her as she fell. She wanted to push away. She wanted to rage and scream, but she was too weak to do anything but sag into that waiting embrace. She buried herself in the familiar scent. It was a touch no one could outgrow. A mother was always a shelter against life's storms—even if her mother had been the one to stir these particular currents.

"No matter what you choose," Agnes whispered, "I will love you forever. For always. But understand I have choices I must make too. I will not abandon our precious work."

Something whispered between them. It wasn't magic. Or at least, no magic that Ren had ever felt before. This was something raw and unspoken and wild. A power as old as time itself. Her mother released her at the *exact* moment that the idea of being touched became unbearable.

Ren stood there in a stupor. After a moment, she wiped the

tears away with the back of her sleeve. Her mother was in the kitchen, fussing over a pot of tea that had come to boil. On the table, she'd left out a large square of red fabric. A perfect match with the one that her mother was wearing now. The same colors that the Makers were reportedly wearing around the city to mark themselves. She reached out and grazed the material with her outstretched fingers. It was deliciously soft. Bright, alluring. It felt like the loveliest sort of trap to fall into. That first touch gave her a glimpse of what would happen next. Like a promise spinning into existence. She would join this rebellion. They would win. They would overthrow the great houses, once and for all. And then the entire city would belong to the people. It all felt so terribly logical.

She had a thousand reasons to flee. Fear of who her mother had become. Anger at how she'd been used to achieve her mother's goals. She knew she should return home. Discuss matters with Theo. Isolate herself from the plague that was already slouching through the streets like some invisible monster. But that smaller voice whispered to reach for the red square of fabric, and so she did. Ren carefully folded the fabric and tucked it into her coat pocket.

When her mother brought over a cup of tea, Ren accepted.

The heat scalded her hands.

The first sip scorched her tongue.

Still, she did not turn to leave.

"Tell me what to do."

Agnes Monroe tilted her head. Once more, it was like she was listening to some distant voice. Ren watched as her mother navigated through the stack of crates in the far corner of the room. She returned with a way candle of all things. Her

SCOTT REINTGEN

mother set the candle down on the table between them and lit the wick.

"Drink your tea. Go back to Theo. Wait for more instructions."

Obediently, Ren sipped. The time it took to finish her cup was nearly an exact match for how long it took for the stub of a way candle to burn down. Ren nodded one more time to her mother before pinching the candle between her fingers. The darkness was like a whisper in her ear. A voice that beckoned and promised and whispered a thousand lies.

And then she was elsewhere.

PART THREE

Burning

25

REN MONROE

Her feet set down in the Heights.

Ren moved quickly. She took the front steps two at a time before knocking. Theo was there, squinting out through the crack, then fussing with the locks to let her inside. She walked past him without speaking. Went straight to the kitchen. She located a pen and an empty notebook. Careful to keep her eyes fixed on Theo, Ren began to write. A detailed set of instructions. It was an enormously difficult task to write it all down while simultaneously keeping her mind fixed on some other thought. But Ren had trained for this exact moment during her time at Balmerick. When she was quite certain all the steps were written down, she slid the notebook to Theo. Again, she made sure not to look at anything she'd written. Theo began to read.

His eyes went wide with shock.

He snatched the notebook and bolted from the room. Ren

could hear him rummaging in the library. *No, don't think about that. Don't think about what he's looking up. Think about . . . Balmerick.* She fixed her mind on an image of the campus at sunrise. How the fog would slowly burn away to reveal the rest of the campus's secrets. She was imagining herself strolling across the main quad when Theo returned. He was clutching the notebook and a book he'd found in the library. Ren kept her eyes averted from the title. She avoided the great temptation to check whether or not he'd found the right text. Ren suspected that this was one of the few subjects Theo had as much training on as her.

A full minute later, Ren felt Theo's first spell strike her in the chest. She sagged helplessly back into her chair and heard the sound she'd been hoping to hear. Like an eggshell cracking. Theo circled quickly then, casting a rotation of two particular spells: stun, summon, stun, summon. On his tenth repetition, Ren heard the cracking sound again. She let out a sharp cry as her entire right pant leg burst into flames. There was a mad scramble then. Ren trying to strip out of her pants while Theo both helped and hindered her.

Finally, she managed to peel them off and rolled free of the licking flames. Theo brought his boots stomping down on the sudden flames, completely forgetting that he possessed an arsenal of spells that could douse a flame far more quickly. The old-fashioned way still worked. The fire went out with a gasp of smoke. Her pants were irreparably damaged. The piece of red cloth had started to burn, too, but it had been salvaged by Theo's efforts.

Ren's thigh looked pink and fleshy. A small price to pay for what she'd just won in return: her mind was her own again.

Theo knelt down beside her. His eyes narrowed in suspicion.

"It's me," she said. "I promise. It's me."

He nodded. "What the hell happened?"

"I was *manipulated*. An incredibly powerful manipulation spell."

Ren shook her head. It was like her mind was waking up, stretching its limbs. Whoever had been inside had moved with flawless efficiency. Closing some doors. Opening others. It was stunning to realize how deeply the magic had infiltrated, and just in the amount of time it had taken for her to return from her mother's house to the Heights. Theo's quick reaction had likely saved her from permanent damage.

"I don't understand. You were visiting your mother. She manipulated you?"

"Yes. No. I don't know. She's the only person I saw. No one else was there."

"But you said she doesn't do magic," Theo pointed out.

"She doesn't. Actually, she can't. My mother was an early test subject for the plague. She hasn't used magic in a decade. The manipulation didn't come from her."

Theo looked confused. "Was there someone else there? Hiding in the apartment?"

Ren shook her head. "No. I would have known."

"Then how were you manipulated?"

There was only one possible answer. Ren's eyes fell to the half-burned scarf on the ground.

"It's a chain spell. Gods. My mother is being *manipulated*, Theo. No wonder she sounded so obsessed. You should have heard the way she talked. I've never seen her like that. Now it makes sense. She's being manipulated by someone. And the spell that's manipulating her . . . it jumped to me."

Theo frowned. "Ren. That would be . . ."

"The most complex manipulation spell in history?" she finished. "Agreed. It would be. Whoever cast this . . . they're brilliant. The spell was really nuanced, Theo. It didn't just try to batter up against my defenses. It waited until I was vulnerable. My mother and I had been arguing and there was this moment where I just . . . I broke down. I was crying. She was holding me. And that's when the magic wormed its way inside. The actual spell is woven into the fabric."

She pointed again to the scarf. Theo took an involuntary step back.

"How'd you know? That you were being manipulated?"

"I've had training. Dockery offered a course on it. Our senior year."

That jolted a laugh from him. "Seriously? You actually took Compartmentalization in Magic? I thought the joke was that no one signed up and he just sat in a lecture hall talking to himself."

"There were only three of us," Ren confirmed. She felt another twinge of guilt when she remembered one of them was Timmons. "All of us were born in the Lower Quarter. I know the great houses train for it at a young age so there's not much point in relearning the theory, but we all thought it was useful. It's all about organizing your mind. Specifically, your arsenal of spells. If you have a particularly complex system, outside forces have a difficult time infiltrating your thoughts. It's kind of like if someone came into your kitchen while you were out. Most manipulators can memorize which cabinet you keep your teacups inside. They know how to set them back in the same place. But if you add another layer—like facing all the teacup handles to the northeastern corner of the cabinet—it's obvious when someone who's not supposed to be there has visited. The same rules apply to the mind. I felt the alterations. I knew things weren't where they were supposed to be."

Theo shook his head. "How is it that you only finished fifth in our class?"

Ren snorted. "One of my credits didn't transfer. I would have been first if the petition had passed. Anyways. The point is that I recognized the manipulation right away. And whoever is doing this must be incredibly strong, because my mother had no idea she was being influenced. It would take incredible skill to sneak past her defenses without being noticed."

Theo frowned. "So that's why she got caught up in all of this?"

Ren knew it would be easy to claim that as the truth, but she didn't want any more secrets to exist between them. Not after a secret almost destroyed their bond. She also knew that she could not be blamed for her mother's action any more than Theo could be blamed for his father's.

"No. My mother has been involved with the Makers for a decade. She truly believes that the great houses must fall, but I know my mother: what's happening right now would bother her. People are dying. Some people were *sacrificed* to spread the disease. Whoever created this spell was smart enough to target a group that was already leaning into revolution. The best manipulation magic doesn't change someone's mind. It works with someone's natural sensibilities. I think this spell is built into her actual beliefs. Think about it like . . . like a hand on her back. It's there to nudge her a little farther than she'd normally be willing to go on her own."

Ren clawed back through her memory for details of their

exchange. There were moments when her mother seemed to retreat. When she seemed less like herself.

"When I brought up Lana, it was like my mother retreated. I was talking about the death of an innocent, young girl . . . and the emotion just vanished from her face. I think that's when the manipulation magic activated. It took over, because I'd touched on the part of what they're doing that my mother would never agree to do. I'm not claiming she's innocent, Theo. She's involved in this, but I think whoever started all of this has finally reached the part where their coconspirators are getting cold feet. It's not easy for someone to watch innocent people die. So, how do you convince them to keep moving forward with the plan?"

"You force them to do it," Theo concluded. "With a manipulation spell."

"Cast on a group of magicless people," Ren pointed out. "And it's not like we can go back to my mother's apartment and snap our fingers in her face to wake her up, either."

Theo was nodding. "That's why the houses train on it. If you don't assess and treat within the first two hours, the magic digs in to the subject and can't be excavated. You can't even sever the connecting thread of magic where it attaches to the victim. It's like steel. You have to go back to the source and cut the thread there."

"We have to find the person who cast the spell," Ren concluded. A shiver ran down her spine that had nothing to do with the subject matter. She looked down and realized she'd been half-naked for most of the conversation. "Let me go get some pants. I have a theory."

26

NEVELYN TIN'VORI

As the days passed, Nevelyn felt as if she were watching the second act of an elaborate play. Almost certainly a tragedy. The Makers—easily visible because of their bright red ribbons—arrived at the same time every day to deliver food to the masses. A seemingly endless supply of noodles and beans and dried fruit. No one ever questioned where it came from, or why anyone would give away so many precious resources at a time like this. Nevelyn watched with a mounting, inevitable dread. The Makers were quietly swaying the populace to their side of the table. When they had enough support, what would the next step be?

"None of it works."

Her sister collapsed into the chair beside her. Ava had recovered in nearly every sense of the word. Her bruises had faded. Her other symptoms had vanished. Only the brain fog associated with the disease remained. Ava couldn't even recall the basic steps of certain spells.

"You're still recovering," Nevelyn repeated. "It will return when you're fully healthy."

Ava refused to take any comfort from that. The fact that the three of them hadn't gotten sick was starting to really grate on her sister's nerves. She felt targeted by fate. As if the illness was some terrible, personal affront—instead of something that had just devastated the entire city.

Their discussions of magic led to another discovery. Josey was completely untrained. It was clear he hadn't grown up as they had. Magic had been an endless resource on the Tin'Vori estate. Their father's magical allotment had been substantial. Practice in the neighborhood archive room? As routine to them as brushing their teeth before bed. Josey only needed one hand to count the number of spells he'd learned so far.

Only *four* in total.

He knew a basic light cantrip that he used to read at night. He also had a rather clever spell that muted the sound of his footsteps. Nevelyn had found that choice rather suspicious. The final two spells were opposites: one for heating and one for cooling. A sensible choice for a boy who'd grown up needing to ward off the peaks and valleys of Kathor's shifting seasons. When Ava pointed out how poor his education had been, Josey had burst into tears. It had taken nearly an hour to extract him from the closet he'd decided to hide in. Surprisingly, it was Dahvid who'd managed to coax him out. Her brother, it seemed, had a small admirer in the house.

"How's Josey?" Nevelyn asked.

"He's fine," Ava said. "Dahvid is running him through the basics."

"Spellwork?"

"Combat. What does Dahvid know about spellwork?"

"Lovely."

She couldn't find a good reason to complain about the decision, though. After all that they'd witnessed from this very window, would it really hurt for the boy to learn how to defend himself? She was about to suggest they search the library for proper textbooks on magic when she spied movement in the streets below. A group of people hustled past. Then another group. And another.

All of them moving with haste. Before long, there was a literal crowd streaming past the front door of the Tin'Vori estate. Nevelyn went to stand by the window. It wasn't flight. She traced a path back to where they'd come from and saw no signs of danger. No fire or threat. The passing faces appeared eager. As if they were all heading somewhere they *wanted* to go.

"I'm going," Ava announced.

Her sister was thundering down the steps before Nevelyn could even turn.

"Ava! Wait a minute!"

Even after suffering through a plague, her baby sister still moved twice as fast as her. Nevelyn muttered a curse. She reached the top of the steps at the same time that Ava reached the landing below. Their commotion drew Dahvid and Josey like moths to flame. Ava started unbolting the extra locks as their entire group converged in the front hallway.

"What's going on?" Dahvid asked. "Is someone here?"

"I want to see," Josey piped in.

Ava ignored them all. She was working through the series of locks like a woman possessed.

"Ava. Hold on. Let's at least discuss this."

Her sister spun around. "Screw that. Whenever we *discuss* anything these days, it's just you deciding what the rest of us should do. Look, you were right. Hoarding food was smart. Barricading in here was the right move. Credit where credit is due. But if you think I'm going to spend the rest of my life trapped in this house, you're wrong. We need to know what's happening."

"I want to come!" Josey added.

All three Tin'Vori siblings shot him looks that would have made their mother proud. He withered immediately, chin dipping to his chest. The boy was smart enough not to ask again.

"I'm our best scout," Ava said, unbolting the final lock. "I'll follow the crowd, gather information, and return. We need to take the city's pulse. You know we do, Nev."

Dahvid stepped forward. "I'll go with you then. For protection."

"Not a chance," Nevelyn replied. "You know you're far too visible. We're not going to risk exposing you to a crowd. Ava is right." Her sister looked satisfied to have someone agree with her for once, until Nevelyn added the last part. "I'll go with you. If things get dangerous, I'm the only one who can hide us."

Her siblings knew enough about Nevelyn's gift to understand what she meant. How many times had she slipped around guards when they were children, without being noticed? She wasn't certain her magic could properly shield Ava, but she knew it was better than nothing.

"Fine," Ava said. "Can you at least try to keep up for once?"

Dahvid snorted. That earned him a kick from Nevelyn. He hissed when her foot connected with his shin. "Gods! Come on! She's the one who said it, not me!"

That had Ava grinning wildly. It was like they were children all over again. Nevelyn quietly adjusted her shawl. "Let's go."

Debate settled, the door to the outside world was opened. For the first time in weeks, Nevelyn stepped across the threshold. Her chest felt tight. She realized she wasn't breathing. Her first instinct was to not take in whatever had grown in the air these past few weeks.

People were still passing their door. Nearly all of them in small packs. Nevelyn and Ava fell in behind a larger group and did their best to not draw attention. The crowd's chosen path wound through the Wedding District. It was clear that other streets were serving as tributaries too. The road grew more and more packed until a proper crowd manifested before them. Ava glided like a shadow through the gathered ranks and Nevelyn was forced to follow with far less grace, bumping shoulders and muttering apologies as she went. The entire time she kept one hand on the dangling charm of her necklace. The shadowed side was facing out. By the time they reached the front rows, her breathing was labored. She tried to settle down while also taking in the sprawling scene.

The mass had gathered in a thick half-moon around the gates of Blythe House.

Named for the original matriarch of the Winters family, it remained the primary residence of the current heir. Nevelyn couldn't remember who that was off the top of her head, but she'd visited the house once when she was younger. Some kind of formal dance. The gates fronting the property were hammered into the shape of the family's house emblem: the knowing eye. It was always rendered in silver instead of gold. A nod to the idea that the Winterses cared more for knowledge than wealth. Judging from the size of the mansion on their estate, that appeared to be more of a clever idea than an actual practice. The massive eye on the gate stared unflinchingly at the waiting crowd.

Nevelyn saw dozens of house guards on the other side of the iron-wrought fence. All standing in formation and properly armored. A man with dark, sweeping hair stood at the back of the group. Even at this distance, Nevelyn could see his eyes were a piercing blue. His gaze swept over the group outside the gates with clear disdain.

"Marc Winters," Ava whispered. "The current heir. His younger brother is the one who died a few years ago. Clyde. He didn't survive that journey through the woods with our old friend."

Their old friend being Ren Monroe. The girl seemed tangled up with every house in the city at this point. She'd certainly weaved quite a web. Nevelyn couldn't help wondering where the little spider was now. Likely barricaded on one of the Broods' estates. Safe and sound.

Nevelyn's attention was drawn to a second group.

A tight circle of people who were all wearing the now-familiar red scarves. Before the crowd could start to grow agitated, one of their number separated from the others. A hush fell instantly over those assembled. He was bald with light brown skin. Unremarkable in appearance, but his voice boomed out for all to hear. Deep and resonant.

"Friends! Thank you for gathering! We are here because the noble houses have abandoned us. When the markets ran out of food, did they share their bounty? When you and your families needed protection in Kathor's streets, did their guards keep the peace?"

He did not need to answer the questions he asked. The crowd murmured the answers for him until they were all stirring and buzzing with discontent.

"We are the Makers," the man said. "Many of you have seen us in the market squares these past few days. We have broken bread with you. Shared our food. Tell me, why have the great houses not done the same?"

He glanced back through the iron gates. Every eye followed his gaze. Nevelyn saw now that House Winters had made a terrible error by trotting their heir out here. Marc Winters provided the Makers a rather appealing target. The cold stare. The pristine cloak draped over his shoulders. All their hatred could be aimed at him.

"In times of peace, you'll see their emblems *everywhere*. The great hawk of House Shiverian. The knowing eye of House Winters. The hammers of House Proctor. The shield of House Brood. The reaping sickle of House Graylantian. Go buy any good at the market, and they'll be there to collect the tax. Cross the canals and their vassals are there, demanding coins for each passage. They have collected our money all these years with the promise that when the time comes—when that peace fades—they'll be the first ones to shield us from danger."

More rumbling from the crowd. It was like watching someone set fire to a field just to see which way the wind would spread the burn. Nevelyn pressed closer to Ava.

"A shield," the speaker repeated in disbelief. "Our hospitals are overrun. Our streets are not safe. Our markets have run dry. But where are the great houses? Have they answered our cry? The promise they've always whispered in our ear is this: if we are strong, you are strong. Well, where are they now? When we *really* need them? Why do they hide behind their gates?"

His questions echoed across the clearing.

"We, the Makers, are officially petitioning the viceroy. We demand that the populace be allowed to vote on a motion of no confidence. If two thirds of Kathorians agree, we can officially remove the current governors. I'm sure it would not surprise you to know that all five positions are members of the five great houses. We can change that! If they will not help us—we must help ourselves. Under new leadership, we can start helping the people who need aid. Officials would be permitted to look through the storehouses on their estates. Any hoarded resources will be redistributed around the city. How many of you know someone who is struggling? Starving? Dying? We cannot just stand by as the great promise becomes a great lie. We must hold them accountable. You have a voice, Kathor. Will you use it? Will you join our cause?"

With the perfect amount of drama, the speaker turned.

He walked up to Blythe House's outer gates. Once more, the Makers' cause was helped by that stunning visual. The pristine silver gate with its priceless metalwork. The distant manse that was far larger than any one family could ever need. All the guards with their hands set delicately on the grips of sheathed swords. And framing it all: Marc Winters, who looked as if he'd never suffered a single bad day in his life. The speaker called out as if he were calling to a god.

"House Winters! Will you help us? Will you be the first house to open your gates? We, the Makers, offer to serve on your behalf. We can organize the crowd. Only families who have nothing will enter your gates. What do you say? Will you keep your promises to the people?!"

Nevelyn saw the guards on the other side of the gate shifting uncomfortably. There was a dark silence in the air. As if history itself were holding its breath to see what might happen next. Marc Winters made no reply. Instead, he raised his chin. Ever so slightly. It was one of the most pompous moments Nevelyn had ever witnessed. And then he began the long march up the hillside. Hundreds of people watched as the fool turned his back on them, and it felt as if all the houses were turning their back on them in that moment.

His retreat took a painfully long time. The hill was steep. The steps fronting Blythe House were many. By the time he reached the front door, the crowd was ready to burn down the city. People were edging forward all around them. She and Ava had been forced a few steps closer to those looming gates. It wasn't a true rush. Not yet. Just the first flexing of a muscle before the actual lunge. When the speaker finally turned back to the crowd, he held up a hand for silence.

"We could break this gate," he said, his voice soft but carrying. "We could sweep forward and take everything that belongs to them. Trust me, I know we are strong enough to do that. But we don't need to resort to violence. Not when we can still use our voice. Go home!" he commanded them. "Tell your friends and your neighbors and your loved ones. Tell them what you witnessed here today. The great houses had their chance to help—and they chose not to. Vote against them when the time comes. Use your voice. We can choose each other. We are the *true* Kathor."

On cue, the Makers at the front of the crowd began distributing two items. There were crates of food, but another group came forward with stacks of the bright red scarves. She watched people reach out and clutch greedily for the small pieces of fabric. Eager to join the cause. Eager to stand with their fellow Kathorians. The food was only claimed by the truly desperate. Somehow the Makers had swung them from violence to charity in less than five seconds.

Before the people passing out scarves reached where they stood, the sisters silently agreed to start the journey home. Nevelyn couldn't help noticing how perfectly the Makers had played their part. Instead of inciting a riot, they'd come away looking reasonable, measured, benevolent. Nevelyn knew better. They were the ones who'd started this plague. She wanted to scream that truth to the crowd. Shake them out of their trances and explain that neither side was worthy of their loyalty.

Protect yourselves, she wanted to say. *Protect the people you love most.*

That was what she planned to do.

27

MERCY WHITAKER

The Safe Harbor morgue became something of a second
home.

Dr. Williams served as her unofficial roommate. The two of
them shared meals, discussed theories, and drank tea. Mercy
was a lightweight compared to him. The coroner seemed to
either be boiling, pouring, or sipping the substance no matter
what time of the day she saw him. Their time in the morgue
would have felt normal if not for the interruptions whenever
a family member arrived to collect the departed. A cousin or
an uncle or a mother. They all seemed to knock on the door
the same way. As if they did not want to bother the rest of the
world with their mourning. Most of them muttered a small
apology before saying the name of the loved one they'd come
to find. Mercy had no idea how to comfort them. What words
would soften a blow that had already struck so deep?

Research kept her spirits up. The feeling that they were

actually *doing* something to answer all this pain and confusion. Williams primarily dedicated his time to studying waterborne illness. Hoping to find some clue from the previous pathogens and their impacts. Mercy's reading focused more on the historical instances of magical disruption. A good deal of what she'd read was terribly anecdotal. A man who lost magic after sneezing one too many times in a row. A woman who supposedly had an orgasm that destroyed her memories of all spellwork. Slowly, their hours transformed into a rhythm of reading and mourning, reading and mourning.

Until a voice interrupted, "Dogs in or out?"

It was early. The voice that asked that question echoed to them from the hallway. She and Williams exchanged a confused glance before she remembered that she'd put in a request to the local kennel. Safe Harbor had contracted with them in the past, but only when a disease required additional tracing. She'd put in the request with almost no expectation of a response. Most of the city was still not operating properly, but here was her request, poking its head around the corner.

"Hello?"

"Yes," Mercy said, shaking herself. "I'm sorry. What was your question?"

"Dogs in or dogs out? I can keep them in the hallway if you like."

Mercy blinked. "Do you have them with you?"

She wasn't really sure what the protocol was, or if the hospital even had protocols anymore. Traditionally, animals were not allowed for sanitary reasons, but at this point, who was going to come down here and scold her for inviting dogs into the morgue?

"Bring them in, I suppose."

The man whistled. Mercy wasn't prepared for the terror of watching three, full-grown hellhounds come slinking down the steps like exhaled smoke. All of them were dark-furred, a brown on the verge of black, with eyes like golden coins. The eyes were too wide and too large on their faces. It had the unhappy effect of making them look adorable, even though Mercy knew the evolutionary purpose was to lure smaller prey into brief stillness. The creatures circled around the room before sitting—straight and regal—along the far wall. Their master trudged into the room with the opposite effect. He looked as if he'd not showered in several days.

"So, what are we tracking?"

"Well, we were actually hoping to take samples today. . . ." She trailed off. The man was close enough now that she could see bruises on his chest, running across his collarbone. "Can you track without magic?"

He offered a crooked smile. "Of course. They're the ones who use magic. Not me."

She sighed with relief. The hounds would be incredibly useful. All they needed now was for the samples to arrive. Absurdly, she heard a knock at the door. She glanced up in time to see a paladin peeking around the corner. "Excuse me? Where do you want these corpses?"

Mercy gestured. The houndmaster made room for them by reuniting with his dogs on the opposite end of the room. If a corpse delivery was surprising to him, he showed no sign of it. Six paladins funneled through the entrance. Each pair ferried a gurney between them, and on each gurney was a covered body. When the final body was set down, the paladins retreated from the room. She didn't blame them for wanting to be gone from this place. These were no ordinary corpses.

"How exciting," Williams said.

Mercy nodded. "I can't believe we found them."

Locating these three bodies had taken an inordinate amount of searching. The city had five water treatment facilities. According to the reports, every building responsible for supplying water to Kathor had been tainted. Corpses were discovered at each facility. She and Williams had risked the streets to hunt down their storage locations. The first four buildings reported that the bodies had been delivered to local morgues. They'd collected addresses and left. When they arrived, however, they were told that hospital personnel had already come by to collect the bodies. All of them had supposedly been transferred to Safe Harbor.

No one was better positioned to know that was a lie than them.

The city wasn't functioning. Their hospital was barely operable. She suspected that Kathor's larger governing entities were faring no better. The normal result of dysfunction was inactivity. She thought it would have been far more likely that these bodies found their way to the smaller morgues, and then were completely forgotten. Maybe—and it would be a big maybe—some official would remember them weeks down the road and rush back to take care of the neglected business. Which was what made these instances so odd. The city's disarray had somehow led to expedited service? And the swift response just happened to have removed very important evidence?

Mercy found that all unlikely. Suspicious even.

Their final visit had involved a stroke of luck. An elderly

woman had come to the door of that morgue. "Bodies?" she'd replied. "Yes, plenty of those."

The bodies from the final treatment facility were still there. Whoever had worked to round up the others had missed these—or else been unable to gain access. She always secretly pictured Nance as her opponent. His failure in this was her victory. Now she adjusted the fit of her gloves, ignored the tingling in her stunted fingers, and nodded to Dr. Williams.

"Let's begin."

He loosened the seal of the first bag and they set to work. The victim was a young man in his midthirties. His hair was trimmed tight. His skin was pale and bloated. Matching slits ran down both biceps. Twin wounds cut across each exposed thigh. Every wound was perfectly identical to the first corpse she'd inspected. Williams leaned close, examining the edges of the lesion by the throat.

"You can't do this with a standard scalpel or knife. Look at how wide the actual incision is. For all of these cuts. Wide, and yet perfectly straight. . . ."

"Could they have been made with a bigger blade?" Mercy proposed. "A broadsword?"

"I'd still expect the wounds to be tighter, but maybe. The chest wound is also odd. It would take enormous pressure to create a wound like that. I wonder how they did it? Some sort of machine?" He shook his head. "The whole thing is strange. It almost feels . . ."

"Ceremonial."

Williams nodded. "Exactly the word for it. Are all three patients like this?"

They carefully uncovered the next two bodies. All of them

had matching wounds. The first time she'd seen a corpse like this, she'd lacked the wider context. Now, she knew that the people involved had been unleashing an illness. The wounds were designed to *spread* something. Mercy knelt down so that she was eye level with the nearest body. There was a reason she'd wanted to inspect these particular corpses. "It's still happening. Unbelievable. Look at that."

A small thrill ran through her. She hadn't dared to hope for this. Recovering the body was one thing, but having access to the substance they'd designed to enter the water? A literal godsend. As she stared, the substance drifted up from each wound. There wasn't as much leaking out as there had been with the first body she'd inspected, but more than enough to gather samples.

"All right. Let's collect as much as we can."

Both of them set to the task. The sealable flasks they used for each corpse appeared empty. Only when she held them to the light could she see the dark swirls. Like some kind of corruption. They took samples from each of the bodies. The houndmaster didn't interrupt them, but a glance back showed that all three hellhounds had altered their stances. Each one was tilting its head to the right. Ever so slightly. The houndmaster cleared his throat when he saw that she'd noticed.

"It has a scent," he said.

"Pardon?"

"Whatever you've got there," he said. "They can smell it."

Until that moment, she would have described the substance as odorless. She tore her gaze away from those unnatural golden eyes and refocused on the task at hand. Williams labeled the individual containers while she secured the corpses back in their shrouds. Once the room was properly tidy, she signaled the houndmaster.

"What now?" Mercy asked. "How do we proceed?"

He shrugged. "You give them the scent and then let them go."

"Right. And the three of us just follow them?"

That drew a snort from him. "Not unless you're faster than you look, Doctor. There's a tracing map in this hospital. These three are linked to it. You can follow their progress there as long as the spell hasn't expired. I'll follow them. Once they reach the end of the trail, I'll send word. Could take a few days. Just depends on how far they have to travel."

Mercy nodded. "Got it. Let's get them moving, then."

"Effie," the houndmaster called, turning. "Go on, girl."

The middle hound broke from its pose and trotted forward. Mercy carefully unsealed one of the sample containers and set it on the ground. The dog was well trained. Focused in an unnatural way. It shoved its nose as far into the flask as it could. Several deep inhalations, and then the creature straightened. They all watched it slip from the room like a departing shadow. Mercy stoppered the container and traded it out for a sample from one of the other corpses.

"Emma."

Another dog came forward. Mercy repeated all the same steps. The final dog—who bore the unfortunate name of Eustace—was the only one who broke protocol. It took advantage of its proximity to her and gave Mercy's palm a quick lick. She scratched the pup behind the ears, then let it get back to its duty. Once all three had vanished, she turned back to the houndmaster.

"You said there's a map?"

He nodded. "Guy I always worked with was short. Bald.

Rimmed glasses. Quietlike. He worked in the back wing. The map is in his office."

A ghost of a smile crossed Mercy's face. "Dr. Horn."

The houndmaster confirmed the name before bidding them farewell. Mercy stared after him, an odd feeling stirring in her chest. It was almost as if an invisible hand had reached inside her and started tightening the screws of her heart. Williams somehow noticed. He was kind enough to set aside the containers and throw a friendly arm around her shoulder.

"Come on. We can go up there together."

She couldn't have been more grateful. Walking into her dead mentor's office was threatening to unmoor her. Only a few months ago, they'd performed a surgery together. And then Horn sent her on an assignment that would echo up and down the eastern seaboard. An assignment that would eventually lead to his death. They found Dr. Horn's office untouched. Exactly as he'd left it. Perhaps a few more folders than normal, as he'd been reviewing several cases prior to his departure. The map in question was hanging over his desk. She couldn't believe she'd never noticed it.

"Do you think that's it?" Mercy asked.

Williams squinted. "Well . . . it's the only one . . . Oh, look! There."

The map *shifted* before their eyes. It had been a wider scope stretching from Ravinia all the way down to the first citadel cities well to the south. Now, the map homed in on Kathor's districts. All of them charted neatly. Three marks appeared. Like burning embers. *One for each hound*, she realized. All of them began inching across the cityscape.

They maneuvered through the Lower Quarter. Then it was

backroads and alleyways to the industrial heart of the city. She saw a long pause there before the hounds were on the move again.

It took another hour for them to reach the city gates. They were delayed there for several minutes. Mercy found herself wondering how they would get through doors or gates or anything that normally required opposable thumbs, but after a short delay, they were outside Kathor proper. The map expanded to follow their path. Slowly widening until they had glimpses of rivers and hills and mountains. She and Williams sat in silence, spellbound by a magic that would have seemed so commonplace just a few months before. She was starting to drift to sleep when Williams spoke. "Look at that."

Slowly and inexplicably, one of the hounds split from the others. It happened just north of Kathor. In the foothills that separated city from farmland. They watched that flickering ember turn inward. Heading west, away from the others. Mercy eyed the foothills in that direction.

Where are you headed? What's out there? Do I even want to know?

". . . pretty good run."

Mercy blinked. "What?"

Williams smiled. "You know, you're a terrible listener. It's a wonder that you ever made it through school. I was saying we've both had a pretty good run. Been at least seven days for me."

"Seven days of what?"

"Not getting sick," he said. "I guess Professor Porthinos was right. Follow the protocols, blah blah blah, wash your hands, blah blah blah."

Williams was fussing with his tea, so he did not notice the effect his words had on Mercy. The way she leaned back into the cushions of her chair, struck by an idea she'd only thought of once in passing. All this time, and still she wasn't sick. Not even a hint of the disease. Who had more exposure than she did? She'd discovered the first body. She'd been with the earliest known patients. She was guilty of drinking water in Running Hills *and* in Kathor. There was no way she'd gone this entire time without being exposed to the illness.

Enough time had passed that Mercy thought she knew the answer. Every disease they'd ever studied—whether a one-off plague or a seasonable illness—shared three commonalities. First, they were all transferable in some way. Whether through physical contact or the air or water. Next, they produced similar symptoms in their victims. The degree might differ, but there would be a consistency across the population. The last component, however, was that every disease she'd ever studied involved a select group that came to be known as the *immune*.

There were some people, for example, who never caught the coastal flu that swept through the city every winter. Doctors in ancient times would have called them lucky. Maybe even favored by the gods. But medical studies showed, time and time again, that some people simply had the genetic makeup to *resist* a disease. Mercy frowned at that.

Williams and I are both . . . immune?

It felt statistically unlikely. Although, now that she considered this angle, she hadn't heard of any other exceptions amongst their staff. Nearly *everyone* had gone home sick. Many had even returned after their recovery to help out. She was debating the odds when the answer hit her in the chest like a two-ton anvil. Even now, Dr. Williams was performing the very task that had saved him.

Sipping tea.

She'd never seen anyone drink as much tea as him, and she realized she'd not seen him drink even a single glass of water. *You've been boiling it out each time.* He might be the luckiest person she'd ever met. Weeks had gone by, but he'd been unknowingly boiling out the pathogens before they could ever reach his body. Until . . .

. . . today. The two of them had just spent hours in a room *full* of the disease. Heavier doses than what would be found in water, in fact. It was possible his mask enchantments might have worked, staved off the illness, but she knew she'd just unintentionally exposed him. She watched him take another sip of his tea and could not decide how or what to tell him.

Better to hold on to hope for now.

The two of them sat in the quiet of that office, watching the three glowing embers work their way across the seemingly endless plains. Mercy found herself dreaming of a world with more answers than questions. More solutions than problems. Maybe, just maybe, the hounds were leading them to that place. Maybe Williams would not get sick. Maybe something would go right.

For once.

28

REN MONROE

". . . now know the disease causes a temporary disconnection with magic. Our researchers are working around the clock on solutions to that disruption. Until then, we are asking anyone who has maintained their magic through the plague to report to Beacon House, effective immediately. This is a citywide mandate. If you have magic: our city needs you. Lastly, a reminder that there's been an official request for a vote of no confidence. This vote would remove all the current governors. . . ."

Ren and Theo leaned against the balcony railing, looking down over the city, as Viceroy Gray repeated the message that had been booming all morning. This was the first break they'd taken from their own research. They'd spent hours reading through books about chain spells and manipulation magic. Everything confirmed their initial guess. Finding the source of the spell would be vital. The problem, however, was that their research also supported the idea that a manipulation spell of this complexity and breadth should not have been possible. There was nothing like it in all of recorded history, which led them to the uncomfortable conclusion that whoever had cast it would be formidable. Ren hadn't been so tirelessly devoted to research since her undergraduate years. Back then, she'd been desperate to prove herself and get a proper foothold with her peers. Revenge had been her entire motivation.

Now her focus was to stop what she'd begun. It truly felt as if finding the right answer to their problem was the only way for Ren to make up for all the damage she'd left in her wake. If her mother's accusation were true—if she'd been the one to leave the door open for this attack—than she'd make damn certain she was the one to close it on whoever was doing this. But the simple truth was that this was not a battle they could fight alone. Theo agreed, activating the resources of House Brood. Vega had winged out with letters for several parties—and now they could only wait. The two of them had stepped outside for fresh air while they awaited her return, and that was when they heard the viceroy's repeating message. His announcement drew their attention to a detail they'd overlooked until now.

"We're not sick."

Ren had been so worried that she'd get sick that she failed to think about how odd it was that neither of them had succumbed to the illness. Clearly, that was rare if the viceroy needed to put out a citywide request for volunteers. Theo considered her comment before responding.

"Lack of exposure?" he suggested. "We were being held captive as the plague spread. Unconscious for most of the time.

It's possible we didn't drink enough water to become infected."

Ren frowned. "Would the amount really matter? We both drank city water before finding the bodies and we both drank city water after finding them. Besides, we were at the actual contagion site, Theo. We have more exposure to this than most people. We just . . . didn't get sick."

"Maybe we're immune to it."

"Both of us?" Ren asked. "That seems pretty damn lucky to me."

The blight wasn't the only subject of the viceroy's message. While Ren worried about the spreading disease, Theo seemed more preoccupied with the official vote that the Makers had forced. The viceroy's message relayed instructions for how citizens should vote, what both options actually meant, and what would happen if the vote succeeded or failed. Ren listened and could not grasp Theo's concerns. Centuries of history were on his side.

"There hasn't been a successful vote of no confidence in Kathor's entire history. None have even come close to meeting the threshold. Your family is the one who rigged those laws so that they didn't have a chance of succeeding. Why worry about that?"

He shook his head. "I was thinking about what I would do—if I were the Makers. You're right. The first hurdle is votes. It's rare that more than half the city's population participates. Most people don't see the point. Many have ties to the great houses. Voting against us—when voting records are public information—doesn't serve their interests. Which means the Makers have to produce the biggest voter turnout in a century *and* they have to get those people to all vote their way.

That would be a difficult task . . . unless you're using magic to manipulate people."

They had watched some of the protests from up in the Heights. A heavy guilt had snaked through her thoughts. Ren felt like someone who'd started a fire, intending to burn out a very specific, invasive plant. It had worked. She'd destroyed Landwin Brood. But now she was watching the fire she'd started spread past the designed burn zone. Catching on the leaves of other trees. Leaping to unintended forests. She could not help wondering how much damage would be done to Kathor if they couldn't put this fire out.

Reports were coming back from some of the gatherings below. The Makers were handing out food and the red scarves that marked their members. Ren imagined the manipulation spell, weaving in and out of the population. Whispering small encouragements to join their cause.

"Even if they get the votes," Ren continued, "it doesn't matter. The vote doesn't actually push the measure through. It just sends the motion to Viceroy Gray. He would have to ratify the people's decision, and we know he's a servant of the great houses. Why would he ever approve a measure that strips your power?"

"He wouldn't—and I'm starting to think that's the point. The results will be public information. The law stipulates that. Let's say it works. They turn out thousands of people and all of them vote in favor of the motion. The viceroy would have to publicly deny the people. I can't think of more perfect ammunition for a rebellion. And this might be the one time in history that the great houses don't have enough power to actually put down a rebellion. It would be anarchy, Ren."

Her stomach knotted as she listened. On the one hand, she felt guilty for the part she'd played in fomenting this rebellion. On the other hand, Theo didn't know just how alluring that all sounded. She didn't need to be manipulated into thinking that a world where the great houses had less power might actually be a good one. The problem, of course, was knowing that the power-in-waiting was just as corrupt. This would have been far more difficult if her mother was taking part in some honorable rebellion. Fighting for a just and noble cause. But Ren had already pulled back the curtain and seen the truth. Her mother—and thousands of others—were being manipulated. Forced to act against their own conscience by a dark puppeteer who still hadn't appeared on the stage. That person, whoever they were, could not be allowed to claim possession of Kathor.

Their conversation was interrupted by Vega's return. Their livestone bird landed on the railing with a resounding thud. Her wings fluttered briefly out for balance, then tucked neatly in against her sides. A crumpled letter was clutched in her talons. Theo retrieved it.

"Several updates: the estate has been secured by my mother. My sister is there."

Ren looked up sharply.

"As a prisoner," Theo read. "She is being guarded. Brood troops have been sent into the city. They'll be securing various properties. Safe houses. We'll have options if it comes to it. Brightsword controls the water treatment facilities . . . and our men decided not to test their defenses for now." His eyes scanned down the page. "Damn. No sign of Zell Carrowynd. Her statues are gone too. This is a hell of a time for her to go missing."

Ren shook her head. "There's precedent there. During the War of Neighbors, the warden vanished and the statues were neutral. They could not harm *either* side in the war—and so they took neither side. It could be she's removing herself from the board."

"That's a loss. A big one. Let's send another letter to my mother through Vega. We can let them know that any 'immune' who remain on the estate should report to Beacon House."

"Does that mean we're going there?" Ren asked.

Theo nodded. "I have a feeling the other houses will be there. Either to show off their strength, or to see who else survived the plague. We need to measure our strength against the other houses—but we also need to measure our collective power. If there aren't enough wizards to stand against the Makers, we're all doomed anyways. Sitting out the viceroy's meeting would just leave us in the dark. I think it makes sense to go."

After that, he made quick work of his letter. Vega winged back to their estate while Ren made some final notations to her research. She could feel a momentum as they prepared to journey to the lower city. Their bond hummed with a frenetic energy. She knew they were still several steps behind the mastermind who'd attacked the city, but this morning felt like the start of a hunt. All they had to do was follow the right trails and they'd find the person. She felt certain of that.

Outside, Ren and Theo paused instinctually on the threshold. The Heights had gone quiet. There were no signs of protest or damage, but nor did the streets look warm or welcoming. It was as if this part of the city was holding its breath and trying not to breathe in what had claimed the rest of Kathor. They safely reached the public access. The building was no bigger than a small shed. No attendant was on duty and just like the station they'd use to travel here, all the way candles were missing. Ren was prepared. She'd brought enough stock for both of them.

Normally, they would have just ported from the safety of their own home—but the public access sites all had portrait galleries. A series of small, painted slates for different sections of the city. These served as mental reminders for anyone who hadn't ported to a particular section of the city very often. Theo searched for a moment before locating Beacon House's outer courtyard. Once it was on display, he arranged their candles and lit both wicks with a warming spell.

Ren had been to the viceroy's residence recently—but not Beacon House proper. She stared at the painting. The sprawling fountains. The arching windows in the background. She was so focused that she almost didn't hear Theo's voice.

"I just had a terrible thought."

Ren lifted one eyebrow. "Oh? That normally falls in my area of expertise."

"Everything's your expertise." He offered a ghost of a smile. "No, I was thinking . . . what if we're the last wizards? What if the plague's effect is permanent? We'd be all that's left."

Ren swallowed. "But future generations . . ."

"Might have magic," Theo said. "But they might not. How could we know for sure? If their parents don't have magic? Would the next generation even be born with a connection to it? And if they are, who will teach them how to use what they have?" He shook his head. "I know it's grim, but I can't stop thinking about what will happen over the next twenty years. The people who are traveling to Beacon House right now . . ."

we could be all that's left of magic in the entire city."

Their eyes returned to the flickering flames. Ren could sense Theo's emotions across their bond. It was like looking into the mouth of a dark cave and knowing just how easy it would be to lose your way if you took one too many steps inside. She needed to pull him back. The way he so often pulled her back from her own darknesses.

"I suppose there's at least one silver lining: you might be the second most gifted wizard in the world now."

That jolted a laugh out of him. "I'll take second place to you any day."

He reached for her hand at the same time she reached for his. A brief fumbling, and then their fingers were laced comfortably together. The candles had burned more than enough to cover their travel through the waxways, but for a stretch of time, neither of them moved.

It was so lovely to sit in the glowing light, hand in hand, and pretend the problems outside that small room were not theirs to deal with. Ren tried to imagine meeting Theo at school. Maybe she dropped her books and he helped pick them up. Going out for coffee, discussing their favorite spells, falling in love the normal way. In that version of the universe, Theo's father would be a kind man. His family's reputation would be for justice instead of cruelty. Ren's father would still be alive. Every night he'd sing songs to her mother as they cooked meals together. And her mother would be happy—not bitter and vulnerable and under someone's dark spell.

When Ren finally opened her eyes, the only thing she still had from that dream version of her life was Theo. His hand nestled warmly in her own. The two of them locked eyes. A quick nod and they were letting go. Reaching for the candles at the same time. The fire burned before pulling them into the lightless nothing. A pain as brief as that other, imagined world.

When their feet set down, Beacon House stood before them.

29

MERCY WHITAKER

Mercy was one of the first to answer the viceroy's summons.

Even in her current state of depression, she could not resist the idea of gathering more data. She wanted to know who'd survived the plague with their magic intact—and she wanted to know why. Would immunity be random? Linked to a specific genetic trait or ancestry? Any answers would be helpful in continuing to form the wider perspective on the disease and its impact on the city.

Besides, what else was there to do?

Williams had woken up that morning covered in bruises. She felt so guilty. He'd avoided the plague for so long. Sipping on his boiled teas. Narrowly escaping one of the most widespread contagions in history. Until she'd been foolish enough to bring live doses to his morgue. Mercy had never been the sort of person who beat themselves up over innocent mistakes.

Logic told her she couldn't have known she was putting him in danger. But she still mourned the loss of yet another partner on this treacherous journey. Devlin was dead. So was Dr. Horn.

I won't let you die, Williams. If it comes to that, I won't let you die.

Her fingers itched every time she thought about it. She had left him nestled in a bed at Safe Harbor. Three pitchers of water on his bedside table. A tray of rations and nuts there as well. After making sure he lacked for nothing, she'd visited Horn's office one more time.

The three glowing embers had finally paused in their movement. It felt obvious that they'd reached their destinations. Two were in Running Hills. A note from the houndmaster explained that he would rendezvous with those dogs first, then head to the second location. That one was still a question mark. Due west of the city. Right where the foothills began to transform into proper mountains. She had cross-checked the location with every map she could find in the hospital library—but there was nothing marked out there. No towns or outposts or natural landmarks. Instinct told her there were answers there. She just needed to figure out how to safely get there.

For now, she quietly sipped a glass of wine and watched the city's other wizards arrive at Beacon House. A dozen other "immune" people were in the room. Every few minutes, there was another arrival answering the viceroy's summons. All of them were offered food and drinks. The "servers" were Brightsword paladins. Seeing their gold-threaded emblems was enough to turn her stomach. She could not help thinking of Devlin. A dead weight that sat in her gut. Conversations swirled around the room. People spoke as if they were distinguished guests, rather than the survivors of some terrible tragedy. As Mercy eavesdropped, she felt a mounting distaste for the entire group.

". . . could be seen as an opportunity. I mean, we're the only ones with magic. We could draw up contracts for specific services? The key will be to avoid undercutting. . . ."

"You can hardly call what I do magic. I just *enhance* other people's magic. It's boring. Pays well, but it's *so* boring."

"My favorite spells are all *purple*."

The last quote, at least, made her smile. It came from a little girl, no older than seven, who had bright curly hair and a wide smile. She was speaking with a boy who appeared slightly older than her. The boy leaned close and whispered that he liked any spells that used *fire*. Her eyes went wide and the two of them appeared to become instant friends. Everyone else in the room felt slightly less redeemable. Mercy sipped and listened until she simply could not bear it any more. The casual conversations. The angles they were taking in discussing how to capitalize on their situation. She realized she did not want to be here any longer than was strictly necessary.

Time to begin gathering information.

She set down her wine and aimed for the nearest conversation. The two wizards were discussing passive magic systems— something about the number of spells that required daily refreshing around the city. Mercy ignored that topic and leapt right in.

"Hello. Do you both still have your magic?"

They looked at her as if she were an idiot.

"Of course. Why else would we be here?"

"Great. Any specialties? What's your focus? . . ."

The two of them were initially taken aback by the way

she'd knifed into their conversation, but Mercy quickly discovered just how much they loved talking about themselves. She learned their occupations: a manipulator and an enhancer. Once she had that information, she moved on. One of them was midsentence. Discussing his connection with one of the great houses. She cared so very little about that. Instead, she abandoned them and went to the next group.

"Hi. Sorry to interrupt. I was just wondering . . ."

30

NEVELYN TIN'VORI

Nevelyn was listening as Josey made a friend.

It was charming to hear them talk. Asking each other about their favorite spells. She heard her ward lie at least three times in less than ten seconds. It was not the devious sort. Just the typical bragging that any child fell into when faced with a peer who was also bragging.

"I almost cast a stun spell the other day."

"I *did* cast a stun spell the other day."

"Yeah? Well . . . I might get tattoos!"

The girl's eyes swung over to where Dahvid stood and she instantly blushed when he met her gaze. Josey was quick to set a comforting hand on her shoulder. "Don't worry. He's friendly."

That drew a snort from Dahvid. Nevelyn couldn't help smiling.

"High praise there," she whispered.

A crowd of roughly twenty people had already gathered inside the western wing of Beacon House. Half of their surroundings were wooden and paneled. A beautiful maple that caught every light and threw it back on the gathered guests. The other half of the room was all glass. It overlooked the nearest street and offered a glimpse of the city. A gradual darkness made it hard to pick out the details. The buildings were quietly converging into a single entity, all capped by the fading crimson of sunset.

They'd almost decided to turn down the invitation, but Ava had insisted they go. Knowledge was power, and this meeting would hand them priceless information about the city as a whole. Not just what they'd personally witnessed from their limited overlook. Nevelyn wasn't really sure what to expect. Would people keep arriving all night? Did the immune number in the hundreds? The thousands? Or was this group of twenty or so people closer to the final count? She suspected they would have an answer before long.

Nevelyn had quietly set her heart-shaped necklace to the darker side. She was not actively casting the spell, but she knew that even when she wasn't consciously using it, the magic still affected how people saw her. If anyone at the party glanced in the direction of the Tin'Voris, their eyes would undoubtedly land on Dahvid. It would take much more focus for anyone to even notice his sister, watching them from the background.

"Did you see the paladins?" Dahvid whispered.

She nodded. "They're all lightless."

An important clue. Nevelyn suspected that the rest of the city's de facto police force had been impacted by the plague as well. After all, the viceroy would want to display whatever strength he possessed tonight. If there were still paladins in possession of magic, they'd be front and center. Visible enough to show the houses and the rest of the city that he held some sway. The fact that they'd been transformed into glorified butlers didn't bode well for their status. Nevelyn was still following that breadcrumb trail in her thoughts when a woman marched right up to them.

"Hello. You're an image-bearer?"

Dahvid nodded. This was nothing new. His magic always drew the eye.

"And what about you?"

She was pointing at Josey. Nevelyn's protectiveness flared.

"Who's asking?"

Her tone caught the woman off guard. Nevelyn watched her blink a few times, as if she'd only just noticed Nevelyn was there. She was shorter with fire-bright red hair. The bags under her eyes told Nevelyn she hadn't slept in some time. She also wore a pair of double-thick leather gloves. She recovered quickly from her initial shock, tapping an emblem on her chest. It showed two hummingbirds in flight, carrying a small ribbon between them.

"I'm a doctor over at Safe Harbor."

Nevelyn nodded. "Does he look sick to you? That's actually why we're all here, isn't it? Because we didn't get sick?"

The forcefulness of Nevelyn's questions drove the girl back a step.

"Of course. I'm just gathering data."

"Try gathering it from someone else."

Another step back. "I . . . I've been studying the place.

Tracing the disease back to its point of origin. I was only trying to figure out if there's a connecting thread between the immune. The more we know about . . ."

"The more you know, the more you can use it against us," Nevelyn countered. "We do not know you. Respectfully, take your survey elsewhere."

The woman held up her gloved hands innocently and backed off. There was a sadness in her expression that Nevelyn could not make herself feel any pity for. A moment later, and the supposed doctor was with another group, asking the same questions. Nevelyn watched for any sign that she was not who she'd said she was. Josey had fallen back to chatting with his friend. A third child their age had seemingly appeared out of thin air. A sharp-looking boy with moon-wide eyes who was clearly trying to figure out how to insert himself into the conversation. Dahvid glanced back at Nevelyn.

"I'd forgotten how good you are at making friends."

She winked back at him. They were not here to make friends. They were here to find out what the hell was happening, and then they would take that information and use it to make sure that House Tin'Vori survived and thrived. That was her only true concern. Nevelyn was about to take another sip from her drink when she spied movement outside.

Two people, freshly arrived from the waxways. She saw their bodies suspended briefly in the air. One was taller with bright blond hair. Pretty, but very distinctly not her type. A boy who looked far too easy to break. The other had straight, shoulder-length hair. She possessed beautiful features, but Nevelyn suspected there weren't many people who would have chosen that as the first word to describe her. So many others fit better: focused, purposeful, obsessive. The girl's right hand clutched a familiar horseshoe wand. It was almost enough to make Nevelyn smile.

Of course you survived.

"Speaking of friends. Some of ours just arrived."

31

REN MONROE

B eacon House was not a house.

It had been once. Generations ago. The first Proctor ancestors to land in Kathor established themselves as the city's greatest builders. No one else could match their skill. Naturally, the secret to their success was magic. It was discovered that the Proctors had hoarded three crucial spells—all to do with the chemical processes of connecting disparate materials—that had given them a massive advantage on their competitors. The other influential houses could hardly complain. After all, which of them had not done the same?

Guile Proctor built the first version of Beacon House. A gorgeous two-story stone building that was perfectly symmetrical. All ten of the front-facing windows were flanked by quaint wooden shutters. Guile's oldest daughter was tasked with improving his perfect design, and she succeeded. She stripped away the stones from each of the front corners of the building and replaced them with sprawling glass windows. These ran in a diagonal line from the bottom corner to the midpoints of the roof. The design formed three flawless triangles. One of stone and two of glass. Occupants could sit in those sections of the house and look out over the entire city.

It went on like that through the generations. Each Proctor tasked with adding their own touches to the communal design. A series of glass bridges connected the original building with new additions. Below these walkways, idyllic courtyards were surrounded by still more expansions. The modern effect was a series of buildings that looked partially suspended in the air. The Proctors went on to donate the buildings as a permanent residence for the sitting viceroy. One of the many benefits that ensured the loyalty of Kathor's public office to the great houses.

Ren and Theo strode through the main entrance. It was flanked by a pair of Brightsword paladins. The emblem on their chests always briefly reminded her of Devlin. Where had he ended up? She had no doubts he'd risen quickly through their ranks, but if these two paladins were any indication, Brightsword's power had been reduced by the plague. Both were lightless. The veins of bright magic that normally ran through their weapons or their armor had all been snuffed out.

Another set of paladins escorted them through a wide hallway that fed into an even wider sitting room. Ren paused there to get a proper glimpse of the entire gathering. Everyone had a drink in hand. They were scattered around the room, attempting small talk, but everyone kept stealing glances at the newest entrants. Ren accepted the first drink offered to her, but didn't take a sip. A standard rule she'd learned from House Brood. It guarded against poison and sloppiness. Ren made a line for the first open space she could find around the borders of the room. She set her back to the bookshelf there and began her assessment of the crowd. If these were the only wizards left in the city, she wanted to know exactly where the two of them stood. The first familiar face was none other than Dahvid Tin'Vori.

Of course you survived.

Their former accomplice was as obvious as sunlight. Dahvid stood a head taller than most of the people present. Almost too handsome. The kind of person you made an effort not to stare at directly. His leather armor was discreet, but still notable in a crowd of wizards who likely leaned toward spellwork instead of physical combat. There were open slashes in the darker fabric that she knew were designed for access to his tattoos. She could see the scarlet traveler glaring out boldly from his chest. A series of concentric circles on one shoulder. Each tattoo housed a powerful spell. Even though they'd worked together, she'd yet to witness him duel. A shame. She'd have liked to take his measure. Anyone who could run a Ravinian gauntlet *and* defeat Thugar Tin'Vori in just a few days was worthy of respect. Perhaps even fear.

If Dahvid was sunlight, Nevelyn Tin'Vori was his shadow. Ren spotted the girl hiding just a few steps behind her brother. Those wide brown eyes assessing the room with the same intentionality as Ren. Her face was partially hidden by a thicket of dark and wildly curled hair. Ren nearly missed the one notable addition. Nevelyn was standing near a boy who appeared to be no older than ten. None of his features were nods to Tin'Vori ancestry. He didn't have their eyes or their noses or their chins.

Who, pray tell, are you?

Nevelyn's eyes landed on her at that exact moment. The other woman took a protective step toward her ward that spoke volumes. She recovered in time to offer a respectful nod. Ren took some small pleasure in seeing how unsurprised Nevelyn was to see her. Where else would they be? Both of them were survivors—above all else. Even fate could not keep them out.

Ren offered a nod in return before continuing her appraisal of the other guests. A quick count had the number somewhere north of thirty. Some were complete strangers. Others instantly recognizable. All five of the major houses had representation, but a glance showed this was not the old guard. Not even close. Over a year ago, Ren had dined in an upper room with some of the city's most influential people. The only surviving member of that group was Gemma Graylantian. According to Theo, she was an incredibly talented manipulator.

Besides Gemma, Marc Winters was the next closest thing to royalty. The current heir of their house—and Clyde's older brother. That thought sent a shiver down her spine. The two had a clear resemblance. Marc had the same blue eyes and dark hair, but a broader frame. He was currently in what looked like a strained conversation with a much younger girl. Ren might not know her name, but she could recognize a Shiverian anywhere. The pointed nose and the scattered freckles. She didn't look a day older than fifteen. Ren was still studying the young girl when a willow of a boy presented himself before them. He offered the world's most absurd bow before righting himself, a shock of bright white hair flopping with each motion.

"Sir. Erm. Master Theo. It's . . . I've been told to report to you. I'm your second cousin. Well, not like you're *second* overall cousin or whatever. More like I'm . . . *a* second cousin. The . . . son . . . of your father's cousin."

Theo was all raised eyebrows. "Gods. Please stop bowing."

Naturally, the boy bowed again. Ren couldn't help butting in.

"What did you say your name was?"

"Theodore." His cheeks went bright red. "I'm actually named after you, sir."

Theo glanced at Ren with a look that said, *Don't you dare*, but she'd already died and come back to life laughing. The boy cracked a smile, though it was clear he wasn't sure what was so funny.

"Named after him? How old are you?"

Theodore shrugged. "I'm thirteen, my lady."

"Don't call her that," Theo warned. "She'll want a crown."

"Thirteen," Ren repeated. "So you were born when Theo was around . . . seven. You know, that sounds right to me. By then, he'd tamed his first wyvern, discovered a dragon's burial chamber, and invented almost a dozen spells. Pretty reasonable for another person to be named after him."

Theodore's eyes widened as she spoke, and Ren realized that the boy actually believed Theo had done all of that before reaching puberty. Meanwhile, Theo's eyes had rolled to the ceiling. He steered the conversation away before Ren could leave the boy even more disillusioned.

"So, you've retained your magic, Cousin?"

The boy looked entirely delighted to be referred to by a familial term.

"Oh, yes, sir. I've still got all my spells."

"Any specialties?"

"Actually, yes. I'm an animator."

That caught Ren's attention. Relatively rare, though not a surprise that he'd be a part of House Brood. They were known for recruiting talented craftsmen, and animators had the rare ability to bring objects to life with magic. Although, as with any magic, there were varying degrees of skill.

"What did we have you working on?" Theo asked. "Livestone?"

Another nod. "Yes, sir. Actually, my father was the one who created yours. The hawk?"

Theo raised an eyebrow. "You're Benjamin Crane's son?"

"Yes, sir."

"Gods. How is he?"

It was Theo's first misstep. Ren had already heard it in the boy's voice—and now she saw it in the way his chin fell and the way his shoulders hunched inward. As if he were preparing for life to deal him another blow, right then and there. "My father passed, sir. A few years ago."

The compassion that Ren felt stir to life in Theo's chest, across their bond, was its own kind of magic. He set a firm hand on his cousin's shoulder. "My apologies. Ben was a wonderful person—and his son carrying on his legacy? Gods, I can't imagine he could be any prouder. It looks like you were one of the few to avoid the plague. That's no accident, Cousin."

The effect of Theo's words was instantaneous. His cousin straightened, clapped a hand back on Theo's shoulder, and then adjusted his body so that the three of them were looking out onto the room together. Theo had won the boy to his side. Just like that.

"What would you like me to do tonight, sir?"

Theo scanned their surroundings. "Honestly? I'd like you to

make friends. Get to know everyone you can. I suspect we'll all be seeing a lot of each other in the coming weeks. It wouldn't hurt to have someone well connected. Especially with anyone here tonight who isn't linked to one of the major houses."

"On it."

It was as if he'd been shot out of a cannon. They watched him walk straight up to the nearest group and offer his hand for an introduction. Theo caught Ren's eye. "Don't."

"What?" she asked innocently. "I wasn't going to do anything."

"I can almost hear the jokes rattling around in your head."

"Jokes? Me? No, I'm not one for humor. But I do love research . . . and the second we get home I do plan to do a little digging and figure out just how many babies were named Theo after your official birth announcement. Do you think the trend began with your transcendent arrival into the world, or would it be after you cast your first spell?"

He shook his head. "Very funny."

From there, it was a quick sequence of introductions and conversations. They spoke with an older, bonded couple. There was an enhancer from House Graylantian, a structural engineer from House Proctor. At first Ren thought their direct line didn't have any survivors, but then she spotted Ellison Proctor sipping a drink on the opposite side of the room. The handsome host who'd worked with her down in the Collective for a brief time and one of their least capable wizards. Their shortest conversation was with a doctor from Safe Harbor. The woman was pale-skinned with fire-bright hair pulled into a tight bun. She wore leather gloves that Ren immediately sensed were a vessel. The girl asked several rapid-fire questions about their magic, then moved on as if she'd grown bored.

Paladins continued to circle the room, functioning as glorified waiters. Their presence started to make Viceroy Gray's absence more obvious. Her final observation was that there were quite a few children present. The boy tucked in beside Nevelyn was hardly the only one. Two attempts to count them landed Ren with a number somewhere between fifteen and twenty. Some were with their parents—who Ren noted were often *without* magic. She saw them framing the edges of the room with the telltale sign of bruises along collarbones or forearms. Interesting that a child would be immune when the parents were not. Ren was attempting another count when she saw the girl.

She wore a simple black dress. Her hair was a familiar, almost ghostly white color. Her parents had put it in a thick braid that the girl couldn't seem to stop fussing with. It was like getting a glimpse of Timmons Devine as a child. The same willowy frame. The pointed chin. Ren's eyes darted up expectantly, but the father standing behind the girl wasn't Mr. Devine. It was someone else. The girl wasn't a relative. She just looked like Timmons. Ren finally realized that she was staring at them and tore her gaze away.

"Everything okay?" Theo whispered.

"Fine," she answered. "Just missing Timmons."

He nodded, clearly confused, but wisely didn't dig deeper. It didn't take long after that for the conversations to grow stale. Everyone had half their attention on the person in front of them, and the other half darting around to check the entryways. Even the more social members of the group were starting to run out of steam. Ren was about to suggest to Theo that they ask one of the paladins how much longer they'd be waiting when magic whispered through the air. Quiet as a breeze.

Everything around them *froze*.

Glasses were still held aloft. Smiles were plastered on certain faces. It was like the tableaus that sometimes started plays. Everyone in first positions, waiting for the curtain to part. Finally, Ren saw movement. The Shiverian girl strode purposefully across the room. Marc Winters trailed her with a dramatic sigh. Gemma Graylantian pushed up from her comfortable chair. Lastly, Ellison Proctor slid through a thicket of immobile figures. One from each of the five houses.

Well, two from House Brood. She and Theo exchanged a glance. Experimentally, she lifted one hand. It moved. She was not frozen like the rest of the room. Both of them had been left out of the enchantment. On purpose. They watched as the rest of the group formed a smaller circle inside the wider gathering. The Shiverian heir was the first to speak.

"Please keep your voices quiet. Limit your overall movements. The less I have to actively hide us—the longer we can discuss matters. My name is Avid Shiverian. I am the daughter of Ethel Shiverian. I have come here tonight to apologize on behalf of our entire house. We made a grievous error trying to sever you. When the dust settles, reparations are in order. It is promised. It is promised twice. From our house to your house, the debt will be paid."

The words represented a rare double vow. Ren had never actually heard one performed in real life by an actual person. She'd only ever seen them in historical treaties. In part because they represented an uncommon admission of guilt. The Shiverians clearly wanted to bury any bad feelings—and fast. They weren't the only ones. Marc Winters spoke next.

"Key financial holdings will be reassigned to the Broods. House Winters will make this right. It is promised. It is promised twice."

Ellison Proctor echoed their words. Attention swung over to Gemma Graylantian. Her eyes were glinting as she met their stares. "All we did was supply a couple of masks. Would we really call that participation? We were more of a *vendor.* . . ."

The glare from Avid Shiverian crackled with magical power. Gemma rolled her eyes, but the quickness with which she acquiesced spoke volumes about her respect for the girl. "Oh, fine. Our apologies. Restitution will be made. Promises and all of that. Now, can we get on with the meeting?"

Avid looked to Theo. "Is it settled? Can we move on?"

Ren snorted. "Really? Just like that? You tried to sever us. If your plan had worked, it's very likely that I would have been executed in secret. Now we're just supposed to forget that it happened?"

"Given the state of the city? Yes." Avid possessed an unnatural calm for her age. As if she'd negotiated on behalf of their house a thousand times already. "We've offered reparations. All the other houses have promised restitution. You're acting like you were the first person in the history of our houses to be kidnapped. This wasn't personal. It was business."

"Right," Ren answered. "Well, as much as I'd like to know how much my life was worth to all of you—I find it far more curious that you've decided to keep this conversation private. Why not apologize publicly? If restitution means so much to you?"

"Because we have matters of state to discuss."

Avid signaled. Everyone in the room remained motionless. The spell was so complex and powerful that Ren could not even begin to extrapolate how Avid had cast it in the first place. Not to mention she was sustaining the magic while holding an intelligent conversation. She'd have to do some research to figure out the underlying magic. For now, she stood there and watched as the person who'd invited them all finally joined the fray.

Viceroy Gray entered the room.

32

REN MONROE

The city's figurehead waded through the sea of frozen figures.

Ren noted that he was wearing the same charcoal suit he'd worn during their last meeting. Some small detail was different, but she could not place it. So much had happened. That was another lifetime, it seemed. The crisp-looking suit was almost enough to hide the fact that the man wearing it was exhausted. The normally perfect hair was disheveled. His eyes were bloodshot and his shoulders slumped. It wasn't surprising. This was the man in charge of a city that had just been punched square in the jaw. Ren doubted that he'd slept since the plague's arrival.

He still had the awareness to glance around the room. She saw how quickly he assessed the resources at their disposal. "This is . . . rather sparse. Are we sure this is everyone?"

"We're missing some," Avid answered. "Like my grandmother.

Too old to travel. We didn't want to risk her getting sick just for appearances—but this is pretty close to the actual number. Our measurements suggested there would be nearly seventy people who were immune."

"Measurements?" Theo repeated. "How could you measure that?"

For a moment, Avid looked prepared to keep that house secret to herself. But the girl was wise enough to understand that now was very much the time for sharing. Trust would be earned.

"We have instruments that measure magical output. Normally, we use them for early training assessments. There are two quantities we can gauge. The first is raw magical output. How much magic does a wizard actually *pull* from the air around them when they channel through a vessel? The second is magical efficiency. It's a measure of how much of the summoned magic actually obeys the commanding wizard. We've always used the tests to help us with recruitment and training."

Ren briefly fell back in love with House Shiverian. The way they approached magic as science—something to be studied, advanced, perfected—had always been so appealing to her. Never mind the fact that they'd just kidnapped her.

"When we found out the plague disrupts magic, we widened the scope of our device," Avid explained. "The goal was to get magical readouts across the city and figure out who was still capable of using magic. Our initial motivation was selfish. We wanted to know if the loss of magic we were seeing in our house was normal, or if someone had targeted us specifically. Our elders wanted to see if any of the other houses happened to avoid the plague."

Marc Winters smirked. "You thought one of us spread it?"

"We didn't rule out the possibility," Avid replied. "But it became obvious that everyone had been impacted. Our measurements aren't perfect, but they're accurate enough to provide a baseline of information. The final estimate was that seventy wizards remained. Forty-three are in attendance tonight. It's always possible we were seeing duplicates. A wizard who cast one spell, then cast another one in a separate section of the city—but the quarantine should have limited overall movement. More likely, there are wizards out there who didn't answer the summons."

Viceroy Gray responded, but Ren was distracted by the barest sliver of movement outside their circle. She thought maybe the spell had faltered for a moment. Her eyes were drawn to Nevelyn Tin'Vori of all people. Her old accomplice was watching their group. She appeared to be frozen in time like the rest of the crowd, but as Ren stared, the girl's throat bobbed slightly.

The Tin'Voris are full of surprises.

She wasn't sure how Nevelyn was resisting the magic, but she decided not to draw attention to it. Better to keep the secret for herself and see if it might be useful later.

". . . any chance of recovery?"

"We can't say conclusively," Avid replied. "But our initial tests are not promising. We took recovered subjects to archive rooms. You know how thorough my mother is. We tested the old and the young. Prominent wizards and people who use a few paltry spells. We even had some of the patients from the original discovery site. Up in Running Hills. None of the patients could use magic. In fact, not one of them could even *see* magic in the air. The archive room was perfect dark for those who'd been impacted by the plague."

Her words were followed by a sort of stunned silence. Maybe—like Ren—they had all been hoping that someone had found some way around what the Makers were doing. An antidote or a cure. Something. Anything. This was the darkest conclusion they could have landed on.

"We have to assume," Avid continued, "that anyone who contracted the illness has permanently lost their ability to use magic. We are the last wizards left in Kathor."

Viceroy Gray swung the group to a new topic. "What's to be done about the Makers?"

Marc Winters scowled. "An interesting name for a group that doesn't seem to make anything at all. Do they even contribute to the city? All I've seen them do is stand on street corners and shout about how unfairly life has treated them."

Ren bit her tongue to keep from responding to that. Thankfully, the viceroy was quick to counter his comment. "They don't use magic, but that doesn't mean they're a group of vagrants. All of our reports on them suggest an emphasis on trade. They thrive on utility. Being useful, above all else. We're talking about dock workers, welders, farmers. And when the plague arrived, they were the first ones out in the markets. Passing out food. Caring for the sick. Look, I know we have no reason to like them, but the rest of the city does."

"Interesting," Gemma remarked. "They have a surplus of food . . . at the exact moment the rest of the city runs out of it? Almost as if they planned it that way."

Ren knew she was right. After all, she'd seen the crates of supplies stacked up in her mother's apartment. It was surprising how quickly the rest of the great houses had arrived at the correct conclusion. "Of course they planned it that way," Marc Winters added. "They're the ones who brought this plague to the city."

Gray considered that. "Do you have actual evidence to support that claim?"

"No, but isn't it obvious? Their group doesn't use magic—and then a plague comes that *destroys* magic. Not to mention their current bid for power. I'd barely heard of them before now."

"That's not evidence," Gray said. "It's guesswork, and guesswork won't sway the populace. If any of you have *actual* evidence that the Makers were involved in this, that would be crucial to our efforts. . . ."

There was an exchange of hopeful glances. Ren supposed this was a group that had long grown accustomed to keeping secrets from one another. Theo probed her across their bond, and Ren realized he was asking for permission to share their own findings. She nodded in return.

"We can confirm their involvement," Theo announced. "The Makers were the ones who spread the plague. We also have reason to believe there is a manipulation spell involved. You've all seen the red scarves they wear? There's magic woven into the fabric. A chain spell. One of the most complex and powerful pieces of spellwork that I've ever seen. House Brood has been working to trace the magic back to its original source."

His words drew interesting reactions from the group. Marc Winters pounded one fist on the nearest table. Clearly satisfied at having his guess confirmed. Avid Shiverian looked deep in thought—as if she'd been presented with a puzzle and couldn't wait to start trying to solve it. Viceroy Gray wore an almost hungry expression. As if this was exactly what he'd been waiting for.

"Evidence?" he asked. "Please tell me you have actual evidence."

Theo shook his head. "No direct evidence, but we do have a lot of testimony. We were the ones who discovered the bodies in that first water treatment facility. We know they were connected to the Makers. All of the deceased were members of the group. . . ."

"These bodies," Gray said. "Where are you keeping them?"

Theo shook his head. "We don't have them."

The viceroy's face fell into his hands. "What do you mean you don't have them? How are they evidence if you *don't* have them?"

Theo wore a look of proper Brood annoyance. "That failure is hardly our fault. We would have a lot more to work with, but right after we discovered the bodies, my bond-mate and I were kidnapped in an attempted coup. Naturally, our investigation was somewhat limited after that."

Gray winced. He glanced around at the others gathered.

"Ah. I see we've discussed the matter," he said. "For what it's worth, I told them it was a stupid idea. But such is the life of a puppet king. No one actually has to listen to what you say."

Gemma rolled her eyes. "We've been listening to you all week, Martin. I can't even take a walk in the garden without your voice thundering at me from the damn bushes."

"Apologies, Gemma. Didn't realize my emergency announcements were marring your morning strolls. If you'd like to write down a few specific times for me, I can prioritize your personal schedule over the rest of the city's safety. Would you like that?"

Instead of taking offense, a slow smile crept over the older woman's face. It was clear that the two of them had dueled like this before. Avid Shiverian interrupted.

"Can we focus? This spell isn't exactly *easy* to maintain. We have more to discuss and I'm actually starting to sweat."

There was, indeed, a single bead of sweat working its way down the girl's right temple. The viceroy dropped his playful battle with Gemma and transitioned back to the topic at hand.

"As I was saying: you'll need more to sway the population. I have the results of today's vote. Nearly ninety percent of the city participated. An unprecedented turnout. I hate to say it, but the Makers were successful. Seventy-seven percent voted for the no confidence measure to pass. All of your houses would be removed from active leadership if I ratified this measure. The results will be public knowledge in less than an hour."

Marc Winters looked annoyed. "Can't we just doctor the results?"

Ren had bitten her tongue earlier, but she could not resist giving the correct answer now. "You can't alter the results of a citywide vote. There are measures in place that keep the houses from colluding with each other. It's been that way since the Anatomy Riots."

Gray nodded. "She's right. Landwin Brood and I discussed the matter once. He was looking for a way to override the current mechanisms, but we couldn't find one. These results will be public-facing. Everyone is going to know the vote passed. The question is: What do you want me to do?"

Gemma snorted. "What do you think we want you to do,

Martin? Sign a document removing all of us from power? Of course we want you to reject the motion."

"And then what?" Gray replied. "Are all of you prepared for what will happen if I block the vote? I'm not trying to be a bastard about this. I'm genuinely asking if you're ready." He gestured around the room at the frozen figures. "Do you really think *this* is enough firepower to hold off a rebellion? Half of the immune appear to be children."

His question echoed. All the great houses had tricks up their sleeves. The people in this room were not their only strength. There were passive magic spells woven around their estates. Trained soldiers sworn to their houses that— magicless or not—could rival any force the rest of the civilians could muster. None of them would collapse overnight. They'd been built too strong for that. But now they were being forced to consider what would happen if true rebellion swept through the streets. If the entire city turned on them— would they survive the longer war? For the first time in over a century, the answer wasn't obvious. Ren was the only one brave enough to answer.

"I think you should pass the vote."

All eyes swung to her. She didn't care about the rest of them, though. The only person who deserved her attention in this circle was Theo. Their eyes met. She didn't see any embarrassment in his expression. Felt no anger across their bond. Instead, a low thrum of pride was stirring between them. The truth was that Ren had been searching for a middle ground ever since the conversation with her mother. She didn't want all-out destruction. She could not bear the thought that her actions might lead to an all-out war. This felt like the right compromise. The actual power of the houses reduced. Civil war avoided. Unsurprisingly, Theo was perfectly in step with her. He nodded once and she listened as the current heir of House Brood took up her cause.

"I agree with Ren. The people have spoken. Even with a manipulation spell . . . this vote is overwhelming. It's clear they want change. And why wouldn't they? A plague just swept through the city and we all retreated to our estates. The only reason their plan worked was because the people who were supposed to help them back on their feet did nothing."

He shook his head in disgust. Ren suspected it was not just for the people in that circle, but rather what their families represented. What he knew his father had done, and his father before him.

"The Makers want us to knock this measure down. It would be the final proof they need that the great houses don't care about the people who serve them. If we do this, it leads to rebellion. The city will go to war with us. But if we let the vote pass, what could they say? That we chose to do the right thing? I believe that we should pass the vote. Accept slightly diminished roles. All of us will still have wealth and power, but we'll also have peace. One day our descendants will talk about the war that almost happened—instead of the war that did."

His voice did not tremble. Ren felt as if they were truly one person in that moment. Body and soul and mind—in perfect concert with one another. She knew that her mother's side in this battle was not the right answer. She still planned to find the person responsible and put an end to the magic they'd woven across the city, but now she and Theo saw it wasn't a binary choice. This situation wasn't the Makers versus the great houses. No, the truth was that Kathor deserved better than both of those options—and she would fight for *that* future.

Marc Winters shook his head. "Is that really you talking, Theo? Or is that what your little pet thinks? I mean, do you even hear what the hell you're say—"

Theo swiped the air with his wand. It was a casual stroke, but the magic that punched into Marc Winters sent him sliding back several paces. His defensive wards caught the blow a split second before it could hit him. Ren saw a massive crack run down the outer layer of magic before it flickered out of existence again. Theo's voice was as quiet as an approaching storm.

"Speak ill of her again, Marc, and I will bury you."

She wasn't normally fond of bravado, but this was definitely one of Theo's more attractive moments. The two of them continued glaring until Avid Shiverian hissed for them to stop.

"I am maintaining a *temporal void*. All of you are currently standing outside the actual fabric of time and space. It would be just *lovely* if you avoided dueling in this space."

Theo lowered his wand. Marc did the same.

"No offense to your bond-mate," Gemma interrupted. "But the answer is no. My house will not be set aside. Graylantian children are still born with calluses, you know. Hardened skin along the upper palms." She held up her right hand for all of them to see. The image might have been more effective if she wasn't wearing an obscene number of golden rings. "We were farmers for so many generations that even after all this time—we come into the world physiologically prepared to hold a shovel. I will not have history remember me as the Graylantian who sent our family back to working in the fields. We earned this crown. If you want it, you'll have to take it from us."

Ellison Proctor looked too embarrassed to make eye contact with Ren.

"Our house politely declines as well," he said.

Marc Winters's opinion was already crystal clear. Avid Shiverian was the last to speak.

"I appreciate your point of view, Theo. But do you really think we'll get to sit back and enjoy our wealth? Do you think they'd allow us to keep our estates? If this vote passes, the new government will waste no time in wielding their power against us. We will be systematically torn down. Piece by precious piece. Allowing our houses to be publicly disavowed? There's no future in that. Not for our houses. Not for this city. House Shiverian votes no."

As the others spoke, Viceroy Gray's eyes had remained on Theo and Ren. There was something unreadable in his expression. "Rebellion it is," the viceroy said softly. "Very well. I can delay the announcement until tomorrow. That should give all of you time to prepare for what's coming. For now, I believe it's time that I make my official appearance at this party. Please do look suitably surprised by my arrival."

He reached up then. As if he were going to adjust something at his collar, but then his hand fell awkwardly back to his side. Ren frowned as he glided back through the surrounding tableau. All the pride that had been roaring between her and Theo just a moment ago was darkening into a shared sense of hopelessness. The great houses had chosen war. A bloody civil war that would claim thousands of innocent lives. It might set their society back by a century, but they did not care, so long as they remained kings and queens. And the hardest truth of all was that Ren and Theo had unintentionally started all of this. Her quest for revenge. Their brief lapse in the city's defenses. It was as if they'd knocked down the first block by accident, and everyone else was hell-bent on seeing the rest of the tower fall just for the pure chaos of it.

Avid released her magic.

There was a sound like a thousand fingers snapping all at once. The room unwound before filling up with sound and movement and echoing clatter. The other attendees were completely unaware that the city's fate had just been decided without them. A bright *tink-tink-tink* sounded.

Everyone looked up. Viceroy Gray was arriving. For the second time.

Ren watched him cross the threshold and it took that repetition—like an echo in her own memory—to recall the detail that had eluded her before. His reach, at the end of their private meeting, had been the only real clue to what was missing. Ren seized Theo's arm. Her grip was so tight that the nails almost dug into his skin.

"Scarf," Ren hissed. *"Theo, he was wearing a scarf."*

At the time, she'd thought of it as a crimson color. The red of a faded garnet or dried blood. That was before she'd seen the Makers walking around the city wearing them. Always tied in knots around their necks or forearms. Sometimes tucked into belt loops. She knew beyond any shadow of a doubt that his was a match for theirs. He must have removed it to avoid suspicion. Ren's fingers curled around the grip of her horseshoe wand. The viceroy was preparing to make his speech.

The room fell quiet.

"He's one of them," she whispered.

33

MERCY WHITAKER

The viceroy waited for silence to claim the room. Everyone turned to watch except for the paladins, who continued filling drinks or removing plates of half-eaten food. She hadn't realized how many of them were on duty tonight until that moment, with the rest of the crowd drawn to stillness.

"Welcome! Thank you for answering my summons."

His voice filled the room. Mercy knew that most of them had been listening to that voice for days now, wherever they went in the city. It hadn't been audible down in the morgue, but every time she'd stepped out to get some fresh air, she'd heard the announcements. Mercy had seen him in person only once before. At her graduation from Balmerick, he'd given the commencement speech. He looked nearly the same as he had then. Perhaps more tired.

"I know this is no small request. Many of you have families who need you. . . ."

One of the paladins glided into her peripheral. She held out her glass absently, without looking. Her hand instinctually braced for the impact of more liquid being poured into what she was holding—that subtle increase in weight. Which was why it was surprising when nothing happened. The waiter didn't pour anything. Nor did he mutter an apology for being out of water.

Instead, he glided past without a word.

". . . houses and holdings that require your attention . . ."

The moment was just odd enough to draw her attention. Mercy glanced back over her shoulder at the exact same time that the paladin glanced over his. He was already ten paces in the distance, aiming for the nearly hidden kitchen doors, but in that brief, shared glance—she saw him. The light brown skin. The soft-set eyes. An open face that had welcomed her with a wide smile the first time she'd seen it. Her brain fractured slightly at the sight of him in the uniform of a paladin. But in less than a breath, she knew *exactly* where he'd gotten that uniform.

It was Devlin's.

"Nance!"

The word came out as something more guttural. Less a name and more of a curse. Behind her, there were shouts and gasps. Mercy thought she heard someone casting magic, but she didn't let that distract her. All that mattered was not letting Nance Forester make it to the kitchen entrance.

Her first stun spell struck him in the side, staggering him to a knee. He caught the second spell with a raised forearm. It was similar to what Holt had done down in the water treatment facility. As if his body was a shield against the magic she was casting. She flung a third and a fourth. He somehow resisted both, all while backpedaling to the exit. His eyes were unnaturally dark as he stared back at Mercy. "Stop him!" she shouted. "Please, someone stop him!"

Mercy cast one final spell—and saw his body *shiver* just before it released from her fingertips. An unnatural ripple of movement. His dark eyes lightened to an almost green. There was a flicker of surprise in his expression, and then her stun spell slammed into him with enough force to crush his rib cage. He launched through the air and crashed down on a cloth-covered table. The feeling of victory was short-lived. There were other spells whistling overhead. Swords were being drawn as paladins flooded the room from all sides. Far more than she'd seen swirling around the room as servers. As if they'd all been waiting for exactly this moment.

The room plunged into chaos.

34

NEVELYN TIN'VORI

It all happened in a breathless instant.

The viceroy arrived. The crowd went quiet. Before he'd spoken more than a few words, two people had moved simultaneously. It was like watching the steps of some strange dance. Ren Monroe had glided forward with her horseshoe wand raised. The annoying girl with the bright red hair had moved the opposite way. Both of them had taken aim. Both of them had released spells at the exact same moment. Their castings were the only warnings of violence.

Nevelyn and Dahvid reacted better than most of the room. One of the few silver linings of growing up as a hunted creature. Her brother summoned his sword. Nevelyn seized Josey by the collar and nearly dragged him off his feet. They cleared the melee just as someone launched right past where the boy had been standing. Ahead, two paladins were plunging their swords into the back of a man with long, dark hair. Nevelyn tried to shield Josey from that sight, but there were violences unfolding around the entire room.

The first paladin to come for them was dissected by her brother with brutal efficiency. She'd always known he was gifted, but gods did he make killing look like art. Two flowing swipes and then he was past the falling man, engaging with the next opponent. The only problem was that enemy soldiers were everywhere. She dragged Josey clear of Dahvid's skirmish and ran right into a new set of paladins. Four of them. They fanned out with weapons drawn. Nevelyn saw that between her and the soldiers were three of the other children. All frozen in terror. All about to die.

Dahvid is not the only one with magic.

Nevelyn pushed Josey to safety and reached for the pendant. A quick turn—from dark to light—and her beholding magic roared to life. She cast the spell at all four of her opponents. It was far more of the magic than she'd ever attempted. Normally, she focused on a single target. She thought this version might result in a weaker spell—but the soldiers went rigid at the exact same time. Their eyes swung to her. All of them wore a blank expression. She could hear Josey screaming for his friends to move! Get out of the way! Nevelyn couldn't let that distract her. All her focus was on maintaining her grip on the magic. She gave her first command.

"Down on your knees."

All four soldiers knelt before her. She was about to tell them to take their own weapons and slit their throats with them— but she felt the magic slip. It was like trying to hold on to a fish fresh out of the water. One of the men, on the far right, was straining. Attempting to stand.

"Dahvid!"

She did not dare take her eyes from her targets. A moment later, Dahvid glided around her. His eyes shocked wide at the sight of the four soldiers. He didn't ask questions or second-guess what was happening. Instead, he quickly executed all of them.

The children were crying. Even Josey. Nevelyn urged them into the nearest corner, one of the only safe spaces left in the room, before spinning with Dahvid to assess the rest of the battle. It was clearly not going well. Ren, Theo, and the girl from House Shiverian were locked in a duel with Viceroy Gray. Nevelyn knew enough about Ren to know that she was a *very* gifted spellcaster. The girl had gone toe to toe with Landwin Brood. Add Theo and a prodigy from one of the great houses, and Nevelyn knew they made quite a formidable trio.

And yet . . . the viceroy was pushing *them* back. Unnatural power rippled out from his wand. Great strikes that hit their protective wards with enough force to reverberate through the entire room. Elsewhere, the paladins were gaining ground. Always fighting with numbers in their favor. If this had been outside, in the open, the wizards would have had a clear advantage. More than enough space for their spellwork to dominate. But in this tighter space, the paladins were quietly beginning to dispatch some of the wizards.

Her first instinct was to run. There was still time for them to save themselves. But the viceroy unleashed a spell powerful enough to knock Ren Monroe off her feet. She watched her old accomplice roll over, gritting her teeth, and unleash her own spell in return. Nevelyn knew this was not a fight they could walk away from. It would follow them wherever they went.

"Dahvid! Help them! I'll take care of Josey."

Her brother shot forward without hesitation, sliding around other fights with all the focus of a revenant who'd come back to life for this singular purpose. Nevelyn needed to believe that he would survive even if she turned her back and stopped watching.

"You will live. You will live. You will live."

And then Nevelyn was moving the other way. She turned her necklace back to the darker side as she reached Josey. There were five children huddled just outside the chaos. They were all calling to a sixth who'd hidden beneath one of the tables and had tears streaming down her face. She looked too shocked to move and no wonder, there were bodies on the floor between them. Blood slowly leaking to where she was crouched. Nevelyn hissed for all of them to shut up.

"Josey, hold tight to the back of my dress. I need you all to link up. We are about to leave this place together—and you need to stay with me. Do you understand? *Do not let go.*"

The five of them fearfully obeyed her. Nevelyn took a deep breath, and then she cast the most powerful version of her other magic that she could. It was the first time she was demanding that the magic she'd used since childhood hide someone else besides herself. And it worked. Nevelyn felt the invisible shield stretch until it covered all of them. Confident the spell would hold, she started walking forward. Josey and the children held tight and it was a lot like towing a heavy bag through a body of water. An extra gravitational pull that she'd never had to account for before now. The door was close. They could escape without being harmed. But Nevelyn aimed them toward the panicked girl beneath the table first. The poor thing was shaking violently. Nevelyn realized that they'd all just disappeared from sight. She probably thought they'd ported away.

It wasn't until Nevelyn grabbed the girl's hand that she *saw* her. Almost as if she were parting a curtain in the magic and saying, *Look here. You are allowed to witness me.* It was enough to break the girl from her trance. Magic exploded overhead. More glass shattering. But now that they had the last girl, they were navigating away from the thicker madness. Toward the back hallway. Nevelyn guided them around bodies. Away from pooling blood. Once a survivor of tragedy, she knew the images of this room would haunt these children forever.

But first they had to survive.

First they had to live.

Nevelyn poured as much strength as she could into the magic. It was starting to tug on her limbs. Weigh on her shoulders. Almost enough to make her faint, but she gritted her teeth and pushed on. If Dahvid could be strong, so could she. Once her head stopped spinning, she guided them out of the nightmare. Into the waiting night. One by one, the children followed her.

35

REN MONROE

Unnatural.

That was the only word for what they were facing. Ren's very first spell had hit the viceroy square in the chest. It was, as far as she could tell, the only spell that had done true damage to him. As if he'd simply not been expecting it, and thus it had struck past whatever impossible defenses were currently making him invulnerable to their attacks. She had unleashed dozens of spells. Theo and Avid were casting a steady stream alongside her. The viceroy's defenses should have been overwhelmed in less than thirty seconds.

Instead, nothing touched him. Spells rebounded, blasting nearby tables into shrapnel. Some appeared to simply *vanish* into him. As he fought, his eyes were dark and glinting and focused. She knew he'd been an accomplished student at Balmerick—but this was beyond anything she'd ever witnessed. It was one thing to resist so many attacks. Quite another to be able to unleash such powerful spells of his own at the same time. It was Landwin Brood's advice to Theo. Keep a man backpedaling, and he wouldn't be able to hit you at full strength. That was true of magic. Barrages like the one the viceroy was facing destroyed a person's ability to counter. One was too busy shielding themselves to perform their own attack.

And yet he was doing exactly that. Fighting with reflexes that not even Able Ockley could have rivaled. Ren was starting to lose hope when she saw Dahvid Tin'Vori join their fight. He swiped one of his tattoos and she watched as *two* versions of him began walking forward into the battle. Spreading out slightly in their approach. The viceroy saw his new opponents a split second too late. He had to choose between them, and he did, blasting the one on the right with a powerful burst of magic. But that left him vulnerable to the other one.

The real one.

Dahvid lunged with his sword. It caught the edges of a summoned ward, but he gritted his teeth and shoved the blade in with all his strength. Just enough to break through. The barrier shattered and the blade slipped into the viceroy's side like a whisper. Not a killing blow, but more than enough to stagger him.

Gray's eyes widened. He seemed to realize he could not beat all of them. Not all at once. Dahvid swung again, but the viceroy blinded the room with a final spell. A concentrated light cantrip like the one that Ren liked to use. She blinked a few times, and then saw him sprinting. Straight for the western entry. Ren knew it led to the glass bridge, and that the bridge led to other parts of the estate. There would be escape tunnels.

Places he could go that they could not follow. Ren didn't hesitate. She sprinted after him.

Theo was a step behind her, their bond pulsing with hunger and fear and adrenaline. Dahvid and Avid joined their pursuit. Paladins maneuvered between them, though, forming a sort of human wall. Ren was forced into close-quarter combat. By the time she'd blasted her way through, the viceroy had a good thirty-second head start.

We can't let him get away.

The hunt began.

36

MERCY WHITAKER

A round the room, the tides began to turn.

Some of the paladins fled with the viceroy, but most were abandoned in impossible positions. The remaining wizards surrounded them, advancing in small packs, until every enemy soldier in the room was subdued. Gemma Graylantian shouted to keep the soldiers alive—and Mercy suspected it was not for the sake of kindness. More likely she wanted to interrogate them.

Mercy fell to triage as soon as the fighting stopped. Cleaning out wounds. Binding the larger cuts. Staunching blood flow. There were a few broken bones that would require more attention—and one younger boy who'd knocked his shoulder out of the socket in an effort to dodge one paladin's attack. It was all comfortable work. The sort of triage she'd performed during her residency. That feeling faded, though, as she began to assess the mortally wounded.

Several wizards were dead. One was Marc Winters—the current heir of their house. Her eyes searched and searched, but thankfully none of the children had died. A short-lived relief as Mercy stumbled across the man and woman she'd spoken to earlier. Bond-mates. The woman had survived, but her husband had not. Mercy could not bear to hear the sounds coming from the surviving wife. She could not watch that sort of heartbreak. Not again.

"Move. Back away. He might not be gone yet . . . let me tend to him!"

The room was still mostly chaos. Others were helping the wounded. The wife moved, but kept muttering. "Dead. Oh gods! He's dead!"

"Someone! Help her! Give me some space to work over here!"

She had the commanding voice of a triage doctor. A few people hustled over, doing their best to pull the woman away. Using their bodies to shield her from the sight of something so terrible that she'd remember it for the rest of her life. Mercy carefully assessed each wound. Took the man's pulse. It wasn't there, but that wasn't the end. It didn't have to be the end.

Quietly, she began casting her magic. Bright flashes that removed infections or sealed some of the internal wounds. Mercy glanced back over one shoulder at the wife. She was screaming at the people who'd dared to get in her way. Everyone was distracted. Mercy hesitated briefly, and then cast the only desperate spell left in her arsenal. She set one hand over his unbeating heart and magic pulsed out from her. Mercy braced herself as the man's entire body began convulsing.

She felt a sharpness in her right foot. A pain so intense and sudden that she bit down on the tip of her tongue. The husband came gasping back. It had worked. The bereft woman sagged to her knees. The two helpers turned to stare as the man rolled over, hacking up blood and mucus and worse. His chest heaved. His eyes rolled wildly around the room. He looked pale as a ghost, but he was here. He was alive. Mercy winced at her own pain before barking out orders again.

"Get him water! Keep an eye on him, please. He lost a *lot* of blood. He's damn lucky to be alive." The poor woman crawled across the floor to her bond-mate. They collapsed into each other. Both of them were weeping, but Mercy didn't have time to watch their reunion. There was too much to do. She made second rounds. A necessary part of any triage effort. Magic had a nasty habit of unwinding itself. Refreshing spells was just as important as the initial castings. Mercy worked her way down the lines, checking and rechecking her work, until the remaining survivors had all gathered around the area. Mercy realized that when the viceroy had fled, several wizards had pursued him. Glancing around, she suspected they were the very wizards who might have taken charge if they were here.

The logistics of what to do next fell to her, a woman named Gemma Graylantian, and a pioneer that Mercy had met earlier. A man called Hurst. Their first task was a body count.

Seven wizards were dead. Over thirty paladins had been killed. That left thirty-one survivors trying to rally themselves, and the first question was where they should go. It didn't take long to arrive at Balmerick as the safest option. The rest of the populace—magicless as they were—could not access the Heights at all. It would be safe and Balmerick's campus was certainly large enough to host a group as large as theirs.

The next question was how the hell to actually get there.

Not everyone had spare way candles. More importantly, there were two groups that could not travel with them. First, the magicless parents of some of the children in the room. A quick discussion took place. Most agreed to send their children ahead to safety. Anywhere but down here where they might be targeted by yet another attack. One mother declined. Mercy could only watch as she put an arm around her little boy and quietly guided him back out into the night.

Be safe. Please be safe.

The second group that could not travel with them—but also couldn't be left behind—were the prisoners. Almost every one of them was magicless, and thus could not be ferried up to the Heights. Mercy saw that one of them was Nance Forester. He wasn't offering her any dark glares or gloating smiles. No, he was huddled and bound with the rest of them, looking like a lost sheep. When no one else offered any alternatives, Mercy volunteered.

"We can take them to Safe Harbor. There are warded rooms there. Designed for when we have to provide medical care to criminals." *Or when you want to falsely imprison one of your own doctors,* she thought, remembering her own stay in one of those rooms. "I'll need a small escort group if . . ."

She trailed off. There was a low buzzing noise. Everyone in the room heard it and all of them went quiet at the same time. Near the front of the room, one of the windows had been broken by a stray blast of magic. Mercy moved toward that spot until the noise resolved into a voice. Words were booming out in the street.

It was Viceroy Gray.

Speaking to all of Kathor.

37

NEVELYN TIN'VORI

When they reached the front door of the Tin'Vori estate, Nevelyn released her magic. All that departing energy dropped her to a knee. She took three heaving breaths before hissing for Josey to knock at the door. *I swear, if Ava left for some reason . . . .*

The door swung open. Ava eyed the pack of children.

"Right. I was thinking we needed more of them."

"Get them inside," Nevelyn gasped. "Now."

She was pushing back to her feet when someone shouted at her. Nevelyn spun, prepared to defend against an attack, before realizing it was the viceroy's voice. The same citywide spell they'd used before. His voice echoed up and down the street.

"Kathorians, this is Viceroy Gray. I have important news for you. The vote of no confidence has passed. Seventy-seven percent of you voted to remove the current governors. I have chosen to honor the will of the people and I have officially signed that measure into law. That means the following governors will no longer rule their designated districts. . . ."

One by one, he listed off recognizable names from the great houses. Every single one of them had just been divested of power. Nevelyn also heard the breathlessness in his voice. His words rasping slightly. As if he'd been running? Had he escaped? All she really wanted to know was whether or not Dahvid was safe.

". . . new leaders will be elected in the coming weeks. But I also come to you tonight with dire news. I do not know if I'll even be able to get this entire message to you. The Kathorian government has been investigating the origins of the plague that swept through our city. We have recently discovered that this disease was no accident. The conspiracy we discovered to allow its spread around Kathor implicated *all* of the great houses."

Nevelyn's breath caught. She knew his words weren't true, but that didn't make the claim any less shocking. First, he'd stripped the great houses of power—and now he was publicly accusing them of treachery. Looking up and down their street, she saw windows open to the night. People were leaning out to listen to his message. It wouldn't take long for this lie to sweep through the whole city. How could they even hope to counter it?

"It wasn't enough to have a monopoly on our magical resources—they wanted a monopoly on *who* was magical. We first learned that the disease removes a person's ability to cast spells. We have confirmed that this is a *permanent* condition. . . ."

There was a great bang in the background of his speech. Followed by a low rumble. When the viceroy's voice returned, he was speaking even faster. His words nearly blurring.

"Anyone with the plague has been cut off from their magic. We now know why. The great houses all chose candidates that would be immune to the disease they were allowing to spread. The plot was designed to force the rest of the city to be even more reliant on magic, and the houses—as always—would be best positioned to reap the benefits. . . ."

More background noises. There were other voices that sounded less distinct than his. She thought she heard the words "now" or "go" in the muddled backdrop.

"When I met with the so-called immune at Beacon House, they attacked me. I escaped but I am on the run. They're coming for me. As your viceroy, I am officially granting emergency . . ." There was wrestling. The sounds of a struggle. And then his voice knifed back in one final time. "Emergency powers to the Makers! They can help us! Our city . . . it's no longer safe! The immune are coming . . . taking over. Oh, gods, someone send—"

His voice cut off sharply. The silence that followed felt like a living, breathing thing. Nevelyn couldn't believe what she'd just heard. It was a damn master stroke. In a single speech, he'd connected all the remaining wizards to the great houses *and* swung blame for the plague to them. As if they'd all somehow planned on being immune to the blight. As if any of them had any choice in what was happening. They would all be targets now. Feared at best and hated at worst.

Ava still stood in the open doorway. The children were huddled in the hall beyond. Her sister was clearly confused about what had happened, about the message she'd just heard, and most of all about Dahvid's absence. Nevelyn's only relief was in knowing that Dahvid was likely safe. If the viceroy had been so desperate to get off one final message, it meant they'd cornered and captured him. But as she looked up their street at all the people still leaning out of their windows, whispering to one another, she couldn't help wondering if the worst was yet to come.

Nevelyn stumbled inside.

"Shut the door."

She was safe. They were safe. For now.

38

REN MONROE

The back wing of the Safe Harbor hospital was quiet, dream-like.

Ren paced the interior of a small office. There was a sturdy desk covered in stray medical notes. Two empty cups of long-forgotten tea. A map hung on the wall, and there were strange, glowing embers marking two separate locations. She eyed those curiously, but could not figure out the significance of either location. Theo was with her. He'd found the room's most comfortable chair and had somehow fallen asleep. Avid Shiverian and Gemma Graylantian were also in the room. Gemma appeared to be meditating. Avid, on the other hand, was perusing a tome entitled *Mathematics and Magic: A Doctor's Guide to Angular Equations*. Normally, that would have drawn Ren like a moth to a flame—but she wasn't in the mood to learn anything new. Not today.

Gods, they've ruined reading for me.

Mercy Whitaker appeared in the doorway. She was framed by Dahvid Tin'Vori and Theodore Crane. Perhaps the most mismatched pair of guards Ren had ever seen. Dahvid was handsome and broad-shouldered. Theo's cousin, on the other hand, looked so thin that if he turned the wrong way he might vanish altogether. Avid Shiverian slammed her tome shut with a loud thud. The noise woke Theo, who shot to his feet, still half in a dream.

"All the rooms are sealed," Mercy announced. "There's no one left at Safe Harbor who can override my access, so unless I'm the one opening the door—no one's opening the door."

Ren nodded. "Good. And everyone is okay with me taking the lead on this?"

Nods all around. There had been a brief discussion earlier. She suspected that Marc Winters would have objected, tried to pull rank on her—but Winters was dead. The others felt comfortable enough to let her take the lead. After all, Ren was the one who'd figured everything out.

The group filed out of the office. The viceroy's holding room was down to the left where the hallway dead-ended. A vertical strip of glass offered a partial glimpse into the now-empty room. Inside, a man sat in a chair, bound and hooded. Ren mentally steeled herself before gesturing to the door. Mercy cast the countercharm to let them inside.

Entering, she heard a low murmur. As if Viceroy Gray were mumbling inside his hood. Speaking to himself. The noise ceased at the sound of their footsteps on the unpolished floors. Ren waited for everyone to take up their positions before removing the hood. The entire right side of the viceroy's face looked like a nightmare. Heavy bruising. Dried blood covering that cheek. He quietly studied his surroundings. Eventually, his gaze landed on her. There was still confidence in his expression. Like he knew something they didn't.

"Viceroy Gray."

"Ren Monroe. Figured it out, did you? I saw you cast that first spell before any of my paladins even pulled a blade. What gave me away?"

"Your scarf. You reached for it even though it wasn't there."

She saw his eyes light up as he pieced the answer together. "I was still wearing it during that first meeting. Of course. When the plague arrived, I put it in a back pocket. Didn't want to risk being associated with the Makers before they took over the city. Clumsy of me."

Ren decided to go back to the beginning. "During that meeting, you tried to delay us. When we brought up those buildings, you were buying more time for your teams to place the bodies in the water supply. It was clever of you. Playing on our sympathies like that."

The viceroy smiled. "Good luck proving that at a trial."

"This is the trial," Avid muttered darkly.

Ren ignored the other girl. Her mind was still carefully tracing back through all the interactions she'd had with the viceroy. There was the first meeting with Theo, but also the private meeting between the houses. Two separate times he'd asked for evidence. Once to Marc Winters and again to Theo. At the time, it had sounded like he was hunting for something concrete to use against the Makers. Now she realized he'd wanted confirmation that they had no way to counter the story he planned to tell the rest of the city. She hated feeling this outmaneuvered.

"So, let's walk through your plan. Step one: create and spread a plague that destroys magic. As that happened, the Makers were uniquely positioned to help, because you've spent the last few years storing up massive amounts of dried goods. You started giving away food to build sympathy with the rest of the population. Before long, you looked like the charitable saviors—all while the houses further isolated themselves."

The viceroy shrugged. "Quite an imagination you have."

"And you knew there would be some people who were immune, because you tested the disease on your own members. The outlying villages as well. A small fraction never got sick. Like you." When he said nothing, Ren went on. "So, the next phase was to gather us in one place. It was a clever pretense: the city needs us. We're the only ones who can save them. It was believable. Desperate without being pushy. And when all of us arrived . . . the plan was what? Just start killing us?"

"Pacify," he replied softly. "That was the order. We did not go there intending to kill anyone. Their orders were to *pacify*. If all of you had agreed to surrender, put down your vessels, then we would have simply made arrests. It didn't need to go the way that it went at Beacon House."

"Right. I'm sure nothing bad would have happened if we gave up our weapons and came peacefully. There were children in that room. Children who have magic."

"Children grow into adults. Adults who will possess magic that the rest of the city cannot access. Are you really going to pretend you haven't thought about any of this? A future in which all of you become gods? That's what will happen if we do not eliminate magic. One day, the people who still possess it will be worshipped as deities. Our great work cannot be accomplished that way."

Ren felt a shiver run down her spine. *Our great work.* Her mother had used those words during their last conversation, and now she'd discovered their source.

"But *you* have magic?" Ren pointed out. "How does that work? Let me guess. You told your followers that you are the exception to the rule. You get to have what you've asked them to set aside. It always goes that way. Power for the few. Nothing but empty promises for the rest."

She felt the others shift around her. Avid adjusting the fold of her arms. Theo switching his weight to the opposite foot. She'd briefly forgotten that she was in a room where those words were true of her allies—not just their current enemy. The viceroy shook his head in response.

"No. I told them that I will use my gift to destroy as many of you as possible—and then I should be killed too. That's the difference between me and you. I've made peace with my death. I know my purpose in this world."

Finally, the zealot was coming out. He must have hidden it so well over the years. Every time she'd ever seen him, he'd come off as polished and professional. A man in complete control of himself. Now she saw he was just a good actor. This was not the kind of person that could be reasoned with. Ren had been hoping for that. A liar, at least, could be bought with enough money. Convinced to go a different way in order to save his own neck. Zealots, on the other hand, would see their work through to the very end—no matter the cost.

"Can I tell you the future?" Gray's voice echoed around the small room. "I have seen it with my own eyes. The people will fear history repeating. What happens when a few power-ful people take control of Kathor again? Wouldn't it be better to just . . . stop them before that happens? One by one, the remaining wizards will vanish. Murders. Exile. In less than twenty years, there will not be a single wizard left in this city. You might think you've won. You might believe that you have power over me—but this future is already written. And I'm the one holding the pen."

Ren offered him a dramatic yawn. "Gods. Sorry. That was just so long-winded. Anyways. You're not wrong. There are people like my mother who want rebellion," she admitted. "She truly believes this world would be better without the great houses. But you know, my mother would never hurt a child to accomplish that. Never. That's where your manipulation spell comes into play, right?"

His eyes narrowed. It was the look of a child who'd been caught doing something they weren't supposed to be doing. Ren held up the scarf they'd removed from his back pocket.

"There's a chain spell woven into the fabric of each one. Manipulation magic that spreads from person to person. It might be the most impressive spell I've ever seen. Complex, powerful. It's the perfect design for people like my mother, too. The magic doesn't activate until they've reached the natural end point of their own desires. Give up magic? Sure. Gather some extra food in the pantry? Of course. Allow your house to be a temporary base? Why not? But there comes a point where what you're asking them to do is too much. The commands start to edge right up against their moral code. It's one thing to ask someone to store extra rations—and quite another thing to spread a plague that will kill thousands."

Ren allowed those words to sit in the air between them.

"That's when the manipulation spell *activates*. Right when they would hesitate, a voice whispers to go just a little further. Dig deeper. The manipulation is powerful enough to take a person like my mother from rebel to zealot. But surely, someone who can create a spell that powerful . . . surely, you see the problem with using a chain spell?"

It was Ren's turn to smile at him.

"We made chain spells illegal because they're so easy to alter. In fact, studies show that the longer and more widespread a chain spell is—the more vulnerable it is to alteration. Now, there are two specific things that you need in order to make an alteration like that. The first is a very gifted manipulator."

Behind her, the others shifted. Clearing a path for Gemma Graylantian. The older woman dragged a chair from the corner to where the viceroy sat. Ren had been surprised that Gemma hadn't chimed in yet. She supposed the woman had been focused on her part in their play. After all, they were not asking her to perform some trifling magic. This reverse manipulation would be terribly nuanced. Difficult enough that few people in the world could do it. Gemma set her chair directly across from the viceroy and took a seat. Ren could feel the subtle waves of magic washing outward from the heiress. Needling carefully at the viceroy's natural mental defenses.

"You also need the originator of the spell." Ren nodded at him. "That's normally the hard part, but here you are. Most manipulators require a single shared moment to make the kind of alteration we're attempting. Maybe an encounter at a tea shop. A quick conversation on a street corner. Truly gifted manipulators—like Gemma here—can make a mental change with a single shared glance. But I'm sure you know that the process is easier when you have an extended period of time with the person. For example, if they were a guest at your home . . . or even a prisoner in a locked room."

A muscle in the viceroy's jaw twitched. Gemma's magic had already latched onto him. Weaving in and out of his senses. Clouding his judgment. Ren saw the woman testing out her magical hold over him. She lifted her chin. In answer, the viceroy lifted his. She looked right. He looked right. A perfect mirror of her suggestions.

"Can I tell you the future?" Ren asked, echoing his earlier words. "I've seen it with my own eyes. We break through your manipulation spell. People all over this city wake up tomorrow morning to find that the voice that's been whispering urgently inside their mind . . . is gone. A few of them will continue on with the revolution. They won't know what else to do with their time. They're already in too deep. But most of them will feel what we call 'waker's remorse.' It's a common term for the post-manipulated. When the magic fades, a person's natural impulses come roaring back—and they almost always move in the opposite direction. Away from what was controlling them. That's why most manipulators are so intentional about being subtle in their work. They know that if they take even one misstep, it could ruin everything."

Gemma performed another test. She rolled her shoulders and he rolled his in response. She raised her eyebrows. He mirrored her. In just thirty seconds, he'd been reduced to a puppet.

"We're ready," the woman announced.

Before Ren could signal to begin, the viceroy began to laugh. A loud and jolting noise. The kind of sound that crawled down a spine and sat right in the gut, twisting a person's stomach into knots. Gemma was trying to regain control, to manipulate him back into silence, but he just threw back his head and laughed even louder. When his head snapped back, his eyes were unnaturally wide. Far darker than the color they'd been before. Ren knew that someone else was looking out at them *through* the viceroy's eyes.

No, no, no, no . . .

"Little Ren Monroe. You have made a grave error," he said. "Did you really think he was capable of *all of this*? Here. Let me show you just how important Martin Gray is to my plans."

The viceroy's eyes lightened. From that unnatural darkness to a molten brown color. Ren saw the briefest moment of terror in his expression—and then his skin started to *smoke*. He let out a terrifying scream, his eyes pinched shut against the intensity of some unseen pain. All they could do was sit there and watch as Viceroy Gray began to burn from the inside out.

Mercifully, Avid cast a spell that muted his screams. Ren ripped her gaze away when his eyelids started melting. Theo drew close to her, trying to whisper comfort, but the casual violence of this moment had cut through all her normal calm. Worse, their only real solution for saving the city had just slipped through their fingers. It was clear now. Gray was not the originator of the spell. She'd been so confident it was him. Especially after witnessing the magic he'd performed at Beacon House. But no, someone else was out there, manipulating hundreds of people. A person who continued to demonstrate that they were more powerful and clever than any of them.

Ren's mind was racing.

Who the hell could do all of this?

PART FOUR

Breathing

39

MERCY WHITAKER

Everyone had different ways of coping.

Mercy needed to keep her hands moving. It felt like her duty to conduct research on the four remaining captives. One by one, she had them escorted into the surgical theater where she'd last worked with Dr. Horn. After securing them to the table, she'd summon the same spells that he had then. Revelation charms tangled with spectral heightening cantrips. Layer after precious layer until the dark room was full of light. She would look up then and see the familiar, magic-brightened threads that connected each subject to everyone they'd ever met.

None of the guards had an *origination* thread. It would have been obvious. Like the thread that exists between the bonded. All the texts described it as a deep silver color. Bulkier than most threads as it extended out of the patient's forehead before diverting in myriad directions. She did notice that each of their captives had a darker thread—like the color of shifting smoke—attached near the back of their skulls. Signs they were actively being manipulated.

Limping across the room, she would attempt to use her scalpel on each of these threads. But every time, the diamond-hard threads began to dull the edge of her blade. This was common with manipulation threads. They were like steel near the subject and like butter near their source. Impossible to sever unless you had the originator of the spell.

Exhausted, Mercy returned the final captive to one of the warded rooms. When she'd brought out Nance Forester to be tested, he'd said nothing to her. Made no apology. Offered no taunting smiles. He seemed almost lifeless compared to the bright creature she'd met in Running Hills. After what they'd just witnessed with Viceroy Gray, Mercy's desire to gloat had vanished too. There was no glory in capturing a man who was apparently already being held captive. After all, how much of what had occurred in Running Hills was Nance's fault? How much of it was the voice in his head? It was growing more and more difficult to parse out who was responsible for what evils.

She returned to Horn's office, still slightly limping. One of the toes on her right foot felt broken. Mercy hadn't had the chance to inspect it yet. Nearly everyone had dozed off except for Ren Monroe. The girl had not stopped to sleep or rest. Her interrogation of the viceroy had been impressive, even if it had not gone as planned. Now she stood in front of Mercy's map. The glowing embers had not moved in some time. Mercy hoped she'd have a letter from the houndmaster before long.

"Any luck?" Ren asked as Mercy came to stand beside her.

"All of them show signs of manipulation, not origination."

The girl nodded. "As we suspected. Gemma said you know one of them. That I wasn't the only one who cast a spell before the paladins attacked. How did you know something was wrong?"

"Nance Forester," Mercy explained. "He's the one who pretended to be our host up in Running Hills, but he was really there to oversee their first test run of the disease. One of his men killed the paladin who was escorting me." She shut her eyes briefly, remembering the way she'd wrapped one arm around Devlin's neck, and how she'd arrived empty-handed back at Safe Harbor. A mistake of moments. "When Nance arrived, I thought he was there to help me get home. . . ."

Mercy thought back to that conversation. It had been such a strange moment that she'd never properly extrapolated the clues. The reveal that Nance was not friendly had clouded her memory of that moment. Thinking back, she saw it more clearly. Nance had modulated his voice. His eyes had shifted, too, as he descended the stairwell. Now that she'd witnessed the viceroy's transformation, she felt confident she'd seen the same in Nance. A darkening of his eyes. An alteration in vocal structure. She should have seen this all before.

"He occupies them."

Ren glanced over sharply. "Who?"

"Whoever is doing this. He's not just manipulating them at a distance. It's like . . . sometimes he steps forward. Occupies one of them at a time. Think about it as this massive web of information. You've manipulated one person, who manipulates another, and another. Essentially, you've built this network of people around the city. As we spoke to the viceroy, he must have been listening somehow—and he decided to make an appearance. He stepped in the room with us. You saw it, right? At the end?"

Ren nodded. "We all saw it. His eyes. His voice."

Mercy's mind was forced back into the dark spaces of that memory.

"It happened at the party, too. Nance . . . he resisted my first three or four spells. It was like the magic couldn't even touch him. But when I cast my final spell, I saw whoever was inside of him leave. Nance felt it too. He had this . . . shock on his face. Like he knew he'd been abandoned, and that was the first time my magic actually hit him. The departure left him defenseless."

Ren appeared to be piecing it all together now. "He left your opponent to occupy mine. I've been trying to figure that part out. My first spell hit the viceroy, but by the time I'd lined up a second, he was basically invulnerable. Nothing we cast seemed to touch him. Normally, dueling works in the opposite direction. The first 'surprise' spell is absorbed by a defensive ward—and then as you break down those wards, they become exposed. I think he was vulnerable at the beginning because the originator of the spell was *elsewhere*. Occupying your opponent."

Mercy nodded. "Which means he shifted to protect the viceroy, because he's more important. But what we're talking about . . . shouldn't be possible."

"I've never heard of anything like it," Ren admitted. "We're no longer talking about manipulation. This is beyond that. Someone powerful enough to occupy another living soul. It's the mind control of hundreds of subjects, spanning across an entire city. There isn't a wizard alive who should be able to perform magic like that."

Belatedly, Mercy realized that Avid Shiverian was listening to them. She found the young heir to be quiet, intelligent, and slightly terrifying. "What if it's something unnatural?" Avid offered. "Like a revenant?"

Ren Monroe shivered. "I've fought one before."

Mercy's eyes widened. She remembered a few details from their survival story out in the woods. She'd primarily been focused on Cora Marrin's death, given how it impacted her own entry into Safe Harbor's medical program. The papers had covered everything. Some stories had claimed that Ren and Theo were pursued by a revenant, but Mercy had never known if that was true.

"The creature we faced had access to unique magic," Ren admitted. "It could absorb the abilities of anyone it killed. It also drew strength from our nightmares. But revenants are usually hyper-specific creatures that are focused on a particular revenge with a particular person. None of this feels specific. Whoever's engineering this is attacking the entire city. You heard the viceroy. Their goal is to destroy *magic*, and we just happen to be the people who still have it."

The three of them fell silent. Mercy could hear snoring. She wasn't sure if it was coming from Theodore or Gemma. All of them looked the way Mercy felt. No wonder it was hard to work out a proper theory. None of them had slept.

"What are these?"

Ren's question broke through her thoughts. The girl was gesturing to the map.

"Oh. Right. Those are hellhound trails. I've been conducting research on the disease. Most of the corpses they used to spread the disease were stolen. I think the Makers were covering their tracks. Maybe the viceroy was behind it. I don't know. But there was one set of bodies they missed. We found them, brought them back to Safe Harbor, and hired hellhounds to track the scent to its original source."

She reached up and tapped the ember glowing to the north. "This is Running Hills. Two of the hounds went there. Which makes sense. It's where I first encountered the disease. But the third one . . ." Mercy let her finger fall to the southwest. "Traveled to *this* location. I've cross-checked it with every map in the hospital. There's nothing of significance marked in this location. I was waiting for the houndmaster to report back before acting on anything. Whatever is out there is worth investigating. If we're lucky, there will be clues that help us."

Their conversation was interrupted by a knock at the door. Dahvid peeked inside, and he had company with him. His sister Nevelyn, who Mercy also thought was quite terrifying. Four children trailed her into the room like a group of over-sized ducklings. None of them were older than twelve. Mercy offered a quiet smile as the group nestled into the room with the rest of the survivors. Nevelyn Tin'Vori crossed the room and Mercy irrationally thought the woman might punch her.

Instead, she opened with an apology. "Sorry about before. I was short with you at the party."

"You were just being cautious," Mercy returned. "I can respect that."

Nevelyn's eyes swung to Ren next. "Always have to be right in the middle of things, don't you, Monroe?"

That earned a snort. Introductions were made around the room. Theo pushed grumpily to his feet before offering to make tea for everyone. He seemed, to Mercy, like the absolute opposite of what she'd always imagined Brood to be. The thought of tea reminded her that Williams was down in the basement. She made a mental note to go check in on him. Lost in thought, she almost didn't notice the boy tapping her shoulder.

"Excuse me, miss?"

Mercy smiled down at him. "Yes, sweetie?"

It was the ward that Nevelyn had been so protective over at Beacon House. He was pointing at the map behind her. She was about to launch into the same explanation she'd just given when the boy cut her off with the kind of startling question that only young children were capable of asking.

"Do you like dragons?!"

Mercy blinked. "Excuse me?"

"Dragons. I always liked them. Even when I was little. My brother, Garth, he's dead now—but last National Day, he bought me a book. He said it was expensive, but that I should own at least one. I read it every night. Over and over again. Learning about different ones. Do you like them too?"

Mercy couldn't quite understand his line of questioning. "I'm sorry," she said. "But what makes you think that I like dragons?"

He pointed to the map. "You have Arakyl's grave marked. I just thought—well, most people don't know about him."

A chill ran down Mercy's spine. "Where? Which mark?"

Like most boys his age, he was skilled in the art of finding ways to make himself taller. She watched him carefully position two thick books beneath the map before climbing on top of them. That small extension of his height was just enough to allow him to stab his finger down on the ember that was glowing out to the west of Kathor. The unmarked second location.

". . . took me a while, but I memorized every burial site. That one is Arakyl's. Oh! And over here is Gathraxes burial chamber. They always fight about who *actually* discovered that one. Because the guy who 'found' it also found a *body* down there, so that obviously means someone else . . ."

Mercy turned away from the boy. Her eyes locked on Ren Monroe with enough intensity that the girl abandoned a conversation she'd been in with Avid Shiverian.

"What?" Ren asked. "What is it?!"

"A dragon," she shouted, awkwardly drawing the attention of the entire room. "The person behind all of this. It's not a person. It's a fucking dragon."

40

REN MONROE

Balmerick.

Ren crossed the quad and the rest of their party trailed her like ghosts walking through the morning fog. The entire escort group was with them. Nevelyn and her small pack of children as well. One of them was the girl who looked like Timmons. The relief that Ren had felt in seeing her safe and whole had been palpable. Even now, she felt a protectiveness over the girl. As if she'd been given one more chance to protect the innocent people she'd failed to protect so far. Their first step in keeping them safe had been to teach them how to actually travel the waxways. The technique was gloriously simple, but it did require focusing one's mind entirely on some distant place. Eventually, they'd all managed the task, though Ren had been forced to promise the last boy that he'd be given candy if he successfully teleported.

Now they planned to reunite with the other wizards who'd

survived the events of Beacon House. There was much to discuss. Ahead, she saw the main dormitory buildings hunched like great stone birds in the still-thick fog. A figure waited on the front steps of the main building. When they drew close enough to see who'd been given guard duty, Ren's eyes swung sharply over to Avid Shiverian. The girl offered a grim little smile.

"As you know, House Shiverian tends to be more cautious than the other houses. We might not have divulged the entire truth to the viceroy during that first meeting. . . ."

Able Ockley came down the steps to greet them. During their private meeting, Avid had led the rest of the houses to believe that Ockley and the rest of the ruling generation of their house had succumbed to the plague. But here he was, the city's most gifted dueler, looking whole and healthy. Almost as if he were flaunting that fact, Ockley raised his wand.

A casual flick of his wrist sent the fog scattering. Ren watched the bottom half of the nearest dormitory emerge. The windows were full of faces. Eyes peering out from nearly every room. *Of course. Why didn't I think of this?* The students would have been right in the middle of a semester when the plague arrived. Some would have gone home, but not all of them.

"How many?" she asked. "How many still have magic?"

"There are twenty-three immune," Ockley answered. "We have them bunked on the second floor. They didn't answer the viceroy's summons because, unlike you lot, they thought it might be a trap. You know how children are. Big imaginations. Think everything is a spy novel."

Avid snorted at that. "This time they were right."

"Combined with the survivors from Beacon House," Ockley

went on, "we're up to sixty-three in total. The future of magic is on this campus. We also have several wyvern riders at our disposal. They're in the campus aerie—awaiting our orders. I did offer them a massive sum of money to stay. So, it would be lovely if some of the houses with deeper pockets were willing to absorb that particular cost."

Avid smiled at him. "If the entire economy does not collapse, I promise that House Shiverian will foot the bill. You have my word."

Theo murmured a confirmation. Ren could feel her heart soaring in her chest. Until this moment, it had felt as if they were losing. Now they had purpose, direction, power. The surviving wizards were all gathered in one place for an impromptu summit. All they had to do was figure out how to stop a dead dragon from destroying them.

"Why don't you all come inside?" Ockley offered warmly. "We'll get a few fires going. Cups of tea all around. I suspect that we have quite a few decisions to make."

Momentum carried their group up the front steps and into one of her favorite common rooms on campus. The western wall was one long run of fireplaces. Each one had a scattering of mismatched but elegant furniture circling in front of it. During the school year, students would study or congregate in these spaces. While she'd spent most of her time in the library, she did occasionally sit in front of these fires. Nearly always with Timmons. Her eyes flicked briefly over to the little girl who bore a resemblance to her old friend.

I will not fail you a second time.

At the very center of the long hall was an old war table. Circular and large enough to fit roughly thirty seats around it. She knew the table had been donated by House Brood. The small emblems of their house were carved around the edges of the table in tight, delicate loops. At the heart of the table, a map of Kathor. Ren knew it was enchanted so that no matter where you sat, it always appeared as if the map were facing your direction.

Once, Theo's grandfather had drawn up plans at this table to defeat the northern farming tribes. It was also the table where he'd go on to sign the accords with the Graylantians. She suspected today's conversation would carry a different tone. This was not a matter of power or rule. No, the question of the day for them would be survival. What was their place in Kathor now?

Ren took her seat as word of their arrival spread. Theo sat beside her and the Tin'Voris claimed seats to his right. Gemma Graylantian, Avid Shiverian, and Ellison Proctor were all present—but she noticed they were the only symbols of power. The people who claimed places to their right and left weren't scions at all. Instead, wizards like Mercy Whitaker and the pioneer she'd met at Beacon House filled in the gaps. It had taken a tragedy to make them the equals they should have always been.

More chairs were pulled in from other corners of the room until the great war table was surrounded by a proper crowd. Able Ockley had a pair of students run up and down the stairs to make one final announcement. A few more students were lured from their beds. Once they were seated, Ockley signaled for silence.

"I am eager to hear an update from the lower city," he said. "We learned a little from the other survivors of Beacon House— but I'm sure there's more to the story."

Ren stood. They'd discussed an order on their way to Balmerick. Avid had offered to close everything out. Mercy, initially, had wanted no part of speaking publicly in front of everyone—but Ren had insisted. Having her expertise mattered. Clarity would be important. For now, it was Ren's job to paint the wider portrait. She cleared her throat and began.

"Last night, there was an encounter at Beacon House. After determining that the viceroy was working with the Makers, we engaged in a duel with him. It became clear that he had arranged for the former Brightsword paladins to attack all of the wizards who'd gathered at Beacon House. He claimed they were only there to arrest us, but after interrogating the viceroy, I'm pretty confident that their eventual goal was to eliminate as many of us as possible. They want to remove magic from the world. That was the goal of the plague. That was the goal of last night's ambush. The viceroy escaped from the main estate. We pursued. . . ."

She had taken speech classes at Balmerick. There had been lessons on tone and storytelling and elocution, but she'd never been asked to summarize something so terrible. The speeches had focused on historical events. Magical theory. Not a tragedy she'd just lived through. Even so, she quietly described the viceroy's capture, the discovery of the chain spell, and their attempts to break that spell. Finally, she shared the gruesome detail of the immolation they'd witnessed. Any playfulness left in the room vanished then. Able Ockley looked particularly disturbed by this turn in the story, and Ren suspected that it was because it was detailing magic that even he didn't know how to perform. Mercy Whitaker took over the next part in the story.

"Right . . . so . . . our current suspicion is that the person who originated this attack is actually a dead dragon. The unconfirmed name we have for the creature is Arakyl. And we know that most dragons connect to emotions. Specifically, the emotions of people who pass by or through their burial chambers. That's, well, the research says that's how they 'awaken' in most cases. Researchers believe they are specifically attracted to *deep* emotions. Anger, excitement, fear. The worst historical incidents with the burial chambers all have direct connections to a person like that encountering the corpse. Most historical cases have the dragon interacting very briefly with the subject. A lot of those instances are fatal. What's happening now would appear to be the largest-scale interaction between a dragon and humanity. Our assumption is that the viceroy is the subject responsible for waking Arakyl. Luckily, we were able to use hellhounds to track the disease back to its source. On the map, the location is . . . here."

She cast a quick spell. They all watched a trail appear on the map in front of them. It led from the city gates and out to the west. The same coordinates that had been marked on the map back at Safe Harbor. "We have the coordinates for the dragon's burial ground and little else. We do not know when the dragon first manipulated the viceroy. We have no idea if he visited the site himself or if the chain spell reached him through other means. We're also uncertain what kind of obstacles we'll face if we engage with the dragon. Is the area defended by the Makers? Or will we be able to walk right up to the corpse without issue? We can't know until we get a team out there."

There were glances being exchanged around the room. Ren knew this part wouldn't be easy. She'd never had to convince a room of people that a dead dragon was fomenting an attack on a city that had stood for hundreds of years. It was her job to fill in the gaps.

"Tracing the disease wasn't the only piece of supporting evidence," Ren added. "Mercy, why don't you share a few of the other details we've discussed."

"Details," Mercy repeated, before nodding. "Right. Well, we know the disease was spread by corpses that were placed in water treatment facilities. All of these bodies had specific wounds. Open sternums, cuts along the upper arms and legs. The coroner who first inspected the bodies noted that each wound was far too wide to be made by a normal blade, but he also noted that the wounds were flawless. Executed with the kind of precision you'd see from a surgeon. Given what we know, I now believe these wounds were made using a dragon talon. It's the only proper explanation for the width of each laceration. Also, the bodies we found perfectly mimicked dragon corpses. The disease was spread from the wounds of the deceased. Gas leaked out from the bodies. It was almost identical to the process that's used for creating the breath."

There was still doubt circulating. Ren knew it didn't feel conclusive, but they'd turned over all the evidence before coming to the Heights. Ren thought their guess was logical. It was just up to them to communicate that to the rest of them. She gestured for Mercy to go on.

"Right. Another piece of evidence is *who* is immune. I haven't had the opportunity to speak with all of the Balmerick students here today, but I'd guess all of you possess a variant magic?"

The question echoed through the crowd. There were whispers,

but no one called out to correct her guess. Ren had *loved* this particular piece of the puzzle and had been so impressed with how quickly Mercy had put together the theory.

"Interesting, isn't it?" Mercy continued. "Enhancers, image-bearers, bond-mates, manipulators . . . every person I interviewed at Beacon House possesses an atypical manifestation of magic. What you do is not just simple spellwork. You have some unique ability or connection. My hypothesis is that the plague didn't impact any of you because the dragon was unaware your kind of magic exists. Variants have become more common in recent years. They weren't really understood when dragons still roamed the land. I believe the disease targeted the most fundamental version of magic. Which is why everyone else had their magic burned away—but all of you maintained possession of yours. The disease couldn't destroy what it didn't recognize as magic."

The first reaction was shock, but that bled quickly into acceptance. Ren guessed there would be several people who were unaware they possessed any unique magical quality. Especially amongst the younger wizards. Still, no one raised their hand to deny the claim. If anything, they were probably tracing back through their life or their schooling, considering the odd moments where their magic had behaved in a slightly different way than everyone else. Ren realized for the first time that she'd never bothered to ask Mercy what her unique ability was. She made a mental note to do that later. She'd been too focused on how irritating it was that her own personal answer for dodging the plague was Theo Brood. It was not that she'd outwitted the disease, but rather that she'd fallen in love with a boy and they'd warded each other by accident. Did the solution have to be so annoyingly romantic? As a gradual buzz seized the room, Mercy glanced over at Ren. They'd agreed that she should present the concluding details.

"The last piece of evidence is the manipulation spell we encountered. It is the most complex magic I've ever witnessed. A chain spell that moves from person to person without any active guidance from its creator. Not to mention the entity who cast it has been *occupying* the manipulated. Not just a whisper or a suggestion. We're talking about literal mind control. The ability to jump in and out of other beings. We spoke with Gemma Graylantian. One of our generation's most talented manipulators. She told us there wasn't a living person who possessed magic like that."

Ockley cleared his throat. "I'll confirm that. What you're describing isn't possible."

"Not for a person," Ren agreed. "But for a dragon? You all know the stories. I'm sure some of you went on field trips to burial chambers when you were younger. The first thing they tell you is to guard your thoughts. They make you wear protective gear and have you cover your body head to toe because even dead, a dragon is dangerous. We have historical evidence that they can manipulate their visitors. Sometimes, the consequences are small. Like the story of the man who tried to walk back through the city gates naked. At his trial, they figured out that a dragon had manipulated him. Thought it would be funny."

The old story drew out smiles around the room. It was a famous tale. Likely apocryphal, but it served Ren's purposes now. "But there have been other reports of people who were commanded to leap off buildings. Ordered to perform dark tasks at the creature's bidding. I feel like we can all agree that dragons are some of the most powerful creatures to ever exist."

One of the students who'd arrived late raised her hand. "I don't remember stories about dragons attacking entire cities. Every anecdote we have points to them manipulating people at a small scale. What you're suggesting feels like a massive departure. . . ."

A quick glance showed that Theo was smirking. Ren thought she knew why.

Gods, did I sound like that when I was a student?

Ren smiled at the girl. "Trust me, I know how absurd this sounds. I've been trying to process all of it myself. All we really know for sure is that we have a hellhound who has traced the disease to a specific location." She pointed to the map. "We also know that we're dealing with someone with powers beyond the abilities of any wizard currently alive. The only other possibility is that there's a person out there channeling the magic of a dragon—and I can't think of anyone who could maintain that sort of power with that sort of control. It's not impossible, but for now, we believe that it's wisest to pursue the most likely conclusion. We could definitely sit here and debate whether or not a dead dragon is capable of something like this—or we can go ahead and send a team to investigate what's happening."

Able Ockley appeared convinced. "Let's accept your premise. A dragon is behind all of this. What's your solution? It's not like we can kill the thing. It's already dead."

The solution didn't belong to Ren. She nodded everyone's attention back to Mercy Whitaker. "We need to send a team to the burial chamber," the doctor explained. "Manipulation threads are impossible to break at the point where they make contact with the victim. It's like trying to cut through steel. It's far easier to attack them at their point of origin. I was trained to perform severance procedures on people. I can't imagine the process would be that different with a dragon. If an escort team can get me close enough to the corpse, I can cast spells that visually display the magical connections between the dragon and the manipulated."

Ren's mind stuttered briefly to a halt. *Severance procedures.* When they'd discussed the matter earlier, she hadn't pieced together what Mercy meant. Her eyes swung over to Theo. He was already looking at her. An instinctual panic trickled across their bond. Mercy was describing the exact kind of procedure that Dr. Horn had attempted. She'd never considered the idea that Horn had worked at Safe Harbor. Were the two of them connected somehow? It was yet another idea she'd have to follow up on. Mercy was still speaking.

"If I'm right, we would be able to begin severing those connections. One by one. You're right. We can't kill a dragon that's already dead. But we could potentially separate the creature from its victims. It won't fix everything. Some of the people who've joined the Makers didn't need to be manipulated. They wanted this revolution. We believe a small group will continue on no matter what, but there are people around Kathor who've been influenced. Those manipulated subjects, upon realizing they've been tricked, will push away from their captors. I believe if we cut those threads, we'll effectively be 'waking up' half the city. It's possible that will be enough for this movement to die out. Hopefully, it's enough to sway them away from the viceroy's final charge."

Ockley snorted at that. "You're referring to the part where

he cast all of us as villains and ordered the city to stand against us? Indeed. It would be a great idea to begin unraveling that thought as quickly as possible. But what you're describing won't be easy. One does not simply walk into a dragon's burial chamber and begin casting revelation charms."

Mercy nodded. "It's a risk. Everything from here on out is a risk. That's why I'm not going alone. I need volunteers. People who are skilled in combat or defensive magic. We don't have any idea what will be waiting out there for us. Who would go with me?"

This was always going to be the hard part. It was one thing to defend themselves from an attack. Quite another thing to walk voluntarily into the burial chamber of a dead dragon. Ren was completely unsurprised to see Dahvid Tin'Vori raising his hand.

"I'll go. I can manipulate my summon sword so that it will cut through the threads you're describing. I assume the faster we work, the lower the risk. I also have a null sword that I recovered from . . . an opponent of mine. It would be effective against what you're describing."

Ren thought it was rather polite of him not to mention that he'd taken the null sword from Thugar Brood's corpse. At the back of the room, one of the Balmerick students stepped forward. She'd apparently been training to be a reaver for House Winters before the plague came.

"Give me that sword and tell me where to swing," she said.

A small unit of specialists began to take shape. Ren was feeling confident about all the personnel decisions until a wave of discomfort swept across her bond. Theo caught her eye, frowned an apology, and then raised his hand.

"I have a talent for defensive magic. Wards and shields. I'll come."

She barely stopped herself from hissing for Theo to shut the hell up. The conversation bounced to the other side of the table, someone else discussing their merits for the mission, and Ren was afforded the opportunity to have a whispered conversation with Theo.

"What the hell is wrong with you? *It's a dragon's burial chamber, Theo.* Don't you remember the one we went in last year? It's not safe. It won't be safe. . . ."

His voice was quiet but steady. "There aren't many things that I'm better at than you, Ren, but defensive magic is one of them. You know I have a talent for wards. It's been the focus of my training for almost a decade. I can help them. Besides, it would be a waste for the two of us to remain in the same location."

Ren frowned. "What? Why would that be a waste?"

"I can pull you," he reminded her. "And you can pull me. Splitting up basically means we have access to both locations. I'm sorry, Ren. It's just sound strategy."

She bit down on her own tongue. Every part of her wanted to tell him that he could take his clever damn strategies and shove them straight up his ass. She wanted to demand that they stay together. No matter what happened. But what would her counterargument be? *Please don't leave, because if you die, I might as well be dead too.* It wasn't a reasonable thing to say to another person.

"It's all settled then," Ockley announced. "We have seven wizards heading west. The next discussion needs to be about where the rest of us will go."

Ren blinked at that. "What? Why would we leave Balmerick?"

"We don't have to yet," Ockley answered. "But this isn't a long-term solution. The infrastructure of this island relies on the city below. There's no agriculture. No way to feed ourselves. Even the water supply depends on Kathor. Life in the Heights depends on a good relationship with the lower city—and with the people who run it."

She hated how logical that was. She'd been so prepared to feel safe here. Balmerick had always felt like a second home. A warm blanket draped over her shoulders. Maybe that feeling had kept her from assessing the realities of what it would look like to carve out an existence here. Not for weeks or months—but for decades. Her eyes cut across to Avid Shiverian. The girl looked as if she'd been waiting for this part of the conversation.

Of course. Shiverians always have a card hidden up one sleeve.

"I'm guessing you have another location in mind?" Ren asked.

Ockley rapped his knuckles on the war table. Magic whispered out from his touch. They all watched the map begin to shift. The view of the coastline slid away. The focus was moving slowly to the north. Slightly inland as well. A small circle appeared in the valley between two mountains.

"This is Meredream," Ockley announced. "Our future."

41

NEVELYN TIN'VORI

Gods, what a terrible name.

Meredream. She'd never heard of it. Judging by the looks around the room, neither had anyone else. Able Ockley took his seat while Avid Shiverian stood to address them. Nevelyn couldn't help wondering where they all learned to look so comfortable speaking in front of big groups. Was there a class for pompous young rulers at Balmerick? Or were they just born looking slightly perturbed by the existence of other people in the universe?

"Meredream is our house's great secret. The only people who were aware of its existence were my mother—Ethel Shiverian—and her sister, Seminar, as well as the builders who received the commission for the work. The contractual agreement was that those builders had to live out the rest of their lives in Meredream. In return, our house would monetarily support their families in perpetuity. We have honored those contracts. We still honor those contracts.

"Over the years, most of the original builders passed away. Right now, just two live there. The rest of the town is empty. Waiting for us. No one has visited except my mother and her sister. This was a secret that they kept even from me—their heir."

Nevelyn wanted to laugh. Dead dragons and secret cities. At least the day did not lack in drama. Theo Brood raised his hand like a child in a classroom. It felt that way, she supposed. As if Avid Shiverian simply knew more about how the world worked than the rest of them.

"How could you build an entire town without anyone noticing? Looking at the map . . . this location is less than a day's journey from the Brood estate. How could my father not have noticed?"

"He almost did," Avid replied. "Several times. My mother and sister are very good at what they do. Or they were . . . before . . ."

It was the first time Nevelyn had witnessed raw emotion in the girl. Her face briefly contorted with pain, and then she smoothed out her features.

"All this to say: the city was never discovered. It waits for us. There is enough housing for nearly ten times the number of people we have here today. Plenty of room to keep growing. There are farms built inside the city's outer gates for sustenance. The town is already stocked. Supplies. Food. My grandmother chose the location because it's atop a magical vein that runs through that section of the mountains. We will have enough magic to last for generations. Archive rooms, too, to keep training the next generation. Meredream was meant to be a failsafe for our house. If true disaster ever struck Kathor—the

Shiverians would fall back to Meredream and survive. Now, we extend that offer to all of you. Our house would not let magic die out. We must survive."

Hope and sadness tangled in the air. This was a real plan. A proper solution that would see them all safe and sound. But there was also the looming truth: they would be exiles. Kathor would no longer be their home. Gemma Graylantian unexpectedly brought one hand slamming down onto the table. She was wearing so many rings that the impact echoed in a jarring way.

"To hell with that. I cannot believe my ears. House Shiverian—the greatest spellmakers in the known world—are giving in to the demands of the mob?! Your ancestors would be rolling in their graves if they heard this. Why should we retreat from the city *we* built? *Kathor is ours.*"

There was a mixed response. Nevelyn saw a few fervent nods. Mostly from people who had direct ties to the great houses. People who still thought of themselves, even after all that had unraveled around the city, as rulers. But far more people around the room exchanged distasteful glances. At best, her words lacked tact. At worst, they represented something that was already dead.

Nevelyn was surprised to find herself firmly in the second group. Less than a month ago, her primary concern had been to restore House Tin'Vori. Rise from the proverbial ashes. Claim their place amongst the city's elite. How could any of that matter now? She wanted peace. A safe place for Josey to grow and bloom. A normal life for Ava. A world where Dahvid didn't need to keep summoning his sword and staring down the next opponent, and the next. This was their chance.

Even Avid Shiverian saw that the world had shifted. "It was

ours," she said. "Once. Not anymore. The viceroy's message has changed everything. A seed of distrust has been planted in the minds of the people. We are no longer wanted. I think the current plan is sound. I have great hope that it will sway the populace—but look to the future, Gemma, and tell me what Kathor will look like twenty years from now."

The older woman was shaking with rage, but she said nothing.

"I'm no prophet," Avid admitted. "But I see two options for us. First, we rescue the city. When the fog of that manipulation spell finally lifts, we tell them the truth. We play the part of humble servants. There are hundreds of passive magic spells operating around the city. Magic that makes life easier for everyone. If we're really clever, we could convince them to let us provide a valuable service to the city. Posture ourselves as civil servants. That role would earn us a few decades of peace. But even then, imagine how they will see us. We will be living reminders of what they will never taste again. Worse, they might actually believe the viceroy: *we took magic from them.*

"It won't matter that it's a lie. Not if enough of them believe it. Every time we perform a healing spell, the person we helped will know there's another spell that could kill them. Every time we fix the foundations of a building, they'll quietly wonder if we also have spells that could bring the walls of their neighborhood crumbling down on their heads. All it would take is one mistake. Just one wizard casting the wrong spell at the wrong time. One accident . . . and they'll turn on us. In that future, we survive for a while. Eventually, they'll decide the world is safer without us. We die—and magic dies with us."

The entire room had fallen under the spell of her words. Nevelyn saw that even Gemma Graylantian had paled as she listened. The future she painted was a bleak one.

"The second option is that we *rule* them. I'm sure that's what you have in mind, Gemma. We use Balmerick as a base of operations and we begin a war with the city below. It would require all of our resources. Looking around this room, I'd bet we have enough firepower to actually win—but only if every-one in this room is willing to slaughter and kill for it. Thou-sands of Kathorians would die. Including some of the people in this room. Our numbers would be reduced. Enough that magic would die out before the next generation. And if we did somehow survive—anyone who still possessed magic would be feared. Despised as tyrants. That's what we'd have to be to keep our grip on the city, though. Tyrants who ruled with an iron fist. Until one day, someone would come along who was strong enough to kill magic for good."

Avid looked around the room. Meeting each person's eye.

"Or we go to Meredream. We make a new society there. We thrive in exile—until the city is ready for magic again. What's the old saying? Absence makes the heart grow fonder? It would work. We would be safe. And then one day, our children's chil-dren could return to the city we all love."

Avid slid back into her seat. The girl's chest was heaving. Gemma remained silent. The woman was looking down at her own hands—bejeweled and ringed—like someone who'd been cursed to watch all the gold they'd gathered over the centuries crumble to dust. Nevelyn almost felt sorry for her, but then she glanced over at Josey. Her ward looked terrified by the futures that had just been presented. She could not bear the idea of him being hunted. She could also not bear the idea of him becoming a hunter. Nevelyn cleared her throat.

"Will the city only be for wizards? Or will nonmagical kin be allowed to come?"

All eyes swung to her. Nevelyn fought the temptation to turn her heart necklace over and cast the spell so they'd all forget she'd just asked a question. Avid looked hopefully in her direction.

"Family would be welcome—regardless of magical status."

Deep down, she knew it would be painful to leave their estate behind, especially after working so hard to take possession of it again. She also knew that Ava hated when Nevelyn made decisions on her behalf—but she truly believed this was what Ava would want. So long as they were all together, what did it really matter? They could make a new life in Meredream. Together.

Nevelyn nodded. "House Tin'Vori will come with you."

If the safest place for their family was Meredream, then they would go to Meredream. Murmurs stirred around the room. People had been rising to leave, but now they paused, falling into whispered discussions. A group of students announced their intentions next. All of them requested permission to come and Avid nodded her thanks. The effect spread across the room like wildfire. A chorus of requests and agreements, requests and agreements. Until it seemed as if every remaining wizard had agreed that this was the answer. They would go to Meredream and make a new world.

Everyone but Gemma Graylantian.

She tapped her finger on the table, causing the overhead lights to dance across all that gold and silver. After a long moment, she rose. They all watched her straighten the gorgeous dress she was wearing. Her eyes glittered like sharpened knives.

"If they want me to leave, they'll have to drag my corpse through the streets."

And with that, she marched from the room.

42

REN MONROE

A sort of organized chaos claimed the entire campus. Makeshift classes were held in the freshman lecture hall for all the children who hadn't learned their foundational spellwork yet. Avid Shiverian taught most of those sessions, which made sense: her mother had invented the standard curriculum. Naturally, the process was a bit rushed. Some of the children would burst into tears when they couldn't get certain spells to work. There were a few, however, who rose to the challenge. Pressure carved them into more. One was the girl she thought looked like a younger version of Timmons. Ren couldn't resist drawing closer to her during the practice part of the lesson. She failed to cast the spell, but then gritted her teeth and dug her feet into the proper stance, attempting the magic again. On her fourth attempt, the girl succeeded in casting a very small but real shield in the air. The girl cast around then, as any child might, eager to see who'd witnessed her success. Eventually, her gaze landed on Ren.

"Did you see that?" the girl asked breathlessly. "It worked."

Ren nodded in approval. "It did. What's your name?"

The girl straightened her shoulders. "Winnie Fletcher."

"Keep practicing, Winnie Fletcher. You're off to an excellent start."

That was all it took for the girl to settle back into her stance and eagerly attempt the spell again. A deep and terrible feeling punched into Ren's stomach as she watched. She had to leave the room to keep herself from crying. This wasn't like her. Not at all. While the children practiced, Ren worked hard to avoid Theo. His crew had spent every waking hour securing the equipment they needed to safely enter a dragon burial chamber. She was angry over his decision. And it made her seethe even more whenever she thought about how rational his choice was. Exactly the kind of decision she would have made. The only difference was . . . that she loved him? Profoundly? Irrevocably?

Gods, how pathetic.

Thankfully, there was plenty to do to keep her mind preoccupied. The first large-scale problem the group was facing was how to get everyone to Meredream. The wyverns had seemed like an obvious answer until Nevelyn Tin'Vori pointed out that repeated flights to the same location would draw the wrong sort of attention. The Makers had been smart enough to steal Kathor from them. They were certainly smart enough to follow a trail, and flying wyverns overhead in the same direction over and over would be more than leaving breadcrumbs. It would be like baking full loaves and setting them out while they were still warm. Someone also pointed out that the wyvern riders were not definitely on their side. None of them still possessed magic. Their loyalty was very dependent on the money they'd been offered. So, what if they decided to turn on the wizards? It would be all too easy for them to remember the route for the next bidder.

The next option was the waxways. It was a small risk for some of the children, who were so fledgling in their magic, to port that far. This wasn't a simple jump from the lower city to the Heights. Any child could travel a short distance. The level of focus required to travel with a standard-sized candle was significantly greater. And that was yet another problem.

"This is the whole supply? It's a school for magic. Shouldn't they have *magical* candles?"

She was staring down at a box of candle nubs. Every drawer and closet had been searched. In total, they'd collected just three of the stock candles. Everything else in the box was leftovers. Ellison Proctor, who had become the group's unofficial accountant, offered Ren a shrug.

"Balmerick students had the portal room," he said. "Or they could walk to the supply station in the courtyard near the front of campus. You went to school here. You know how it goes. Most of them just used the enchanted carriages."

Which no one knew how to safely drive. None of the immune were professional carriage drivers. It was a very nuanced magic. One that often was passed down through generations— father to son or mother to daughter. Avid promised she would read up on the subject, but then they'd have to find an actual carriage in the lower city and get up to the Heights without drawing attention.

Ren decided to order their search for way candles to span outward. Once more, her scouts came back empty-handed. A few of the abandoned houses were explored with candles in mind this time instead of food, but none were found. Next, they attempted to knock on the doors of the houses that were still occupied. Almost no one would open their doors. Ren understood their caution. Wards worked almost like passwords. They were sealed safely inside as long as they didn't grant access to anyone. It was fair to not completely trust a pack of people who'd randomly started roaming the gilded streets you called home.

In total, five people opened their doors. All of them had gotten sick and were living off a healthy supply of stored goods. Some were carefully rationing each day. Speaking with them, Ren couldn't help thinking about the fact that they were *stuck* here. The waxways were not an option for any of them. They would need a wyvern or a carriage—or a long rope.

One problem at a time.

Ren noted that sympathies were in their favor in the Heights. Most of these people—magicless or not—had been wealthy merchants. Scions of the great houses. Their success was distinctly tied to whether or not the great houses survived all of this. Some even went as far as whispering that they didn't believe the viceroy's claims. Their kindness was welcome, but it didn't solve the actual problem: no one had extra candles.

After failing to resupply in the Heights, Ren returned to headquarters and suggested sending down a search party to the lower city. Ellison Proctor volunteered to go. He'd been keeping fastidious notes of all their supplies, and suggested that he keep an eye out for the candles and a few other items they needed to refill. He also claimed to be nondescript enough to blend in with a crowd, whereas a pack of wizards might draw unwanted attention. She thought that was a stretch—given he was one of the better-looking people in the city—but after seeing him with his hood pulled up, she agreed a more discreet route would be best. Not to mention they didn't want to waste more candles than strictly necessary. When he ported away, the room fell to silence. Avid Shiverian was reading a book that Ren assumed would have detailed spellwork about flying carriages. Able Ockley appeared to be meditating. She leaned back into the comfort of her chair and began her own version of a meditation.

Ellison's return woke her up. He'd managed to secure just two candles.

"I checked four different markets," he reported. "None of the normal way candle vendors are there. It's like the supply ran out. Which makes sense, I suppose. The factory isn't one of those passive-magic places. The candles have to be handmade. I'd guess it shut down after the plague, and it's not like people are clamoring for more way candles. No one down there can even use them. Still, it's strange the original supply vanished. . . ."

His words caught Nevelyn Tin'Vori's attention. Ren must have been sleeping when she'd returned. Her old friend had volunteered with the children all morning. A surprising choice. Nevelyn didn't strike her as the motherly sort. Really, she seemed more of the "get those children away from my garden" kind of lady. It was one of the rare instances where Ren didn't mind being proven wrong. "Wait," she said. "You're looking for candles?"

Ellison nodded. "I just searched the lower city markets for them. We don't have enough to cover travel for the entire group. Not even close. We could always port to a location outside the city gates. Walk the rest of the way . . ."

"Shit. That's what they were doing."

Ellison and Ren both looked at her.

"What who was doing?" Ren prodded.

"I saw the Makers distributing food in the market—but there was one day where one of their members traded crates of food for candles. Hundreds of them. I didn't piece together that they were way candles. I mean, why would they buy them? They don't use magic."

"A defensive move," Ockley offered. His eyes were still closed as if he were meditating. "The waxways are a tactical advantage for us. If it ever came to open warfare, our ability to port around the city would have left them vulnerable. It's clever. Hamstringing us before the race even starts."

Very clever.

Ren was tired of being outmaneuvered by Arakyl—if that's who was truly behind the attack. There were rumors that the dragons existed outside time. Some philosophers believed that was the explanation for how they could still interact with the world, even though they were all dead. It certainly felt as if Arakyl had glanced into the future and planned out every possible detail. And that thought made her stomach turn even more.

What if he knows Theo is coming? What if he planned for that, too?

Avid Shiverian had been half reading and half listening. The girl pushed to her feet, dog-eared the page she was on, and set the book on the table.

"Give me three of those candles," Avid requested. "I know what to do."

Ellison Proctor slid the box in her direction. All of them watched as she lit one of the candles with a quick wave of her hand. The flame danced back and forth. Ren shook her head.

"Come on. There's no way you figured out how to drive a flying carriage that fast. . . ."

Avid winked at her. "I'll be back soon."

Before Ren could ask anything else, she snuffed out the flame and vanished with an echoing whisper. Ockley leaned back into his chair with an exaggerated sigh.

"You know, they're all that way. Geniuses, but do they ever stop for a few seconds and just tell you what the hell they've figured out? Do they pause long enough to just explain it? No. Never. Not one time. It's always, 'Able, be a dear and come clean up this mess.' 'Able, would you mind fighting this warlord for us.'" He let out another sigh. "Guess I'll get to enjoy another few decades of that. Just lovely. All right. I'm going to get a drink."

Ren almost pointed out that it was a dry campus, but she suspected if anyone knew where to find a secret stash of liquor at Balmerick—it would be Ockley. He aimed straight for the kitchens and the doors closed behind him with a resounding thump. She was about to lean back and sleep some more when she felt a pull across her bond. Theo was asking for her. It was more than that. A true need. As if his entire body was aching to see her. She smirked to herself, thinking it was a different sort of need, but then she realized what it really meant. His group was ready to depart.

The campus aerie hardly lived up to its name. It was located on the highest hillside, near the very north end of campus. A rising cylinder with great openings for the wyverns to fly in and out of whenever they'd operated in the Heights. The entrance wasn't even a door. Just a gap where the stones had been scuffed with hundreds of claw marks over the years. Ren could see their party through that opening. Theo appeared. He eagerly trotted back down the hill to meet her before she could reach the entryway.

"What? Didn't want the rest of them to hear me shouting at you?" she asked. "Or maybe you were embarrassed by the idea of—"

He ended her sentence with a kiss. Their bond pulsed and it was that same hungry feeling from before. As if she could not taste enough of his lips or feel enough of his hands on her skin. She kissed him back and that brief sand in the grains of time seemed to tumble slower than the rest. For a moment, only they existed. There wasn't a dead dragon to fight. There was not a spell that needed to be unraveled. No wars to fight or people to rescue. Just them.

All magic ceases, though. Even the best spells end.

Ren kissed him one more time and then Theo pulled away. His side of the bond thrummed with confidence. An assurance of purpose. He knew he was doing the right thing—which meant she knew she was doing the right thing. He started marching back up the hill. The rest of the crew had started loading onto the wyverns. Theo glanced back, about to call out to her.

"I know," she said, cutting him off. "I love you too."

He grinned wildly before vanishing inside the aerie. She could not bear to watch for a moment longer. Her heart might actually burst in her chest. It was easier to retreat. She'd almost made it back to the main building when she heard them. Great wings pounding the air in a slow but steady rhythm. All three creatures soared upward. Ren felt Theo's breathless adrenaline and even thought she heard a few of the riders whooping with the sudden freedom of flight. She'd initially been worried that their bond would take years to repair. That Dr. Horn's attempted severance would reduce it to something small or feeble. It was clear, though, that the setback had been temporary. She knew the magic coursing between them had never been so full, so rich, so deep.

But it didn't take long for Theo's adrenaline to fade. It was replaced by a slow-forming dread. A twin emotion had been stirring in her own thoughts. The person she loved most was heading for a dragon's burial chamber. One that had proven powerful enough to launch an attack on the greatest magical city to ever exist. She found herself hoping they would circle back for some reason. One of the wyverns would be sick or a storm would appear on the horizon. Anything.

Instead, they winged on.

43

NEVELYN TIN'VORI

Nevelyn raised one eyebrow when Ren Monroe took her seat in the war room.

"I'm surprised you stayed."

Ren frowned at that. "Why wouldn't I stay?"

"Because you're in love with him. He's going to fight a dragon. I just . . . I would have put money on you going with him."

Unbidden, she saw a glimpse of Garth. Not the version she'd grown fond of either. No, she was forced to see him the way she had at the end. His throat slit. His eyes lifeless. She had to physically shake her head to get rid of that image. She'd suspected Ren might try to sneak away with the other crew, because Nevelyn would do anything to see Garth again. Ride a wyvern. Face a dragon. Fight an army. All she had left of him was Josey, and she was already fiercely protecting him. Fighting to keep that last talisman of the one person who'd really seen her as she was, and loved her as she was. It felt ridiculous to hold anyone else to the same standard, but she'd simply assumed Ren would do anything to stay by Theo's side. The girl seemed to read her thoughts.

"We aren't ever fully apart."

Nevelyn frowned. "Like . . . spiritually?"

Ren snorted in response. She looked as if she were going to keep whatever secret she possessed, and then thought better of it. "No. We are bonded. Magic always develops oddly between two bonded people. There are always unique traits that develop. Ours is that we can pull each other across the bond. From location to location. Think of it as a private wax-ways. I can get glimpses of what he's doing, hear what he's saying, but I can't communicate back. It's only ever activated during moments of heightened emotion."

Nevelyn leaned back in her chair, mind racing. She considered keeping her own secrets—and then realized Ren was trying to build trust. She didn't know what she'd gain from keeping this girl as an enemy. In every sense, their fates were now tied together.

"So, that's what happened with Ava."

Ren went very, very still. Nevelyn knew this was a girl who'd spent most of her life hunting or being hunted. She was quietly calculating how to respond. Finally, she spoke.

"Your sister . . . who I assumed was dead until about half an hour ago."

Nevelyn raised one eyebrow. "How do you know she isn't?"

"You asked about nonmagical family members," Ren noted. "There's literally no one else who that could be. Josey has magic. Dahvid too. I assume that Ava . . . somehow survived?

She reunited with you. And *somehow* you kept her hidden all this time, but she caught the plague. Which means she's currently waiting out at the Tin'Vori estate for further instruction."

Nevelyn leaned back in her chair. "Gods, you really are annoyingly smart, you know? Yes. She's waiting on our estate. I've sent a letter letting her know about our plans to travel to Meredream. I hold no ill will about what you did. You didn't know who she was—and even if you did, she was about to kill Theo. You did what you had to do. Ava might . . . dislike you?"

Ren snorted. "Well, I can handle that."

"She tends to communicate her displeasure with her knives."

"A Tin'Vori who holds a grudge. How unsurprising."

It was Nevelyn's turn to snort. "You're one to talk."

"Fair. Speaking of surprises, I'm dreadfully curious about what happened at Beacon House."

"Noticed that, did you?"

"Barely. How'd you resist Avid's spell?"

She tapped the charm dangling from her necklace. "My magic is tied to this. One side allows me to push someone away. I can ask them to ignore me—or to forget me entirely. That's the spell I used on your mother last year in Ravinia. It was a useful gift, growing up the way we did. On the move from town to town. If I encountered a bully, I learned how to just . . . slip by them. But that's not my only gift. It took years to figure out the other half of my power."

"You can pull them too?" Ren guessed.

One day, Nevelyn would grow accustomed to the girl always being right.

"Yes. I've always called it my beholding magic. I don't use it very often. It's not as comfortable. The curse of being an introvert, I suppose. I prefer *not* being seen. But if I want to, I can make someone see me. Force them to focus all of their attention on me. I can . . ." She lowered her voice. They were alone at the table, but it wasn't something she cared to share with anyone else. "Sometimes I can make them obey me. Bend them to my will."

Ren was nodding. "Your magic hid you from Avid's spell. That seems . . . useful."

This time Nevelyn snorted. "It is."

The two of them were quiet for a moment. Nevelyn had always felt a begrudging respect for Monroe and that feeling had only grown in the last few minutes. There was just one fence left to mend. "You tried to kill my sister," Nevelyn said. "Left her for dead in the snow. Why?"

"Because she was about to kill Theo. He . . . pulled me across the bond. Like he had before. Only this time I was standing there watching him die. I was so desperate that I actually physically traveled to Nostra. I hit her with a spell. I'm sorry, Nevelyn, but I didn't know it was your sister. I just knew that Theo was about to die. What would you have done?"

Nevelyn would have done anything to save the people she loved.

"That's interesting," she said.

"Is it?"

"Yes. Last year, under threat of death, you told us you didn't love him."

Ren nodded. "It was true."

"I know it was. Otherwise you would have lost a limb. But it's not true now."

The girl's eyes flicked over to the windows. The wyverns

had faded from sight. Nevelyn had watched them leave too. Ren's eyes fell to the floor.

"No. It is not true now."

A deep chasm seemed to open up in Nevelyn's chest. She completely understood Ren's position—and she also despised her for being able to say what she'd just said. Why had the person she loved been spared? Why had Garth had to die? Sweet Garth. Nevelyn's eyes swung back to the window again. The empty skies. Maybe Ren would know that pain soon enough.

I hope no one has to know this pain.

Before they could say more, the air around them *fractured* with magic. Two figures appeared in the small gap between the table and the back wall. Both were frozen in a dangling sort of limbo. Their feet hovered just above the ground and their eyes were eerie, unfocused. Nevelyn recognized that brief moment where the body arrived before the mind.

Avid Shiverian had returned. Hunched at her side was an elderly woman who bore all the same physical features: a small nose, a sharp chin, crystal-bright eyes. The two of them had looped their arms delicately together. It was clear Avid was offering stability to the older woman as their feet finally set down on solid ground. Ren was the first to break the silence.

"I completely forgot about your grandmother."

Avid was helping the older woman into the nearest chair. Ren's comment drew the attention of their new guest. Her eyes were that creepy, piercing blue that Nevelyn had only ever seen in the elderly. "Oh?! Am I *her* grandmother all of a sudden? Gods help us all. I'm sorry, but when did we start defining the older generation by the younger? My name is Ingrid Shiverian. When *my* granddaughter here invents the

foundational spells for isometric physics, you can start referring to me as *her* grandmother. Until then, show a little damn
respect."

Well, I like her already.

Nevelyn and Ren exchanged smiles. As soon as the woman
was properly settled in her chair, she looked around, baffled by
what she saw. "Well? What the hell are the three of you waiting
for? Do I need to blow into a horn to get you moving? Bring me
the maps. Go on. Get moving."

Avid gestured for them to both stand and follow her. "We
need to go to Balmerick's main library. There should be topo-
graphical maps of the surrounding regions. My grandmother
needs the most up-to-date versions. If we can find the correct
information, she might be able to adjust the wax sculpture in
the portal room so that it features the area near Meredream.
Then everyone would just have to light the candle for that
location and wait for the portal spell to activate. Solves our
supply issues."

Ren always shivered a little at the thought of using the portal room, but that unnerved feeling was quickly snuffed out by
the possibility that the sculpture she'd used week in and week
out could be altered after all this time. "How can you alter the
magic? Wouldn't you need the original artist? I thought someone named Gothen made it."

She only knew that because Theo had mentioned it during
his argument with Avy. A justification for why he should be
allowed to put his boots on the wax. The sculptor was a "family friend." Ingrid Shiverian offered Ren a mysterious smile in
return.

"I have always said that you want to be the right amount of

powerful. Too much, and your enemies will posture against you. Too little, and they won't respect you. Gothen is the name we used to veil some of our talents. An effort to maintain that delicate balance. You do need the original spellcaster. Luckily, you have her."

She gestured to herself—and then dismissed them with one of the rudest backhands that Ren had ever witnessed. Like someone shooing servants away from the dinner table.

"Now, be a dear, and go get what I asked for before I fall asleep."

44

MERCY WHITAKER

Mercy had never flown on the back of a wyvern.

She likely never would again. Her stomach turned uncomfortably with every drop or rise in altitude. The creatures had always seemed beautiful to her, but at a distance. All sweeping wings and bright colors and breathless speed. There was nothing beautiful about the way she was currently bouncing against the wyvern's backside, uncertain if the ropes fastening her to the creature's back had been tied tightly enough to withstand their velocity. Nor did it help that she was pinned in beside Dahvid Tin'Vori, who appeared to have somehow fallen asleep.

Their crew of seven was split across three wyverns. They were the most formidable hunting party she'd ever traveled with. Theo Brood was the governing leader of one of the great houses. Dahvid had supposedly won a Ravinian gauntlet, which everyone knew took more than a smile. The other four members of their party weren't famous, but that didn't make them any less useful.

Margaret Woods was the only student who'd volunteered to come. She'd won every junior gladiatorial contest in the city over the last year. And now she was armed with a null sword. Two of the crew were siblings—Win and Guion. One had a talent for long-range spellwork while the other was specifically trained in close-range combat. They were bonded. A rarity between family members, but their father had been training them to join an elite battle squad for one of the great houses. He thought the idea of bonded warriors would make them more appealing recruits. The final person to volunteer was a pioneer named Redding. Mercy thought his skill set—survival techniques and a familiarity with mountains—might prove the most useful of all. They still didn't know if the location was deeper into the mountain chain, or in the foothills below.

She'd not received any more letters from the houndmaster. That troubled her. She worried that she'd sent him into unnecessary danger by letting him travel to Running Hills. What if the Makers had intercepted him there? Hopefully, he'd survived the initial journey and was now escorting the other two hounds to the same location that they were currently flying to. In a perfect world, they'd have the dogs to help them navigate down into the actual burial chamber. Mercy had read a little about them before their departure. The chambers were dragon-made. The best guess of "experts" on the subject was that dragons, upon sensing their coming death, would burrow underground. Once there, they'd carve away the stone and the dirt and make a burial chamber in which to die. No one actually knew if this was true, however, as no one had ever witnessed the actual process.

Gods, we're actually going down into a dragon's burial chamber.

There was no one to blame for her situation. This had all been her idea. Now she was stuck *leading* an expedition into a cursed place to execute magic she wasn't entirely sure would work. It was one thing to perform a severance procedure in ideal operating conditions. Quite another to attempt the same on a dead dragon. Before long, the mountains began to loom larger on the horizon. Each individual peak growing more distinct. Mercy glanced over and found Dahvid's eyes were finally open. A striking blue color that reminded her of the ocean. She was trying to think of something to say when he turned his neck as far as the harness allowed, and vomited.

She'd seen many disgusting things working at the hospital, but she'd nearly always been masked and gloved. The wind-caught splatter of bile on her forehead was less than ideal. She couldn't even reach up to properly wipe it away. Dahvid shouted an apology before slamming both eyes shut again. So, he hadn't been sleeping. He'd been nauseous. Mercy buried her own face against the wyvern's bristle-furred back in an effort to wipe it away, and then spent the next hour dreaming of a warm bath.

The first sign that they were closing in on the right location came from the wyverns themselves. Mercy's stomach dropped as they pulled into a sudden turn. Their mount widened its wings, peeling off in a new direction. The rider tried to turn the creature back. It worked, but only for a moment. Once again, the creature pulled away—all while making squabbling sounds that reminded Mercy more of a giant chicken than a creature that could eviscerate her with a single strike from its claws. A quick glance showed the other wyverns were behaving the same way. The riders exchanged a series of hand signals before beginning the descent.

That was the worst part yet. A tight coil that had her stomach turning and turning. They set down with a jolting thud. As the wind subsided, Dahvid started a proper apology, but Mercy was rushing to unclip herself. She'd managed to loosen just one buckle before spewing her own breakfast over the right wing—and on Dahvid's boots. It was instant relief. She wiped her mouth with a sleeve before looking up at her riding partner.

"Guess we're even."

He grinned at that. The others were dismounting, but again she saw the wyverns giving their riders trouble. Resisting basic commands. All three of them lowered their heads to the ground. Once the riders were clear, they put their wings out too, flattening them against the earth. Almost as if they were trying to blend in with the rocky hillsides. Their crew gathered off to the side, eyeing their surroundings. It took a few minutes for the head rider to settle his mount and join them.

"I'm sorry—they won't fly any closer. They sense something dangerous in these hills. Doesn't matter how well we've trained them. Their ancestors knew that when a dragon was nearby, you don't go any closer. You either hide or you run. That's what they're doing." He gestured to where the wyverns were cowering in the grass and dust. "See the lowered heads and wings? We don't teach them that. They're born with the instinct."

Mercy nodded. "So, we travel the rest of the way on foot. Do you have coordinates?"

The head rider nodded. "I can aim you the right way, but the rest is up to you. Here."

Before he could dive in too deep, she waved Redding over. She felt it was best if the actual pioneer in the group received their bearings. The rider walked him through the landmarks. A specific tree in the distant hills. A gap between two mountains. He carefully aimed them like an arrow—and then gave them a rough estimate of the expected paces. Redding noted everything in a small journal before nodding to the rider. Mercy thanked him.

"Ockley wanted two wyverns to return to Kathor," she said. "Do you think you'll be able to keep one of them this close to the burial site? Or are they going to be spooked the whole time?"

The rider turned, orienting himself with the landscape behind them, before pointing.

"I'll wing my wyvern back to that overlook. See it there? With the jutting rocks? A little distance should settle him, but we'll still be close enough to help. Remember there's a radius around the burial site that my wyvern won't enter. If you need me, you'll have to backtrack outside that circle and we can pick you up."

Mercy nodded. "Thank you. And sorry about the . . ."

He waved her off. "Everyone spews on their first ride. Happy hunting."

His wyvern had started issuing a high-pitched whine. She watched him rush over to comfort the creature before turning back to her own crew. Preparations were underway. Theo Brood had unloaded a reinforced chest. He popped the lid open and began passing out cloaks and gauntlets. As well as a number of half shovels. It had taken a few days to secure all the necessary equipment. Some of the spell-woven clothing came from the Shiverian family's personal armory. A few other pieces had been donated by the Winterses and Proctors. They wouldn't even be able to approach the chamber without them.

"One cloak for each of you," Theo said. "They have sensory dampening charms woven into the fabric. Your magical output won't be impacted, but it will keep the dragon from sensing your spells right up until the moment they depart from your vessel. It should be enough to let us safely cast magic inside the burial chamber. Just make sure to put your suits on first. The cloaks won't fit inside them. . . ."

The smoke-gray jumpsuits had been specifically created for the government workers who tended to one of the dragon burial sites located just outside Kathor's city limits. Mercy—and so many other Kathorian children—had visited that location on field trips growing up. It was almost startling now to think that they'd been allowed so much proximity to such a powerful creature. Although, if memory served, that dragon had been almost completely drained by drug farmers. Most of its scales removed. The talons all stolen. When she'd first seen it in person, the corpse had been little more than a skeletal frame slumped over the barren stones. Their dragon was likely to be far more intact. It was possible it hadn't been harvested at all.

"Arakyl," Margaret tested the name aloud. "I don't remember that name."

All of them were working to get their jumpsuits on over their clothing.

"I didn't either," Mercy admitted. After Josey's revelation, she'd done her best to research the name and the grave location. Ren Monroe had been incredibly helpful for that part. Really, she'd commandeered the entire process and found twice as much information in half the time. As if she'd been born inside a library. Together, they'd pieced together a rather imperfect portrait.

"The burial chamber was first discovered twelve years ago. It is the most recent discovery by a few decades. There were articles printed, a lot of excitement, but only during that first week of discovery. The city claimed the rights to the location. For magical research. Harvesting was scheduled for later in the year—but then the ceremony was cancelled. Someone supposedly 'debunked' the site as not being real dragon bones? Interest fell away after that. There's not a single mention of the location in any report. Not even in the private documents we read from the great houses. It's like everyone decided to ignore the place. The dragon's life is a mystery too. We could only find one story that even mentions the name."

Everyone was adjusting their suits. Tugging at sleeves and pulling zippers up to their throats. Margaret was the only one who really didn't have a perfect fit. Being a head taller than the rest of the group left her ankles exposed. Mercy offered her the spare pack of bandages.

"Wrap your ankles with this. You don't want any direct exposure to the gases in there."

Mercy watched as the girl began winding the thick fabric around each ankle. Everyone else offered a thumbs-up. They were armed and ready. Dahvid's deeper voice broke the silence.

"What was the story?"

She'd been half hoping no one would ask. Ren had found the tale in a book that primarily focused on how to create and sustain villages. The bulk of the book had focused on survival methodology, but each chapter opened with a short anecdote. There was no way to verify the story they'd found—but that hadn't stopped Mercy from memorizing what she read, hoping for clues.

"Once, a man got lost in the woods. Two dragons stumbled upon him at the exact same moment. As the terrified man stood there, cowering before them, the dragons debated who should be allowed to eat him. One was named Arakyl. The other was called Provenance. After a lengthy debate, Arakyl suggested that Provenance eat the man first. Once he was finished, they could go back in time and then he would be allowed to eat the man the next time. Provenance agreed to those terms. He devoured the man—bones and all. When his stomach had settled, the dragons used their magic to travel back through time. Of course, the man had also heard their plan. As soon as he appeared in the woods, alive and whole, he bolted through the forest, sprinting all the way back to his village. While the memory of being eaten alive haunted his thoughts, he also believed he'd been clever enough to avoid death. Little did he know, the dragons had been searching for his village for months. It was well hidden . . . until his panicked escape led them right to it. That night, they feasted on the entire town."

Margaret frowned. "Why couldn't they have just let him go right from the start? Wouldn't he have run back to the village anyways?"

"That would have been suspicious," Win commented. "If a pair of dragons just let him go for no reason. He would have suspected something, right? The time-magic tricked him into thinking he'd actually outwitted them."

Guion shook his head. "It's just a story, you prat."

Before the brothers could dig into a proper fight, Theo spoke. "Those stories aren't meant to be taken literally. They're just shadows of a bigger truth. You have to extrapolate. There are two lessons: the first is that Arakyl was working with another dragon. That's rare. Most dragons were solitary creatures. Wandering the land alone. The second is that he was patient enough to delay his hunger for a far larger prize. That's also rare. Think of all the other stories. A lot of them focus on how impulsive dragons are. But Arakyl was patient enough to follow a bigger plan. Which means he'll have considered what to do if someone attacks his burial chamber. We need to go in there understanding that he's probably two steps ahead of us."

Nods all around. Mercy didn't bother pointing out that the lesson she'd taken from the story was that Arakyl was uniquely violent. Most of their stories about dragons didn't involve entire villages perishing. Dragons normally viewed humans as interesting toys. They would hoodwink them or take away their most treasured possessions. A taunting of sorts. Like cats playing with mice before eating them. There were even stories about dragons taking a particular interest in one person. Torturing them over time, for no apparent reason. She could not think of any tales where dragons hunted at such a large scale. But she didn't say this to the group. Better to let Theo's cautionary charge lead them onward.

The group began walking west, over the rolling hills, and the air grew colder as they went. She couldn't help thinking of the old maps that the first Delveans had drawn of this continent. Before they'd ever dared to sail here. There were always three words written in the upper corners. A warning for sailors to not approach the very place they would one day settle and claim. The only land she had ever known.

Here be dragons.

Now she intended to ignore that same advice—and find one for herself.

45

NEVELYN TIN'VORI

Nevelyn had not known how breathlessly complex magic could be.

The core of her own spellwork had always been so simple. She could either fade from existence or consume someone's attention entirely. Push and pull. Her reliance on those two powerful spells meant that she'd never really devoted time to learning more. Aside from a deep dive into the world of weaving magic, she'd never had any additional education.

The truth was she'd been denied the opportunity. When they fled from Kathor, they went to places that were best for hiding—not training young spellcasters. Even Ravinia, a proper city, had nothing like Balmerick. And if they had, what school would have accepted a trio of orphans who had no money to pay them with? She'd spent two days at Balmerick and it took about that amount of time to realize just how much she'd missed out on. First, she'd listened in as Avid—a girl who was not a day older than fifteen—taught foundational spellwork to children. The structure of her lesson had been stunning. How certain spells could be built upon. How one sort of knowledge led to another and another. And Nevelyn knew that Avid's lessons were merely a test of that world. Designed specifically so that *children* could process the information.

Now she watched Avid's grandmother flex those basic concepts to their natural breaking points. It was devastatingly complex. The old prune could hardly walk across campus, but the moment they set her before the great wax sculpture in the portal room, she began dismantling decades-old spells with little more than a flick of her bony wrist. Bright sparks splashed into the air every few seconds. Nevelyn couldn't understand what each color and shape meant. Ren Monroe, on the other hand, seemed to be reading what was happening like someone perusing an enjoyable book. Written in a language she was intimately familiar with. Every now and again, Nevelyn saw the other girl nod in approval at a certain spell Ingrid was using. On the far end of the room, Avid Shiverian was seated—and hiding yawns.

Gods, she's bored with magic I can't even understand.

After dispelling the magic built into the surrounding walls, Ingrid began to focus on the wax sculpture itself. Here, she finally began to struggle. Avid noticed. The younger girl snuffed one final yawn, crossed the room, and set a hand on her grandmother's back to keep her steady and upright. Nevelyn saw movement bubbling along the surface of the wax. Almost as if they'd lit a fire beneath the entire sculpture. Slowly, it was becoming more malleable. Flattening into a shapeless mass.

On her first two attempts, the map shivered back to its original form. That flawless layout of Kathor with all its buildings and canals and districts. Ingrid unleashed some of the more inventive swear words that Nevelyn had ever heard. When she finished cursing the universe, she'd resume the task as if she were beginning for the very first time. Her third effort crossed a threshold the others hadn't. The sprawl of buildings melted fully down into the overall surface of the sculpture. Bubbling until the land was just one, featureless sphere. The way it might have looked before any of the great houses arrived in Kathor. A land ruled by dragons and the wild.

It was then that Nevelyn noticed the sphere was *turning*. Almost too quick to notice at all. The entire object, rotating beneath Ingrid's pruned fingertips. She waited until just the right moment and then stabbed her wand down straight into the wax. The vessel nearly cracked. Nevelyn heard it. That first creak of wood on the verge of giving way, but then magic forked outward. Tonguing like lightning through the sphere itself. Avid was forced to plant her feet as the reverberations from that magic nearly buckled her grandmother's knees.

But it was *working*.

Nevelyn saw little hills spawning across the surface. Mountains rising like the teeth of some slumbering beast. Hundreds of saplings grew into hundreds of trees that formed dozens of forests. A single candle appeared—wick and all—at the heart of the display. That was when Ingrid lost her grip on the magic. The spell slipped away from her with a whispering snicker. Like someone had punched the room in the stomach and all the wind had gone rushing out. Ingrid staggered into the nearest chair with Avid's help. Ren frowned at the final display.

"It's incomplete."

She was right. That much was obvious. The central area of

the display was flawless. All the forests surrounded a sloping hill that led right up to the outer wall of a city: Meredream. The candle had risen just outside those looming gates. But the farther the eye moved from that location, the less defined everything looked. Ingrid's chest was still heaving. Those ice-blue eyes were wide and unfocused. It took a moment for her to recover. When she did, she scowled at her own creation like an artist who'd just used the wrong color.

"Well. Best I can manage," she replied. "It should work just fine."

Nevelyn couldn't help echoing that word. "Should?"

"If you can improve it, be my guest," the old woman replied. "Now, I'd like some tea. Fetch me a cup. None of that flavored garbage, either. I want something dark and strong. Bring me a proper mug for it too."

Nevelyn felt like the old woman might deserve a cup of tea thrown in her face—but thankfully, Ren Monroe replied before she could suggest that. "I'll get the tea."

"I'll help," Nevelyn said, eager to escape.

As they retreated, she heard Ingrid muttering to her grand-daughter.

"Takes two of them to make tea? I'm starting to doubt that magic will survive, dear."

Ren apparently heard too. The two of them smirked at each other. Once they were out of earshot, Nevelyn nudged the other girl's shoulder. "Hey. Do you really think that sculpture will work? I'm not eager to let Josey get lost in the waxways because that old crone can't finish a spell."

"The underlying magic is sound. I was following every casting, just in case. She hasn't lost her touch. I'm pretty sure Avid was doing the same. It will work. It might just require a longer burn than—"

Monroe was cut off by a distant rumble. A second one. A third. The ground beneath them shook with the impact of some distant explosion. Both of them held out their arms for balance, and then their eyes met. "That's up here," Nevelyn said. "How else would we feel it?"

Two buildings—the library and the dining hall—were cutting off their view of the rest of the Heights. Ren led them, jogging to the right in an effort to maintain their current elevation. Slowly, the answer came into view. Fires were raging through the neighborhood she'd heard others refer to as the Pearl Quarter. Once, that portion of the city had been heralded as the single-greatest architectural accomplishment of the magical era. But as she watched, the white-walled exteriors blackened. Flames roared higher and higher—until the wards between houses *shattered*. The magic had been designed for exactly this moment. If one house went up in flames, the others would be spared. The problem was that there were little fires everywhere. Pressing in on the wards from too many directions. Draining the magical defenses slowly but surely.

All they could do was watch as the fire leapt from one house to another to another. Great clouds of smoke began to churn in the sky above. It was like watching the end of the world.

46

MERCY WHITAKER

Their search party moved cautiously across the hillside.
No one knew for certain where the chamber was located.
They had no information on who might be there to guard the
place. Nor did they even know if the dead dragon was truly
responsible for the plot that had stolen their city. What if some
other perpetrator had created the disease in secret here—and
that was the reason the hound had come? She wanted some
sign that they were on the right trail. It was Redding who spotted the first clue. "Look at that section."

All the forests in the area were sparse. Never more than a
few trees standing tall together. Redding was pointing to a place
where the trees were inexplicably *small*. There was growth,
but it didn't come close to the rest of the surrounding forest.

"It burned down," Theo said. "When the dragon buried itself
here."

Of course. The lives of trees were not measured in days—

but in decades. Mercy could see that this was the right place. The burn, whenever it happened, had spanned two hillsides and a lonely valley. It was still a fairly large stretch of land, but she was glad to have their search narrowed. Even the air felt fractious—as if time were standing still. Their group widened out their approach, eyes open for any sort of clue. Mercy found herself searching for any sign of the hound.

Where are you? Where's your master?

It took Margaret tripping over something to find the next clue. She fell and rolled and nearly cut herself with the null blade. Guion and Win exchanged grins before helping the poor girl to her feet—but what she'd tangled in wasn't natural at all. Everyone circled around as Theo reached down and began tugging something. It was nearly the same color as the ground, and it had very little give. Moss had grown in and around it. Dirt had filled in what holes remained.

"Fabric," Theo said. "Someone covered this spot with fabric."

Without a better lead, they passed out the half shovels and began digging. Working away at the spot, removing great strips of fabric that was starting to feel endless in length. The manual labor only really looked natural for Dahvid and Margaret who would use their boots to drive the tools deeper into the ground before sending great chunks through the air behind them. Everyone worked up a sweat before the ground finally gave way to what waited beneath: darkness.

"That's the main boring tunnel," Theo noted. "It's the entrance that dragons leave unsealed when they die—to encourage future visitors. Someone obviously tried to cover it with fabric."

The tunnel ran diagonally into the earth. The original must

have been much wider, but time had slowly sealed in the edges, like a wound patiently healing shut. It was wide enough for two of them to descend, side by side. Standing there made Mercy feel as if she were about to crawl down the throat of some terrible beast. A feeling that was only made worse by the great belches of hot air that kept wafting up from below.

"So, they find this place," Mercy said. "It's reported back in Kathor. The city claims it—and then someone says that it's fake. Everyone starts ignoring it. And someone covers the entrance with, what, some kind of tarp? They didn't want anyone else finding the place."

No one questioned that theory. When they all just stood there staring into the dark for long enough, Dahvid broke the silence. "Aren't we going in?"

Theo shook his head. "I'd rather find a secondary tunnel. This one . . . it would be like knocking on the front door. The dragon leaves it behind on purpose. It's enchanted so that he'll know we're coming. We want to go around the back of the house. Break into a window, so to speak. There should be other tunnels. Wild animals are attracted to burial chambers for the same reasons that humans are—they are nexuses of power and magic. Maybe we can find an old wolf tunnel or something. . . ."

Dahvid was staring at him. "Why did you make us do all that digging then?"

"Oh." Theo looked around at their abandoned shovels, the sweaty faces. "Well, we had to at least confirm *where* the chamber is. Now we know."

Before Dahvid could reply, movement drew their attention. All of them saw the distant figure at the same time. Or figures, rather. A man stumbled over the top of one of the distant hillsides. Maybe five hundred paces west of their location. He was trailed by three hounds. Mercy let out a massive sigh of relief. This is what she'd needed. Something to go in their favor.

"That's the houndmaster I hired," Mercy said, already starting to walk in that direction. "One of his hounds tracked the scent to this location. I'd imagine they can find one of the tunnels you're talking about, Theo. Far easier than we could. It'll save us a few hours."

She'd taken a dozen steps before realizing the houndmaster had not moved. He was just close enough that she could make out his figure, but too far to see any nuance in his expression. As she watched, he raised one hand to his lips. There was a sharp whistle that echoed through the valleys around them, carried by the wind.

All three hounds shot forward.

Running at a full sprint. At this distance, they looked beautiful. Poetry in motion. But she knew from their introduction in the morgue that those creatures weren't pretty or elegant. They were hunters. Trained to track scents, seek out prey, and kill if necessary. She watched in confusion as their movements triangulated. One dog took the lead. The other two looped wider and she finally realized they were moving to *hem* something in.

It took Dahvid's grasp on her arm to realize *they* were the something. He hissed in her ear to start moving and to start moving now. A final glance showed that the hounds had already covered nearly half the distance. Their great flanks rising and falling. Their eyes glowing like half-dead embers in the fading light. When the terrain took them out of sight, Mercy ripped her gaze away and ran back to the others. A decision had already been made.

Theo didn't like it, but he didn't protest, either, because what option did they have? Their crew began the descent into the main boring tunnel. She heard a whisper of magic and saw Theo setting barriers up at the entrance. Something to slow the hounds down once they arrived. Mercy's heart was beating fast in her chest. Louder than she'd ever heard it before. It took several minutes of dark descent to realize the beating she was hearing did not belong to her. Something else was waiting for them. Down in the bowels of this place.

Thump, thump, thump.

The darkness welcomed them with open arms.

47

REN MONROE

Her first thought was to mobilize as fast as possible. Any wizard who knew the standard deoxygenation spells. Even water-shaping magic would be useful. She thundered back into the war room, ready to join the others, and found Able Ockley sitting idly, watching the fires burn through the window. No one was rushing out to stop the fires. They were just . . . watching it happen.

"What is this? Why aren't we getting people out there?"

"Because it's too late," he replied.

"Too late? We have magic. We can put those fires out."

"We could, but the damage is already done. Look up."

Ren crossed the room to get a better angle. Of course. The Heights, being so exposed to the elements, had been created with a highly regulated atmosphere. The system cycled through preset weather patterns that were designed to support the general vegetation and appease the wealthy residents who called the Heights home. Regulation like that could only be executed in a small, controlled environment. To achieve that, they designed a massive sphere to enclose the floating section of the city. She knew from her studies that the initial casting had required hundreds of wizards, alternating shifts for days.

It was not something they could replicate if the current sphere failed. Above, dark clouds of smoke were gathering. Pressing up against the edges of the barrier before pooling into a faux thunderhead. Clearly, there was no release valve. At least not one large enough to handle the amount of toxins that had start spilling into the air. The dome would have been designed to handle a few fires—not dozens all at once. Which meant the same spells that kept out brutal chills and harsh storms for nearly a decade were now trapping noxious fumes. How long before the air they were breathing was unsafe? Her mind went straight to solutions.

"What about Winslow's dispersion charm? If we have enough people . . ."

"Where would the toxins disperse to?" Ockley asked, and it was clear that he'd been sitting there thinking about the problem since the fire began. "Dispersion magic relies on an endless atmosphere. We don't have that in the Heights. There are release valves at the corners of the dome, designed for air rotation, but they're not large enough to matter. Not with that much smoke."

Ren felt helpless. "Why not destroy the barrier?"

"And expose a floating city to the elements that exist at this height? Besides, that would require *power*. We'd need almost everyone casting spells around the clock to actually destroy the thing. No, there's only one option."

Ren stared at him. "Leave. As soon as possible."

She'd secretly been hoping that wouldn't happen until Theo returned. The journey to Meredream felt like one they should take together. A new place, a new home, a new life. She quietly set that ideal version aside, setting it on a dusty shelf in the corner of her thoughts. The fires were forcing their hand. There was nothing else to be done.

"I'll spread the word."

It didn't take long for Balmerick to fall into a frenzied panic. People were shouting down from windows, bellowing across hallways. Gathering all their personal possessions and more. There was no longer a guarantee that what they left on campus would remain safe. If they wanted something to survive, they had to take it with them. As everyone scrambled, a stream of new people began arriving at the edge of campus. Able Ockley took a small group down to greet them, worried it might be an attack, but it became clear they were trying to survive the same fires. These were the residents who'd watched them uncertainly from their windows. They'd come hoping for rescue, but the problem was that none of them had magic. When Ren and the rest of the wizards ported to Meredream, all of them would be stranded here.

"I'll check the aerie," Ren said, when Ockley returned. "Keep everyone moving to the portal room, and tell them to only bring what they really need."

Small packs of wizards began making their way across the main quad. Ren saw Nevelyn Tin'Vori fronting the entrance to the portal room. She could hear her friend giving repeated instructions about what to do and what to expect. In the other direction, the nonmagical survivors were huddled, looking miserable and uncertain. That was fair, given they were now trapped on a floating island that someone had set on fire.

Someone.

Ren actually stopped walking for a second, struck by that thought. There had been several explosions. Fires were spreading more quickly than normal. The only way to break through the wards up here would be to coordinate several fires that slowly drained the magical barriers from several directions. Either the Heights had just suffered the unluckiest catastrophe ever—or someone had designed this attack. She made a mental note to ask about who'd been away from campus. But as she started walking again, she realized she had little time to play the role of spy.

When she made it to the aerie, she saw one wyvern had returned.

Finally, a stroke of good fortune. Ren found the rider halfway through stripping out of his gear. His hair was wild and windblown. He also smelled like the inside of a barn. The sort of thick animal scent that undoubtedly meant his mount had worked hard to wing their crew out west—and even harder to get back with haste. She hated to demand more of them.

"Can you manage a few more flights? Short ones this time."

The rider didn't complain. Instead, he nodded and put his gear back on. The rescue was arranged. She just hoped the creature had enough energy to wing the entire group to safety. It would likely take a dozen flights to get them all to the lower city. And it didn't help that the number of people crowded by the front of campus had already grown.

Next, Ren rendezvoused at the portal room.

A proper crowd fronted the building. At least forty of the

surviving wizards were already gathered. Nevelyn had been busy organizing the children. She'd apparently assigned them "buddies," which Ren thought was a clever system. Most of their parents had approved travel to the Heights. They all believed their children would be safer there than in the city below. None of them had been notified about the change of plans to take everyone to Meredream. There wasn't time for that. All they could hope was that the parents wanted their children in the safest place imaginable.

"Head count?" Ren asked when she reached Nevelyn.

"We've got forty-eight of fifty-six . . . I think. The children are so damn squirmy."

"And yet, you're quite good with them."

Nevelyn offered her a world-class scowl. Ren grinned back at her. She'd grown to like her former accomplice. They were as close as two people could be who naturally kept the rest of the world at arm's length. "Could you do me a favor?"

Nevelyn nodded without hesitation.

Ren kept her voice low. "When the count's close to the full number, let me know if anyone is missing—or if you see anything odd. Those fires were no accident." She eyed the waiting group. There were students she didn't know, as well as the people she'd met at Beacon House. No one that she instinctively trusted or distrusted, which unfortunately made everyone a suspect. "It might be easier once everyone's inside. What are we waiting for? Is Ingrid still working on the magic?"

Nevelyn shrugged. "I don't know. I was just standing here and people kept assuming I was in charge for some reason."

"Well, you are in charge."

"I don't want to be in charge. You be in charge."

Ren grinned again. "Right. So we're waiting for no reason then?"

"Gods. Feel free to make an announcement."

More chaos ensued as everyone funneled from the courtyard and into the narrower confines of the portal room. Ren thought that Ingrid might still be touching up her spellwork. Instead, she found the old woman snuggled into one of the chairs, tucked beneath a blanket, and very soundly asleep. Ren's second concern was that the room would not accommodate a group of their size. She'd only ever seen packs of six or seven students use the portal at once.

She watched as every seat began to fill.

Avid was at the very back of the group filing inside. She was struggling under the weight of a massive pack. "I pulled every important text I could find. I thought they'd be safe up here, but now I'm not sure. If the Makers start burning libraries in the lower city, we'll have copies of the most important magical concepts. For future generations."

Ren nodded at her thoughtfulness. The girl found an empty seat next to her grandmother as Nevelyn performed yet another count. Ren could hear her hissing threats at a few of the children who'd made a game out of swapping seats. It might have been funnier if they were not all heading into a forced exile. The reality was starting to set in. Like a stone in the pit of her stomach.

The wax sculpture vanished.

Ren frowned, and then finally felt the familiar pull across her bond. The walls crumbled to dust. The faces and lights around the room blended into something far darker. Ren's feet set down inside a dark cavern. Someone had cast a light cantrip. In its glow, she saw the escort group. Her intuition about the bond had been correct. Whatever damage Dr. Horn had done was fast-healing. At least enough for her to be pulled across the world to witness what Theo wanted her to see.

No one appeared to be hurt, but where were they? Already underground? The air felt thick with heat and . . . something else. Ren felt a sudden tightening in the center of her chest. As if someone had knotted a rope around her heart and was now tugging it, patiently, hand over hand, in a direction that she did not want to go. It was a particular feeling of helplessness. Similar to how she'd felt on the table before their severance procedure or in Della's half-house moments before being tortured. Like there was some inevitable *presence* that had been waiting for her arrival.

But then Theo stepped into her vision. That helpless feeling faded. He was wearing his protective suit and the cloak the Shiverians had provided. All the additional layers were dark fabric, which drew out the brightness of his hair and the paleness of his skin. He looked terribly handsome.

"We're in the main boring tunnel," Theo said, clearly speaking aloud for her benefit. "We have a few unexpected guests, but we're safe for now. Our plan is to navigate down to the main chamber and begin soon. Is everything okay there?"

Of course. He must have felt the rush and panic of the last hour. All of that would have found its way across their bond. As raw feeling at the very least. Ren knew she could not speak to him in this form—so instead she pressed her current confluence of feelings across the bond: persistence, determination, steadiness. Yes, there were fires, but they had a plan: Meredream. Theo glanced directly at her ghostly form, nodded once, and then cut off the connection.

She could still see his eyes—like burning embers—when reality doubled back. The sculpture and the people and Nevelyn Tin'Vori hovering over her, frowning.

"What was that then?"

Ren blinked, her head suddenly swimming. "The . . . what I mentioned before. Theo and Dahvid and the others. They're in the main tunnel now. About to make their approach."

Nevelyn nodded. And then cursed. "Damn it. Lost the count. Let me start again."

It took another loop for her to report back. They had fifty-four of the fifty-six wizards in the room. Ockley was still outside, overseeing the wyvern departure, which left one straggler.

"Someone is missing," Ren whispered.

"Which could be suspicious—or it could mean someone slept in."

Ren nodded. "Let's have everyone light their candles."

Her mind was racing as Nevelyn called out the instructions. Who was missing? If it was one of the students, she'd have no way of cross-checking the person. Able would potentially know them all, but even that felt unlikely. Was it one of the survivors she'd met at Beacon House? Ren tried to mentally walk back through that evening, every face and conversation, but her mind was tangled up in all the other logistical constraints.

The process of lighting the candle began. One of the Balmerick students detached the ceremonial rod hanging from the far wall. The lone wick was lit, and then they handed it off to the next person. Ren watched as Ellison Proctor repeated their motions. A pretense of lighting the candle that would serve the same function as actually lighting it. Slowly, the rod passed around the room clockwise. Some people were nervous, their hands trembling as they reached out. Ren watched it all and kept hoping some small detail would be jarred loose.

A few seats down from her, Ren spied the girl again: Winnie Fletcher. Her right leg was shaking nervously. She was also fiddling with her ghost-white braid again. The same way she had at Beacon House. Ren realized that her father was not here, and could not be here, as he lacked the magic to port up to the Heights. The poor girl was about to travel away from him and everything she'd ever known. No wonder she was afraid. Ren quietly slid from her seat and crouched down in front of the girl.

"Hey. There's no need to be nervous," Ren whispered. "This spell lets us all travel together. It's easier that way. Strength in numbers. We'll get there just fine. I promise."

Winnie nodded. "It's just . . . one of the other boys, he told us someone died in here."

Ren's heart sank into her stomach. The girl looked terrified as she recounted the rumor.

"He said there was this accident and the magic didn't work and someone *died*."

It was hard not to feel as if Timmons's ghost were hovering behind the girl, watching and waiting for Ren's answer. She steeled herself before looking Winnie in the eye.

"I will not let anything happen to you. I promise you. I promise it twice."

She had no idea if the girl understood that Ren was making a double vow, but the words earned a firm nod from Winnie. Ren nodded back before taking her seat again. Even though she was sitting perfectly still, her heart was thrashing wildly in her chest. Aside from Theo's survival, nothing right now seemed to matter more than what she'd just said to that little girl. It felt like the only road that might lead her away from her revenge and her guilt and back to something whole.

Halfway through the lighting process, Able Ockley returned. He offered her a perfunctory nod before dropping into his seat beside Avid. At least that meant one task was finished. The nonmagical survivors of the Heights were safe in the lower city. Ren's turn arrived. She took the lighting rod and the echo of this moment was not lost on her. Two years ago, she'd stood in this very spot. Sat in this exact chair. Ren took a deep breath, lit the waiting candle, and handed the rod to the next person. She was quietly brooding when she noticed that Nevelyn was in an intense, whispered discussion with her ward. Josey nodded emphatically about something, which had Nevelyn rising and crossing the room to speak with Ren.

"Theo's the one who's missing," she whispered.

Ren frowned. "Well, of course. He's with the hunting—"

It finally hit her. Nevelyn didn't mean her Theo. She meant the boy. The one who had made Ren laugh so hard down at Beacon House. Supposedly named for Theo Brood. A serving member of their house—and someone they'd never once thought to question or double-check, because his existence had felt like a punchline. Ren stood. She made her own scan of the room and confirmed that the boy wasn't here. She crossed over to where Ockley sat.

"What room did you assign Theodore Crane?"

He frowned. "Third floor. Back wing . . . I think it was room 307."

Her eyes swung to Avid. "How long do I have? Before the spell activates?"

"Less than thirty minutes."

"I'll be back. Keep everyone calm."

Nevelyn looked ready to come with her, but Ren reassured her with a quick nod. She knew she would be fine. She'd gone toe to toe with Landwin Brood. She wasn't afraid of Theo's cousin. She didn't even think it was likely that she'd find him. If he was responsible for the fires, she suspected that he would have already ported back to the lower city to rendezvous with whoever had assigned him that terrible task. But she knew that searching his room could lead to clues. She walked back across the quad, her feet aiming her toward that distant dormitory. Adrenaline pumped in her chest as she gripped and regripped her horseshoe wand. The feeling matched what was churning across her bond from Theo. Both of them were on the precipice of something terrible and uncertain. Both of them were unsure of what danger lurked around the next corner.

And still—they kept moving forward.

Into the unknown.

48

MERCY WHITAKER

They'd not reached the actual chamber yet, but Mercy could hear a voice whispering to her. Just on the edge of hearing. She thought she heard her name. Spoken in her grandmother's voice. Then in Devlin's. She didn't listen to their silent pleas because she knew they weren't real. The others showed varying degrees of agitation. The only solution was to keep moving.

"Once we're inside, we'll need warding spells up and ready. We're going to force Arakyl to feast on that barrier of magic until I've established all the visualization spells. Then we'll work on cutting away the manipulation threads. When that first shield fails, we rotate a new pair in to cast the next ward. Theo, you wanted the first casting?"

He nodded. "I'll partner with Redding. Remember, it's not just about creating that initial shield. We have to actively keep feeding that magic. Bolstering it. Even dragons follow Wickham's law of aggression. That means each new shield has to be powerful enough to keep Arakyl from focusing on the spell that Mercy creates—or else he'll attack the one person we can't afford for him to attack. Guion and Win, you'll be in charge of that second casting. Dahvid, if you—"

"I will focus on destroying the threads," he said, cutting off the possibility of being commanded. Mercy thought it was clear that the two of them had some sort of history. He was certainly not eager to take an order from a Brood. "We will focus on the threads until those dogs get down to the main chamber. Then we'll all need to tighten our formation and focus on the immediate threat first."

When everyone felt confident in the plan, Theo and Redding maneuvered to the front of the cramped antechamber. They began their spellwork. Mercy took a deep and steadying breath as a nearly invisible shield formed in the air. She felt a dark foreboding. As if the eyes of some ancient creature had flickered open and were slowly turning to them. The shield stretched, gossamer and trembling, across the entryway. A final pull on the magic locked the spell into place.

Whispers sounded in the air. Hundreds of different voices. From her past. From her present. From her future—if she even had one outside these walls. Mercy heard them whispering different fates. Ones where she died and worms ate her corpse. In others, she grew immeasurably powerful, ruling over entire kingdoms. Just as suddenly, the voices fell away, leaving a terrible silence. Theo turned back to look at her and his eyes were two lightless pits in a waxen face.

"Come all this way to die?"

Mercy blinked. "What?"

His features had smoothed back out. "Are you ready?"

She knew it had to be Arakyl. Attempting to plant seeds of darkness between them. She offered Theo the most confident nod she could manage and the group began moving. They were greeted by a slight deepening of shadows. Without the light cantrip, she could only see the person directly in front of her. The walls tightened too, forcing them into a crouching walk. The tunnel wound back and forth. It was like they were walking through the belly of an impossibly large snake. Finally, the trail opened back up, depositing them in the main burial chamber.

Light emanated from the dragon's corpse. Nearly enough to reach where they stood—and from that angle, the chamber appeared untouched. All the normal infrastructure—great steel doors or filtration systems—were absent. The lack of human interference left the air pregnant with heat and bright with twisting colors that kept flickering in and out of her vision, depending on which direction she looked. She felt the substance needling at her protective suit. Probing for weaknesses.

The chamber itself was massive. Large enough that she could only just make out the far wall through the churning fumes. Her eyes finally focused on what they'd come to see. A dragon.

Arakyl.

Even thinking his name felt like a mistake now. An invitation into her mind. Mercy was forced to watch a black-scaled dragon wing through an empty sky. The creature was so large that it blotted out the sun. She knew she was witnessing another time, another world entirely. Before her ancestors ever arrived on this continent.

The same force that had guided her away set her back down like a rag doll. She barely kept her feet—and in the same moment, Theo and Redding's shield flickered. It was warding off the dragon's mental attack. With her clarity returned, Mercy performed a quick assessment of the corpse. His size dwarfed the wyverns they'd just ridden on. Most of the dragon's flesh had rotted away, but only a few of the scales were missing. She counted three or four at most. Those spots were backlit by a purple flame. So, too, were the empty eye sockets. The light made it seem as if he were watching their approach. Still alive. A half-rotted neck ran in a sinuous line back to the body. Mercy was surprised how defenseless he seemed. All that stood between them and Arakyl's corpse was a slight descent and roughly fifty paces of packed mud. Could it really be this simple?

And then the dead dragon raised his head.

The great skull twisted ever so slightly to face in their direction. Mercy thought she was imagining it. Dragons were known for feeding human minds illusions. But then she heard Theo Brood say in a breathless voice, "*Gods, it can move!*"

The arcane fire swirling inside the creature flashed in warning. She knew those bright swirls were exactly the sort of thing dragons had always used to hunt. A bright light designed to briefly paralyze their prey. Humans had only survived because they were smarter than other creatures.

"Everyone get moving! Now, now, now!"

Her voice was a shove back in the direction of their purpose. Theo and Redding fell into lockstep with one another. Dahvid flanked Mercy on the right. Margaret on her left. She could not see them, but she knew that Guion and Win were quietly bringing up the rear. All of them were moving with a single directive in mind. Halfway across the room, Arakyl unleashed a stream of purple fire at them. The blast struck the center of the shield with force. Theo and Redding barely set their feet in time, skidding back a pace, but it was enough. The shield held. The purple light dispersed. It would have been easy to stare at their back and forth. Watch them pour magic into the shield's layers as Arakyl prepared another blast of purple light. But that was not her purpose here.

Mercy emptied her mind.

She pretended she was in the operatory with Dr. Horn. Going through the routine list of spells. She was just a doctor. This dragon was just a patient in need of a severance procedure. Mercy's first spell had that familiar, silver light creeping into the air. She had to work harder than normal to maintain her radius, but the magic held. She pushed it outward before using the next spell to cocoon her and the others from its effect. Before she could cast the third layer, Dr. Horn appeared in her vision. He was walking forward, inspecting what she'd cast. She heard him whispering to remember balance. It was shocking to see him there. Even more shocking when he turned to her, his face covered in those terrible bruises, his jaw dangling unnaturally.

"I will kill you, Mercy Beatrice Whitaker. I will bury you in the darkest part of the earth. Leave you rotting in a place where no one will ever find you . . . where no light will ever touch . . ."

There was another blast of purple light. Mercy shook herself. Dr. Horn wasn't there. It was an illusion. She gritted her teeth, so hard her jaw started to hurt, and began her work again. The sphere she'd cast was thick enough now for the next phase. Distantly, she heard Theo calling out for Guion and Win. They were about to perform the first rotation. Mercy ignored their voices and their movement. Her work was all that mattered.

She set both hands to the edge of the floating sphere. Splayed her fingers as far as they could go—her stunted ones protesting the movement. And then she gave the waiting magic a push. Several things happened at the same time. There was a flash of bright light. A hot white color that briefly blinded all of them. Then the first shield shattered. Guion and Win stepped forward as Theo and Redding retreated. All with flawless timing. Their shield roared forward and it was more than enough to keep Arakyl's attention. A second later, her own spell found its equilibrium. The magic rippled outward—like a stone thrown into water—and a third light filled the room.

Threads.

It was just like being in the operatory. Bright silvers and fickle reds and luminous yellows. Magic that had always been there. Her spell simply made them visible. She watched them slowly populate around the room. Dozens of threads . . .

. . . and dozens and dozens. Mercy watched with growing horror. The spell was revealing more threads than she'd ever seen in any human patient. Great ropes of beaten gold. Smaller cords that looked like slashes of sunrise. The thickest thread she saw protruded from Arakyl's chest and was a sort of burnished bronze. She knew she wasn't the only one who could see them. Everyone in their group kept stealing glances up at the complex web that was weaving itself in the air. Even Arakyl seemed briefly distracted. Mercy knew she should keep moving. Rattle off orders to Dahvid and Margaret. But the threads were *still* appearing. Her last patient had a few hundred. This was well into the thousands. Her task could no longer be called difficult. It was impossible.

I might as well go home. Give up. Surrender to the majesty that is . . .

"Mercy."

Dahvid was there. She felt his breath against her neck. A faded mint. He was so close to her, in fact, that she could feel his heart beating against her shoulder blade.

"Mercy. Do not listen to that voice. We need you now. Do you hear me? We need you to tell us what to do. You haven't moved in over a minute now. Stop listening to him. Stay with us. . . ."

It had seemed like a moment. Mere seconds. Mercy focused on Dahvid's touch on her shoulder. That mint that smelled so much nicer than the rotting corpse in the room. She slid one hand down to the enchanted saw blade tucked into her belt loop. As her fingers closed around the handle, her confidence returned. It was like setting her feet back on solid ground.

"Tell us what to do first," Dahvid repeated. "Just guide us."

She was nodding. "Keep the shields rotating. I need to test the threads. Once I know which ones coordinate with the manipulated, we can start eliminating them. . . ."

But the colors were all wrong. She'd learned the patterns with previous patients. Silver for mentors and teachers. Kin were always some variant of red. The colors she saw filling the room now were different from any she'd seen before. An entirely new pattern. It could be that the fumes were altering their appearance. Or that dragons were different from humans?

All she could do was test them, color by color.

She seized a thread of faded gold. Carefully, she lined up the edge of her handsaw and began to cut. The enchanted teeth caught. Back and forth. She was rewarded with a glimpse: Birds. Dozens of birds in midflight, and then she blinked back to the present. Mercy spied another thread that was the same color just ten paces to the left. She went to it and repeated the same motion. This time she saw a stag, bent over a stream, lapping the water with its pink tongue.

"Animals," she announced, mostly to herself. "Those light gold threads are for animals. Maybe prey? Remember that. . . ."

Dahvid nodded. She tried to ignore how closely he was watching her as she seized yet another thread and began to cut. Silver threads were for other dragons. She was gifted glimpses of conversations, aerial battles, and more. She heard voices that she knew the world had forgotten long ago. Those threads left her the most disoriented. Twice she needed to be steadied by Dahvid.

At some point, Guion and Win had switched out again. Theo and Redding stepped forward with their group's third shield spell. Great bursts of purple flame continued striking the edges of their barrier, and Arakyl's magic seemed to be corroding their defenses faster each time. As if the dragon was learning their magic, adapting to it as any intelligent creature might.

White threads for landscapes. Red threads seemed to connect back to younger versions of Arakyl. She saw what he looked like as a hatchling. No bigger than her. Finally, Mercy found the threads that connected to people. A putrid yellow that looked like pollen. Four testing cuts revealed a pattern. She saw a man sitting on the ramparts of a castle, tapping a bored rhythm against the stones. A woman on a morning walk in a forest. Each image a confirmation, because in each one she saw the familiar red scarf that was being used to spread the manipulation spell.

"It's these ones," she announced. "Any that are this shade of yellow."

Now that she knew the right color, she stepped back and tried to consider the overall portrait again. Just like before, she found the sheer amount staggering. There were hundreds that were that shade. At least one third of the visible connections. She knew there was nothing else they could do but begin. Mercy found the spot where she'd performed the test cut and began sawing back and forth, back and forth. Far less delicate strokes than she'd use in a normal surgery.

Finally, she was through.

The thread writhed briefly in the air. Like a snake rearing back to strike—and then it vanished with a brief gasp of pollen-like dust. Behind her, Dahvid and Margaret had already set to work. She saw them lining up their blades before taking massive swings. Their blades made far quicker work of the threads than her saw.

Another shield failed. Theo Brood called out the transition. Mercy felt a brief wave of heat—but it was met with another new shield. At least their first phase in the plan was working. Methodically, they eliminated every single thread in the section that was blocked off by the summoned ward. "Theo!" she called. "We need to shift. I need access to more threads."

Dark laughter filled the air. The sound snaked through

Mercy's gut. All of them looked up in time to see a figure high-stepping over the skeletal neck of the dragon. Three shadows glided after him, moving with deadly efficiency. The houndmaster had arrived.

49

REN MONROE

Ren had lived in this dormitory her sophomore and junior year. Unable to afford any upgraded amenities, she'd been placed on the very top floor in one of the most cramped rooms on campus. Still, it had been hers. She'd relished the freedom, the privacy. A space that she could form to her own liking.

Now she walked the same stairs she had then. Her wand up and ready. She tried to remember everything she knew about Theo Crane. He'd claimed to be an animator. His father, Ben, had apparently built Vega—who even now was clutching at Ren's shoulder. That felt like a strangely deep connection for someone who turned out to be a traitor. Didn't Crane stand to gain far more from House Brood than the Makers? The only possible flaw she could find was Theo's misstep at the party. He hadn't known that the boy's father was dead. Could that be it? Maybe the Broods had neglected the Crane family during their time of mourning, and maybe Theo's mistake had salted that wound? If the death had happened anytime in the last year, either Theo or Landwin might have been too distracted to properly honor their family.

Ren considered those possibilities as she ascended to the third floor. The landing offered a full view down the dormitory's upper hallway. Rooms flanked both sides running the entire length. The room Ockley had guessed would be roughly halfway down. Evens were on the left. Odds on the right. Ren adjusted the grip on her wand and started walking.

317, 315, 313, 309 . . .

It was unlocked. Left open, in fact. She could see just a sliver of light through the crack. Ren performed a quick probing spell. Testing for counters and traps. There was nothing cast across the entrance, though. She opened the door slowly, wand raised. No one sprang out from the corner. No one shouted for her to get out. There was no sign of Theo Crane sleeping on his bed in the corner.

The room was empty.

Only the desk displayed signs of occupancy. She glided across the room, drawn to the open books and journals and pencils. It almost looked like the occupant had been right in the middle of exams and had stepped out to get a quick cup of tea. She was wondering how to confirm this had been his room when her eyes landed on initials, stitched into the bottom right corner: *TC*.

"What were you up to, Crane?"

One of the pages of the nearest textbook had been dog-eared. It detailed a number of conflagration spells. The exact kind of information someone might need if they were hoping to create and spread a fire. Ren frowned before turning through the pages. Why leave the books like this? It would have been obvious to anyone who stumbled into the room. Maybe he simply hadn't been planning to return? But then how had he departed from the Heights? She supposed it was possible he could have pilfered one of the candle stubs. It wasn't as if she'd been there to monitor all their gathered supplies.

Another textbook caught her eye. The page was turned to an essay on the historical development of insurrections. Really? Crane was just casually reading up on the exact sort of revolution that he'd joined? Then, inspired by that reading, he'd taken it upon himself to go start a fire that would eliminate one of the best outposts for the surviving wizard contingent?

This scene felt contrived. Meant to be found. The only real thing, she realized, was Crane's journal. She flipped through the pages and saw that the handwriting didn't match the other notes around the table. "Shit." Turning, she began calling his name. "Crane?! You in here, Crane?"

Ren moved from room to room. Each time she would call his name—and then listen as the echoes faded. It wasn't until she reached the end of the hallway that she finally heard something. A terrible scratching sound. It took time to calibrate the direction of the noise—and then she was moving, hunting. There was a broom closet back near the stairs.

A quick spell blasted away the door's handle. She yanked it open. There were abandoned mops, scattered cleaning supplies, and Theo Crane. He was bound and gagged. Ren could sense a few layers of muting spells in the air. He'd wormed his way from a back corner. In the dark, he'd managed to roll to one side so that his hands, bound as they were, could reach the door. He'd been using his nails to scratch the wood. Any other sound he made would have been muted, but the wards his captor had set couldn't account for sounds the door itself made. It was clever of him.

"Who did this?" she asked, tearing away his gag. "Who was it, Crane?"

The words came tumbling out after a few ragged breaths. "Proctor. Ellison Proctor. He's sold the other houses to the Makers. When he . . . was down in Kathor. He made a deal with them. Deliver the other houses, and the Proctor family's holdings would be left untouched. Ren. I think something terrible is about to happen."

"I know, I know. He's already done it. The fires he started have been spreading across the Heights all morning. The atmosphere up here is wasted. Unlivable. We're going to Meredream. The portal room is already active, Crane. We'll have to deal with him when we get to the city. . . ."

But Theo's entire face contorted. "No. That's . . . first phase. I was following him, Ren. I was suspicious of him. He passed all the information back to the Makers. They wanted him to destroy the Heights, but that's only because they know about Meredream, too. He sent them the location. The coordinates. He was taking notes this whole time. In that journal. They know, Ms. Monroe. They know where we're going. They know everything."

Her heart stopped beating in her chest.

"When did he get them the details?"

"Days ago. It was days ago, ma'am."

Meredream was at least a full day's travel from Kathor on foot. Perhaps longer. Her instinctual thought had been that it was simply too far for the Makers to make good use of the information. Sure, they might eventually track down the city and set up an army outside the gates—but by then, what would it matter? The wizards would be safely inside. There were farms that could sustain them for years within the gates. But now she knew that several days had passed since the first reveal. If Proctor had managed to hand them that information early enough—the Makers might already have assembled a small army. What if the place they were porting to was surrounded?

"Shit, shit, shit!"

Ren turned and sprinted. Crane was smart enough to not ask questions. He ran after her. She reached the stairs, taking two or three at a time, and nearly sent herself sprawling over one of the railings. The boy had gained on her some by the time they reached the bottom floor. She started running down the main hall before Crane shouted, "This way! The back door! It's faster!"

He was right. She'd forgotten about the back hallway. Her left knee nearly buckled as she cut back in that direction. Crane was shouldering through the door and she darted through the gap with him. Both of them were already breathless, their chests heaving, but they kept running. All the way across the quad. He crossed the threshold just before her. The hallway leading into the room offered Ren a partial glimpse of its occupants. Ellison Proctor was sitting in that distance. When he saw Theo barreling in his direction, his eyes shocked wide.

"It's a trap!" Ren screamed. She was staggering down the hallway. Nearly there. "Ellison! Everyone needs to get out of the—"

Before she could say more, Ellison leapt the hip-high barrier. He scrambled over the wax sculpture, nearly on all fours, and lunged for the candle that everyone had so carefully lit. The flame pinched between his extended fingers. There was a gasp of smoke. Nothing happened. And then everything happened. The room's exterior lights flickered in rapid sequence. The warning she'd seen a hundred times. Ren saw—in that split second—a square of red fabric poking out of Ellison's coat pocket. That would be his sign to the Makers. A visual letting them know he should be spared. Ren staggered one more step before magic thundered through the room. Power. Raw, untethered power. Ren felt the sudden force shoving her back. Like an angry god turning away a supplicant who'd prayed the wrong words.

No, no, no . . .

Something was wrong. That magic should have swept her off her feet. She should have felt her body compress, tightening into too-small spaces, as she raced through the waxways. Instead there was a deafening roar. Everyone in the room vanished. Nevelyn Tin'Vori and Able Ockley and Winnie Fletcher. All of them gone. Everyone except for Ren and Crane. The wind briefly buffeted her back into the nearest wall, and then everything went silent.

Perfectly still.

"It's a trap," she said, to no one at all.

50

NEVELYN TIN'VORI

Nevelyn vaulted through the soundless dark.

Her father had once taught her that a divided mind was a dangerous thing to take into the waxways, but that was exactly how she felt. One part of her mind was thinking of Ava and the fact that she hadn't been able to write her sister a second letter to say they were leaving for Meredream sooner than expected. She was also trying not to worry about the fact that her sister hadn't answered the first letter she sent. Ava was smart. Hopefully, she'd see the Heights on fire and know what to do. Another part of Nevelyn's mind was with Dahvid in that distant burial chamber. She hoped her brother knew she could not live without him. That his goal wasn't to play the hero, but to survive. All these thoughts echoed in that lightless place.

And then her feet set back down. A grass-covered hillside. Forest on their right and left. A slight slope leading to a nearly hidden rampart. Meredream.

It looked like a dream—until she saw Able Ockley. His lips were so bright and red that he looked as if he were wearing lipstick. And then the lipstick dribbled down his chin. *Blood*, Nevelyn realized. *That looks so much like blood.* An arrow had punched through his throat. A second one in his chest. A third in his abdomen. Ockley stumbled past Nevelyn, raised his wand, and cast one final spell. The magic didn't thunder or roar or pulse. The spell that issued forth didn't even make a sound. She watched a crescent moon form on the tip of his wand. A small flick of his wrist sent the magic racing into a group of charging soldiers. She watched as the magic *unmade* them.

There was no other word for it. The way their limbs suddenly abandoned them. How their bodies quietly crumbled to dust. Ockley collapsed sideways as his spell sent shockwaves back through the ranks of the surrounding army.

Army. There's an army here. Waiting for us.

Nevelyn's mind finally caught up with her body. Ren Monroe had come bursting back into the room. She'd screamed that this was a trap. Ellison Proctor . . . he had . . . crawled across the sculpture. Extinguished the flame. Accelerated the spell.

This is a trap.

Ockley's spell saved her. It was just enough of a distraction that she could get her bearings. Enough time to cast a shield spell as another volley of arrows thrummed in from the tree lines. Her shield caught one that would have been a death blow. Others weren't as lucky. She heard screams. The birth pangs of true chaos. Nevelyn whipped around, searching for Josey, and nearly trampled him. He was down on the ground . . . but alive. His face full of terror.

More arrows came. Nevelyn pulled the boy to his feet, tucking him protectively into her, and began slowly backing up to where the other wizards had formed a makeshift defense. A few of them had cast wards just in time. Avid Shiverian was now gliding through their ranks like a seasoned general. Nevelyn knew enough about magic to understand that she was using binding magic to seal the edges of their shields into one larger barrier. Nevelyn and Josey plunged inside that protection as more arrows whistled overhead. There were bodies everywhere. People down and wounded.

But as she looked out, she saw chaos there too. Ockley's spell had backed them up. No one was eager to face the same potential fate. She also saw people fleeing. Abandoning the gathered army and running away. She didn't understand why. All that mattered, however, was that far more were staying. The Makers had somehow gathered a literal army—and the bulk of it sat between the wizards and Meredream. Projectiles were still being launched from both sides of the forest. Most were deflected, but each one caused the larger ward to flicker. Small cracks were already starting to form. They were cocooned safely away thanks to Avid, but how long would the shields last?

A great horn sounded. There were shouts from the enemy generals. Once more, the army began its approach. A slow march toward their circle. Nevelyn knew they couldn't ward off projectiles *and* close-range combatants. If enough of the soldiers pressed in on them, their shields would shatter and the battle would be reduced to tighter skirmishes. Fights that favored hand-to-hand combat. The surrounding circle that was slowly tightening into a hangman's noose.

"Add layers to that outer ward!" Avid was shouting. "I've bound them together, but we need a second layer. Make them pay for every step! Projectile magic at the ready! Wake up! We did not come all this way just to die!"

Her voice was like a welcome sort of lightning. Loud enough and bright enough to shock some of the wizards back to life. Nevelyn saw them stagger into position. Casting additional wards or regripping their vessels. The tightening of their ranks made the one flaw in the formation all the more obvious: Ellison Proctor was making a break for it.

The handsome boy with the bright curls had betrayed them. She watched him sprint through the barrier, his red scarf clutched in one hand, held high enough that everyone could see it waving in the air. Nevelyn couldn't think of a spell to stop him in time.

Damn it, he's getting away.

But arrows punched through his chest. Ellison staggered, two steps to the right, and then he fell. Nevelyn's eyes shocked wide. They hadn't spared him. Even though he'd clearly given them this location for the trap—still, they hadn't spared him. *Which means they won't spare any of us.*

"Children to the center!" Nevelyn screamed, realizing that this was life or death. There would be no mercy for any of them. "I don't care if you think you're ready for a fight! There are about to be soldiers crashing through the wards and they will not hesitate to gut every single one of you. I cannot allow that. You are our future. Get to the middle and have your vessels ready. If the lines break, be ready to cast your own wards! Get moving! Now!"

Avid Shiverian offered a grateful nod. The children started

scrambling to the middle, but the larger problem was still coming. The army was only twenty paces away now.

"Anyone with combat experience," Avid shouted. "Get to the outside of the formation. You have magic. They do not. It's time to use it. Hold *nothing* back! Punish every step they take. I want Balmerick students layered in behind the first group. Let's keep communicating. Call out any breaks in the line. Everyone else—children and the elderly—"

The young girl cut off sharply. Nevelyn saw why. Another figure had separated from the group. It was not the same jolting sprint as Ellison Proctor. Instead, she watched the frail figure stumble outside their protective wards: Ingrid Shiverian. Nevelyn's first thought was that the older woman was confused. That she'd stumbled out beyond the safe zone by accident.

But then fire raced out from her raised wand with terrifying speed. The burst forced back the approaching soldiers. Ingrid took advantage of their hesitation. Her next spell was a comet of fire. It streaked over their heads like it had been shot from a cannon. The spell hit the largest tree in the forest. Ingrid swung her ward the other way and cast the same spell.

Fires ignited instantly. Spreading from branch to branch, limb to limb. The first soldier who lunged for the old woman caught a third bolt of fire right in the chest. The fire spread from him to the two closest troops. There were screams. Ingrid looked like she might cut a path through their entire army—until the first arrow caught her in the chest. Then a spear plunged into her stomach. She lost her grip on the wand she'd used her entire life, then fell. Avid didn't scream. She didn't fall to her knees. Instead, ever efficient, she sounded the order for the first attack.

"Projectiles! Now!"

Her grandmother had provided an opening. The first line of wizards took a step outside the barrier, and then streaks of every kind of magic cut through the air. Soldiers crumpled beneath blows of invisible force. Some were launched backward. One fell to the ground, writhing as his skin burned with some kind of acidic magic. Ingrid's fires were working too. Most of the enemy archers were too worried about the fire-eaten branches above them to keep firing. At the edges of the group, she saw a steady stream continuing to flee from the battle entirely. Several dozen at least.

We're winning. We have enough magic to win.

But then soldiers from the waiting ranks stepped up. Every single gap they'd just made, filled in an instant. Beyond them, rows of soldiers waited to do the same. Her eyes traced outward and she finally saw that they would need to win hundreds of battles, back to back to back, just to have a chance. Her next thought was much darker than the first.

We've already lost.

51

MERCY WHITAKER

Look at the mortals. Come all this way to kill what has already died!"

Mercy knew it wasn't the houndmaster's voice. There was a darkness in it that she recognized from their interrogation with the viceroy. Arakyl was using him like a puppet. Speaking through him.

"I know you. I have seen every life you would have lived! Theo Brood. He killed his own father. A weakling. A man who can do nothing on his own. Dahvid Tin'Vori—a coward who could not even save his brother. Who sacrificed his lover to win a battle! Look at the trail of dead you've left behind! Mercy Whitaker, how many have you ignored over the years? How many more souls could you have saved? You are selfish. A sniveling worm. You live a lie! They knock and knock and you will not answer! Guion Prather . . ."

Before he could reveal the man's secrets, Guion stepped

forward and unleashed a bolt of magic. It was a bright stream of silver light. A projectile that hissed across the room with so much speed that it was hard for the naked eye to follow. It should have struck the houndmaster square in the chest. Instead, the dragon's eyes flashed in answer. Powerful, hungry. Mercy saw that he'd been baiting them. Hoping for a reaction. Any small lack of discipline. It had worked.

The bolt of magic froze in midair.

She could see it spinning ever so slightly, the tip as sharp as any spear. Time stood still, however. The bolt failed to reach its target. And then magic *raced* back in their direction. The spell she saw was the color of a bruise. It filled the air with a corpse-like scent. Something dark and rank and long buried. Arakyl used Guion's spell like a road. All that darkness completely ignored their summoned ward—as if he'd opened a door for it—and the magic hit him right in the gut.

She expected an explosion. For him to go flying back against the cavern wall. Instead, he crumpled inward. Crushed from the outside by an invisible hand. His blood vessels bloomed suddenly before exploding. He was dead in seconds. Mercy knew it was true because Win—bonded to his brother—dropped down to his knees and let loose a bloodcurdling scream.

Arakyl took advantage of the distraction.

Another bolt of purple light spewed out from those skeletal jaws. This was the most powerful spell yet. It slammed into their current shield, shattering it to pieces. Mercy heard Theo calling to Redding to summon another one—but before they could, great shadows cut through their ranks. Teeth glinting in the fickle light. Mercy tried to call out a warning, but too late.

The hounds were amongst them.

52

REN MONROE

R en paced back and forth.
Like a caged animal.

Theodore Crane was seated. He kept rubbing his wrists where the bindings had left cuts and irritations. They'd both used the ceremonial rod to light the candle again. The room's spell had activated. Time was counting down. The required burn for two people wasn't nearly as long, but any delay was enough to fill her mind with the darkest possible thoughts.

What was happening? Had an army ambushed them? Would they arrive only to find all their fellow wizards already slain? Or had the others ported and found Meredream waiting for them in the distance? The summoned army too late to stop them? There was no way of knowing. Panic and uncertainty drummed inside her skull. She also felt Theo across their bond. Her own heightened emotions had muted her normal sense of him. Over the last two minutes, he had moved from adrenaline to panic—then panic to fear. She found herself desperately hoping he had the good sense to pull her across their bond. She could help him.

I need to do something. Let me do something.

Crane broke the silence. "Are you sure we should go? I just . . . if it's a trap, aren't we porting right into it? The two of us . . . we could still survive."

Ren didn't shame him for saying the truth out loud. She'd already considered and dismissed the same idea. In fact, there was some former version of Ren Monroe that would have already plotted her own escape. Save herself. Survive and see tomorrow. Crane was right, after all. There was a possibility that when the portal activated, they would arrive in a field full of corpses. A feast for crows. And then it would be the two of them against whatever was left of the waiting army.

Could they really survive that?

She doubted it. But there was also a chance the other wizards were still alive. Fighting back against the Makers. Ren imagined Avid and Able and Nevelyn casting protective spells. She could see the children—Winnie Fletcher amongst them—huddled behind the older wizards in terror. In that version of the world, Ren's choice still mattered.

"If we save even one of them, it will be worth it."

She could hardly believe those words had come from her. *Gods, I've been spending far too much time with Theo Brood.* Crane only nodded in response. His eyes were still on the ground. Ren decided to offer him a way out. After all, he was not responsible for any of this. He wasn't the one who'd spent a decade plotting out a revenge. He had not bonded with a boy, fought an empire, and weakened it to the point that some outside force found a way in. That was all her fault. Not his.

"Look, you don't have to go. I promise you, there is no shame in it. We are knocking on death's door. It is very possible that we will port and be dead within minutes. I can't tell you what will happen. All I know is that I have to go. It is not a choice that I can make for you. As one of the heads of House Brood—I command you to do whatever you want. There will be no punishment if you leave now. No judgment at all. Theodore, the choice is yours."

Ren turned and began pacing again. She listened for the scrape of his footsteps. The sound of him retreating from the room. It never came. When she glanced back, he was rubbing his wrists, crying quietly to himself, but the true measure of Theodore Crane was that he didn't leave. He stayed in his seat and braced himself for the unknown. Only thirteen years old—and marked by a bravery few would ever know. Ren nodded to him before taking her own seat.

The exterior lights flashed again. About five minutes left. She tried to settle her mind. Think through spells. What to do if they ported into a long-range battle versus close combat. She mentally rehearsed the steps she would take. How she would react to someone with a sword or someone with a spear or someone with a hammer. All the small variations. Unbidden, she saw an image of her mother. How would she react if that was the face she saw across from her on the battlefield? Desperation flooded her senses. A primal fear. What any animal felt just before it faced its own death. Ren thought the feeling was coming from her own thoughts until she sensed it.

The sharp and familiar tug from Theo.

Ren allowed herself to be pulled through space and time, but the expected sensation of *arrival* never came. Her eyes opened to inky darkness. She could not see her own feet or her own hands. Darkness stretched in every direction. A realm of endless shadow.

Am I in the waxways?

Ren's thought was answered by movement. Two eyes flickered open and they looked like twin flames. The purple light was bright enough for her to make out the edges of that hulking form, where shadow ended and dragon began. She knew without asking that this was *their* dragon too. The dark puppeteer behind the attack on the city—behind the manipulation of her mother.

Finally, I come face-to-face with my creator.

She heard laughter in the words. Ren had been prepared for sharp-edged threats or gilded promises. Dragons were famous for their guile. Luring people like her into a false sense of security. Was that what he was doing? She mentally steeled herself before locking eyes with the great creature.

"What's that supposed to mean?"

Another laugh. It tolled in the air like a broken bell.

It means what it means. You are the one who brought me back to life, Little Ren Monroe.

The words echoed. Back at Safe Harbor, the voice speaking through Viceroy Gray had called her that too: Little Ren Monroe. She'd found it odd then, but she'd lacked context. They hadn't yet solved the riddle that a dragon was involved. Putting those pieces together made the moniker feel even stranger. Why would an ancient, dead creature call her by that name? Arakyl spoke again.

I have known you for a long time, Ren Monroe. I was born the day that your father died.

Ren felt an initial jolt of confusion. That was followed by a slow-burning anger. She hated when people tried to use her past against her. The dragon's tactics seemed obvious. Maybe he was reading her mind? Pulling out sensitive memories and wielding them like knives.

There it is. That rage of yours. It burns, doesn't it?! All the way down into the bones.

"Shut up," Ren said, her chest pumping. "Just shut up."

Distantly, she felt Theo. He was still trying to pull her across the bond. Still asking for her help. She knew that if she leaned into that feeling, it would work and she would leave this place and this conversation and this looming hatred behind—but her anger would not let her go so easily.

"You're a liar," she accused.

I've never been as good at lying as my brothers and sisters. Rage always suited me better than guile. Besides, I've no reason to lie to you. Not now. I tell you a truth: our kind live on in these temporal spaces. The waxways as you call them. Do you understand? We cannot fully depart from the world. We are bound by the magic we used in life. And so our souls are buried in the dark. Left in perfect silence. Unless someone comes along. Your kind are like . . . lanterns. A light by which we can see again, even if it is only for a short time.

Ren had researched as much as she could on the subject. None of the most renowned experts on dragonlore had described this—but Arakyl's claim did sound like a match for what she knew. Dragons reacted to people, and they specifically reacted to two types of people: those who came in close proximity to their burial sites and those who felt the deepest emotions.

Fear or delight or . . . anger.

"But I've never been anywhere near your grave. . . ."

And yet . . . I felt you. The burning rage. The righteous fury. You burned so bright that the other dragons all hesitated. I claimed you before they could recover, because I knew that if I let you . . . you would bring me back to life in a way none of the others could. You opened the door—and I have FINALLY figured out how to walk through it.

Ren felt the pulsing again. Theo was pulling her harder than he ever had. There was a tremor of panic laced through his emotions now. She had no idea if she had been in this place for a second or a minute or an eternity. Time in the waxways was notoriously fickle. She did notice, however, that Arakyl had been slowly closing the gap between them. Inching ever forward through the shadows.

"Even if that's true . . . I'm here to close the door. I am done with revenge. I am done watching others die because of me. We will not let you win."

That terrible laugh again. She saw the dragon's teeth glinting like knives.

But is it ever done? Are we ever sated? Come now, child. I am the unspoken secret that has wormed its way to the very center of your heart. I am the truth you've never told anyone else, even though you've thought it a thousand times. I am the voice that whispers . . . kill them all.

Ren wanted to tell him that he was wrong. Scream that the words were not true—had never been true, but what he was saying crept through her like a paralytic. Overwhelming and terrible and familiar. It was a truth that she'd been keeping even from herself. Hidden away so she would not have to face the worst part of herself.

You pretend to be tame for him. Your precious Theo. You act as if your rage has actually been sated. As if it were truly enough to simply kill Landwin Brood. To trade one father for another! But deep down, you want them all to burn. Every house left in ashes. Every piece of gold melted down for scraps. Every single man and woman who walked over your father's grave . . . LET ME FINISH WHAT YOU STARTED.

LET ME . . . BURRRRRNNNNNNN.

There were tears racing down Ren's cheeks. The dragon's jaws opened and she knew if she said yes—Arakyl would consume her. She could hear that whispered promise in her mind. That he would make her into the same sort of god that he once was. The rest of the world would burn and maybe, just maybe, the world *she* wanted would rise from the ashes. She felt the darkest parts of her waking up, stretching their limbs, ravenous for all that power.

Until a hand gripped her shoulder. Painful. Real. She looked over to find Theo with her in the dark—and he was just strong enough to pull her away.

53

MERCY WHITAKER

One of the hounds had Win by the leg.

His screams had transformed. From mourning to pain. A small voice whispered that she should help. Cast a stun spell. *Do something! Do anything!* But she also knew that if she did that, she would lose her grip on the magic that was illuminating the threads around the room. Would she be able to cast that set of spells again? In all this chaos? It was a split-second decision, but Mercy decided to hold tight to the current spell in the air. Win kicked and screamed and writhed. His outer suit was slowly being shredded. All the layers beneath, too. The hound had sunk its teeth into the meat of his calf. Blood was everywhere.

Dahvid, Margaret, and Redding were trying to hold off the other two hounds. She saw them swinging their weapons in exaggerated arcs to keep them at bay. All while Theo attempted to summon a new barrier. Mercy saw Arakyl gathering himself for another attack. The bright flames churned inside his chest and up his throat. There, the light gathered in a tight sphere before it hurtled across the room.

Theo caught it with his ward—but this time all it took was one blast to shatter the entire thing. He was flung onto his back. Hard. Mercy was about to let go of her own magic and rush to his defense when other figures came streaming past her. Two and then four and then a dozen of them. She saw them as brief slashes of color and movement. Joining the fight so quickly that her mind could not even process who they were. Not until someone strode into her peripheral.

Zell Carrowynd.

The city's warden was there. The taller woman offered Mercy a tight nod before shouting commands to her squadron of livestone creatures. "Take that first one! Put them down if you must! Get our man out of there and get him out *now*."

The tides couldn't have turned any faster. A gargoyle pinned the nearest dog. The same two panthers she'd seen slinking around the docks as a child were there, too, cornering a second hound. Win limped clear of the fight and Mercy saw that his leg looked like an absolute nightmare. She reached into her pack and tossed him some gauze. Every part of her wanted to go to him. Help treat those wounds, but she knew if she took her focus off the magic it would slip away. Even now she could feel it trying to worm out of her grasp with everything happening around them.

Her eyes swung back to Theo, thinking he still might need help with the shield, but Mercy saw there was yet *another* figure with them. Theo was sprawled on the ground. A livestone hawk had landed on his chest. Impossibly, Ren Monroe had appeared in the room. There were several odd details that Mercy processed in rapid succession. First, the girl's face was streaked with tears. Second, the bone-thick bronze thread Mercy had seen before . . . was connected to Ren Monroe? It linked her and the dragon for some reason—heart to heart. What in the world was that?

There was no time for Mercy to solve the riddle, however, as Ren positioned herself between the dragon and Theo. She raised her horseshoe wand like a sword. A massive ward thundered out. Mercy felt herself knocked back a step by the magic. She watched Ren cast a few more layers and Arakyl's next blast—which would have been a death blow—caught against the summoning. Ren's ward didn't so much as flinch.

There was no celebration or triumphant shout. Instead, Ren quietly set about the task of casting even more layers. Spell after spell spun from the tip of her wand. As easy as breathing. When the girl finished, she turned back to Theo. Mercy couldn't hear the exchange. Just a few words and then—without any warning— the girl vanished again. Gone as quickly as she'd arrived. Mercy was still staring at the empty air when Zell called out again.

"Who's in charge here? We need to set up a perimeter!"

Theo was back on his feet, but looked dazed at best. The others had won their respective battles with the help of Zell's statues. Mercy saw two of the hounds escaping back up the main boring tunnel—a few of the statues in pursuit. Before Mercy could respond to Zell, there was a scream of rage from the houndmaster.

"Enough games! Let us put an end to all of this."

Mercy felt the hairs on both arms stand up straight. A great surge of power filled the room. Mercy briefly saw all the remaining yellow threads begin to flicker. In that moment, she knew that Arakyl was drawing on the connections. The final secret of his power was being revealed. The threads weren't simple manipulation threads, which normally allowed magic to flow in one specific direction. The puppeteer could use those threads to feed directives to the puppet. That was how every manipulation spell she'd ever studied worked. Now, however, she watched as Arakyl *reversed* that magic. "He's pulling power from them!"

Dahvid was the first to understand what she meant.

"Everyone to me!" he shouted. "Now!"

The image-bearer backtracked so that Win was just a few paces away from him. The rest of the crew obeyed. Even Zell Carrowynd and her statues edged as close as they possibly could. The dragon was raising its head. The backlit eyes stared at them through the slight distortions of the shield. When everyone was close enough, Dahvid swiped the tattoo on his exposed shoulder: a set of concentric gold rings. Magic whispered past and through her. A golden sphere circled a golden sphere circled a golden sphere—and all of them inside that protection. The world outside went silent. Mercy realized that the whispers that had been needling at every thought, filling the space between every noise, were also gone. Dahvid had somehow sealed them off from everything.

Just in time. Arakyl unleashed an attack unlike anything so far. Everything in the room was *pulverized*. The shield Monroe had summoned smashed into bits. The houndmaster was flung like a rag doll across the room. Two of the livestone statues—the panthers—had been returning from the main tunnel. Zell let out a too-late cry of warning as both of them *melted* into nothing.

Dusted in seconds. Only Dahvid's golden shields held. And barely at that. Arakyl's spell bent the golden magic inward, denting on all sides, before passing through the rest of the chamber.

Dahvid said, "This spell will hold for thirty seconds. We need to organize."

Zell Carrowynd's chest was heaving. The woman was staring out as if two members of her family had just perished—rather than statues. Theo noticed too. "Their sacrifice will not be forgotten," he said. "Zell. Thank you. You saved us. How'd you know that we were here?"

After a long beat, she turned back to them. "I didn't. The statues sensed a threat to the city weeks ago. We followed the trail up to Running Hills first—and then traced it to here."

Theo nodded. "Lucky for us. Thanks again."

"We're glad to have you," Mercy agreed, eager to catch the woman up. "There's a manipulation spell linking this dragon and the Makers. Hundreds of them are acting on his behalf. I also think these threads are fueling this awakening. He's pulling power from them. Severing the threads will free people back in the city *and* cut Arakyl off from his source of power. We've already started the process of cutting those threads. You can see what's left. Hanging in the air."

Zell glanced up, nodded. "We have to destroy all of these?"

"Just the yellow ones," Mercy replied. "But there's still a lot to do. We need someone to tend to Win. We're also going to need a new shield when this one falls. Everyone else is on the threads. Locate, confirm, destroy. Don't cut any of the other threads. . . ."

"There is one other that I need to destroy." This came from

Theo. All attention swung in his direction. "The bronze one. Right there. Ren told me it needs to be cut too."

Mercy had seen the girl appear. She had a dozen questions about that—and a dozen more questions about the bronze thread that she'd seen *connecting* the girl to the dragon. It clearly wasn't the same as the others. Ren wasn't being manipulated, but then what was their bond? Her curiosity would have to wait, though. None of those questions would matter if they didn't do what needed to be done to survive the next thirty seconds.

"Then we cut that one too," she finally said. "Let's get ready."

Everyone moved at the same time. The golden sphere was a tight space, which made it slightly awkward, but all of them fell to the necessary tasks. Zell knelt down beside Win. There was a mixture of grieving and pain in the noises he made. Mercy had been so focused on surviving that she hadn't thought about the fact that Guion was dead. Her fingers itched as she glanced over at his mound of a body. The pain in her right foot flared too. There was a brief internal debate and then Mercy remembered she couldn't perform any other magic. Not without losing her grasp on the visualization spells.

Theo and Redding were huddling together to create a new shield. Margaret had her null blade up and ready. Dahvid was tightening his grip on his own sword. The golden sphere flickered. Zell finished wrapping Win's leg and turned back just as the golden barrier vanished. Mercy expected a barrage. Gouts of bright flame. Instead, they were left in darkness. Only the threads glowing in the air around them. It was just enough light to see the dragon's massive corpse.

The light that had been glowing in the dragon's eyes was

gone. Mercy frowned. Was it over? Had the dragon pulled too much power from the Makers and burned his final bridge to this world? No, this was something else. Her thoughts went back to Beacon House. She'd seen Nance when he was occupied by the dragon. How he resisted every spell. How his eyes had changed colors at the last moment, when Arakyl had abandoned him to occupy the viceroy's mind instead. It took that chain of thoughts for her to understand what she was looking at now.

"He's not here. He's elsewhere! We need to get moving. *Now!*"

No one needed to be told twice. Everyone moved with haste. It didn't take long for them to build a sort of rhythm. Working around the room. Finding threads. Calling them out. Letting Dahvid and Margaret hack away at them with great sweeping blows. Theo and Redding helped with the identification, both of them waiting patiently to cast the ward when the time came. It didn't take them long to finish one section of the room and move on to the next one. Finally, it felt as if they were actually progressing. They'd severed some fifty threads when Theo looked up sharply. His face twisted in anguish. Mercy thought that Arakyl might be manipulating him. Whispering into his mind and showing him things that were not real. Instead, she noticed that the bronze thread had started burning brighter than the rest. Almost too bright to look at straight on. When Theo spoke, a chill ran down Mercy's spine.

"Oh gods. She's going to kill them all."

54

REN MONROE

Her mind shattered.

Or maybe it was her body? Both? Ren couldn't be certain. All she knew was that Theo's initial pull across their bond had landed her a face-to-face meeting with Arakyl. A private moment in the waxways that was still haunting her thoughts, creeping through her mind like poison. Her guilt about what was happening in Kathor multiplied, spreading across the infinity of her thoughts.

All of this is my fault. All of this is my fault. All of this—

Not only had she weakened the city's defenses to allow the Makers to infiltrate—but now she was supposedly responsible for the dragon's awakening in the first place. The creature had been feeding on her revenge this entire time. Gaining strength for this exact moment. Her hatred was like a fire that had spread too far. It was burning the beautiful parts of the world now too. Was she too late to stop him? Or would Arakyl burn until everything she loved was ashes?

Theo had pulled her free at the very last moment. Ren's feet had set down in the burial chamber, and it was no small glimpse of his surroundings this time. If they needed proof that their bond was properly restored, this was it. She'd been pulled fully across space and time, right into absolute chaos—but Ren Monroe had always thrived under pressure. She'd cast wards to protect Theo, turning away a blow that might have killed him, and then when she was certain he was safe, she'd told him two things: cut the bronze thread and push her back. Really, she'd begged him to do those two things. And Theo Brood, for all his family's sins, had never failed her.

Obediently, Theo had used their bond to do just that. A shove back to where she'd been standing just moments before. She heard a whisper of Arakyl's presence in their private waxways—but she was moving far too fast for him to capture her again. Ren's feet set down in the portal room for exactly one second. A single grain of sand in the hourglass, and then she was pulled *again*.

The spell had activated with perfectly imperfect timing. The claws of the portal room seized her. It was far too much push and pull for any one person. For a brief moment, her consciousness fractured—completely detached from every world, every plane of existence. She was . . . nowhere. Not in the waxways. Not in the portal room. Not in a dragon's burial chamber. Not even outside Meredream—her actual destination. The place she found herself in was a void. Empty of all life. Absent of all threat. Home to only Ren Monroe. She might have stayed there for the rest of time, untouched by the real world and all its torments. It was a comfort to think that she might be safe here. Safe, but alone.

It was that final thought that sent her sprawling through the waxways at last. She could not leave Theo behind. Not after all they'd been through. Not when she still needed to try to make good on her promises. Her feet set down on a hillside. The trees around her were swaying. They were also . . . on fire. There was blood. Bodies spread over the ground. Most of them, thank the gods, belonged to the Makers. She saw their red scarves. Her eyes dragged upward from the dead to the living. She'd been set down in the same location the others had—but it was clear that the army had pushed the wizards back. Pressed after them and up the hillside. Which meant Ren found herself standing behind enemy lines.

Some one hundred soldiers stood between her and the others. All with their backs to her. She couldn't believe the wizards were there. Still alive! Behind their wards, fighting to keep the enemy at bay. She saw their numbers had been reduced. Only half of them were still on their feet. The others were down. Wounded or worse. Her eyes found Winnie Fletcher in the middle of that sprawl. The girl was slumped down, holding one of her friends, who'd taken an arrow in the stomach. Ren's entire body went perfectly still. The other little girl had attended Avid Shiverian's classes too. Ren remembered that she'd been quite good at the elementary wards, but that had not been enough to save her. Her face looked paler in death. Winnie was clutching the girl tightly, almost as if she might keep her in this world a little longer if she just held on.

"No more of this," Ren whispered. "There will be no more of this."

Her hand tightened on the grip of her horseshoe wand. Dark rage was trembling through her entire body. The world must answer for such things. Ren would be the one to make it answer. No one had seen her yet. None of the enemy soldiers had bothered to look back. The first soldier was awarded a killing spell right in the back. She saw his spine fail him. The man crumpled with a scream. Ren hit the next with a stun spell so violent that he was thrown out of one of his boots. The rest was action and reaction. Her magic took on the shape of poetry. The soldiers were no more than paper on which to write the most elegant words she could think of. She ducked under a sword swing and hit the man point blank with a blunt-force punch of magic. Turning, she cast her favorite binding spell, unexpectedly pulling one woman toward her. A quick side-step brought the same woman's sword into her fellow soldier's stomach instead of hers. She blasted both of them away with an outstretched hand.

A voice in the back of her mind whispered that this was a terrible thing too. These people were not themselves. It wasn't fair they should suffer. "But the children must live," she whispered back to that voice. "The children must live."

She slit the next soldier's artery with a downward slash. Another caught the same invisible blade across their chest. When enough of the army had turned to face her, she cast the concentrated light cantrip. Nearly thirty soldiers, blinded in an instant, temporarily stumbling around. Panicked, they began taking wild swings where she'd stood—all while Ren rotated off to the right, casting stun spell after stun spell into their vulnerable flank. The goal wasn't to kill them. Most would be wounded. And the truth was that she relished their pain.

The sounds of bones breaking. The great ripples across their skin as her magic punched again and again into their ranks. Finally, she was unleashing everything she'd held in for so long. One man was desperate enough to throw his sword at her. She caught it with a quick ward and sent it spinning right back at him. Ren marveled at how easy it all felt. Magic was a scythe. She was the reaper. Her enemies became faceless. They fell, flower-cut to the ground. Ren was about to begin another sequence of spells when she realized that she knew the face standing in front of her. It was familiar. Her wand hand trembled, then lowered.

"Nevelyn? What are you doing here?"

Her friend grabbed her by the shoulder. Together, they ducked back inside the waiting wards with the other wizards. Ren didn't understand. There had been so many soldiers on that hillside. How had she gotten through them all? Had she somehow ported by accident? She didn't understand until she looked back. Theodore Crane was picking his way across the battlefield. His eyes were wild and darting. Like an animal who'd just heard the first, hair-raising howl of a wolf in the distance. Except no one was hunting him. Only dead soldiers lay before him.

Ren had . . . she had . . .

"Shit."

Nevelyn barely kept her upright. Ren had nothing left. She'd just emptied out all that she was onto that hillside. Every burning thought. Every bright rage. Logically, she accepted that these people would have killed her if they had the chance. She knew they would. That's what they were here to do. But what she'd just done was not just defensive magic. It was not blow for blow. She had cut through them with the same terrible power that the viceroy had told them to fear. If ever they needed an example of why all the wizards should die—this was it. Nevelyn kept whispering that it was all right. It would all be all right. Avid caught her eye and nodded once. As if this terrible display of power had been necessary. Crane came gasping into the safety of their wards. All around them, the army had paused. Soldiers at the edges of the group were fleeing. Ren wasn't sure if it was what she'd just done scaring them off—or some other reason. Those who remained settled back into their stances. Ren could not stomach the thought of more battle. More dying. And for what? A dragon's grand trick?

She just wanted Theo. Needed him like she needed air. Ren tugged at the ever-present strands of their bond, but she couldn't feel him. It was almost as if he was hiding from her.

Hiding from what she had done.

55

MERCY WHITAKER

They were past one hundred threads severed. Mercy wished she could see the impact this was having around the city of Kathor. She could not help imagining the Makers, waking up suddenly, aware that the voice they'd been guided by for months or years was now absent. She hoped they would spread the word. Share their stories. A reversal within the Makers might just be their only chance to survive the years to come. It also gave her hope that Arakyl would not have the power he needed for another attack. All they had to do was finish their work.

As many as they'd severed, roughly the same number remained. More perhaps. They were trying to work in quadrants. A systematic approach. But every now and again, she found herself squinting at a section she'd already cleared, unable to find new threads.

Mercy was sawing at another thread, her arm weak and

cramped, when purple light flared in the room. Arakyl's body was glowing again. Those backlit eyes swiveled to focus on them. Without the houndmaster to speak through, his words whispered into their minds instead.

Very well. You have earned my attention.

There was a scraping sound. Mercy's eyes swung back to the entrance. Two creatures were worming their way through the narrow entry tunnel. As soon as they were through, their wings swept wide. "Oh, shit . . ."

That was all Mercy managed to say as two full-grown wyverns descended on them. Their riders were gone. Their harnesses had been cut. Arakyl had restored them to the wild creatures they'd once been. Before someone had come out to the Dires and tamed them. And gods were they massive. One landed on the ground beside Win. The group had left him at the back of the cavern. They'd thought he was safe there. Now he held up his hands and screamed. Blood spattered in a dreadful arc. The lionlike mouth clamped down and he was dead. Just like that.

Zell's statues were the first to react. They didn't possess the animal instinct that forces a smaller creature to pause when it sees a larger one. The gargoyle led the charge against the other wyvern. It leapt through the air and wrapped itself around the wyvern's right leg. The effort was enough to drag the creature downward. The other statues took advantage. As a group, they pinned the creature's wings. Dahvid was there first. Mercy had to blink, though, when a *second* Dahvid whispered out from the first. The wyvern let out a screech, lashing out with his claws, as both versions of the image-bearer jabbed at the creature with their matching swords. Margaret and the second wyvern entered the fight at the same time, crashing in from opposite sides.

It was all limbs and claws and wings. Mercy saw Margaret fumble her sword. The girl rolled to one side just as blasts came in from the right. Theo and Redding were advancing, their wands raised. They cast projectiles instead of focusing on wards. It worked. Driving back one wyvern as the other fell with a piercing scream. Mercy could have watched them battle for hours, but she'd come down here with purpose. No one else was cutting threads. She was reaching for the closest one when it *pulsed* brighter. Another surge of power ran across the length of those makeshift bonds. Moving in the direction of Arakyl.

"Theo!" Mercy shouted. "Wards back up!"

She expected arcane fire to come pouring out again. Last time, Arakyl had unleashed a massive spell. Instead, the voice returned. Rattling through every corner of her mind.

Enough of this.

Arakyl was rising. The threads around the room *burned*. No one alive had seen a living dragon. She wasn't really sure that's what they were seeing now, but it was close enough. The great skeletal frame pushed up to its feet. His neck writhed before straightening. The purple-bright eyes stared down at them with true hunger now. As if he had been waiting a century for this particular feast.

Theo was the first to rush forward.

It was brave—and foolish. He cast another shield and they all watched Arakyl punch straight through it. A strike that happened in less than a blink. The great claws closed in around Theo's midsection. Puncturing his back. Arakyl shook him from side to side, and then slung his body to the right. Dead.

He went for Dahvid next. Mercy saw the warrior's eyes widen. He reached up and swiped the red flower painted on his chest. Easily his most visible tattoo. Mercy had no idea what it did but she felt power pulse outward and she briefly hoped—beyond all hope—that maybe it was powerful enough to actually stop a fully resurrected dragon.

Nothing seemed to happen, though. Instead of unleashing a great burst of magic or summoning a new weapon—Dahvid's eyes swung in her direction.

"You have to run, Mercy. You're our only hope. *Run now!*"

Arakyl brought one claw smashing down on top of him. Crushed him into the stones the way a wagon might crush a mouse as it rumbled down the road. Zell and the rest of her creatures were next. She let out one final battle cry, and was forced to watch as Arakyl spewed that purple fire, melting the statues that didn't scatter in time with a single continuous blast. Dahvid's final words were still ringing in Mercy's mind.

You're our only hope.

Of course. Mercy didn't know how he knew that, but *of course*. She turned and sprinted for the entrance. She ignored the sounds of crunching bones. The final scream of the wyvern as Margaret plunged her sword one final time into its chest. She knew that all of them would die. That was the only way forward now. They had to die. And she had to live.

It looked like cowardice. She didn't care. She made it up the first ramp and found herself squeezing through the entry tunnel. Ahead, she thought she saw one of the livestone creatures escaping but it was hard to tell in the dark. She wound back through the twisting caverns. Behind her, she heard screaming. Redding? Margaret? Zell? It didn't matter. Dahvid had turned and told her to survive. She knew that was the only way to win. She found herself in darkness. Groping against the walls. She didn't dare light a cantrip. Not now. Instead, she reached the antechamber they'd gathered in. Halfway up the boring tunnel, she'd seen an opening. Some kind of animal nest. She went to that side of the tunnel, set one hand to the dirt wall, and started walking. As fast as she could. Until her hand found empty air.

There was a burrow. Hardly big enough for her, but she crawled inside it. She had to scrape at the dirt until there was enough room for her entire body to curl inside that dark space. Unseen. She released her grip on the magic she'd been holding on to all this time. The visualization spell down in the chamber would vanish. She could still hear screams. The sounds of her brave group dying. They had lost.

Or they would if Arakyl found her. Mercy tried to keep her thoughts calm. She settled her breathing the way she would before an operation. It took time, but her heart rate slowed. Even now, knocking on death's door, her hands didn't shake. And then she heard the voice.

Come now, little one. What use is hiding? Do you think there is anywhere in this world that you could go—and that I would not find you? I am Arakyl. The first and last of my name. I . . . will . . . FIND . . . YOU.

There was a deep rumble. As if the earth itself were opening up. She didn't think Arakyl could navigate the same tunnel she'd used, but he was also a dragon. He would have other ways to pursue her. She needed to remain steady. Perfectly quiet. Offer no sign of her existence to him.

If you come out now, I will let you live. I will allow you to witness my return. It is near enough. All this work. All the effort. Your friend opened the door and now I am nearly through it. As your magic fades—I revive. Do you see what I have done? Can you even comprehend the breadth of this plan? Come out here. Witness the first dragon to be born in centuries.

More rumbling. Mercy kept her eyes shut. Her mind closed. No matter how fascinating she found his words, she would not engage. Curiosity was like planting a seed. If she did that, he might take root. Make a home in her thoughts forever. She nestled deeper into the darkness and waited.

Fine. I will wait for you. I have waited for so long, after all. What is one more day? One more eon? I slept in the nothing for nearly three decades. Spoke only with the shadows, and they are such boring company. Sometimes, I would whisper to the wolves who ranged above me. Enter the thoughts of wyverns as they winged overhead. I would ask them questions about the world above. They would tell me of the sun, the mountains, of your kind . . .

Mercy felt a sudden wash of heat. As if the great dragon was breathing down on her neck.

It was so hard to fathom. Your species had survived ours? You have weak bodies. Even weaker minds. How was it possible? The only answer I found was magic. Stolen magic. I waited so patiently— and she woke me up. From across the continent, her anger was like the brightest flame breaking the longest night. Enough for me to find my way back to my body, and all I needed then was for someone else to find it. It took years, but some whelp and her father stumbled into this chamber. They reported the location of my grave site. And when your city's precious leader arrived, I saw a path forward. A future that was to my liking. I bent him to my will. I began spreading this whisper of an echo of a curse. I planted just one seed in his mind—and look at how it bloomed! Now, as magic dies in your kind—it returns in me. I will be the first dragon to walk the earth in . . . I don't know how long. Others will follow. Or not. Maybe I will rule the land alone. I can hunt you—one by one. I'm not sure. All I know is that I was in darkness, and a door was left open. I am finally prepared to pass through the realms. And you, Mercy Whitaker, are one of the only things left in my way.

The heat intensified. Her eyes were pinned shut, but she thought she could see the glow of that arcane fire. There was a burst of energy and she thought she was about to die. Instead, the magic struck some distant wall. She heard rocks stirring and tumbling and falling still. He repeated that same routine three times. Whispering threats. Firing spells. Missing her over and over again. Not once did she move or speak or think. She would not be broken. He'd have to get lucky and actually hit her with one of his blasts.

Coward! They're dying, you know? As you save yourself? THEY ARE DYING.

Mercy experienced a forced glimpse of some distant field. All the wizards they'd left at Balmerick were there—crowded behind makeshift wards. There were bodies everywhere. Hundreds of soldiers surrounded the group. A killing field. In the distance, she saw Meredream. She shook herself away from that vision. He was lying to her. Showing her something to draw on her desperation. She offered him no emotion. No response or thought. Nothing at all.

When I find you, do you want me to eat your body first? Or your soul?

The shuffling sound grew more distant. The rumbles grew less pronounced. Everything went quiet. As if he were waiting for her to reveal herself. Crouched somewhere in shadow. After a minute, he began moving again. Returning to the lower chamber. The air boiled with his frustration. Mercy knew that if she waited long enough—he would return to that other battle. His attention would be elsewhere. Quietly, she began to count.

56

NEVELYN TIN'VORI

A horn sounded.

Loud enough to halt every action, every shout, every
spell. The enemy lines parted to allow someone through. Nevelyn assumed this would be their leader. And so it was a shock
to watch Agnes Monroe march forward. The woman was outfit-
ted in some of the finest leather armor Nevelyn had ever seen.
Bone-handled daggers were sheathed at both hips. She looked
like someone who'd grown up traveling in a mercenary army.
Nevelyn's eyes swung over to Ren. Her friend had slumped
down to her knees. Her eyes wild. Almost rolling.

"I . . . I can't feel him . . . ," she muttered to no one. "I don't
understand. *I can't feel him.*"

Nevelyn didn't know what those words meant, but it was
far too clear that the girl hadn't recovered from the bloodbath
she'd just left behind. There was no way she was fit to perform a negotiation. Nevelyn's feet carried her to the edge of

the wards. The other wizards parted to allow her passage. Taking a deep breath, she stepped through the trembling magic. Exposing herself to an army that seemed hellbent on removing all of them from the face of the earth. Agnes Monroe mirrored Nevelyn's steps until they were no more than ten paces apart.

"My daughter won't speak to me?"

"Right now? I don't think she can. Try again in a few years. After the dust settles. Come knock on Meredream's door and see if she'll let you in. Maybe you'll be a grandmother by then."

As intended, that word cut through Monroe's mental armor. A dozen different emotions flickered over her face. Her eyes moved from Ren in the distance then back to Nevelyn.

"Your . . . is she . . ."

And then her expression neutralized. The sharper emotions faded. There were whispers in the air between them. This would be the manipulation spell. Carefully pulling her back to the plan.

"You must surrender," Agnes said suddenly. "Or more people will die."

"Yes. Come quietly, so that you can kill us all later, right?"

Agnes made a show of looking wounded. "Do you think I would let that happen to my only daughter? No, there would be trials. The worst that any of you would face is prison. Sentences for insurrection. After a time . . . you'll be released. Free to live a normal life."

"Free," Nevelyn repeated. "As long as we give up our magic."

"The Great Balancing must reach its natural end point. A magicless world. Would that really be so terrible? People are tired of living in fear—and your magic is the last thing they have to fear."

The words were almost reasonable. Very nearly convincing, if Nevelyn didn't know there was a dragon whispering lies from across the continent. "You don't want us in Kathor. That's fair. Allow us this self-exile. We will go to Meredream. Let us pass. We can live in this city and you have our sworn word that no one will return to Kathor. Not unless you ask us to come back."

Agnes Monroe nodded. "An enticing promise. How many generations do you think will actually keep it? One? Two? Come on. You know that someone will eventually try to take back Kathor. All it would take is one powerful wizard—or maybe the entire next generation grows up thinking of it as a birthright that was taken from them. I see Shiverians in your group. Proctors. Graylantians. Winterses. Even Broods."

When she said the last house, her eyes drifted to Ren. The accusation was clear. She saw her daughter as one of them now. She was no longer a Monroe in her mother's manipulated eyes. Nevelyn decided to cut straight to the most reasonable offer.

"The children then. Let the children through."

For the second time, Agnes Monroe faltered. The easy confidence slipped. An expression of utter despair crossed her features. Like a shadow of the true self. The part of her that knew that all of this was so wrong. That they had gone too far. Killed too many. Nevelyn raced to take advantage of that flaw in the armor.

"One is already dead." She pointed back to the girl with the arrow in her stomach. "And you know that's one too many. Let us pass. We will escort the children to Meredream. Once they are safe, we will surrender. It will be exactly as you've asked. You can drag us back to the city, perform whatever trials you'd like. I do not care. You once told me that the great houses must fall. They have fallen. Truly, they are no more. But the children must live—or your society begins with the same blood on their hands."

Tears streaked down Agnes Monroe's face. She started to nod. It was such a reasonable compromise. The children would live. The children *should* live. Agree, and the armies on both sides could set down their weapons. They would even have prisoners to take back to Kathor as proof that they'd won. But as she waited for a response, the woman's eyes grew dark. From light brown to shadow black. More tears fell down the woman's face. All that pain, but it didn't matter. Arakyl was here. Taking over. Nevelyn began to backpedal. She was face-to-face with a demon now.

57

MERCY WHITAKER

Mercy counted to one hundred. When she reached that number, she crawled out of her hiding place. Brushed off the dirt and the debris and began the descent once more. Quiet as a field mouse, she maneuvered through the snaking tunnel. A glance confirmed that Arakyl had returned to his original position. His diamond-shaped head was slumped back on the stones. All around him was carnage. No one from her party had been spared. Death and death and more death. Normally, she would mourn them. Whisper a quiet apology for those who'd passed on to the next world.

Instead, Mercy removed her gloves.

It always felt so lovely. The open-air breathing across her knuckles. Sometimes, she went an entire day without taking them off. As a student, she only ever removed them in the privacy of her own room. And the handful of times she made love to Devlin. Gods, she'd always been so afraid of what he would think. After they'd been together for a while, he finally was bold enough to ask her. What had happened to her fingers? She told him she'd been born that way. Buried the truth inside another truth. That way no one would ever see the real Mercy.

Now, she stretched both hands. Attempted to splay her fingers out. The two dead ones on her right hand refused to cooperate. Her pinky and ring finger. Both were the black of ashes. Dark stubs that were shorter than her other two fingers, because they had not grown since the incident. No blood pumped through them. The nails had fallen off and never returned. Mercy had also discovered there was no way to be rid of them. They could not be severed with a blade. The fingers were permanent, because they'd come from a curse.

This was her secret.

One summer, her family had visited her aunt's farm. Well south of Kathor. She'd snuck out at night with her two cousins. All of them younger than ten. There was a pond on the property. Back through the woods. They fancied a midnight swim and so they took turns watching for the adults. Keeping an eye on the trail that fed through the woods. Mercy had backtracked, just to see if any of the house's lights were on, when she heard stillness. A dreaded quiet.

One of her cousins had swum too far down. At the bottom of the pool, he'd accidentally stirred a nest of slipsnakes. They'd wrapped around him. His arms and his legs. Pulled him down to the bottom. When he didn't surface, his brother dove after him. For every snake he ripped off his brother, another wrapped around his own limbs. Mercy didn't know what had happened, but when she sprinted back to the pond's edge, she found them both floating facedown.

Her first instinct was to rescue them.

It took all her strength to drag their bodies back to the muddy bank and flip them over. She tried everything she'd ever heard adults talk about. Breathing into their mouths. Pumping her hands down against their bird-thin chests. Nothing worked. Desperate, she'd grabbed one cousin by the collar and started shaking him. Unleashing screams that were full of anger and fear and fury. Magic came pouring out of her. Wild and reckless and free.

It was the first spell she'd ever performed. Easier the second time. All she had to do was call on that waiting magic and pull him *back* from wherever he had gone. She didn't piece it together then. The truth of what she'd done. All she knew was that she had to save them. Both of her cousins returned from the dead. Just like that. And that's when the pain came.

Mercy screamed as something bit down hard on her hand. A searing, hot-white sort of pain. She thought that the snakes had surfaced. Maybe one was clamped down on her hand. But when she looked, she saw that two of her fingers had withered. From pale white to a dead black.

Her cousins weren't great witnesses. Mercy told her parents what happened, but they couldn't confirm the details. Her insistence on the true story—that she had brought the boys back to life with magic—only seemed to bother her aunt. The adults were quick to shut her up. Repeatedly told her not to tell that story, even though she'd been taught her whole life not to lie. It was as if she'd done some unthinkable thing. Something to hide. Rather than saving two boys from dying. They never went back to visit her aunt's house again. Her boys, Mercy heard, became outcasts in that town. Rumors had spread. No one could believe that they were normal. Her aunt seemed to be waiting for some dark power to manifest in them. As if they were more revenant than human. It took Mercy a very long time to understand the truth of what had happened.

She had performed an *exchange*.

Life traded for death. She could resurrect someone, but only if she offered some small part of herself in the trade. Something of hers had to die. Her first thought had been of power. And what little girl wouldn't think that way? She fancied herself as a potential hero. Imagined all the ways she might help people. She even spent time in the library, secretly reading about necromancers. There were dozens of examples in Kathor's history, but she discovered that what she had done was incredibly rare. Bringing a person fully back to life without curse or consequence? There had been necromancers who could raise the mindless dead to do their bidding. Others she read about could allow a loved one to have one final conversation with the departed. But there were almost no instances of someone dying and coming back to life exactly as they had been.

Mercy's magic was an exception.

All the thrill vanished, though, when she remembered the cost. Every time she saved someone, a part of her would die. And she had no way of predicting which part. Her fingers had withered during that first incident. One for each cousin. She already felt self-conscious about the way they looked. Other children stared when they noticed them. What would the magic demand next? Her bright red hair? Her vision or her hearing? Even worse, Mercy could imagine what might happen if others learned of her gift. People would be knocking on their door day and night. Begging for her to restore this child or that husband or this sister. How could she ever choose who should return? Didn't hundreds of people die in their city every day? And how long before the exchange claimed some part of her that she could not live without?

Mercy learned to hide her power instead. Always wearing her special-made gloves. Never mentioning the story about her cousins. She didn't use the gift again until she was a sophomore at Balmerick. One of her friends overdosed on a bad batch of the breath. They found him unresponsive in his bed. As other students sent for the medics, Mercy slipped into his room. She worried that it had been too long since she first performed the magic. That she might not remember how to do it. But the spell came naturally. Like breathing.

She resurrected him. This time it cost her an organ. Mercy felt her appendix rupture just seconds after he gasped back to life. When she checked in at Safe Harbor to be treated, the doctors told her that her appendix had not simply burst, as it did in most cases. Instead, the organ seemed to have withered into a husk inside her. It was the trade again. Life for death. Mercy studied each event closely. It seemed to her that the magic was choosing less crucial parts to kill. Two of her smaller fingers. An organ with very little functionality. She wondered then. If she used the gift a dozen more times, maybe she wouldn't lose anything that mattered.

But what if she was wrong? What if her heart burst next? There was no way to know. No way to test out the hypothesis without inviting greater risks. Guilt pushed Mercy to switch majors. From structural magic to anatomical. If she could not use her gift to save people, she would find some other way to help them. At least that was the idea. Nothing completely absolved her from that hidden shame.

During Mercy's senior year, her grandmother passed away. She'd always assumed that her parents had dismissed and forgotten about her gift as the imagined claims of a little girl. Yes, there was the strange incident with the cousins. And of course, they'd heard about the situation at Balmerick. But Mercy hadn't bothered to tell them the truth that time around. Which made it all the more surprising when her mother came to her before the funeral.

"I want you to bring her back."

Mercy had been too shocked to reply. Her mother accused her of playing dumb—and then of being selfish. When Mercy explained how the gift worked, her mother had pressed on gracelessly.

"Maybe it won't be bad this time," she said. "Since you're doing me a favor. Maybe the magic will just take your eyelashes. You can live without eyelashes."

"Yes, I could," Mercy replied softly. "But what if my eardrums rupture and I can never hear anything ever again? What if a capillary in my heart bursts?! Grandmother lived her life. She was a good woman and it is time for us to mourn her."

She didn't say: *If I bring her back, won't she just die again?* It was not like her cousins or her friend from school. This wasn't a person who had an entire lifetime stolen from them. The argument broke their relationship. Her mother seemed incapable of seeing the danger of what she was asking. Nor could Mercy see—at the time—how desperate grief can make a person. How it consumes their better judgment and forces them to demand the unthinkable.

No one else ever knew about her gift. Devlin had come the closest to finding out. When she started falling in love with him, imagining how their courtship might one day be a marriage, she'd nearly come out and told him everything. Countless times. The memory of her mother's scorn had always stopped her at the very last second.

Working at a hospital should have pressed her right up against the discomfort—but it hadn't. Every patient she lost during her training had been elderly. Or else they suffered from a disease that, if she resurrected them, would only kill them a few months later. She knew she would have used her gift if a child had died at the hospital. Some accident that grated against her sense of fairness. But years passed at Safe Harbor without any such incidents.

She didn't consider using her power again until Devlin. What a catastrophe that had been. Mercy had already made up her mind about it. She would get him back to Safe Harbor. If the antidote saved him, all the better. If it didn't, then she would have intervened. Sacrificed some small part of herself to keep him in the waking world. Fate had laughed at her good intentions. Devlin took his last breath just before she'd reached for the candle. Everyone knew the dead could not travel. A body couldn't port, because when a person died, the magic inside them ceased as well. Mercy had teleported away and in that split second she had also lost her chance to bring him back.

"Not again."

The dead waited for her. As always, she could sense them. Spirits hovering near their bodies. As watchful ghosts or potential revenants. A soul always tarried. It waited to make sure it wasn't needed, perhaps. Or maybe the soul needed to say goodbye to the body? She wasn't sure. But she had felt it with the bonded couple at Beacon House. The husband who'd passed away. His spirit had been tormented even more by his wife's anguish. The bond magic that had connected them. Mercy couldn't stand the way that had felt—and so she had intervened. Pretended to do some basic spell while activating magic only she possessed. Now she would do it again.

The souls in the cavern remained in agitation. The closest body to the entry ramp was Guion's. Mercy took a deep breath before kneeling down beside him. She set one hand above his unbeating heart—and then her spell began. There was a brief hitch, as if the magic was waking up, stretching its limbs. But then she felt the exchange. Life trading places with death.

Guion came gasping back to her. The resurrected always had a wild-eyed look to them. Lost and found all at the same time. "Mercy?" he croaked. "What . . . oh gods . . . what happened?"

She ignored his questions. It was easier to ignore that than the sudden itch spreading across her scalp. Slowly, her hair began to fall to the ground. A very small and very vain part of her hated that it had to be her hair. The bright red locks that she'd always loved so much. A more logical part of her understood this was *good*. Better hair than her frontal lobe. Rose-red strands fell to the floor as she walked. Great clumps tumbled down. Before Guion could say anything, she knelt down beside his brother—Win. These wounds were more substantial. Mercy suspected that wouldn't matter.

She placed one hand over his heart.

Come back to me.

He did. The great wounds across his chest puckered shut.

When he saw his brother walking toward him, he began weeping. Such an impossible thing. She hoped they would wrestle with the impossibility for years to come. Mercy crossed the room. As she went, she felt a sharpness in her jaw. The taste of blood. Reaching up, she pulled an incisor that looked rotten all the way through. Bone blackened by the curse. She tossed the tooth onto the floor.

Margaret came next. The young girl came back more violently than the others. She woke up screaming. The terrors of life and death still tumbling her like a stone in a river. Mercy gestured for Win and Guion to take care of her before moving on to the next corpse. Both of them looked shocked. Really, they looked scared. They'd finally realized what she was doing. Finally understood where they had been just moments before, and the impossibility of where they were now.

Mercy's entire right calf seized with enormous pain. The muscle was dead. It was a struggle to stay upright. But she had a good leg. She shifted her weight to it, set one hand on the nearby wall, and limped onward. An absent muscle would change the rest of her life, but she would trade it a thousand times over for Margaret. Next up was Zell. She felt the others watching her and knew this was what her life would have been if she had ever revealed her gift. If anyone had ever learned the truth. Did they think of her as something unnatural? Would they think of themselves that way? It didn't matter. Not really. In a way, they *were* revenants. She'd brought them back for a specific purpose. She knew she needed all of them to finish this.

Zell returned with a look of pure calm on her face. As if she'd simply dozed off in her bed and was being woken by a roommate who was eager to get to class on time. Mercy finally felt pain that couldn't be ignored. Her right eye *ruptured*. It felt as if someone had lined up a knife and carefully pushed it into her pupil. Warmth gushed down that side of her face and she dropped to a knee. Zell rushed to her side.

"What the hell? Mercy? What the hell is going on?"

She shoved back to her feet. Away from the other woman.

"Get them ready," she said. "Everyone get ready!"

One eye still worked. Mercy's head spun with the pain, but she grunted once and started across the room. Dahvid Tin'Vori's body lay slack across the stones. He was as pretty in death as he was in life. For the first time, Mercy hesitated.

Hair then a tooth then a muscle . . . and now an eye? Is it getting worse each time? She couldn't help the tremor of fear that ran through her. No one would fault her for stopping now. She'd already done the impossible. And these next three resurrections could keep ramping up. Was death angry with her? Was it, even now, preparing to punish the next theft she committed? Mercy realized she was crying.

"Keep going," she whispered to herself. "Finish what you've started."

With a hand on his heart, Mercy brought Dahvid back. She prayed that it would be an eyebrow or an earlobe or another tooth. Maybe that was a mistake. Maybe fate heard her. Mercy's left eye burst. The darkness came with terrible swiftness. A vast and all-consuming void.

Dahvid actually caught her. Dead one moment and the swooning hero the next. Mercy almost wanted to laugh, because as strong and fine as his arms felt, she knew she was probably bleeding all over him. Dahvid didn't ask questions.

He didn't demand explanations like the others. Mercy realized it was because he'd known this would happen. Somehow. He'd *seen* this.

"I have you," he whispered. "It's okay. I have you."

Magic curled into the air. Dahvid must have swiped one of his tattoos. Mercy could feel it trying to reach her—and failing. "I'm . . . I'm not sure. I'm trying to heal you. . . ."

"It can't be healed," she whispered back. "These aren't ordinary wounds. Please. Just take me over to Redding. Guide me there. Please, Dahvid."

"Take you to . . ."

"Now."

Her voice didn't leave room for argument. He slid one arm beneath her and guided her through that darkness. She was in too much pain to think through the rest of her life. What this meant for her future. All that mattered was *here*. All that mattered was *now*.

"Redding is in front of you."

"Guide my right hand to his heart."

Dahvid obeyed her. Mercy repeated the spell again. Damn the consequences. There was a satisfying gasp as the pioneer returned to them. Dahvid's voice was low. Near her ear.

"Your fingers . . ."

"I'll be fine," Mercy replied. "I'll be just fine. Take me to Theo."

He was the last one. Dahvid positioned her again. Accepting that she might die this time, Mercy leaned down and performed the final exchange. She waited for the feeling to come. A burn in her throat. A slice across the abdomen or in her heart or down her spine. Nothing. Did it not work?

And then she heard Theo's voice.

"I don't . . . what the hell is going on? What happened?"

Mercy straightened. She could not see any of them. She couldn't see herself. The pain pressed in, threatening to shut her mind down, to let her slip into unconsciousness. She could not allow that. Instead, she pushed the pain aside and cleared her throat.

"I brought you back," she said. "Do not waste this. I swear to every god that has ever existed—if any of you die again in this chamber, I will find your soul in the afterlife and kill you a second time. Arakyl thinks you're all dead. His attention is focused elsewhere right now. This is our chance. I am going to cast the visualization spells. My tools . . . someone can borrow my tools. Margaret, get the null sword. Dahvid, summon your weapon. We need to move with haste."

She shoved Dahvid away from her and nearly collapsed.

Gods, I feel like death.

That thought almost had her laughing. Almost. Mercy began the familiar steps of the spell. Even without her sight, she knew what she was doing. How to control the magic. She could hear the others whispering. There was no time for more explanations. She focused on finishing the casting.

It worked.

She knew it worked—and began weeping uncontrollably, because even though she could not see Dahvid or Theo or the dragon corpse—she could see the magic. Every remaining thread appeared in that darkness. It was an unexpected, overwhelming gift. Mercy looked up at those bright colors and gave the others a final command.

"Finish what I started."

And then she was falling through the earth itself.

58

REN MONROE

Her mind refused to piece itself back together.

Half of her watched the conversation between Nevelyn and her mother. The other half was focused on finding Theo. She couldn't feel him. There wasn't even a flicker of his emotions across their bond. Had he traveled out of range? Was Arakyl disrupting their connection? That guess felt wrong, too, though. The revenge that bound her to the dragon felt like scorched earth. Almost as if they'd both burned through the power at the same time and there was nothing left between them at all. She couldn't summon hatred or rage. All she wanted now was to live with the people she loved, safe behind Meredream's pearl-white walls. But each time she reached for Theo and came back empty, a terrible feeling formed in the pit of her stomach. It was not something she would even allow herself to think—for fear that saying the words even to herself might make them come true.

And then her mother brought down her right hand. A signal to the surrounding army. Ren had assumed this was a negotiation. That the two sides would speak and then return to discuss matters. Instinct had her shoving back up to her feet. Nevelyn was out there. Completely exposed. An answering war cry sounded from the Makers. Every remaining soldier launched into motion. Ren saw their ranks bending like a compressed moon on Nevelyn's position. The girl was backpedaling, her hands out helplessly in front of her. Ren wasn't the only one who came to the girl's defense.

One soldier collapsed at random, a knife in his back. Another dropped beside him. Ren watched as one of the red-scarfed figures began cutting back through the lines. Her first thought, when she saw the girl's face, was: *Is that Dahl Winters?* And then she remembered that no one with that name existed. Ava Tin'Vori was here. She'd somehow smuggled behind enemy lines and now was fighting, daggers in both hands, to get to her sister before the other soldiers could. But there were too many crashing down on their position. Too many to fight alone.

Ren and Avid Shiverian stepped through the outer wards at the same time. They both raised their wands and power thundered out, bright streaks cutting paths through the coming soldiers. Punching into chests. Smashing into kneecaps with bright bursts of light. Ren cast again and again until they'd reached Nevelyn. The nearest soldier lunged and for once Ren was too slow. The tip of his sword caught her in the side. Ren gasped, the blood spurting from her wound, until he was blasted backward by another spell. Ren turned to see Theo was there. Impossible. Mere seconds before she'd feared that he was dead. She could not reach him across their bond. His eyes were full of bright fury. He had come for her. He was alive. She had somehow pulled him to this bloody hill without even thinking about the magic at all.

And that was when all hell broke loose.

They'd exposed themselves too much. Soldiers swept in from all sides, swiping desperately with swords and spears. The other wizards responded. She watched them come pouring out from behind the wards. Their wands desperately slashing the air. One soldier was punished by his own, struck in the chest by a stray arrow. Ren slid past him and cast another spell, careful to keep her back pressed to Theo as they navigated the madness together. His spellwork was always a fine complement to hers. She would go on the offensive and he would shield her. In and out with perfect ease. Stray spells whispered over their heads, just narrowly missing them.

"Push for Meredream!" Avid was shouting. "Everyone move! Now!"

Ren thought she saw the logic. If they stayed out on this hillside, they'd have to continue fending off the entire army. Exposed. This maneuver would at least give them a chance to fight their way to Meredream. One desperate push. If they could somehow break through the Makers' ranks, it would be a footrace to Meredream. Ren and Theo kept casting, moving in step with the other wizards. She made sure that Winnie was moving and was relieved to see the girl on her feet, stumbling along with the other children. As Ren followed, she almost tripped over her own mother.

"Ren?! What . . . what is happening? Ren, where are we?"

It wasn't an act. Something had happened. Arakyl had abandoned her—or maybe her mother's manipulation thread had finally been cut back in the burial chamber. If Theo was here with her, their mission must be going well. Ren grabbed her mother by the collar and pulled her to her feet. "Stay with me," she hissed. "Whatever you do, stay close!"

With Theo's help, they kept moving forward. Other wizards filled in the gaps. Arrows had stopped flying, because the combat was too thick. Far too difficult to hit the right target. Ren could also see more and more Makers fleeing the scene. She felt certain that was Mercy's doing. They were clearly cutting threads. Freeing people from Arakyl's magic.

"Keep pushing!" Avid screamed. "Don't leave anyone behind!"

Their group did not have the advantage of the terrain. It was an uphill push. But magic was one hell of an equalizer. Each successful spell split the enemy's ranks. Ren shoved their leftover wards at one group and they were pummeled backward. Ava's knifework was enough to finish anyone who avoided the major spells. Miraculously, they'd nearly managed to punch all the way through. She saw just one more line of soldiers. Meredream glinted in the distance. Ren and Theo started to turn as the rest of the wizards kept pushing, knowing their rear would be exposed to the soldiers they'd just passed. That single turn was enough to show her the mistake they'd made.

It was a miscalculation. The Makers had allowed their progress. That was clear now. All while they pivoted the battle. There were still far too many of them. Flanking on both sides— and now the wizards had left the safety of their wards. This was a trap. The jaws were about to close in from both sides and all of them would die. Their best chance was a dead sprint for the gates. Ren looked up and her heart fell. The city was too far away. They could not reach it without the soldiers pursuing them, picking them off one by one. She was about to call for the ranks to form up again. They needed to start casting wards. But Avid was shouting something. Ren could just barely make out the word.

"Nevelyn!"

In the chaos, she'd lost sight of the Tin'Vori girl. The brief glimpses of Ava fighting beside them had convinced her that Nevelyn had been marching with them, but now Ren saw her.

They all did.

59

NEVELYN TIN'VORI

She had backpedaled as everyone else flooded forward.

The spells had cut through the enemy ranks. A call had gone out to charge uphill. Why keep fighting out here when they could make a run for Meredream? Nevelyn had been too shocked to follow. She watched them rush forward. Ava was with them, fighting fiercely along the front lines of the charge. Josey was there too. She saw him running, linked arm in arm with the other children. Their little legs trying to high-step corpses.

God help us all.

People were dying. People were *dead*. It all felt so senseless. For some reason, she kept backpedaling. Away from the terrible nightmare. She was so very tired. Even as a voice whispered that Josey and Ava weren't safe, that she needed to protect the two of them. From her angle, she could see the enemy troops turning. Circling around to re-form their ranks.

The wizards seemed to be making good progress. Forcing a path to Meredream. But gods, it was still so far in the distance. She saw there was no chance they would make it.

All of this? Just to die on some random hill? To see more loved ones buried too soon?

Nevelyn reached for the charm on her necklace. It was turned to the dark side. She knew she could cast that spell and leave. No one would even notice. She could walk back to Kathor and pretend that this had never happened. Use her magic to survive whatever happened next.

Instead, she turned the charm to the lighter side.

"Look at me."

The first wave of magic was like a whisper. A few heads turned. It was not enough.

"I SAID LOOK AT ME!"

Magic burst out from her like sunlight. Power beyond anything she'd ever summoned before. No one on that hillside was spared from it. She held out her hands and watched as every single enemy soldier turned to look at her. Their swords briefly slumping. Their jaws lulled open. She had their attention. Finally, she had their attention.

"Good. Keep looking."

Nevelyn put all her remaining strength into the spell. Blistering light pulsed out. Bright enough to blind the entire hillside. She could tell it was working. Too well. All the wizards had paused too. Taken in by the demands of her magic. They were beholding her too. It took what little energy she had left to cast more nuance into the spell. A minor change that very nearly bubbled out to the rest of the spell. It worked, though. She saw the wizards shaking themselves free of the magic.

Ren Monroe was staring back in horror. Ava was screaming something Nevelyn couldn't hear. Turning as if she might make one more rescue attempt. Nevelyn shook her head, though.

"Go!" she shouted. "Save them!"

One by one, the enemy soldiers began walking toward her. Nevelyn kept her own feet moving. Backpedaling to lure them farther and farther away. The archers began knocking their arrows. Soldiers raised their swords. Nevelyn felt like a goddess as she lured an entire army to her like sleepwalking dreamers. Beyond them, she could see Josey and the children and all the others running. Covering the distance to reach the gates easily. No one followed them. She made sure of it. As the first wave of soldiers reached her, and as arrows raced through the sky, Nevelyn Tin'Vori couldn't help smiling. "There. Now you see me. Now . . ."

60

REN MONROE

M eredream was a fitting name.

The roads were carved from polished white stone. The survivors followed the main thoroughfare, passing idyllic cottages and more utilitarian public buildings. At the heart of the city, there was a small crystal-blue lake from which a myriad of streams ran. The Shiverian ethos—which emphasized precision and usefulness above all else—could not have been more evident. Even the courtyards had been set in strategic positions, drinking in maximum sunlight, and always doubling as gardens for specific crops. Ren saw great tomato vines with their fruits on the verge of bursting. She noticed there was a stasis enchantment layered over the entire section. They'd grown them to the point where they were nearly ready to be picked, and then magically frozen them in time. Similar wonders were everywhere, waiting to be discovered, but now was not the time for exploration. Their first task was finding a proper graveyard.

Thankfully, the Shiverians had thought of that too. A small field had been set aside near the western gates. After taking a moment to tend to their own wounds—which included the relatively deep sword puncture in Ren's side—the surviving wizards spent the next few hours after the battle ferrying the dead up the abandoned hillside, through the main gate, and to that sunlit hollow. Trails of blood began to mark their passage over the once-white stones. At one point, Ren found herself staring at a bloody handprint someone had left on one of the doors and she knew this place would always be half-haunted for them.

Nevelyn's sacrifice had been the turning point. After seeing that the rest of the wizards had reached Meredream, the opposing army had crumbled and fled. Some of them, like her mother, had remained behind to help with the dead. Their senses returned after having their manipulation threads cut in that distant burial chamber. Others were too confused or afraid to do anything more than disappear into the surrounding forests. Ren knew there would be a reckoning at some point. Not everyone would abandon the cause they'd fought for on this hillside. A few would go back to the city and whisper that they should finish what they'd started. The wizards, they would say, were too dangerous to be left alone. Fear would spread until there was a clear divide between the people who had magic and the people who didn't. But for now, none of that mattered.

Ren and Theo trudged side by side, completing tasks together. She felt tension across their bond. Something unspoken. She could only assume it had to do with the connection between her and Arakyl. Maybe he thought he'd seen the worst of her in his father's research. He'd forgiven her for that, only to be rewarded with something worse: the truth that the woman he loved was responsible for the fall of Kathor. When they stopped by one of the city's fountains to wash their hands of blood and grime, Ren could not stand the silence any longer.

"The bronze thread," she said. "You're wondering why I asked you to sever it."

Theo looked over in surprise. "Am I?"

"You're not?"

"Well, no. Not really. I figured that part out. Dragons are attracted to deep emotions. After seeing the thread, I just assumed that your anger was a latch-point for Arakyl. Which means he used your anger to power his manipulation efforts and then when he'd built enough other connections, he started drawing on them as well. Seemed pretty straightforward."

Ren stared at him. "You already knew all of that?"

He snorted softly. "Why are you always surprised when I know things? You realize that I was ninth in our class, right? It's not like I got bad grades or something. I'm pretty smart too."

His tone was light and calm and didn't match the tension in their bond at all.

"So, that's why you're upset?"

Now he frowned. "Why would that upset me?"

Ren gestured around them. "Because I'm the reason all of this happened."

"Do you really believe that?" The question made Ren feel childish and small. Theo didn't give her the chance to answer it either. "If it wasn't you, it would have been some other kid from the Lower Quarter. Someone else who lost a loved one to my father's cruelty. Or someone who was wronged by the

Graylantians or the Proctors or the Winterses. Ren, look at the army we just faced. Arakyl didn't make them feel small and powerless. He didn't plant hatred in their hearts. *We did that.* For centuries. My father was always so fond of talking about you reap what you sow—and this is a generational reaping." He shook his head sadly. "Arakyl lied to you, Ren. This isn't your fault. Trust me, that's not why I'm upset."

She couldn't help focusing on those words. "But you *are* upset?"

"Well, yeah, but not with you. I'm upset because I died, Ren."

It was such a shocking claim that she snorted out loud. "Died? What are you talking about? You're here right now, Theo. Walking around. You're not dead."

He kept his voice low. "I know. That's because Mercy brought me back. She's a very powerful necromancer. None of us ever asked what the variation was in her magic. Remember that night at Beacon House? She went around asking everyone what their variation was, but no one remembered to ask her."

Ren realized that was true. She'd made a mental note to inquire, but had never followed through. That realization hardly mattered compared to the larger truth of what he was saying.

"That's why I couldn't feel you across the bond . . . you were actually dead."

And he would still be dead if not for Mercy. Before Theo could reply, she wrapped him in a bone-rattling hug. The two of them were sweaty and dirty and it didn't matter. Theo held her tight and for a moment there was no other world outside of his arms. He kissed her forehead and Ren pressed as far into him as she could. He let out a wince that turned into a laugh.

"Hey now. Take it easy on me. Dying hurts. My body is still mending. My mind, too. Sorry for being distant. I guess I was just trying to . . . take it all in. All these bodies. My own death. I guess I was just trying to figure out what it all means. What we do now. All of that."

"Of course. Don't apologize. I'm sorry, Theo. I didn't realize. Gods, you know I hate being in people's debt, but I guess I owe Mercy Whitaker drinks for the rest of time."

A shadow crossed Theo's face. He shook his head. "I'm not sure she survived, Ren. The magic she used . . . it had a cost. Every time she raised one of us from the dead, I think some part of her died in exchange. Before you pulled me, I saw her collapse to the ground." He shook his head a second time. "I don't know. I hope she's alive. I hope all of them are."

It took longer than expected to learn of their fates. According to Theo, two of the wyverns had been killed during their battle with Arakyl, which left just one of the winged creatures available to retrieve the other group of survivors. They sent the rider winging south and all they could do was hope for a swift return. There were plenty of tasks to help them pass the time.

First, graves were dug, marked, and filled. Word was sent back to Kathor that any living relative of the deceased could come to Meredream and reclaim their loved ones. All they had to do was bring a wagon to the front gates and the wizards would help them load the bodies without argument. Only one casualty from the battle remained unburied: Nevelyn Tin'Vori.

The rumor was that Ava Tin'Vori had nearly knifed the person who tried to bury her sister before Dahvid could return to say goodbye to her. There was also some interest amongst the other survivors of paying tribute to the woman who'd sacrificed herself to let the rest of them escape. A polite suggestion was made that they could store her temporarily in the morgue.

Ren found herself walking through the small building that the Shiverians had designed to serve as the town's hospital. She passed through empty rooms full of shining, untouched instruments. Stairs led to a sublevel. She took them and the air grew cooler with every step. Nevelyn had been set on a stone table against the far wall. Ren saw that they'd commandeered one of the enchanted shrouds that were often used by undertakers to keep the dead from rapidly decomposing. A gossamer material that stretched from head to toe. Both Ava and Josey were slumped in one corner under a pair of thick blankets, their snores tangling in the air.

Ren crossed the room as quietly as she could. The other survivors had been visiting, paying their respects. She'd delayed because she couldn't bring herself to say goodbye to another person she thought of as a friend. Time hadn't helped. She had no clever words or heartfelt sentiments. Besides, she had a feeling Nevelyn would only smirk at anything serious she tried to say. Ren began crying and settled for placing one hand on the dead girl's shoulder. The fabric felt like a silk barrier separating their world and the next one.

"She liked you."

The voice was close enough to make her jump. Ava Tin'Vori had maneuvered quietly across the room. When Ren glanced back, she was grateful to see the girl wasn't armed. Her stare was weapon enough at this distance. "Even though you threw me off a mountain . . . she liked you."

Ren started to apologize, but Ava dismissed the idea of apologies with a backhand.

"Save your breath. You're not sorry. You'd do it the same way a hundred times over if it meant saving him—and gods know that I'd gut you to save any of mine. You really want to bury your guilt?" Her eyes swung to Josey, who was still fast asleep. "Train him. Teach him everything you know. Give him the same tools you've got—and I'll consider that blood debt settled. Forgiven and forgotten."

Ren wiped her tears away. "Done."

"Oh. And maybe you could bring us some food? Josey won't leave. I'm worried about him not eating enough. He's all skin and bones."

Ren offered the girl a nod, whispered one final word to Nevelyn, and left.

61

REN MONROE

There was no end to the list of other tasks they needed to perform. The city might be brand-new, but that didn't mean it would run itself. Theo shouldered a lot of the organizational work. All that education he'd undergone to be Kathor's warden was finally put to good use. The surviving wizards were all assigned specific cottages that became theirs the moment they crossed the thresholds. Any children who'd come alone were appointed guardians until their parents could make the trek to Meredream. Meetings were arranged. Votes taken. Weary as they were from the recent battle, they were not immune to different opinions and arguments.

The first big decision focused on what to do with the Makers who'd stayed behind to help bury the dead. Were they guilty of crimes? Victims themselves? It was terribly complicated to navigate what a just punishment would be for a group who wanted revolution—but who wouldn't have committed murder if they hadn't been manipulated by a demigod.

Theo proposed the Recanting Protocol. Any of the Makers who were willing to publicly deny the original goals of their group and pledge support for the surviving wizards would have their charges erased. Anyone unwilling to do so would be imprisoned to await further trials. Thankfully, of the thirty or so Makers who'd stayed, none put that side of the equation to the test. Her mother even led a burning ceremony where the famous red scarves were all tossed into a bonfire. The public display eased tensions, but there were still wounds that only time would heal. Ren was walking evidence of that. She'd still not found the courage to sit down and speak with her mother.

Another meeting was held about what to do with the great houses. Names that had loomed large in their world for centuries now: Brood, Proctor, Shiverian, Winters, and Graylantian. Word had come back from Kathor that House Graylantian had already been sacked. Gemma had led a failed charge on Beacon House—and their holdings were already being divested. The other houses had also been publicly ordered to distribute their wealth to the struggling families in Kathor who needed it most. But those estates had elaborate wards that made enforcing such an order difficult.

As a show of goodwill, the highest-ranking member of each family sent letters back to Kathor. Ren watched in disbelief as they signed their names to those documents. While they could not force their families to acquiesce, their signatures were a powerful statement. The only wizards left in the world were agreeing to the idea that the wealth they'd earned over centuries should be redistributed. In exchange, they asked for peace. A letter eventually came back from the newly appointed grand emissary of Kathor. Theo read the letter aloud as people gathered in the amphitheater. There would be no ill will between the cities. A tentative peace had been reached. For the first time in Kathor's long history, there would be no ruling elite. Ren knew that a new world was in the process of being born. Even now they were all witnesses to its first, ragged breaths.

On the third day since their arrival in Meredream, a wyvern was spotted through gaps in the surrounding trees. Theo tried to keep everyone calm, asking for the bigger crowd to disperse, but no one would listen. They'd been waiting for this moment too. Ren's heart lightened when she saw the wyvern rider wasn't alone. There were two others tucked into the harness straps.

Dust stirred as the wyvern's wings swept wide. Her heart leapt again at the sight of Dahvid Tin'Vori pressed tight to the creature's neck. Nevelyn deserved to be put to rest and her brother's return signaled an end to Ava and Josey's prolonged vigil. Ren started striding out to where the wyvern was landing before stuttering to a halt. The other survivor was . . . Mercy Whitaker.

Ren actually covered her mouth at the sight of her. There was no one else it could be—no one else they'd sent matched her size and frame—but the transformation from who they'd sent to that burial chamber and who they saw now was the most startling she'd ever witnessed. Ren shot a look over at Theo, who nodded a confirmation. He'd told her there was a cost to the magic, but she'd never imagined what it would actually look like.

Mercy wore a blindfold. Ren's first thought was that it was designed to ward off the moving sickness of wyvern flight—

but then she saw the bruising at the edges of the fabric. Bits of dried blood. Clearly, something gruesome had happened to both of her eyes. Her bright red hair had completely vanished as well, leaving the woman pale and bald. Nor could she stand on her own. Dahvid half carried her in the direction of the waiting crowd—and it seemed one of her legs wasn't functional. The initial shock had kept the waiting group silent, but a whoop from the back led to another and in seconds the entire group was clapping and cheering for the people they knew had saved their lives, one severed thread at a time. Dahvid nodded gratefully, but it was clear his attention was on Mercy. He whispered quietly to her before they made their limping way through the group. He only paused when he reached Ren.

"All the threads were severed. The dragon is no more powerful than any other corpse now. It is finished," he reported before searching the crowd again. "Where are my sisters? And Josey? Why are they not here?"

Her jaw quivered slightly. "Follow me."

Only when they'd passed through the small hospital and reached the stairs leading down into the morgue did Dahvid seem to understand where they were going—and why. He led Mercy tenderly down the steps before turning and passing the doctor's weight off to Ren and Theo. She saw tears were already streaming down the warrior's face as he made his way across the room. His heavy footsteps woke the other two, who rubbed their eyes before trailing cautiously behind him, like two birds afraid of flying too close to the edges of a storm. Dahvid made a strangled noise before tearing the front of his tunic down the middle. He staggered, on the verge of collapse, but Ava and Josey kept him on his feet. The three of them slumped against the stone table, one in their grief. Their pain pointed Ren sharply back to her own pain. How many friends were gone? How many loved ones had died? And every single one of those griefs led like markers down a long, winding road to the first grief: her father. His limbs bent wrong-ways in the canal. A few days later she'd stood there, watching as they lowered him into the ground, and she still remembered thinking it was a terribly small space for the undertakers to try to fit an entire world.

Now she watched the Tin'Voris try to make sense of that same equation. How a world could simply vanish without warning. "Who is it?" Mercy whispered. "Did both of his sisters die?"

"No," Ren whispered back. "It's Nevelyn. Ava survived."

Mercy's head tilted. For a moment it seemed like she was watching the scene unfold in spite of her blindfold. "How did she die?"

That, at least, was an easy question to answer. "She sacrificed herself to save us. She used her ability to draw the entire army's attention while we escaped." Dahvid was still unleashing great sobs. Loud enough that Ren felt she could speak without offending them. Her eyes flicked briefly to Theo before settling back on Mercy. "I understand you made a similar sacrifice, Mercy."

The doctor stiffened. "It was the only way. Anyone else would have made the same choice."

"I agree that it was the only way—but if you think everyone would have made the choice that you made, you're wrong. Same with Nevelyn. Both of you . . ."

Mercy waved the thought of her own heroism away. Clearly,

all this talk and attention made the woman uncomfortable. "I need to rest. Is there somewhere I can sleep?"

Theo answered, "We can assign you to a cottage. You'll have the entire place to yourself."

Mercy shook her head. "Surely there's a bed here? Isn't this some sort of hospital wing? There should be a gurney upstairs. I got used to sleeping in them when I was doing my residency. Besides, I'll need a draft for the pain. If they have a powder case here, I can walk you through the steps."

The three of them left the Tin'Vori family to their grief and walked back upstairs. Mercy was right. There was a gurney waiting in the back corner of one of the rooms. Theo handed off the draft-making duties to Ren while he ran around fetching pillows and blankets. Mercy thanked them, looking eager to be alone. Ren couldn't simply leave her like this, though. She decided to briefly lean back inside. Offer one final word of encouragement.

"Your plan saved the city. It saved us. It saved magic."

Mercy's face fell. Ren thought that she'd somehow said the wrong thing, but after a moment, the doctor nodded. "Thank you."

The next wave of arrivals didn't come on the back of a wyvern. Instead, they scaled the outer gates and had two of the newer guards ringing the bells to alert the city of an attack. The commotion was quelled quickly enough when everyone realized the livestone statues had been sent ahead by Zell Carrowynd—who had every intention of making Meredream their permanent home. After a brief word with the guards, the gargoyle led the other surviving statues inside the city. Their numbers had been significantly reduced in the battle with Arakyl, but Ren knew their city could use every loyal guardian they could find.

Over the next few hours, the statues were seen roaming the streets, getting to know the stones, quietly claiming which areas they wanted to watch over. Ren hadn't realized they could swear allegiance to a new city—but maybe that wasn't exactly right. Maybe the heart of Kathor had simply moved here. Or maybe their true allegiance wasn't to a place, but to magic itself, and the protection of the people who used it now. Ren wasn't sure, but whenever she saw one of them perched on the ramparts or a rooftop, the city felt more like home.

Their warden wasn't long behind them. The wyvern returned in the late afternoon with Zell and the bonded siblings—Guion and Win. The only person from their party who was still missing was Redding. Zell informed them that he'd refused to leave without marking the area surrounding the burial location. Ren appreciated that. The last thing they needed was another random soul stumbling unaware into Arakyl's chamber. Severing the threads had been enough to cut him off from his power. He had no access to Ren's rage or their magic anymore, but that didn't mean that he was harmless now. Redding's efforts were the first step toward making sure that Arakyl never returned.

All three of the fighters claimed cottages for themselves. Ren couldn't help noticing that they had the same wide-eyed expressions. Like deer who'd had their necks inside the mouth of a predator only to be unexpectedly released. It seemed the world they found themselves in was constantly surprising. The sun a bit too bright. The people all too real. Ren knew it was a confirmation that Mercy's power had truly brought them all back. From somewhere beyond. When the crowd finally started to disperse, she slid an arm through Theo's and they strolled back to their own cottage. At ease for the first time in days.

"Mercy's gift . . . I'm surprised she never told anyone about it."

Theo shook his head. "I am too. I'm sure it took incredible restraint, but keeping it a secret saved her life. A skill like that? There would have been a bidding war for her talents unlike anything Kathor's ever seen. What enhancer could compare to a necromancer that brings back the dead? Without any consequence to the deceased? She would have been rich—and whoever won her contract would have slowly killed her. Piece by piece. And not to save people who really deserved it, you know? They would have used it to keep their ancestral lines healthy and whole. Resurrecting whoever they wanted, whenever they wanted. I'm glad she was smart enough to hide it."

Ren glanced back over one shoulder. Guion and Win were still there, chatting amicably with some of the other survivors. "Well, it's not hidden anymore."

Theo nodded his agreement. "That's a bridge we can cross when we get to it."

"Spoken like a true city planner."

That had him smiling. The cottage they'd chosen wasn't anything like the villa they'd enjoyed together in the Heights. It had no first editions on its shelves. All the antique furniture had been replaced with simple, functional pieces. The view was not a sprawling city, glinting below their feet like a sea of diamonds. Instead, their lone window looked out at a tree in full bloom. One of the city's many creeks looped in and out of sight. Somehow that felt right to Ren. Like they were being called to witness the beginning of something that would only keep growing if they let it.

As they prepared dinner, Ren set the table. She hesitated only briefly before adding a third plate. A third set of silverware. A third glass. Theo watched her, nervous energy humming across their bond, but he was wise enough not to nudge her about it. He allowed her the space to decide if this was the right choice, the right moment. When the table was set, Ren quietly slipped back out into the street. It was not a long walk to the cottage she had in mind. Three knocks, then a door was opening. Her mother's eyes immediately fell to the ground. Her shoulders slumped slightly. As if she knew Ren had come to deliver a condemnation for the part she'd played in what had happened.

Instead, Ren moved close enough that she could reach out and raise her mother's chin. Then she used the other hand to straighten her mother's back. "Remember. A Monroe stands tall."

Her mother cried then. They embraced and whispered apologies and started walking before the tears had dried. Not everything between them could be healed. It would not be perfect, Ren knew, but for now they needed each other's strength. And so, she led her mother back to their cottage.

Inside was warm from the burning stovetop. There was cinnamon in the air and something else she couldn't recognize. Theo glanced up from his cooking and looked relieved. Clearly, he'd been hoping this was the guest Ren had in mind. Outside, the sun had set. The three of them began a quiet and enjoyable meal. How close it was to feeling right and whole.

But as meaningful as it had been for Ren to offer an olive branch and put out that third place setting, her eyes began to linger on the fourth spot at the table. An empty chair. With no other warning, Ren began to violently sob. Theo reacted, the bond magic pulsing between them, but it was her mother who got their first. Those familiar arms wrapped patiently around Ren's shoulders.

"Come now. What's all this, my love?"

She felt childish as she pointed to the empty seat. "It didn't bring him back. No matter what I do . . . he's just gone."

After all this time, she was still that little girl who missed her father. Roland Monroe would never return. The death of Landwin Brood had not restored her father to the realm of the living. The fall of the great houses hadn't brought him grinning back through the door to claim his place at their dinner table. He would never make small talk with the man she loved. Never catch her eye across a room and offer one of his famous winks. Even Mercy Whitaker's powers could not reach back through time and whisper life into the man whose absence had quietly defined her entire life.

"He's gone," Ren repeated numbly. "And Timmons and Cora and Avy and all the others. They're all gone. Gods, what did I do, Mother?! What did I do?!"

Agnes clutched her tighter. "My sweet girl, you did what you thought was right. Landwin Brood deserved to die. For what he did to your father—and for a thousand other sins. You're smart enough to know that no one else would have punished him. He would have gone on living that way for years. Perhaps decades. Justified. Arrogant. Cruel. No one is doubting what you did to him. But the others?" Agnes pulled back now to look

Ren dead in the eye. "Those are ghosts you must learn to live with. You'll never be able to make those losses right. Ever."

Ren's bond with Theo surged again. Sympathy came thundering across. He looked ready to say something to soften the blow, but Ren knew her mother was speaking a necessary truth.

"But open your eyes, sweet girl. Didn't we teach you to see the entire picture? You did the right thing until you realized it had gone too far—and then you were brave enough to stop and turn around and look for the *next* right thing. Do you know how many people would rather watch the world burn than admit that they were wrong? Gods, Ren, I would have kept going. I know I would have. I did. . . ."

Her voice broke off momentarily. She shook her head before continuing.

"The very moment you realized it was wrong—you stopped. You did everything in your power to keep the fire from burning even farther. Do you have any idea how many people survived because of you? If all of this comes down to a single battle instead of outright war, then this moment will be remembered as one of the most peaceful transfers of power in history." Her mother's grip on her tightened. "Sweet girl, you are only letting the worst things carry weight on the scales. Open your eyes. Look around. You found Theo through all of this. You saved the wizards out there who might have been killed otherwise. You changed the entire fabric of Kathor. Do you really want to know what Timmons and Cora and Avy would want you to do now? What your father would ask you to do?!"

Even through tears, Ren nodded.

"They would want you to keep going. There was once a man

who said, 'Who you are in times of peace is more important than who you are in a fight.' We've already seen who Ren Monroe is when she has to fight. We know you'll win nine times out of ten. But now I think it is time to see who you are when you get to put the weapons down. For the first time in your life, the question isn't: How will you win? The question now is: What will you grow? It might take some time to figure out what the answer to that is, but gods know, you always seem to find the right answer."

Her bond with Theo had evened out to a steady hum. Ren wiped at the tears in her eyes, nestled once more into her mother's arms, then pulled away. She couldn't resist asking.

"Who said that? That quote?"

"A little-known historian," her mother replied. "Named Roland Monroe."

When dinner ended, her mother departed with a final hug. Theo received a brief pat on the cheek, as if he were a Lower Quarter boy who'd done a good job at the docks that day. Ren could feel the compartments of her mind reorganizing. A quiet adjustment of ideas and priorities, hopes and dreams. Her mother's words had given her permission to alter . . . everything. She knew now it would never be perfect. The past could never be made right, but the present did not demand perfection from her. No, all she was being asked to do was wake up tomorrow and pursue the next right thing. Whatever that was. And she suspected she would not be alone in her pursuit of it.

When it was just the two of them, Theo slumped into the most comfortable chair. Ren ignored the other chairs in the room and nestled into the same seat as him. He looped an easy arm around her waist and she set her head on his chest. There was a sort of magic in the quiet between them. Their bond rumbled pleasantly. Out of the corner of her eye, she saw Vega asleep, perched on the window sill. For once, her mind accepted the simplest answer for what she was feeling. She didn't need to assess secondary theories or perform additional research or find corroborating evidence. The answer to this was simple. As perfectly imperfect as it could be.

She was home.

Finally.

62

MERCY WHITAKER

Mercy pretended to be asleep when she heard Dahvid Tin'Vori's footsteps. They were easy to recognize. Heavy and purposeful. The sound of a man who moved deliberately through the world. She could feel him lingering there, watching her, debating whether he should wake her up and see how she was doing. He had not stopped taking care of her since they'd left the burial chamber. Even blind, she could sense the weight of his attention. It took all the restraint she possessed to not turn and ask him to come closer. She felt that if she so much as breathed the wrong way—Dahvid might be foolish enough to sit down at the foot of her bed. Maybe he'd even be foolish enough to stay there for as long as they both should live.

And that she could not abide.

Not when she had one more task to complete. Which meant that she breathed in and out and pretended to be snoring until it was no longer a pretense. Sleep claimed her greedily. A dreamless few hours—and then Mercy woke to pain. A throbbing headache that stemmed from the ruptures in both eyes. There was a terrible tightness in her dead calf. Itching all along her scalp. She had very specifically misled Ren Monroe, walking her through the steps to make a draft that would dull the pain for only a few hours. It was far less than she would have prescribed to a patient who needed a full night of sleep—because she'd had no designs of sleeping through the night.

The truth was that Ren Monroe had helped Mercy make up her mind. She'd already been leaning in one direction, but that weighty thank-you had told her everything she needed to know. People would call her a hero after what had happened. Undoubtedly, rumors of her gift would spread. How long would it take for someone to beg her to be a hero again? Mercy knew in that moment that she'd spend the rest of her life deliberating on who was worthy and who wasn't. Deciding which lives to save and which lives to pass over. Like some terrible angel of death. It was a burden that she knew she could not bear.

Carefully, she sat up in bed. Listening for sounds. There was some kind of mountain insect making noise through the closest window. She maneuvered off the gurney. Her good leg could not suffer all her weight. She was forced to slump down to hands and knees. Still listening, she crawled in the direction of the door. It was open. Her hands felt the frame, calibrating the direction of the hallway. Again, she paused to listen. There was snoring, but farther down the hallway. Maybe in one of the other rooms? She crawled in the opposite direction. On and on until the air grew cold.

A draft was coming up from the morgue.

There was no graceful way to maneuver down a set of stone stairs on hands and knees. Mercy did her best, keeping each thump as soft as she possibly could. At the bottom, she paused once more, listening. No footsteps answered. No voice called after her. Dahvid was asleep. It took time to cross the room, but eventually she reached the back wall. Pulling herself up from the ground was the most difficult part. She managed it, grunting against the pain and the sudden vertigo. She probed with her hands and found fabric. Then the body beneath it. Limping, she repositioned herself so that she could set both hands over Nevelyn Tin'Vori's heart. Mercy's entire body felt as if it was on fire. It used to be that her fingers would throb and itch whenever she was near the dead. Whenever she sensed a lingering soul hoping to cross back into the land of the living. Now *all* of her burned and it was the most unbearable kind of pain. Maybe she was being a coward—or maybe she was being brave. It was not Mercy's place to say. All she knew was that it felt right to her. She would bring back the one person who'd willingly sacrificed herself so that everyone else could live.

"All right then," Mercy whispered to the ghost. "Come back to us."

She unleashed her magic. Nevelyn had been dead for several days. Far longer than any person she'd resurrected before— but as the magic coursed through her veins, Mercy Whitaker's hands did not shake. An exchange was made. She heard that quick gasp of breath at the exact moment that a terrible sharpness knifed through the right side of her head. Pain so intense that it stopped being pain after the first few seconds. It became a bridge that led to another world—and Mercy knew beyond any shadow of a doubt that she was ready to see what waited there for her.

And so, she began to walk.

63

EPILOGUE

"Now . . . tell me, why is it a monster?"

Ren waited for her class to respond. Each one of them had finished their drawings and were now studying them with new eyes. She quietly sipped her tea as she circled the room. The class sizes were naturally small at their school. Due to a lack of students, they'd been forced to merge the freshman through senior age groups. It required some serious educational differentiation—adding layers to certain assignments to challenge the older students—but most of the students were so relieved to be alive and practicing magic in a safe place that they rarely complained about having to work with each other.

Naturally, Theo had pressed her into this role. She'd started out tutoring Josey to fulfill her promise to Ava. Then she'd added a few extra sessions for Winnie, who gravitated to Ren every time they were in the same room. It took her a month of working with the two students to realize that she *liked* teaching. The only thing better than knowing the correct answer, it turned out, was sharing that correct answer with everyone else. And as pleasurable as the basics had been, she found that diving into theoretical magic, pushing the boundaries of deeper concepts, actually suited her skill set best. That realization had somehow led to this moment: a younger boy politely knocking on the door to the classroom and calling her by a title she'd never envisioned for herself.

"Headmistress Monroe?"

Gods, it sounds more pompous every time I hear it.

"Yes?"

"It's Mr. Brood. He's waiting for you at the front of the school."

Ren nodded once before letting her eyes sweep back over the students. She felt that small thrill of power that every teacher feels. Their fates in the palm of her hand.

"Very well. Class will be dismissed early today."

There was a raucous cheer that she stifled with one raised finger.

"However. You will write a full page answering this concept. You are to provide at least *three* examples backing whatever theory you propose. And Lawrence, please for the love of all that is good in this world, do not copy Hanna's work this time. Changing a few words does not suddenly make the essay yours. Have these on my desk by tomorrow morning. Understood?"

There was a chorus of murmurs and agreement and maybe one or two groans. Ren was going to follow them out before remembering she had an easier method. She reached across her bond. It was like knocking on a door that always opened.

Reality briefly flickered and she was outside with Theo in the blink of an eye. He smiled at her. Their bond had continued growing. The powers waiting between them were more powerful, more accessible. It didn't hurt that every time she ported, his hand was there waiting for hers.

"They're already here?" she asked.

He nodded. "Just arrived. We've sent word to the chosen representatives."

"To the wards, you mean?"

Theo scowled. "Ren, we agreed. . . ."

She reached for his tie, tugged him downward, offering the lightest kiss on the lips.

"Only joking. Come on. Let's go look official."

Her fingers laced easily with his. Matching bracelets, woven using the same thread and decorated with two halves of the same stone, dangled on both of their wrists. These were the traditional wedding bands worn by people in the Lower Quarter. Her mother's dragon bracelet had just been a fancier version. Ren had elected to keep her own last name, but she did not mind the idea that everywhere Theo Brood went, anyone who set eyes on him would know that he belonged to someone—and that someone was her.

Five years had passed since their arrival in Meredream. A span of time that was marked by both good and bad. It turned out that a pristine city that was the last safe harbor for magic was not immune to crime. People still stole from each other. There were still drunken arguments that turned into drunken fights. Even the occasional duel that went way too far. It did not help that their population was so dreadfully small. Like a country town where everyone vaguely knew everyone's business—and thus mistakes or quarrels felt magnified. The only counter to that problem was the small, but steady trickle that continued flowing from Kathor to Meredream.

At first, it had mostly been parents eager to reunite with children who'd been immune to the plague. Then there was a wave of folks who were smart enough to understand that a brand-new city would be full of opportunities. Certainly, there was more room to grow than in an older city that was more established. Over half the cottages remained empty, but Ren held to the hope that other residents would come. The world would continue to find its balance.

Balance. That might as well be the word of the day.

Ren and Theo aimed for the front gates. The familiar gargoyle was perched in the distance. Hunched on his favorite rampart. There were people bustling up and down the streets, their baskets full of this vegetable or that fruit. Harvesting the city's food supply had turned out to be such a massive percentage of Meredream's required work that it was the only task every citizen was conscripted to perform. All of them took shifts. Even the livestone creatures helped, because feeding the city was currently a bigger priority than defending it from outsiders.

After all, the only threat to Meredream was Kathor.

Everyone had feared an attack in the first year. What if the Makers changed their minds? What if they decided to march an army of ten thousand right up to the gates? Or even fifty thousand? The wizards had survived the first battle, but those kinds of numbers could sway the odds beyond anything they could hope to survive. All it would take was one distrustful generation and the wrong dictator to set the gears of war into motion again. Today was a step in the other direction. A move to solidify their fledgling peace.

"Open the gates!" Theo called.

The two of them took their places with the rest of the party. Ren eyed the waiting ranks. The five official volunteers stood at the front. All of them had agreed to leave Meredream for Kathor. It turned out that some of the passive magic systems in the city had started failing. The Makers' dream of being a society that didn't rely on any magic hadn't accounted for just how much of Kathor relied on spellwork that was woven into every facet. The failed magic was causing enough disruption that Kathor's leaders had reached out to Meredream—hoping for an exchange. A sign of good faith.

Five wizards would travel to the city. They would spend the next year working for the citizens who had once tried to kill them. Fixing what was broken. Repairing magic wherever they went. Restoring what had been lost—in more ways than one. In exchange, Kathor would send five of their own people to Meredream.Historically, this would have been called an exchange of wards. After some of the larger-scale wars, the losing side would send their young princes or princesses to the victor. It was an incentive for the new vassal kingdom to obey the edicts of the treaty. If they stepped out of line or outright rebelled, the ward they'd entrusted to their enemy would be executed. If they obeyed, however, then the ward would be fed and kept in good condition for as long as they lived there.

Which was precisely why Theo didn't like using the term "ward." There was a whisper of threat behind the word. Instead, he wanted to treat them like scholars. A chance to learn from each other and build bonds between once warring kingdoms.

The first volunteer had been Avid Shiverian. A perfect fit. She knew more about passive magic systems than any of them. Beside her were two of their younger wizards. Their parents waited patiently behind them. Both children had family they hadn't seen in five years. Siblings who'd remained in Kathor for one reason or another. Ren knew those reunions would be sweet and long overdue. While the children weren't as skilled in magic, there were plenty of basic tasks they could complete while they were there. The fourth volunteer was a middle-aged woman named Maya Ruminas. She'd served as a structural engineer for House Proctor and would likely have the widest understanding of the various problems they'd face as they made repairs. Last was Redding. The pioneer had returned to Meredream, but he'd found the town too quiet for his liking. He'd asked if his time in Kathor would allow him the freedom to roam the countryside on his days off. Both sides had agreed that would be just fine.

Behind the main group, Ren saw all the other town officials had gathered as witnesses. All of them had stepped up into more official roles over the years. Her eyes were drawn to the woman standing like a bookend on the opposite side. A nest of curls framed a skeptical expression. Nevelyn Tin'Vori caught Ren staring and made a face at her. It took effort to not laugh. Aside from Theo, Nevelyn was her best friend by far. She worked at the school some with the little ones, but most of her focus was on acting like a mother hen for Josey. Every time Ren saw her—or Theo for that matter—she felt like she was witnessing a miracle all over again.

Finally, the gates finished their grinding movement. A matching group to theirs waited outside. One woman detached from the others. There was an emblem on her cloak that was new. It had been on the last few missives as well. A lion at the center surrounded by swords waiting to be unsheathed. The lion's claws gripped a flag with the smaller emblem of a crown. An emphasis, Ren thought, on the idea that Kathor's strength now rested in what it could physically do. Her stomach churned uncomfortably at the sight of it—but the face above that emblem was smiling.

"Hello. Thank you for inviting us. I would love for you to meet your new recruits."

Introductions were made. The woman, it turned out, was the actual grand emissary. She'd traveled all this way to make sure that the meeting went well. Ren liked her. She had her misgivings about all of this, but they were growing quieter with each passing minute. Their five wizards eventually went forward. There was no trap waiting for them. No ambush sprang out from the woods. Instead, the emissary chatted amicably. Her excitement was clear—which meant Kathor was truly desperate to have their services. A promising start.

Ren joined Theo in welcoming the five recruits sent from Kathor. Theo had walked her through their decision-making. First, all of the recruits were young—between sixteen and twenty. That idea had come from Nevelyn, who thought the younger generation would be more open-minded about magic. If they could plant a seed that wizards weren't some distant evil growing behind the gates of Meredream—it would go a long way to building a future together.

The second request was that each recruit be an artisan of a specific trade. Ren spotted the girl who was the blacksmith. She could tell just by the muscled forearms. The others ranged from bakers to butchers—and again there was purpose behind each selection. Theo had wanted them to learn valuable skills from every recruit who came.

Final farewells were made. Other wizards stood on the ramparts and waved down to the five who'd been chosen to leave. Ren could tell there was a communal sense of hope and dread in the air. That same mixture, in fact, was thrumming across her bond from Theo. This could be everything. Or it could go terribly wrong. Their duty was to make sure *this* side of the equation worked. And so, Ren and Theo swept forward to welcome their new recruits.

The first matter of business: a tour of the city. The curiosity on the recruits' faces was evident. Ren was sure this felt like walking right into a myth from a storybook. The fabled city where all the world's wizards lived. They asked questions about the cottages and all the crops they saw. The blacksmith was the only one who didn't speak, though Ren noticed the girl darting nervous glances at her every now and again. The group walked until they reached the crystal-blue lake at the very heart of Meredream. Sunlight angled from the distant mountains and across the water. It was a lovely day. One of those rare times in spring where it feels like summer in the sun and winter in the shade.

When they'd first arrived, the lake had been set apart. Completely on its own. The only small change that had been made since then came from Theodore Crane. The boy had a talent with stone. While most of his training for House Brood had been with livestone in mind, he'd quickly found that the citizens of Meredream would pay him for a different sort of work. Not livestone, but statues that honored their lost loved ones.

Now his work could be seen along the trail that circled the lake. There were full statues and smaller busts, depending on the requests that had been made. All of them a nod to someone who'd been lost on the journey to Meredream.

Theo deliberately picked up the chatting when the recruits reached the section that had become hallowed ground for Ren. He could no doubt sense that she didn't want to talk, not on this section of the lake. Her only commission stood to the right. Sunlight shone down on four faces: Timmons, Avy, Cora, and Clyde. Every time she passed the statues, she would whisper a quiet promise. Her mother's words remained true. There was still pain in their absence. Gaps that nothing could ever fill. And while those feelings would never fully fade, it also felt as if there was an understanding between them. A wordless reply in their blank stares that said simply: *Keep going.* Her mother had been right. It was past time to see what Ren Monroe could grow out of the ashes of all she'd burned.

The group paused naturally at the very tip of the lake. There was a bridge that spanned one of the larger streams and standing on it was the city's most famous statue: Mercy Whitaker. Crane had carved the familiar medical kit at her hip, as well as the thick gloves she always wore. This version of Mercy was looking eternally up at an unseen foe, forever determined to win a fight she'd already won for all of them. Theo caught Ren's eye. It appeared he'd reached the end of his speeches and stories. It was time to show the recruits to their cottages. Ren was about to announce that when the blacksmith girl finally spoke. She blurted her question out.

"Hey. Can you show us magic?"

Ren blinked. To her surprise, all the other recruits were

nodding. Theo grinned at Ren as if he'd somehow been in on this. It was clear from the girl's expression, though, that she was hungry to witness something that hadn't happened in Kathor in nearly half a decade. Ren glanced around, wondering what the best first spell to show them would be, when her eyes found the lake again. As they'd circled, their angle to the water—and to the sun—had changed. The light was stretching from the opposite side of the lake to where they were standing. Like a bridge.

Ren grinned. "Come with me."

Theo figured out what she was doing a few seconds later. Ren felt a curious mixture of emotions across their bond. Tiny threads of grief as he remembered the moment that this echoed out from. The people who had been there to witness the magic, but who were no longer with them. The grief, however, was quickly overwhelmed by a joy that was as bright as the waiting sunlight. For the first time, Ren realized that was the moment he'd fallen in love with her for good. She could sense the truth of it across their bond. It might have taken Ren longer, but here they were, all these years later, alive and in love and standing on the cusp of another new world.

She performed the steps of the spell. A visual ripple raced across the water. The golden road tightened and straightened. It had looked fickle before. Something they had to pretend was a road, but her binding spell solidified every particle into a single entity. Ren carefully anchored it to the other side and the only thing missing in this moment was Timmons's hand on her shoulder.

The recruits let out predictable gasps. Even if they'd grown up around magic, none of them would have ever seen a bridge made of sunlight. Ren delighted in their reactions. This was one of the things she loved most in the world: these moments where a wizard could do the unthinkable. She held the spell tight in her grasp before locking eyes with the blacksmith.

"What are you waiting for? Go ahead."

The girl had been too shy to ask as many questions as the others, but that didn't mean she lacked in bravery. All of them watched her walk to the edge of the lake. She cast one more glance back over her shoulder at Ren, making sure this wasn't a trick or a joke, and when Ren nodded—the girl stepped out. She looked surprised when the bridge held, but her next step was more certain. And the next and the next. Ren and Theo shared a smile as the other recruits followed her across that sunlit bridge. This was magic. Breathless, impossible magic.

ACKNOWLEDGMENTS

My favorite spell in this series is Ren's bridge-of-light spell. She performs it twice. First, she uses it to help her crew across the river out in the Dires. It's this breathless magic that temporarily saves the day for them. She uses the spell again at the end of the story as a demonstration of hope for the next generation. I've had an idea for that spell in my brain for about a decade—and I think it's very symbolic of the sort of magic that's also performed by a publishing team. The way they make a bridge, seemingly out of thin air, that readers can cross to properly enjoy an author's work. This book would just be wild magic without them.

In this metaphor, my editor, Kate Prosswimmer, is the one who first realized we *could* make a bridge of light to cross to the other side. Simply put, *A Door in the Dark* would not exist without her. And certainly that first book would have never transformed into a series if not for all the advocating she did in-house for it. She's the one who took the first steps onto that bridge of golden light—and I'm so grateful that I had her vision guiding this series.

The rest of the team followed in her footsteps, believing that the spell we'd cast was steady and firm enough to take us to the other side: Justin Chanda, Karen Wojtyla, Jen Strada, Greg Stadnyk, Tatyana Rosalia, Nicole Fiorica, Andrenae Jones, and so many others. Thank you for being in step with us the entire way—and I'm also rather grateful there wasn't a revenant trailing us across this metaphorical bridge!

Another credit is owed to the cover artist: Justin Metz. Most folks, when they look at my covers, see this perfect set of images that all fit seamlessly together. Very few people know that they are three different covers by three different artists. The ability to mold your art to fit our needs, while still bringing to life one of the most insanely gorgeous covers I've seen, is just incredible. Another shout-out for Chris Brackley, who continues to do amazing work on the maps in this book and is an absolute professional who has me double- and triple-checking the math I've created in my own imaginary world. Thank you so much.

I always have to tip a hat to my family. Thank you to Grammy, Dr. J, Nana, and Nonno for helping to watch kids during writing sessions or tour travel. Thank you to my wife, Katie, for always listening even when I changed a character's name for the thirty-fifth time. And thank you to my three wonderful children. You're all wild as can be, and I need those moments of wild to keep me going in between writing sessions.

I'm also grateful, as ever, for my writing group: K. D. Edwards, York Wilson, Paige Nguyen, Jen Perez, Caitlin Poole,

Tyler Ellzey, and Ali Standish. Keith, you sat with me at the Open Eye Café and listened as I rambled on and on about a dragon manipulating a cult to spread a plague. That normally would get someone kicked out of a coffee shop, but you patiently listened and gave me courage. Collectively all of you offered the confirmations I needed to push forward with this story concept. And some of you even read this story in its original version, back when it had a different title and a different main character. Thank you for helping me carve out the parts that were worth keeping and set aside those that didn't belong.

Last but not least: a thank-you to Kristin Nelson and the entire team at the Nelson Literary Agency. This was book number fourteen for us. I like to think that means that the two of us have now walked across the river fourteen times together. We seem to keep finding the other side, don't we?! Thank you for all that you've done to keep me thriving.

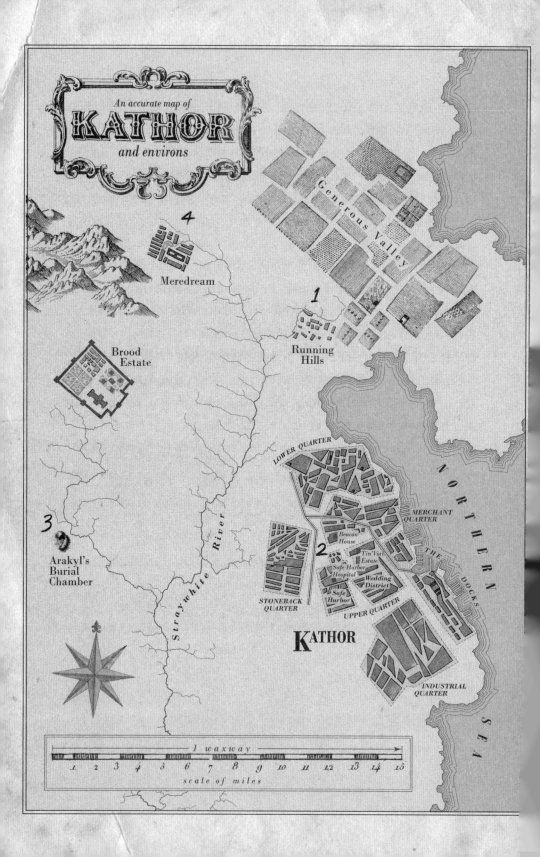

"These annotations are intended to provide context for recent events through a historical lens. While it is tempting to think we have lived through some unique era, experiencing what no wizard before us ever has, the truth is we are nearly always walking in the footsteps of those who came before us. Rare is the wizard who turns the wheels of history and takes the world in an entirely new direction." —Ren Monroe

1. The Water Treatment Facility — This building was first investigated by Dr. Mercy Whitaker. Inside she found a mutilated body that was specifically designed to spread the plague to the surrounding village. The first group to employ a similar chemical warfare was none other than House Brood. Near the turn of the century, their army found a worthy adversary in the Graylantians, who'd managed to merge the northern farming tribes and successfully train them in the tactics of open warfare. Stymied on the battlefield, the Broods eventually turned to poisoning the Graylantian water supply using the enchanted organs of dead wyverns. Ironically, they used the exact same stasis spell that was used on the bodies in the treatment facility, and I suspect the Makers drew direct inspiration from their tactics decades earlier.

2. Beacon House — Developed by the Proctors and eventually donated to the Kathorian government as the official home of the viceroy, this house added to its historical record by becoming the site of the first bloody battle between those with magic and those without. Led by a manipulated Viceroy Gray, the former paladins responsible for acting as the city guard participated in an event that now stands as the second-highest body count in Kathor's history. There have been several bloodier battles outside the city walls, mostly perpetrated by House Brood, but within city limits, only the Harpy Murders were worse than the Battle of Beacon House. The former incident centered around a disgruntled makeup artist who poisoned her boss's clients—killing seventy-three people.

3. Arakyl's Burial Chamber — In retrospect, the most interesting detail about this chamber is that the great houses collectively let it slip through the cracks of their attention. It was, after all, the first dragon's burial chamber discovered in over seventeen years. While that would seem to merit more attentiveness, the houses all assumed someone else would handle the arbitration of assigned roles. This collective belief allowed Arakyl to operate in secret, occasionally manipulating anyone who showed interest in the site. Unfortunately, there are hundreds of examples of similar governmental oversights. My personal favorite is a man named John Strawbridge. He worked as a canal attendant, maintaining a particularly busy dock that fed directly into the Merchant Quarter. The only problem was that he didn't actually work for any of the great houses. One day he was eating his lunch in that location, legs dangling down in the water, and a merchant requested access to unload. John waved him forward, thinking nothing of it, until the merchant slipped him a docking fee for his troubles. From that day on, Strawbridge would arrive at that location every day, advertising direct access to the local market, always claiming to be from a different house, depending on who owned the approaching boat. Using the collective disregard of the great houses, he collected enough money to retire two decades earlier than he would have otherwise—all because his clients assumed he must be attached to someone of consequence.

4. Meredream — Secret cities have long captivated the imagination of Kathorians. When our ancestors first began exploring the eastern seaboard, the rumors were that "secret cities" possessing "great quantities of magic" might already exist there. Similarly,

once Kathor was established and the great houses raced ahead of everyone else in terms of wealth, they were all subsequently linked to the concept of secret cities. House Proctor, famed for their building and infrastructure, was believed to have as many as a dozen secret villages in the distant Dires. House Brood was commonly linked to a "northern city of great wealth" that turned out to be Ravinia. While the Broods did have connections in the free port, the rumor that they were building an army there in order to launch future attacks on Kathor turned out to be unfounded. House Winters was famously thought to have a "secret garden" where they grew rare herbs for medicine that only the members of their house could access. Shrouded in a similar mystery, the Graylantians were believed to have built an underground city to the north connected by an endless warren of tunnels. Naturally, House Shiverian, the only family that wasn't the subject of those early rumors, turned out to be the house that actually did build an entire settlement in secret. Perhaps they believed some of the other rumors, and never a house to be outdone by their peers, hastened to build a fallback option of their own. The result was Meredream.